Karina May is a Sydney-based magazine journalist turned digital marketer and writer of lively love stories that span the globe. When she's not dreaming up her next meet-cute, you'll likely find her rescuing her paperback from the bath, or out guzzling espresso martinis in the name of research. *Duck à l'Orange for Breakfast* is her first print novel.

Duck à l'Orange FOR Breakfast

KARINA MAY

MACMILLAN
Pan Macmillan Australia

First published 2023 in Macmillan by Pan Macmillan Australia Pty Ltd
1 Market Street, Sydney, New South Wales, Australia, 2000

A catalogue record for this book is available from the National Library of Australia

Typeset in 12.5/16 pt Sabon by Midland Typesetters, Australia

Printed by IVE

All emojis designed by OpenMoji – the open-source emoji and icon project.
License: CC BY-SA 4.0

To my parents, for everything.

And to Donna. Your hair looks amazing.

Every woman should have a blowtorch.
Attributed to Julia Child

Prologue

On the morning of her brain surgery, Maxine Mayberry awoke to her 6 am alarm, showered, wiped her body down with chlorhexidine antibacterial wipes, applied a thick coat of fragrance-free moisturiser to her face, slicked her hair back into a low bun and dressed carefully in stretchy activewear.

Then she checked Tinder.

Chapter One

Three months earlier

Let the record show that when downing an entire bottle of cheap chardonnay in two minutes flat, I'm classy enough to use a glass. One of my treasured Murano glasses from our trip to Italy, when I'd decided that mouth-blown Venetian glassware was definitely worth a fortnight of eating stale paninis for dinner. Scott hadn't agreed. Especially as he was the one tasked with keeping the glasses safe in his overstuffed backpack while his stomach simultaneously 'ate itself'.

Down go five consecutive glasses of warm wine, poured in quick succession to hold back the flood of rising bile. The vomit comes anyway. Right back into the glass. That is also a rare triumph. A slippery hole in one.

It's the glass with the crack in it, I realise now, my fingers tracing the fracture. From when Scott's backpack had mysteriously launched itself off the top bunk in our hostel and connected with the concrete floor.

We'd fought about it – Scott's lack of regard for our valuables. I can see now that it was my fault, really. For attaching myself to him in the first place. For thinking he was capable of caring about something other than himself. Someone other than himself.

I'd ignored plenty of red flags. Because he made me laugh. And he had endless potential. I was the one who decided to put in the work required to polish him up.

On that day in Venice, we'd stood, transfixed, watching the Murano artisans working the glass. It darkened as it heated over the flames. Light blues turned to cobalt, pinks transformed into ruby reds, and copper into smoky browns. They layered colours on top of each other, adding thin sheets of silver and gold to create sparkly flecks. Every glass was unique; each with its own imperfections.

'What else can you make?' Scott called to a rosy-cheeked older man as he pulled a steel rod vined with molten glass from the flames.

'Signore, you tell us what you'd like.'

Scott cocked his head at me, eyebrows wriggling, then turned back to the man.

'One duck, please.'

'Duck?'

'You know, quackity quack.' He clapped his hands together in front of his face like a bill.

'You look like a piranha,' I said, laughing. 'You're going to give him nightmares.'

For the entire ferry ride back, I was conscious of the tiny, warm yellow duck nestled inside my bag.

'Let's name him Duck,' Scott had said.

Duck. The Duck. Poor Duck. It wasn't his fault that five years later, Daddy decided to bail.

I'm still cradling the cracked, vomit-filled Murano glass when my parents arrive.

The fluorescent hallway lights flicker on as Mum and Dad storm in, ready to carry me back to the safety of my childhood home, a world where I lounged in front of Saturday morning cartoons without a care.

Suddenly, I am a voyeur, watching my own life play out in front of me.

My mother cleans and carefully bubble-wraps and packs my Murano glasses. The moving van comes the next day for my belongings. On my instruction, they leave poor Duck, the couch – the yucky, pilled one that has seen years of foreplay – and one fork. The fork that has most likely been in *her* mouth.

PART I

Flambé

/flɒmˈbeɪ/

(adjective) Doused with alcohol and set aflame.

Chapter Two

Now

'Who orders a bloody coffee at the movies? Psychopaths, that's who!' Alice hisses at me as we wait for my oat latte. 'I thought you'd want something stiffer to celebrate your big day. That's why *I* drove.'

I shrug. 'I guess I still don't feel like it.'

'I'm surprised you're even here when you could be having post-production drinks with Zac. He loved your copy, Max. *Your* words!'

Zac is one of the models Slice Agency regularly books for ads. This morning I'd been giddy at the thought of spending all day on set with him, but somewhere over the course of the shoot I'd realised that an exciting workday was the highlight of my life right now, and it had hit hard. Not even an offhand remark from Zac complimenting the script I'd personally penned could fix things.

'Yeah, my whole four lines of utter drivel.'

'Don't be like that, Max. I know you're still feeling shit, but you have to take the wins.' Her irritation is palpable now.

'Seriously, though, did you have to ask for oat milk? Not even regular milk?'

'I'm sorry. I didn't think it would take this long.'

Alice is one of my tent poles. The load-bearing centre pole, in fact. My tent poles have helped keep me upright for the past few months (well, as upright as I can possibly be while laying down), but I've noticed that even the strongest poles occasionally strain to prop me up and buckle under the pressure. So I can't begrudge Alice her impatience. And oat milk or not, this really is becoming a ridiculously long wait.

'What are they doing, sacrificing a goat back there?' says a voice behind us.

We spin around to see a man in a striped shirt and beret. All that's missing from his ensemble is a baguette sticking out of his satchel. He's very obviously gotten the French film memo.

Alice elbows me. 'He's cute . . .'

I grab her arm and turn us back towards the coffee machine, completely mortified. He definitely heard us.

'Absolutely not,' I hiss in her ear. I know exactly what she's thinking. 'For you, maybe.'

'Not my type,' she responds matter-of-factly.

'Oat latte?' the guy behind the counter bellows.

'Halle-fucking-lujah,' Alice calls back.

~

Half an hour later Alice is apologising profusely to me. 'I'm so sorry, Max. I had no idea this movie was about an affair.'

'It's fine,' I mutter.

But it's not. There's something about the way the movie's star, Raphaël Personnaz, twists his face into a familiar look of cruel contempt that makes me want to throw up. In the last few months of our relationship, I went from being Scott's muse to a sharp pain in his side.

'I was too busy checking that none of the characters had a stupid pixie haircut,' Alice adds.

'You have a pixie haircut!' I can't help but exclaim.

'Shushhh!' huffs someone a few rows in front of us. I slump in my seat, cowering in the darkness of the cinema.

'That's why they annoy me so much,' Alice continues loudly. 'I don't know why I ever went pink – I look like a bloody tampon, yet they get to flounce out of their four-poster beds in their charming Parisian châteaux looking perfectly tousled.'

'CAN YOU SHUT THE HELL UP DOWN THERE!'

The heckling is now coming from behind us. I lean further back into my chair and sip my stone-cold coffee.

'Wanna duck out and go for burgers instead?' Alice asks.

I nod eagerly, and we stand. It's unfortunate that she booked us the best seats in the house, in the very centre. I take my lead from her and shimmy out, grazing an assortment of knees on the way. I can practically hear the theatre breathe a collective sigh of relief as we reach the end of the row and make our way to the exit.

We head to the burger joint next door and scoot into one of the booths at the back.

'I'm going to have the sliders. What do you want?' Alice asks.

'Like your burgers like you like your men, hey? Lots of choice!' I tease.

She's shagged so many different guys recently it's like our flat, the Nest, has a revolving door. Yesterday I found myself wondering if the rooms get together while we're out to gossip about it. I imagined the bathroom saying to the bedroom, 'I wonder what kind of penis she has in store for us next? Banana-shaped? Pencil? A hammerhead?' and the shower screaming out, 'Please, no curly pubes or chest hair. These old drains can't handle any more!' I've officially lost the plot.

Alice gives me a fierce glare. 'Getting brain surgery is no reason to be an arsewipe,' she says.

Shit. She's right.

'I'm sorry, A. I'm not sure what's going on with me.'

'I do,' Alice says. 'You're going through that stage where you lash out at everyone who's been good to you because you can't lash out at the person who hurt you most.'

'When did you get so wise?'

'Oh, you know, about the same time my heart was smashed into tiny pieces.'

Alice rarely speaks about James, her ex from a few years back who'd decided to pick up and move to London without so much as a conversation with her. But I can't remember her ever really getting super mean.

'I just didn't realise that you'd branched out into slut-shaming,' Alice continues.

I groan and rest my head in my hands. 'Oh, God. Who even am I?'

'Not that you deserve to know, but I'm actually seeing just the one person.'

'Really?' I peer through my splayed fingers. It hadn't occurred to me that the multiple Mr Late Nights could be the one Mr Serious. 'That's great news,' I add hurriedly, sitting up straight.

Have I really been so caught up in my own misery that Alice has started dating someone and I haven't even noticed?

'When can I meet him?'

'Soon . . .' she says with a coy smile.

The waitress approaches our table to take our orders, and we quickly rattle off our requests. When it's just us again, Alice leans across the table.

'Are you really okay, Max?'

'You mean about Scott, or my impending brain surgery?' I quip.

'Both.'

'I don't know. Fine, I guess.'

I look down at the table, then take a deep breath and continue.

'Sometimes I feel nothing at all, and for a while I think it's the numb moments that are the scariest. Then something sets me off again, and I'm in a world of pain. I mean, how on earth am I supposed to make it through the next three weeks when I can barely sit through a movie without it upsetting me?'

Alice is quiet for a moment, her eyes full of understanding. I'm glad I've regularly been candid about how I've been feeling the past few months, so she knows just how fragile I am.

But instead of reaching out to grab my hand, Alice's fingers flutter on the tabletop. *Tap, tap, tap, tappity tap.* Then a mischievous expression dances across her face.

Oh no, what is she up to . . .

'I have an idea,' she exclaims. 'And I want you to hear me out before you shut me down, please.'

'Okay . . .' I say, cautious.

'Tinder.'

I laugh. 'Sorry?'

'Tinder. It's the perfect solution. You don't need to meet up with anyone – in fact, I'd advise against it. But I think some fun, flirty banter with a cute guy, or a couple of cute guys, would do wonders for you!'

'I don't know, A . . .'

I'm feeling the exact opposite of my most fun, flirty self. And what would I even talk about with a cute stranger? The fact I'm about to be wheeled in for brain surgery in a few weeks' time? How sexy does that sound? NOT.

'Oh, come on, Max! If the tables were turned, you'd be giving me the same advice . . . And you just said that you don't know how you're going to keep yourself distracted! Hellooo, anonymous hot guys!'

I laugh again. If I'm honest, it's the most I've laughed in weeks.

'I feel like I failed you by taking you to that stupid movie tonight,' Alice says. 'Please let me make it up to you. I'll set everything up, choose your very best thirst-trap pictures – we could even do a shoot at home. Soft lighting, a juicy pout, and that beautiful mermaid hair out. Then I'll leave you to have all the fun! It'll be a nice reminder that there's still a life to be lived out there. I want you to remember that, Max.'

Alice's big, brown eyes plead from under her shock of pink hair. Those damn eyes have always made it near impossible to refuse any of her requests, no matter how ridiculous.

'Okay,' I relent.

'Perfect! Phone, please.'

'You mean now?'

'Yes.'

With my phone in the palm of her hand, Alice punches in my birthdate and quickly navigates to the App Store.

'Now, it's like thrift shopping, but for human beings,' she schools, as Tinder is downloading.

'So, everyone is worn-looking?'

'A little. But that can also be part of the charm.'

Great. She's really selling this thing, I think.

'I'm going to set your filters to ages thirty to thirty-five and up to fifty kilometres away. Not that it matters – you're not going to actually meet up with them. Now, a word of warning: don't, under any circumstances, hand your phone over to any of your smug coupled friends. It's like a fun sport for them, and they'll have you on a date with a man with a mullet because he has "kind eyes" before you can say, "I'm just browsing, thanks."'

Not so long ago, I was half of one of those vomit-inducing couples. Our classmates in first-year Performance Studies could attest that Scott and I had clicked from the moment we'd been paired up to attend and critically analyse a performance of *Waiting for Godot*, although it wasn't until the very end of that year that we worked out our connection was romantic. I now wish I'd never stepped foot into that class.

'What if it's an ironic mullet?' I ask. 'Like, they've grown it to raise money for a charity or something?'

'No, Max! The correct and only answer is always NO. Honestly, it's slim pickings on dating apps, but if you dig around enough, you'll find some decent second-round draft picks. You know, those great guys who've been benched for no reason except that they were too quick to settle down.' Alice is trying her best to sound optimistic as she swipes.

'Ohhh, see . . . What about him!' she exclaims, flashing the phone at me.

I lean in to inspect a photo of a man in a dark denim shirt.

'A memologist? What sort of occupation is that?'

'Whoops! I didn't see that . . .'

'See, I'm a quick learner. The words are just as important as the pictures.'

'Spoken like a true writer. Let's keep swiping, then.' Alice's thumb moves towards the screen.

'Wait!' I blurt, snatching my phone back.

'Oh! Look at that. Not even one minute on the thing and I've done my job.' A smug grin stretches across Alice's face.

With his peppery hair and curly beard, Johnny, the thirty-year-old memologist, looks like a scruffier version of Scott, but I know better than to say that out loud. Alice is treating me with kid gloves, but brain tumour or not, she'll lose it at any mention of Scott.

'I guess you have,' I say instead. 'I feel better already.'

Chapter Three

The Frisky Flutter 2000 is whirring like it's about to take flight. It's fresh off the charger. I hadn't realised its recent performance had been so subpar; I'd just thought I hadn't been in the mood. I reach for the remote to dial it down. Sex toys are at the frontier of solo female empowerment, yet somehow I've ended up with a vibrator specifically designed for two.

It had been Scott's idea to buy it, to liven things up in the bedroom. But tonight, when I positioned the pink rubber butter-fly on my clit, I realised I'd now have to operate the remote myself, which basically rendered it useless. I'd been at it for a good ten minutes and felt nothing yet. *Stupid couples' vibrator.*

Can Alice hear the vigorous buzzing from her spot in the living room? She's set up on the couch with a wine and her laptop, finishing some work.

She seems to be getting enough sex for the both of us lately. Whoever this mystery man is, he's certainly keeping her satisfied. Her door is closed most nights, and I'm treated to frequent high-pitched moans through the paper-thin walls.

I'm only surprised that Maggie, our uptight downstairs neighbour, hasn't been banging on her ceiling again.

I quite enjoy the orgasmic moaning in the background. For now, anyway. It makes the Nest feel more festive, in the same way that I find watching re-runs of *The Bachelor* therapeutic. The show is ninety-nine per cent heartbreak with the tiniest sprinkling of hope. I put in some solid viewing hours over the Christmas break and have almost finished the most recent season. I'm not sure how I'm going to keep myself distracted for the next few weeks after I'm done.

I sink back into the downy pillows, close my eyes and apply more pressure to my clit. *Focus, Max, focus. You still need to sort your finances tonight.* I have to email Scott too – he owes me eighty dollars for our last electricity bill. Call me petty but I can't afford to write it off. Even with health insurance, the surgery is going to have some out-of-pocket expenses. I could get a week in Bali at a luxury resort, cocktails included for the cost of one night in the ICU! *Gah, stop thinking about medical bills.*

I try emptying my mind, and an image of Zac's bronzed face on the set of last week's shower gel ad appears.

Ohhh, yes, thank you. That will do nicely.

His bicep bulges as he runs a hand through his perfect, sun-kissed hair, then he opens his mouth and begins reciting my words. He delivers the lines like smooth, flowing caramel that drizzles all over my body and laps up between my legs. The image plays on a loop until the lapping of the caramel rivers culminates in a delightful explosion that ends in uncontrollable shivers from the very top of my head to the tips of my toes.

Orgasm done, I flick off the Frisky Flutter 2000, roll over to pop it back into the drawer of my bedside table and check my phone.

A notification from Tinder.

I swipe before I really register what I'm doing. A new message. From the memologist.

Hey Max, nice to match. I'm Johnny. You've got pretty eyes

Oh, shit! Should I go and consult Alice? But, I find myself typing straight back.

Hey Johnny! Max here. Sorry, hardly original. Where are the conversation prompt thingys? I obviously need them!

He replies instantly.

Pfft, prompts, you don't need prompts. Your profile says you're a writer

Hopefully Alice only mentioned that I work for an advertising agency and said nothing about my unfinished novel.

I'm still all about the convo starter templates, I write.

Really? That's pretty lazy

It was a joke

Am I not doing this right? I wonder. Maybe I should have used a winky face emoji. Or would that have been too suggestive?

Sure it was, comes his reply. **So, what are you up to?**

I can't tell him what I've really been up to. Oh, you know, just getting myself off. Although I'm sure he'd love that. This may be my first time on Tinder, but I'm not an idiot. It's why I ignored his 'pretty eyes' comment – if we went straight to chatting about my appearance, it'd be a slippery slide down into a dick-pic ball pit.

Just having a quiet night in! I type.

Very generic, Max. Give me details. I like details

I glance around my bedroom for ideas, my gaze landing on my laptop resting on the end of my bed. Nope. Work chat is boring. I scan again, my eyes reaching my jam-packed bookshelf, where the black-and-gold spine of *The Laurent Family Cookbook* glints at me. It was a Christmas gift from Scott's mother, Helen – along with a plane ticket to Paris for her sixtieth birthday celebration. It's funny how you can want something so badly and then, in an instant, it can go from meaning every-thing to absolutely diddly squat.

I'm making dinner, I type at last.

What's cooking?

Ah, shit. I'm a terrible cook. I've never even cracked the cover of *The Laurent Family Cookbook* – Scott and I broke up a couple of hours after Helen gave it to me. It had been bundled into a box during my parents' rescue mission and somehow made its way onto my bookshelf at the Nest.

I panic.

Duck a l'orange, I type.

The Laurents' signature dish. Hardly a Monday night meal.

Fancy, Johnny says.

We're already at one-word replies. Surely this isn't a good sign?

Ah, shit. Am I a Tinder failure? I ask.

Huh?

You're monosyllabic . . .

So she is a writer!

Of ad copy

I see. Working for the devil, then!

Hardly. Luxury beauty brands, mostly

The same thing, no? And I was monosyllabic because I was tossing up whether or not to tell you that I actually live above a cooking school

Why wouldn't you tell me?

I was trying to decide how stalkery you seemed

Oh, I'm very stalkery

Perfect. Well, I won't tell you then

Wait, does that mean you're a chef? I thought you were a memologist

I see, you read the fine print

Always! So what's a memologist?

I make memes for a living

LOL, wow

Did you really just LOL?

Shit, that was certainly cue for an emoji. I'm enjoying myself far too much to stop and select the most appropriate tiny yellow face to mock his made-up internet job.

LOL, I type again.

Don't laugh. I make a lot of money from it

Sure you do

I do! Check out the Mother Ducker. Oh shit, you'll definitely stalk me now

I'm already in your front yard

You are? In that case, don't judge my bins. Busy week. I promise I normally recycle

So your memes are all ducks? I thought cats ruled the internet?

It's time for ducks to have their day!

You're an interesting one, aren't you, Johnny?

Right back at you, Max

A strange thrill runs through me. Bantering with this random man on the internet has completely derailed my plans for the evening. I can't put down my phone.

Aren't you going to ask me for a boob shot? I type.

And why would I do that when you're already in my yard and I can invite you straight into my shower?

Wow. I'm getting out of my depth.

I need my volumising shampoo, I tell him.

Drats, I'm all out

It's on special at Aldi, FYI

So if I run out and grab a bottle, you'll crawl out from behind my bins?

How do I even respond to that? My Tinder training wheels are most definitely off!

I navigate back to his photos and pinch the screen to zoom in. Johnny is very good-looking. A disarming smile that isn't cocky. You can tell that, stripped of his beard, he'd still carry himself well. It's simply an accessory, there to accentuate his features rather than bear the weight of them.

I've hesitated too long. Another message flashes up on the screen.

So . . . I haven't told you what I'm looking for on here. I'm seeking something casual

Right, yes. Of course he is. Isn't that what Tinder is all about? And isn't that what I'm seeking? I wonder if I could actually go through with a random hook-up with this Johnny guy just to prove to myself – and to Scott – that I've moved on.

Alice would be completely shocked. Delighted, but shocked. What an amazing story it would make!

Still, seeing it typed out like that makes it seem so crass. Like our banter has just been poured from an expensive crystal decanter back into its three-dollar bottle and returned to the cleanskins bin.

Love the disclaimer, I write.

Just your standard t&cs

I'd recommend more direct language, like 'currently banging other chicks'

Thanks, editor! I take it you're not currently banging a bunch of other dudes?

That I'm not

Figured

Why?

You don't seem like that kind of girl

Now he's irked me.

You don't know the first thing about me

I know that you're a writer who cares an infinite amount about the fluffiness of her hair. You have beautiful hair btw. Almost as lovely as those eyes

Wow, you nailed it! Me in a nutshell

It's settled then, he writes.
What is?
We'll be pen pals
Huh, pen pals? What am I supposed to say to that?
You can't resist the chat, I type.
It's true
So we'll write to each other?
Si
That's SO romantic
Like the olden days, he says.
Horse and cart optional
Ye olde nudes allowed?
Don't push it, disclaimer guy
I'm smiling so widely my face might split in two.
Haha, okay
And to think this all started with my pretty eyes
I can't believe I've made it this far without ruining things with some embarrassing reply. I need to quit while I'm ahead.
Night, Johnny
My breath catches as I wait for his response.
Night, Max XOXO
I exhale deeply. Not only have I survived my first experience on a dating app, I loved every second of it.

$\sim$

'Ew, Max. "Your pretty eyes"? Really?' Alice can't withhold a groan.

I'm tucked up next to her on the couch, phone surrendered.

'I know. That's why I steered the convo away from my eyes straightaway. I'm not as clueless as you might think, you know. And it's not like he mentioned my boobs or anything.'

'What would he say? "Love myself an ironing board, fancy doing my shirts?"'

'Rude.'

But my A-cup tits are beside the point. The truth of the matter is that I am completely clueless, and Alice knows it.

I'd been with Scott since we were both nineteen, so my only dating experience has been by proxy – mostly watching *The Bachelor*. And I know that in real life, first dates typically feature way fewer candles and fewer fire wardens on stand-by.

Scott and I didn't even go out much. When he wasn't on tour, he liked to grab Oporto's – the burger meal with extra chilli – to eat in front of the telly. Whereas Johnny seems like the kind of guy who'd sling me on the back of his bike and speed down some rain-slicked coastal road, *Dirty Dancing* style. Yes, I have already cast myself in the role of Baby.

Alice continues making lots of 'hmmm' sound effects as she scrolls through my conversation with him.

'Huh,' she says. 'He's funny. Though not as funny as you.'

I never feel like I'm funny. Scott was an aspiring stand-up comic – in fact he's relatively well-known now – so he always got to be the funny one in our relationship. I guess that's what you get for dating a comedian.

'So I have your permission to play on?' I ask.

Alice's brow furrows. 'I'm not too sure that's a good idea. He sounds like a massive player, Max . . . But I'm proud of you for giving it a go.'

'It's not like I'm actually going to date the guy,' I say. 'If it's just meant to be a distraction, does it really matter if he's a player?'

Alice considers my point for a moment. 'You're right, Max. That was the purpose in the first place, wasn't it?' She hands back my phone and stands up. 'As you were.'

Chapter Four

The padded envelope was a casualty of last night's down-pour, so sits damp in my hands. It's thick – so thick that I had to tug at it to retrieve it from the letterbox flap. When I turn it over, I see that it's secured with a wax seal. A familiar wax seal.

Legs suddenly weak, I kneel on the pavement. I'm out the front of our building on Crows Nest's busiest road, with Sydney traffic roaring past.

I rip open the envelope and unfold a piece of paper covered in cursive handwriting. My heart lurches as I scan the words.

Dearest Maxine,

Sorry that it's taken some time to get in touch, dear. We were so saddened to hear about you and Scott, but I suppose the heart wants what the heart wants.

Since you will no longer be joining us on our trip to Paris, I'm enclosing your Christmas present from us.

I hope you will wear it and think of our family.

Love,
Helen Laurent and family
PS – I left your Tupperware at your mum's door.

I scoff. Why the fuck would I want to think about them?

Oh, to have been a fly on the wall as Scott explained his version of our break-up to his family. If I'd had the strength, I'd have returned to the Laurents' on Boxing Day and barged into their lounge room – without removing my shoes – to let Helen know exactly the kind of man she had raised. A man-boy who didn't have the guts to tell me that he'd met someone else.

I empty the contents of the envelope into my palm: it's not a dainty chain but a colourful beaded necklace, likely purchased from one of those charity handicraft stores. *Thanks, Helen,* I think. *What a wonderful person you are, supporting underage girls in third-world countries. Your son's fuckery is all but forgiven!*

Besides, Helen has already given me a Christmas present: the book filled with family recipes, passed down through the generations, as sacred as the Colonel's eleven herbs and spices. I plunge my hand into the bottom of the envelope and feel around, sure that I'm going to find another padded bag, this one self-addressed, with a note asking me to return the cookbook – but there's nothing.

So why has she sent me the necklace? Is it a peace offering, or maybe a bribe, so I won't turn up at the airport and create a huge scene? It's unlikely I could, even if I wanted to, but they have no idea that I'm now scheduled for brain surgery just four weeks before their trip.

Besides, I'm sure my ticket has been transferred into *her* name anyway.

If I were the vindictive type, I'd post their precious recipes on the internet. I can see it now. My blog would be a huge hit with scorned women everywhere. Once you've cooked your way through the entire catalogue, your heart is miraculously healed! Joy!

'Can you please move?' says a stiff voice.

I look up to see our neighbour, Maggie, standing over me. Her dark brown hair is slicked back in a tight bun, emphasising her angular features, and her bulldog is panting at her side.

'Sorry,' I mumble, and shuffle out of the way, still on my knees. How can a woman my age intimidate me so much? I bet she works in finance.

Maggie huffs as she leans down and unlocks her letterbox.

Is now the time to confront her about the aggressive note complaining about 'excessive noise' that someone slid under our door last month? There was no name or flat number – a complete coward's act – but Maggie was suspect numero uno. I think about it, then decide I don't have the energy to deal with an altercation right now.

As Maggie checks her mail, her dog jumps up and mounts the bank of letterboxes, vigorously thrusting his hips. At least the dog has some personality.

'Down, Thor! Down, boy!' Maggie yanks on his lead and steps back from her letterbox.

'Sorry about that,' she says.

'No problem.' I manage a weak smile. What a surprising turn of events, to actually be spoken to, politely.

She hesitates awkwardly, as if she has something more to say. 'Well, you have a good day,' she says eventually, then turns and stalks off into the street, dragging Thor behind her.

My knees are starting to hurt, so I pull myself up off the ground. As I stand, I instinctively slip the necklace over my head.

It feels like a noose around my neck.

~

One hour later, I'm stripping down to my undies and pulling on a hospital gown. I've had enough of these scans over the last few months to have worked out that the method I use to endure a bikini wax is transferrable: I go in with a full bladder, so that all I can think about is not pissing my pants, in the hope that it will distract me.

At first I assumed it was stress at work causing my headaches. I was barely eating, after all. But when, after a few weeks, the intermittent dull thudding gave way to blurred vision and constant pain, my GP sent me for a scan. As it turned out, it wasn't just that I kept forgetting to eat – the scan showed a small tumour at the base of my brain. Likely not cancerous, the GP explained. These types of rare tumours generally aren't, he told me – but they couldn't be sure until it was removed and the cells were tested.

The tumour – about the size of two peas fused together – was pushing on my optic nerve, causing the problems with my vision. Not to mention the stabbing headaches, often so bad I was nauseous. It was also secreting hormones that were messing up my whole system. I'd been on the pill for years, which had masked the early warning signs, like missed periods. It was slow growing, which meant it had probably been humming along for years already.

Within a week of the diagnosis, I had a surgical team: a perfectly lovely but also very business-like endocrinologist, a smiley ENT with terrible veneers and hair plugs – and Alexander, my ridiculously dreamy neurosurgeon.

Alexander had a last name, of course – and the important title of Doctor, too – but at my initial consultation he had insisted I call him by his first name and I'd happily obliged. Basically, I'd fallen in love with Alexander before he had even saved my life.

While explaining my diagnosis, he'd nudged a photo of his perfect wife and a pair of golden-haired kids to the side to make way for an anatomical brain model and, with steady hands, calmly demonstrated how he would extract the tumour by pulling it out through my nose, like he was plucking a grape from its vine. By the time he advised me that he'd also be prescribing something in the interim to help with my headaches, I was head over heels.

'Right, are you all set in there?' the technician calls through the curtain.

'Yes. Coming.'

Before stepping out, I run my fingers over my earlobes and the back of my hair to make sure I've removed my earrings and bobby pins.

The technician leads me through the double doors into the room with the MRI machine, and I lower myself onto the table.

'You know the drill, right? Lie down flat, and we'll put an IV in now. We'll introduce the contrast dye about halfway through the scan. You might start to feel a bit warm then, and get a metallic taste in your mouth. You'll be in there for about thirty minutes.'

'Right. Thank you.'

'Want to pop these in your ears first?' She hands over a set of foam earplugs and I stuff them into my ears. A disposable blue hair bonnet and a pair of bulky, wireless headphones complete my look.

I wince as the needle pricks my skin. I need to get better at this.

The technician exits the room, and the table slides into the metal cylinder. The chamber is about the width of two rulers, perhaps a little wider. I can barely hear the Top 40 tunes playing through my headphones over the loud thrum of the machine starting up. It sounds like I'm being sucked into the depths of its powerful magnetic field. I squeeze my eyes shut and try to focus on Kendrick Lamar, but his raps have nothing on the 130 decibels bouncing off the chamber's metal walls and vibrating through-out my entire body.

Feeling anxious, I open my eyes to peer into the tiny mirror just above my eyeline, angled so that I can see my toes. A reminder of a world outside this close, narrow coffin. *Not a coffin yet*, I remind myself. *A brilliant machine built to keep me out of a coffin. If I'm lucky.*

I want to shake my head to free it of these thoughts, but I have to remain as still as possible. This is the final scan before my operation. The scan that tells Alexander exactly where to use his scalpel. I can't risk messing it up.

I really need to pee. My bladder feels like it's on fire, like I have a raging urinary tract infection. Perhaps this strategy isn't the wisest, after all.

Heat from the dye rushes down my arm, then up my legs. I imagine my torso as a waxy candle, my neck the wick and my head the white-hot flame.

Shit. It's never been this hot before. I'm not sure I can bear it.

I try to steady my breathing, cheeks burning. How can I stay calm when I'm seconds from being burnt to a crisp, like bread stuck in the toaster?

I don't understand why –

Then it dawns on me. I reach for my neck, urgently grasping the beaded necklace with its metal clasp sitting innocently under my hospital gown. I tug once before changing tack and clamping down on the emergency buzzer.

Fuck that family. Seriously.

I don't need their support, but it would be wonderful if they'd stop trying to kill me.

Chapter Five

IKEA's perfectly plotted paths drive normally functioning humans to despair. Me? I can't get enough. The lavishly deco-rated rooms, reminiscent of movie sets, can be relied upon in a way so much else in the world cannot. IKEA is the place I seek refuge. Which is why I drive straight to the Tempe store after my MRI appointment. To the mothership.

My IKEA obsession started a few years ago – well before my diagnosis – around the same time Scott and I moved into a nearby apartment. Rather than retreating to the bathroom whenever we argued (where my rage was fuelled further by the erect toilet seat), I would walk it out around the neigh-bourhood. One stinking hot summer's evening, I ducked into IKEA and found that the industrial-strength air conditioning cooled not only my body temperature, but my nerves. Soon, I started detouring there for a pick-me-up after creatively stifling workdays, just to relax before going home. It's where I came up with the idea for *The Doors*, my fantasy novel about escaping to new, magical worlds – kind of like

Narnia or the Faraway Tree, but through IKEA display room doors.

It's been five years, but I still haven't made much progress on my novel, preferring instead to make up little stories about the characters I see at IKEA. At last count, I have twenty IKEA-inspired vignettes. Scott used to laugh when I read them aloud, but I stopped doing that months before we broke up.

Still a tiny bit shaky on my feet from my MRI disaster, I take a deep breath and step out of my silver Mazda and look up at the familiar blue structure. A banner strung over the front of the building instantly lifts my mood.

Cfofee tbales from $29

Who is the copywriter who comes up with this stuff? It's brilliant. I make a mental note to research the agency working with IKEA. The ad asks the reader not just to consume its message, but to engage with it. To invest time and effort creating the whole from its parts. It's the same psychological trick that keeps us buying IKEA's furniture: you place a dispro-portionately high value on something you've created yourself, even if all you did was assemble it. The $29 coffee table isn't just a pile of cheap laminate, it's something you built. Or better yet, something you and your significant other built together. Is that why I was so attached to Scott? Because I had such a hand in building him that it became impossible to see he was disposable junk?

The escalator carries me up to the entrance, and I grab a yellow carrier to loop over my arm. There's a small, round bandaid in the crook of my elbow, marking the spot where the needle went in. Once the beaded necklace had been disposed of – into my locker first, though later I threw it in the rubbish bin next to the hospital's revolving doors – they were able to redo the MRI. *Happens all the time*, they said. *No damage done.*

I follow the arrow past the first kitchen display and feel an immediate sense of calm as I take in its sparsely filled shelves. The glass-fronted pantry is stocked with dry pasta and spices, the jars lined up in neat rows, and sparkling utensils hang from a rack affixed to a white-tiled splashback, adding to the sense of order. My hand trails over the spines of the vintage recipe books arranged on the counter.

I take a step into the living space, in which a gallery of air-brushed Swedes in frames fill every inch of wall space. Just as I plonk myself down on the modular sofa, my phone buzzes. I retrieve it from my bag to find a new Tinder message.

Hey, pen pal!

A smile creeps across my face.

I swipe open the app and type, **Hey yourself!**

His reply comes instantly.

So, have you given any thought to how you plan on convincing me?

Huh? What's he on about? I try to recall how our last chat ended. Nope. I'm still drawing a blank.

Convincing you to do what?

To meet up. As if you don't secretly want an in-person rendezvous . . .

The hide!

Oh pls . . . I have way too much going on

Shame. I could have had my arm twisted

I was actually going to suggest that we double-down on this pen pal thing, I type, improvising on the spot. **And keep it completely anonymous**

Ooh, I likey. How kinky of you, Max

I can feel myself blushing.

Perfect. Let's vow not to stalk each other online then

Deal

So what exactly do anonymous pen pals talk about? I ask.

Anything and everything. Depends. Whatever's going on, really

You're telling me that this is the place to bring my woes and my worries. Like an agony aunt?

Sure. I'll be your agony aunt, green eyes

How many Tinder pen pals do you have? Do you collect us?

No collection. But I want to be straight with you, Max

His use of my name makes my stomach flip-flop, even more than when he called me green eyes.

Yes, Johnny?

I'm seeing a few other women. Casually, I mean

I sit up straighter. Interesting.

Busy boy

Does that bother you?

I play it cool.

Not in the slightest. You do you, boo

☺ So what have you been up to today?

Gah. Imagine if I actually told him.

Not much, I lie.

Where are you?

IKEA

Brave

I thought so

Why would anyone choose to go to IKEA?

I'm not ready to share my feelings for IKEA with him. It's too soon.

It's so hot outside, and it's a perfect 19C here

Seriously, fuck climate change. My new thing is to shower and then stand in front of the fan

I hesitate for a beat before typing. *Yeah, why not*, I think. I'm going to go for it.

I bet it is, I type. Since my new theory is that you're 50 and live in your mum's basement. Not much ventilation down there

Oh, real-ly?

Shit! A photo is coming through! What if it's a dick pic?

When it loads, I feel a pulse deep in my underwear. Johnny is staring straight into the camera, like he's looking directly at me. There's no denim this time; he's wearing a simple white T-shirt that perfectly complements his olive skin. He's cradling a coffee mug like it's a rescue kitten, two fingers looped through the handle, and his thumb resting on the lip.

Alice needs to see this. I screenshot the image, in case it suddenly disappears.

Aren't you supposed to hold something up? I type, still trying to play it cool. **That could be your son**

I get up off the couch and quickly rearrange the decorative pillows. I've just realised it's 2 pm. I need to get back to the office and finish the copy for a cologne ad. I continue on the marked path past the bedrooms and bathrooms, towards the market hall.

What do you mean, hold something up? he asks.

I dodge a toddler having a tantrum in the middle of the aisle.

You know, like a newspaper with the date

OMG, you're ridiculous

I laugh so loudly that the couple in front turn around to look at me.

Funny suits you, he says.

En route to the registers, I grab a pack of Swedish meatballs, then try to decide which queue to join.

Why thank you. All right, I'm at the checkout

What are you buying?

Dinner

Yuck, don't do it. Pegasus begs of you. Those meatballs are made of horsemeat, you know

Ew. Really? I dump the meatballs in the bin of miscellaneous items near the counter and grab a lilac-coloured eggwhisk instead.

Just joking. I was here for some new cooking gear

Right. See you for dinner, then?

My heart races. Has he already changed his mind about not meeting?

Sorry?

A snap of your dinner. Tonight. 8 pm

Before I can reply, he sends another message.

Best dish wins the right to ask a question of their choice

This feels like a trap, I say.

I'll be waiting, Max

Chapter Six

Alice storms out of her bedroom, tote bag in hand. The bells on her red-and-green striped elf socks jingle uncontrollably as she charges towards the kitchen, sliding to a stop in front of the packed bench. 'Whoah! Look who transformed into Martha-fucking-Stewart overnight!'

I glance down at my smorgasbord. It had gotten out of hand rather quickly. It all started with a practice batch of packet-mix brownies I found in the back of the pantry, just to check I knew how the oven worked. Things had escalated from there. Next came a simple caprese salad, before I embarked on a classic lasagne.

'What happened to my "two-minute noodles are a meal" flatmate?' Alice asks as she swipes the edge of one of the brownies and sticks an icing-covered finger in her mouth. 'Ohhh, yummm. Okay, Martha Stewart can stay.'

Pride washes over me. Yes, the brownies are from a packet, but they're edible – which is more than I can say about the gluey scrambled eggs I made this morning, an attempt to start my day right before I left for the hospital. I blamed MRI anxiety for the curdled creation.

That was before my new lilac eggwhisk. Before the challenge.

I'd been surprised at how much I'd enjoyed cracking the eggs for the brownies, measuring out the milk and melting the butter to add to the chocolate powder. I'd found an old wooden spoon at the back of a drawer and stirred until the mix smoothed and thickened. The wooden spoon hit the side of the ceramic bowl over and over with a rhythmic thump that was oddly meditative.

'Don't get used to it. I'm kinda doing an assignment.'

'Pray thee, do tell?' Alice wriggles an eyebrow. I laugh and turn to open the fridge, crouching down to the bottom shelf to retrieve a bowl of béchamel.

'Okay, now you're taking the piss!' Alice exclaims as I rearrange the bench clutter to make room for the new bowl.

I get to work spreading the sauce and meat mixture over the lasagne sheets. I'm careful not to overdo the fillings. There's a fine line between 'bountiful' and slapped together by a teenager with the munchies. 'You remember that Tinder guy?'

'Guy? As in just one guy? It's been days, Max. Shouldn't it be guys, plural, by now?'

'I don't know. We got chatting, and I'm kind of enjoying it.'

'Okay, I'll allow it. Let's ease you in. Provided you're not talking to Scott.'

I focus on wiping up a splodge of béchamel and don't answer right away.

'That was a question, Max.' Alice looks at me sharply. 'You're not, are you?'

'No. No.'

A few emails don't count, I tell myself. We still had that electricity bill to sort out. Plus, I've been ignoring the emails not related to household expenses.

'Good,' she says, but she still looks suspicious. 'So, what's all this for, then? What's your assignment? Is Tinder guy giving you homework?'

'He suggested we share pics of our dinner.'

Alice frowns. 'Is he trying to wife you already?'

'Nooo, it's not like that!' I protest. I'm actually semi-enjoying myself for the first time in a long while, and I don't need her poking holes in my fleeting happiness. I try to change the subject. 'Why are you wearing those socks? Christmas was months ago!' Anything Christmas-related still triggers a trauma response.

But Alice is not ready to drop it. 'I hope you're not selling yourself as some domestic type, or he'll be bitterly disappointed.'

'Okay, harsh. But also, of course not. It's just some fun. Johnny's sending me a pic too.'

'Oh, it's Johnny now? You're not supposed to call them by their real names. Until further notice, he will hereby be known as Duck Boy.' Alice stamps her foot on the ground, bunny-hopping into a little elfin jig.

I laugh again. 'Careful. The she-devil from downstairs will be banging on our ceiling again.'

Alice dismisses my warning with a flick of her hand. 'Don't worry about her – I've got it handled.'

'Did you tell the real estate we're being harassed by our neighbour?'

'Mmm, something like that,' she says, backing out of the kitchen.

I sprinkle a handful of grated cheese over the final layer. 'If you're good to wait forty minutes or so for this thing to cook, there will be plenty for both of us.' I bend down, open the oven door and push the lasagne tray onto the top shelf. 'Hey, do you know what sort of an oven this is? Is it fan-forced?'

I'd somehow managed to burn the brownie edges, and I wasn't sure why. I had to cover the blackened bits with a thick lick of icing. The kitchen had always been Scott's domain. It's his lasagne I've just put in the oven.

'I don't know,' Alice says. 'Isn't it like a hybrid?'

I roll my eyes. 'It's not a Prius, A.'

'Well, I'd love to stay and feast, but I'm on my way out.'

'Wearing that?'

In addition to the socks, Alice has on bike pants and a holey sweatshirt. She looks like she's about to roll a spliff under the covers in her university dorm. Alice is a successful advertising account manager, but she also has no desire to grow up. Even when we met, working as interns at the same ad agency at age twenty, Alice insisted that she was 'twenty-teen', and now, standing in the kitchen with her sweet pixie haircut and elf socks pulled up past her knees, she certainly resembles one of Peter Pan's lost boys.

Alice pokes out her tongue and jigs over to the door. 'Save me a piece for breakfast?' She slides her feet into her Birkenstocks.

'So, you're really not telling me where you're going?'

'No, sir,' she says, performing a final jig before disappearing out the door.

If I didn't have to keep an eye on the lasagne, I'd be tempted to follow her. I hadn't even had a chance to fill her in on how today went – and tell her about the joke of a necklace!

Exactly thirty-eight minutes later, I'm opening the oven door and feeling triumphant about the bubbly, cheesy, oozy goodness that greets me. I leave the lasagne to cool for a bit before arranging it on a plate with the caprese salad on the side and brownies artfully positioned in the foreground.

Then I sit and wait.

Right at 8 pm, my phone pings.

Okay, whaddya got for me?

My stomach gives an excited flutter, but I manage to wait a few moments before sending through my carefully composed shot.

Impressive, comes the reply.

I barely have time to enjoy the compliment before another message comes through.

Now I need to see the proof

Proof? I reply, confused.

That it wasn't ordered from Uber Eats

I smile, despite myself. I turn to survey the kitchen and see the sink piled with dirty dishes. I flip the camera around to selfie mode and snap a quick picture of myself and the sink and press send before I can give it a second thought.

I wait what feels like an eternity for his reply. *Come on! What the hell are you doing over there?*

I click to inspect my picture. Not bad. Not bad at all. My eyes are bright, cheeks flushed, nose scrunched, and my blonde hair is knotted messily on top of my head. I look angelic. A picture of health. How ironic.

Hey, green eyes

My heart almost leaps out of my rib cage. I imagine his voice, deep and gravelly, delivering the message.

Hey back, I type.

My mind is whirring with idyllic fantasies. Heads on pillows. Early dawn light. Eyes cracked, bed hair, sweet morning cuddles.

That plant looks like it needs a drink

I come crashing back to reality. I examine my photo again and see that I've managed to capture Alice's dead succulent.

Stop buying time, I say. **Your turn**

A few moments later, I'm staring at a picture of a shiny layered pastry with crushed nuts of some description sprinkled on the top.

A pastry?

Baklava. It's Greek

That's not dinner, I type.

It is in my world

What is his world? I zoom in on his photo for clues. The plate of baklava sits on a stainless-steel bench, and in the background is even more stainless steel. It looks like a commercial kitchen.

That's not your house, I say.

Got a good look at the kitchen from the bushes the other night, did you?

I love his continual references to our previous chats, and that we already have our own ridiculous in-jokes.

Ping! My phone chimes again, and I feel my dopamine spike. It's all very Pavlovian, really.

I live above a cooking school

Oh yes, he had mentioned that.

That doesn't seem fair, I reply.

Why lasagne? he asks.

I hesitate.

My ex used to cook it

Ohhh, THE EX

Yup

Isn't that kinda masochistic? Or did you stay friends?

I actually found it therapeutic. And no. Definitely not friends

Why did I mention Scott? I want to keep our chats bright and breezy. Yet Johnny seems to have a knack for extracting personal details.

So, who's the winner? I type, before he can get me to reveal anything further.

Ah, she's a competitive one

How does he do that? Read me so perfectly through a phone? My mind flashes back to my last holiday with Scott, in Hawaii, and the giant pineapple maze. I had commando-crawled under the spiky bushes in an effort to beat a pack of teenagers to the exit, emerging with scratches all over my arms and legs. I even ripped my sundress. Scott laughed at me for letting the kids get under my skin, but I was laughing too. I remember the warmth of his gaze, and how happy I felt with the tropical sun glowing down on us.

Johnny's right. I am competitive.

I made multiple dishes, I fire off.

It's quantity over quality with you, is it?

You're the one who collects women, I joke.

He takes way too long to reply. Oh, God. I didn't mean to push the parameters of our teasing. Isn't this how banter works?

His message finally comes through.

So, me seeing multiple women does bother you, he says.

Not at all

I'm not going to be on this app long enough to care . . .

Right, back to business. I start typing again.

It's not really a fair competition, is it?

How do you mean?

Well, since we're not tasting each other's dishes, all we really have to go off is looks

There's another pause. I visualise him feverishly stroking his beard in the way Scott had whenever I challenged him. Is that why I like Johnny? Because he reminds me of Scott?

So, how do you propose we get around that? he asks.

We could cook the same thing, I suggest.

Johnny replies in an instant.

Of course. Excellent solution. Jamie Oliver? Donna Hay? Margaret Fulton?

Too well known, I type. **How do I know you haven't cooked the recipes before? Can't have you cheating over there**

Any suggestions, then?

I glance up at the shelf above the fridge, where there's space for cookbooks. Instead, it houses another dead plant and a collection of empty wine bottles that Alice keeps saying she's going to repurpose into candles. I think fast.

The Laurent Family Cookbook, I write.

Never heard of it

I got it for Christmas

I squeeze my eyes shut while I wait for his reply. What am I even doing? My phone vibrates in my hand.

Interesting. How do I know you haven't cooked the recipes before and this isn't a ploy to win?

You'll have to trust me

I know the taste of the recipes in that book by heart, but I've never attempted them. The decadent crème brûlée, the slow-cooked beef bourguignon, the moreish French onion soup and, of course, the *pièce de résistance*, duck à l'orange.

Go on . . .

I hesitate, wondering whether or not I should send the next message. But I want to be completely honest with him.

The Laurents are my ex's family

Three dots appear. Johnny is typing. Words flash up on my small screen.

Well now, isn't this a turn of events?

I picture his pearly whites, framed by wild facial hair. Irresistibly smug and rugged.

I know it sounds wack, I type after a beat. **But for some reason it feels necessary. Like I'm rewriting my own story by claiming a piece of theirs**

Okay, I'm in

That giddy feeling from earlier is back.

That was easy

On one condition, he adds.

Yes?

That I'm declared the winner of this round. My baklava was *chef's kiss*

Haha. Sure

That means I get to ask you a question

I'd forgotten all about what was at stake.

All right, then. Shoot

Why did it end between you and the ex?

I wait until my hands stop shaking to reply.

Because he cheated and ripped my heart in two

I hold my breath. He was probably after some witty answer, and I've served up an overshare instead. Then my phone buzzes.

That skato!

I'm assuming that's not a good thing . . .

No. It's Greek for piece of shit

Funny, that's exactly how Dad describes him.

Haha yes, that's fairly accurate, I type.

Right, well, let's go ahead and FORK HIM then

I put my phone down on the bench and cut into the lasagne. An avalanche of meaty filling oozes out the sides, and a grin dances across my face.

Let's fork him, indeed.

Chapter Seven

IKEA was the logical choice for the cookbook drop. I've come straight from work, a wad of photocopied pages from *The Laurent Family Cookbook* stuffed into my laptop bag.

My heart is hammering in my chest as I step onto the escalator. I have to remind myself that it's just plain old adrenaline doing its thing and nothing to do with my tumour.

I didn't say a word to anyone at work today and – unsurprisingly – Alice didn't return for her piece of breakfast lasagne, so I haven't had a chance to fill her in on the plan. A good thing, really – if I'd told her I was off to plant a copy of my ex's family recipe book in an IKEA display kitchen for my internet pen pal to retrieve and work his way through like a deranged version of *Julie & Julia*, she'd have staged an intervention and locked me in my bedroom.

Once Johnny and I had nutted out the details of the IKEA plan last night, I couldn't resist sending one more message as I'd climbed into bed, smug and satisfied from the lasagne.

You're in trouble, I typed.

Is that so? came his reply.

I think I may have unlocked hidden talents. My dinner was delicious

I received similar feedback on my baklava

Feedback? Of course. He'd told me he was seeing other women. But my stomach still dropped at the idea of someone else's lips around Johnny's baklava.

Stepping off the escalator, I grab a bag and stuff the photo-copied pages inside, keeping a watchful eye out for Johnny. On the off-chance he's come early to catch me in the act, I want to spot him before he spots me.

Fork Him project, Day 1: Max drops the pages at approx-imately 1800 hours; Johnny retrieves them just before closing at 2100 hours. I could stop at the cafeteria for a plateful of meatballs and there'd still be no chance of any crossover.

Still, I've worn some pink lippy for the occasion: 'Love on Top', the same shade I wear for my appointments with Alexan-der. I've also dabbed some concealer under my eyes and a swipe of bronzer across my cheeks. Just in case. I'm not sure if I'm terrified or excited about the prospect of a Duck Boy run-in.

I survey the shoppers playing house in the first display kitchen. There's a red-headed couple in their twenties – who would be amazing contenders for my favourite Instagram account, Siblings or Dating? – running their hands over the faux marble countertops and ooh-ing and aah-ing about how durable they feel.

Pace yourself, darlings. Things always feel indestructible in the beginning.

Over by the sink, a mother is wrangling two small boys.

'But I'm thirstyyy!' the older one is screeching.

'Harry, I've told you that the taps are pretend. There's no water. We'll get you a drink at the kiosk soon.'

'I want it nowww!'

Harry throws himself on the floor at his mother's feet. I admire her ability to continue appraising the chrome finish on the faucet as he attaches himself to her leg.

It's a relief that Scott and I weren't quite at the kids stage. We had talked about it often, as couples do, but we never went further than picking our favourite names. Scott would joke that he wanted to name his son T-Bone, which, of course, horrified me. I had swooned over old-school, bookish names like Audrey, Sylvie and Persephone. If we'd had a baby, we'd have been linked forever. Scott would have loved that. The strongest card in his deck of reasons to take him back.

My eyes flick around the space. We agreed I would do the drop at the first Billy bookcase I came across. I spy one instantly to the right of the island bench with the faux marble top, but the young lovers are in my way.

I hover around the magnetic spice rack and wait for them to finish fondling benchtops. Harry's mother is still examining the taps, and his little brother has chimed in too, so now both boys are demanding soft drink. I imagine that T-Bone would have behaved even worse, taking after his father.

Come on. Move it along, peeps.

This is not how I thought things would go. I thought I'd be in and out in a hot minute like a stealthy, sexy spy – James Bond style.

I wander over to the freestanding oven and start fiddling with the knobs.

'Can I help you?'

I startle, then freeze as it occurs to me there's a chance the person standing behind me, mere centimetres away, is Duck Boy.

No! It can't be . . . I imagined his voice to be much deeper. A rich, distinctive bass that would slide down my back like warm honey.

God, maybe he's catfishing me. He did send through a photo that matched the pictures on his profile, but that could have been ripped from anywhere. *At least we're in a public space*, I think.

I turn around slowly, my heart in my throat.

A pudgy man with a moustache stands in front of me, the yellow 'Hej!' employee shirt stretched tight over his belly. I recognise him as one of the regular evening workers, but he's never approached me before.

'Our ovens are top of the range.'

Since when does IKEA have customer service? You can be lost in the labyrinth of aisles looking for the coordinates of a particular item for hours before finding someone to assist you. Then, once you've managed to flag them down, they're off again before you realise your box is on the top shelf.

'Amazing, thank you,' I say.

'Swedish designed and engineered.'

'Yes, thank you.'

'This one is called the Görlig. All curiously named. Sounds like pig Latin, doesn't it?' he says in his broad Australian accent.

'Hmm.'

He takes a step towards me, and I clutch the IKEA bag to my chest. It's like this guy has a sixth sense I'm up to something suspicious. Except – as I remind myself – I'm leaving something, not taking something.

'Well, please come and find me if you need any assistance. The name's Dennis.'

'Will do, thanks,' I reply.

Under his breath he says, 'There's some lolly in kitchen sales for me, you see. Janice and I are particularly skint after Christmas.'

Of course. Commission.

I watch as Dennis makes a beeline for the red-headed couple. A few minutes later, he's leading them to see a 'far superior benchtop material a few kitchens over'. Bound to be a far superior price, too. You're doing God's work, Dennis. You've earned yourself that commission through your divine intervention.

The mother and her whiny kids have finally moved on – she could do with some divine intervention too, the poor thing, or at the very least a post-checkout hot dog.

I plunge my hand into my bag to retrieve my lippy. Once I've reapplied a fresh coat, it's show time.

The bookshelf is decorated with Scandinavian knick-knacks: a golden hand sculpture, a geometric deer figurine and a photo of a shiny, smiley couple in a frame. Interspersed between them are several all-white books that stand to attention like dominos. I reach for the thickest book at the end of the middle shelf and pull it down.

Simple gold lettering decorates the front cover, and matching type runs up the spine. *The Tales of Mother Goose*. I open the cover and flick through the pages to find maths problem after maths problem. The rumour I'd heard about IKEA covering old Swedish textbooks with new sleeves is evidently true.

I check over my shoulder for Dennis – or one of his commission-hungry colleagues. Coast looks clear. I pull the thin sheaf of papers from my bag. Fourteen recipes from *The Laurent Family Cookbook*, each carefully selected. Fourteen days until my surgery. I hesitate, then dip back into my bag to retrieve a pen and scribble on the front page:

Johnny
xoxo

Then I fold the recipes in half, slide them between the pages of the faux *Mother Goose* and put the book back on the shelf. I love the idea of French silk pie sitting alongside mathematical pi.

Mission complete, I stride away, following the arrows through the tableware department, then past the desks, wardrobes and the home textiles section.

By the time I reach the bedroom department, I'm practically floating – high on a mixture of adrenaline and excitement. I'm sure there's a goofy smile plastered across my face, too, like I've just had a mind-blowing orgasm in one of the display beds.

Chapter Eight

2 1:05.
  21:06.

Our oven clock ticks over painfully slowly. Alice purposely juts out her bum to obscure my view as she cleans up after our Mexican kit dinner. I told her about the Fork Him project over our tacos. I could tell she wanted to advise caution, but once we locked eyes, the sparkle in mine must have stopped her. It didn't stop her teasing me, though.

'Earth to Max! The best flatmate in the world has just cooked you what some would consider award-winning tacos, which you barely ate because all you can think about is Duck Boy.'

I'm about to deny it when my phone pings.

You smell nice

'OMG, he messaged!' I cry.

'Yasss!' Alice drops the bowl she's washing into the sink, sending soapy water spraying like a blowhole, and lunges towards the couch. 'Give it here!'

I reluctantly hand my phone over. Johnny's messages were starting to feel very much for my eyes only. The kind that make you want to crawl into bed and read them under the covers, not in front of an audience. Even an audience of just Alice.

'What does he mean, "you smell nice"? I thought you said you hadn't met this guy? Ma-aax, I really don't want to be a killjoy, but surely you don't need the complication?'

My face reddens. I hadn't sprayed my Dior perfume directly onto the pages – I just spritzed the air and wafted the pages through it. A subtle hint of me. Or so I thought.

'I don't know what he's talking about,' I say, snatching my phone out of her hands.

'Okay, settle down, Rambo. I'll leave you to message Duck Boy in peace.' She backs away from the couch. 'Provided you do the drying up and fill me in on every last detail in the morning.'

'Deal,' I agree. I'm aware that I'm hard to live with, with my moods dancing around constantly. Alice never knows what version of Max she's going to get. Truthfully, nor do I. And it changes hourly. But right now, it's the happy, excited Max. Hopefully she'll linger for a while.

'Night, Martha Stewart,' Alice calls on her way to the bathroom.

'Night,' I murmur, already distracted.

I sink into the couch cushions, my heart racing.

I'm glad you think so, I type back.

He replies in a flash.

So, chocolate souffle for dessert?

I'd put the chocolate soufflé recipe right at the front, where he'd see it first, and was hoping he'd take the bait. If we're going to cook through all fourteen recipes before my surgery, then we need to start today.

Sure, I say.

Great. I'll be home in 10 mins. Give yourself a head start

I don't need it

Despite my words, I spring off the couch and start assembling the ingredients on the countertop. I made a stop at the supermarket on the way home and selected the most expensive cooking chocolate I could find, denoted by its shiny gold packaging. It was time to graduate from packet mix. Before I made it all the way home, I realised I'd need an electric mixer, so I swung by my parents' house. Predictably, they'd wanted to chat about how I was feeling. The top line was 'quite well, all things considered'. I was slowly marking off all my pre-surgery appointments and doing a good job of keeping myself distracted. How I really felt about things was future Max's problem. Present Max's only issue was how to transform her bag of groceries into a gooey, chocolatey soufflé.

I'd eaten the Laurent chocolate soufflé more times than I cared to remember. Afterwards, I'd end up moaning in pain while Scott rubbed my belly and teased me for having the self-control of a four-year-old. How ironic that, in the end, he was the one lacking any real self-control.

I'd managed to make a quick getaway, with the beater tucked under one arm, by promising Mum that I'd call her straight after my endocrinologist appointment tomorrow.

Now it's time to get down to business. I chop my expensive chocolate into tiny squares, drop the pieces into a saucepan and melt them with sugar and milk.

Next up, I beat egg whites and a pinch of sugar together until soft peaks form, then, with Mum's mixer still running, I slowly add the remaining sugar and whisk until the peaks stiffen.

Burning, I can smell burning.

Oh, crap! I forgot the chocolate. An unpleasant dirt smell curls up my nostrils. Hopefully there's not enough smoke to set off the fire alarm or rouse Alice from her bedroom sexting . . .

Despite my questionable cooking skills, I'm enjoying my solo kitchen time.

Luckily, the chocolate mixture looks salvageable and ten minutes later, once I've carefully added in the egg yolks and flour to create a paste, and then folded in the beaten whites, I spoon it into ceramic ramekins (another loan from Mum). I have followed the Laurents' recipe to the letter. So much so, there's a fat, chocolatey fingerprint marking one of the pages.

Okay, Max, you're doing well, I tell myself. I slide two soufflés into the oven: the real deal and a back-up. If *Master-Chef* has taught me anything, it's to always have a back-up. I double-check that the temperature is 190°C and set the timer for twenty-five minutes.

Now I just have to cross my fingers that the burnt smell hasn't permeated through the whole mixture and that the damn thing is going to rise to greatness. Even with the best photography, there'd be no disguising a deflated soufflé. Just like Tinder, our challenge is all about appearances. We haven't discussed scoring, but I'm assuming presentation will be paramount, with taste just an optional extra.

My phone has been completely silent while I've been hard at work perfecting my soufflé. I check the screen again, just in case I didn't hear it ping over the thrum of the beater. Nope. Nothing.

For all I know, Johnny has arrived home and fallen asleep. Or decided that this whole thing is silly and he wants no part of it. I really hope that's not the case. Like, really, really.

At least I've occupied myself for the night. Once the sun sets and night takes hold, my mind tends to wander to dark places – especially when Alice isn't home. I imagine couples and families cosied up indoors, laughing, kissing, cooking, doing the washing-up. That's the thing – I know chores are being done too, but that's also the stuff I miss. The simple act of being together in the mundane. My life now consists of going to work, coming home to the Nest, dinner and (when she's home) chats with Alice, then bed. I'll forever be grateful for my time here – to even have a home to come home to – but I miss what I once had, before Scott left me to do the washing-up and face my surgery alone.

I drum my fingers on the benchtop, trying to drown out the intrusive thoughts. They are not welcome. Especially when I have gorgeous soufflés (hopefully) puffing up in the oven. I pick up my phone and promptly put it down again. I could message Johnny, but I don't want to be a nag and risk taking the fun out of this thing we're doing.

I don't know what to do with myself. Where to put myself.

I walk over to the couch and flop down.

A delicious, rich chocolatey scent wafts over to me, and my tastebuds zing to attention. *The soufflés might turn out okay after all*, I think, swallowing the saliva that's pooled in my mouth. I don't dare step back into the kitchen. The temptation to open the oven door and let out some of the precious hot air 'just to check on them' is far too strong.

Instead, I instinctively reach for my laptop. Before I realise what I'm doing, I open a new Word document and begin to type.

The couple

A life uncomplicated suddenly made complicated the moment they impulse-purchase a modular couch.

They step outside of IKEA, hot dogs the colour of their hair in hand, excited and proud to own their first piece of furniture. They could have scored a second-hand couch from a friend, but this is better. It's brand new, periwinkle blue, and it's theirs.

It's not until they pull their Hyundai hatchback up to Click & Collect that they realise there's an issue.

The couch doesn't fit. The staff laugh when they suggest they'll strap it to the roof.

She cracks first, calling him moronic for not thinking about how they were going to get the couch home. He yells, wondering why he's the one who has to think of such things. Don't get her started. She organised the rental inspections, secured a property, signed the contract, paid the bond, picked up the keys, scrubbed the place from top to bottom.

Okay. He'll sort it. A van is sourced. He can't drive a manual, so she'll drive. Traffic is bumper to bumper, he tailgates her in the Hyundai and almost runs up her back. TWICE.

Finally, they're home. Silence as they carry the couch up the long drive and manoeuvre it up three flights of stairs.

They're too tired to admire their new couch. Too tired to sit. The van needs to be returned.

The apartment is quiet, save for the occasional faint whimper of Thor downstairs. Maggie must be out. I quietly delight in reading back the words that have poured freely from my fingertips. After months and months of nothing I've finally written my twenty-first IKEA story. I'll soon have enough for an anthology! Now if only I could focus on *The Doors*. But it's something – I've written something. *Let's just hope it doesn't foretell the actual fate of that sweet couple*, I think as I save the file.

I check my phone. No message from Johnny, and only five minutes left on the timer. It's nearly 11 pm. Why haven't I heard anything from him? Disappointment builds. I want to hear from him. In fact, in this moment, I have never wanted something more.

My fingers itch to type 'Mother Ducker' into Google's search bar, but I manage to resist. We have made a pact not to look each other up, and I refuse to let my anxiety make me go back on my word.

I open my email instead. My heart hurtles into my throat when I spot yet another email from Scott. Can't a girl have a quiet, drama-free evening in, cooking soufflés?

But after my writing win, I finally feel ready to find out what he's been sending all those emails with no subject lines for. I take a deep breath.

Hey Max,

Sorry if you feel like I'm hassling you. I had a moment of panic yesterday morning at Hype. I was looking at all the sneakers and felt crippled by a fear that you wouldn't like the pair I selected. It really crystallised just how much I want to be back in your life, and how far away I feel from that ever happening.

I know I've made mistakes, I know I've hurt you, and I know you feel betrayed, but I am certain you are my soulmate, certain that I love you, and certain that we have a once-in-a-lifetime connection. I have never stopped loving you. The little pinkie of our relationship contains more happiness and love than most of the relationships that other people settle for.

I know it won't happen overnight, but I'll do whatever it takes to get back with you.

I can honestly see us getting back on track and having a wonderful future together, one that is better than ever.

Trust me, Max, I never lost sight of how wonderful you are. I did take you for granted. It kills me to admit it, but it's true. But I never stopped loving you, and I never forgot how special you are.

Please give me a real and honest chance to fix this and make it up to you. Please, please, please!

Scott x

Ugh. I push my laptop away. It takes considerable self-restraint not to throw it against the wall. How dare he? I can only imagine how thick he'd be laying it on if he knew about my tumour. I wish I could believe his words; I really do. But I'm not sure that I can believe a single thing that comes out of his mouth ever again.

I could end the flood of words now by blocking him, yet for some reason I don't. I don't want to hear from him, but I don't *not* want to hear from him. Go figure.

My thoughts are interrupted by sharp pinging. I jump up off the couch, relieved, and scurry over to the oven. I scrunch my eyes closed and pull open the door, suspense building, like the lead-up to an impressive magic trick. A wall of thick heat slams me in the face, and I slowly peel open my eyes.

'Wow. It worked!' I exclaim as I inspect the luxurious-looking desserts. The soufflés have risen a few centimetres above the edge of the ramekins and appear light and fluffy.

I grab some oven mitts and carefully pull them out. It would be devastating if they collapsed. As I'm placing the ramekins on the bench, my phone lights up. Johnny!

I rush to remove a mitt so I can swipe open his message.

It's a photo, almost identical to the view in front of me. Maybe I needed that head start after all.

I quickly snap a photo of my own creations and press send. I mimic his approach, not adding any accompanying text. I wish I had more time to style the shot properly, but I can't have him thinking he's that much speedier.

While I'm waiting for his reply, I take a teaspoon from the drawer. The soufflés are rich in colour and blissfully spongey with a crackly top. *I hope they have gooey centres to match*, I pray. I select the best-looking soufflé and plunge my spoon deep into its heart. Success! I snap another photo and forward it to Johnny. Surely that's worth extra points? I take a tentative lick at the chocolatey goo on the spoon. As suspected, it's still very hot and, disappointingly, has a distinct smoky flavour. Damn it. Thankfully there's no taste-testing involved. That's a definite upside to this arrangement.

My phone flashes with another message from Johnny. A photo of his gooey centres. This time, with text: **The Devil's Chocolate Soufflé**

I snort.

The Devil? I like the name

I'm glad. I figured it needed a rebrand

My stomach flip-flops.

I've added some extra icing sugar on the top, Johnny says. **I wanted to guarantee it was more delicious than any sex you ever had with what's-his-name**

Holy shit. My heart is beating so fast it feels like it's going to fly straight out of my chest. I did not expect that.

Haha thanks, I reply.

I wish I had something smart to say, but my hands are shaking so badly as it is that I can barely type.

Bon appetit, Max x

Bon appetit x

Chapter Nine

We're at Day 5 of the Fork Him project, and my cooking skills have not improved.

Day 2 was a beef bourguignon with a 'splash' of pinot noir, which I somehow ended up drowning with a whole bottle. Day 3's bouillabaisse was edible; the accompanying cheesy croutons, less so. And my cassoulet on Day 4 was burnt to a crisp. I blame Johnny for that one. I was too busy laughing at his new name for the recipe – Crap Comedian's Cassoulet – and the beans caught on the bottom. That was my favourite of his new names so far. It was the alliteration that sealed the deal, narrowly beating out the Dishonourable Beef Bourguignon and the Vile Bouillabaisse.

I wonder what name Johnny will bestow upon tonight's French silk pie? It's a dessert-for-dinner kind of day. I can barely wait to get home and into the kitchen and start my routine marathon texting session with Johnny. It's getting harder and harder to keep things from him. The other day, when he was messaging from the grocery store to let me know that Bakers

Delight's day-old one-dollar sourdough would make perfect croutons, I was waiting for blood tests.

Thank you! I'll swing by a Bakers Delight once the vampires are done with me

Luckily, I'd caught myself in time and deleted the second sentence before pressing send. Johnny didn't care what was going on in my life. Sure, he knew vaguely about my ex – I'd mentioned in passing that he was a stand-up comedian – but that was how I wanted to keep it. Vague. There was nothing sexy about the details.

I pick at the small round bandaid stuck in the crease of my inner elbow. The nurse really did a number on me, pulling the needle out and then sticking it back in multiple times, seeking a plump vein. A black-and-purplish bruise has ballooned down my arm. I should have worn a long-sleeved dress.

It's imperative that I look and act professional today. Like I truly have my shit together. Scratching at my skin like a junkie isn't helping. But at least it's giving me something to focus on, other than the exact coordinates of Raffie.

The studio lights beat down on me. Even from my position tucked up against one of the far walls, I feel claustrophobic in the heavy heat, like I've just disembarked a flight in Hawaii and am now navigating the sticky tarmac. We're still waiting for Zac to emerge from his dressing-room and take up residence on the stool in front of the cameras.

A week ago, I was right alongside all my other colleagues, waiting for the moment Zac peeled his shirt off so we could ogle his abs. Today, I'm too anxious about seeing Raffie to care.

I slump further into the wall, trying to make myself invisible, then throw a subtle glance across the room to where Raffie is adjusting Zac's stool. I have been acutely aware of her presence since she first entered the room. She's been shuffling the stool over a few centimetres, then back again, for a solid twenty minutes.

I'd be lying if I didn't admit to getting some joy out of seeing her so flustered. I would still give everything in my being for her to be shipped back to New York. Why couldn't she have just stayed there indefinitely? She was the creative director of this shoot, so I'd arrived knowing that there was no avoiding her today – but that didn't make me any more prepared.

What was it about her that had made her so irresistible to Scott? Was it her obvious ambition, or her uncanny similarity to his mother? I've spent months analysing the 'why' and still not come up with any airtight theories. It just doesn't make sense to me.

I let out a loud sigh, and Raffie's head snaps up.

Shit, shit, shit!

A swarm of butterflies start flapping in my stomach, and I quickly divert my gaze, looking over Raffie's head to the catering station behind her.

'Nerves getting to you, Max?' Raffie calls out to me.

'Oh, hey, Raffie. Welcome back. And no, not at all,' I respond with false cheer. 'Just thinking about lunch already.'

Wow, we're really doing this. Playing the game that everything is okay.

'How was New York?' I ask.

'Fabulous. You'd love the set-up. They have an in-house barista, so bagels and coffee on demand. Keep up the great work and we'll send you there on secondment, too.'

'Sounds great.'

Like most young creatives, my dream had also been New York. Now that, too, had been sullied by Raffie. I didn't solely blame her, of course. She should have had some common decency, but it was really Scott who owed me loyalty. It was hard not to wonder if his flurry of apology emails would even have started if Raffie had been in the country. Though she was back now, and the emails were still coming hard and fast.

I had ignored two more from him this week. I wasn't game enough to ask her if she'd spoken to him. Whether she was still with him. Whether she was going with him and his family to Paris.

Today was all about getting through work and remaining as professional as my shaky legs would allow. Now that Raffie was back, there would be many days just like this, so the sooner I could master a state of cool indifference, the better.

'How are you feeling, Max?' Raffie is walking towards me, a look of concern in her eyes.

My heart quickens as she approaches. *Does she really want to do this here?*

'I'm fine. Thank you.'

'You know, I have tried to reach out. Eve said that you're not responding to her messages, either.'

My throat feels thick as I picture Scott's sister, and I struggle to swallow the lump.

'I've needed some space.' My voice sounds robotic.

'Of course,' Raffie says, twisting the trio of gold bangles that wind like a serpent up her long, slender arm. 'I just want you to know it really was just a few times. He was lonely because you weren't around. But I'm still so sorry.'

I nod. I don't trust myself to speak.

Her eyes move to my bruised arm. 'Are you sure you're okay?' Her tone shifts, like she's suddenly concerned about more than just my broken heart.

As a member of the agency's upper management team, Raffie has access to the staff leave calendar. She could easily have found out that I'm taking six weeks' leave soon but would know none of the detail. I haven't shared what's going on with anyone at Slice except Lucy – which I'm already regretting. As a fellow writer with a shared dream of leaving the agency world, Lucy is a genuine friend. Just not in the way Alice and I were when we'd worked together. Lucy is my replacement Alice: a version with loose lips and a demanding four-year-old.

I'd prefer my team think I'm having some banal surgery, like getting my wisdom teeth pulled. Although I realise that six weeks off for dental work would be extreme. I just don't want them to look at me differently – like I'm a ticking time bomb – when I already feel like one anyway.

I clench my teeth, prepared to respond again, when Zac glides into the studio.

He's clearly gotten some sun over the last couple of weeks. His skin is a delicious golden brown, and his hair is streaked with the odd highlight, like the sun has literally bowed down and kissed his head. He's also sporting an effortlessly cool beard. A razor is hardly a priority when there are surf reports to check, frothies to scull and beaches to be barefoot on. It's the kind of beard Scott had aspired to, cultivated by lifestyle, not clippers.

Zac greets the room with an easy two-finger salute.

'Hey, guys,' he drawls.

'Morning, Zac,' we all chorus. There are about ten of us in the room, including the hair and make-up team and camera operators. Somehow I'm still standing next to Raffie.

'You want me here?' Zac asks as he slides onto the stool, and turns his attention to the teleprompter. My butchered words have already started scrolling across the screen. It had been another case of copy by committee.

'Ready whenever you are, Zac.' Raffie beams.

It's cologne, not shower gel today. Zac begins delivering his lines, seamlessly throwing in the occasional lopsided grin and flick of his hair.

Did he or didn't he?
So seductive, only the bottle knows for sure.

A real man doesn't need cologne.
He is wild.
That's what you smell.
Carefree, easy . . . animalistic.
Antaeus, a breezy scent for the modern man.

I wince. This script is particularly cringe-worthy. That's what happens when you work for an agency where the motto is 'all creativity is billable'.

'Animalistic, hey, Max?' Zac curls his fingers and swipes his hand through the air like it's a lion's paw.

I wait for the usual rush of excitement. Not only has Zac noticed me again, he also knows my name . . . But – nope – I feel nothing.

'Why don't we take some behind-the-scenes footage for socials? The actor and the writer,' says Raffie. 'I'm sure Antaeus will appreciate the extra content.' Next minute she's behind me, pushing me towards the bright studio lights, bangles jangling.

'No, thank you,' I say, digging my heels into the floor.

What the hell is she trying to do?

'Come on, shoot your shot, Max,' she whispers in my ear. 'You and Scott weren't right for each other anyway.'

Chapter Ten

'Alice! Are you home?'

I push open the front door and rush down the hall, stopping outside her room.

'Alice?' I call again, pummelling her door with my fists. 'Are you in there?'

I need to calm down. The fifteen-minute uphill trek from the train station usually helps sweat away any stress from the day, but today it has had zero effect.

'Alice?' I call out once more. There's silence on the other side of the door.

It's 3 pm. Of course Alice isn't here. She's still at work.

It may be midafternoon, but it's also rosé time. I back away from Alice's door and head towards the kitchen.

In front of the fridge, I hesitate. Is it too early for a drink? No, not after the day I've just had. Plus, apart from Raffie terrorising me, I've had a surprising reprieve from my usual thumping headache. At least that's something. I retrieve an open bottle of rosé from inside the fridge door, then stand on my tiptoes to open the overhead cupboard. Ever since that fateful night, I've committed to consuming my wine out of glasses – no matter my state of despair. I make a point of reaching for one of the Murano glasses. They're so beautiful, I refuse to let memories of Scott taint them. He got the stupid duck; I got the thousand-dollar hand-blown glasses. A small price to pay for sticking your dick into someone else's vagina, really.

I plonk myself on one of the bench stools and take a measured sip of wine. I feel instantly calm, not from the wine – it needs a few minutes to do its thing – but because the kitchen is so familiar. It feels like one giant, warm hug. From the lilac-painted cupboards with the ceramic knobs that Alice found on Gumtree to the timber countertop that she'd lovingly sanded back and stained, the warm, comfortable aesthetic would be right at home in any Nora Ephron film. Even the dead succulents somehow have their place. It's so different to the kitchen in the apartment I shared with Scott. That was a modern, soulless space I rarely stepped foot in.

In contrast, I've spent so much time here in the last week that I know every nook and cranny and all its quirks by heart: the oven that only catches alight if you fan the gas flame with the door; the drawer that won't close properly without an act of bodily violence; the rangehood that whirrs so loudly it sounds like you're blasting off into space . . . I love it all.

I trace the rim of the glass with my finger and smile. Who would have ever picked that I'd feel most at home in the kitchen? But here we are.

I polish off the glass of wine and top myself up. I don't mind the idea of tipsy baking. How much damage could I really do? A burnt crust is one thing, though – setting the Nest alight is something else entirely. Perhaps I should go easy . . .

I abandon my glass and walk to the pantry. It's too early to start on the pie, but I need to do something to keep my hands busy and stop myself from checking my inbox for another of Scott's emails.

Countless times over the past couple of months, I've dreamt of forwarding them straight to Raffie. Would she be surprised by his persistent declarations of love for me? I have no idea if there is anything still going on between them. They've both said it is done, but at this point, words mean nothing. I haven't told a soul about Scott's emails, and I've resisted that urge to send them to Raffie. I still very much need my job – and my sick leave.

I groan. Who knows what sort of dire position today's storm out has left me in? Do I even still have a job? I shouldn't have let Raffie's words chase me away. I stop my hunt for ingredients and return to my wine. It's so easy to drink away any thoughts of work, Scott and Raffie. And my broken brain.

As I take a sip, my phone lights up with a new message from Tinder. My palms are suddenly sweaty, and the Murano glass almost slips from my grasp. It's too early for our nightly meal pic swap . . .

How is your week treating you?

There's no mention of any Bakers Delight sourdough specials or substitute ingredients for this evening's French silk pie. Just one, simple question, laid out bare.

Should I be honest? *Fuck it. What do I stand to lose?*

Awfully, I type back.

Oh no, really? What's going on?

I'm just my own worst enemy, that's all. Sorry, therapy session time, LOL

Please don't apologise. Work got you down?

Kind of. It's work-related

Let me guess, your boss is a low-grade narcissist and went mental on your arse?

Good guess. I would have preferred a psychotic boss to a day spent with Raffie.

Not quite. More that I work with the girl my ex cheated on me with, and we had our first encounter since the break-up today

Oh, shit. That would do it

Yup

Do you mind me asking where you work? Or does that breach our anonymity clause?

I've already told him about my work. Has he forgotten? A sign, perhaps, that Johnny is not as into me as I'd like to imagine?

Sure ☺ I work for a creative agency

Ah, that's right. A slave to the devil

The real devil is the other woman, who IS also kinda my boss

Tell me there was blood spilled today?

How is it that he's managed to elicit a grin out of me?

If there was any spilled, it was mine

I don't believe that for a second

Really? I'm a big ol' weakling

I haven't seen any evidence of that

I did sort of storm out when she tried to set me up with the talent

Do you like him?

No. Well, yes, we all have crushes on him, but that's not the point

I understand the problem here

You do?

Yup, it's pretty simple

Okayyy. What is it?

It's you

Ah, nooo. I want to turn away from my screen. *Please* don't ruin this, Johnny.

You can't see what other people see when they look at you, he types.

Holy shit. My insides are a mess. Where did this insightful Johnny come from, and where did light-hearted, sling-me-on-the-back-of-your-bike Johnny go?

Okay, Aristotle, I reply, in an attempt to lighten the tone. Writing to Johnny is supposed to be fun.

What are your dreams, Max?

Wow, he's really doubling down on the intensity. This is starting to feel a bit too personal now.

What do you mean?

When you lay your head on your pillow at night, what's the one thing that keeps you up?

I obviously can't say that it's mostly thoughts of dying on the operating table. But when I picture life on the other side of my surgery, I always see myself sitting in an overstuffed armchair at the back of a bookshop, a long queue stretched in front of me, at my book launch.

I take a deep breath and type, **I guess I'd love to be an author. But it's hard to find the time to write between work and life**

And heartbreak and brain tumours, I think, but I don't dare add any more.

You need to make the time

Yeah, I know, something always just crops up

Something will always crop up

Yahhh, yahhh

He's hit a nerve.

You really want to hear this from me, right? Some anonymous guy on the internet. I'm sorry

No, I appreciate it. But it's not really things just cropping up. I suppose it's more that I don't think that I'm good enough

Well, I know that's not true

How would you know that?

I could give him a list of ads to watch and advertorials to read, but they're hardly an accurate representation of my skills. I feel like I've used it all up – my talent, my creativity. I'm not sure what I have left, nor what will remain once Alexander and his scalpel are done with me.

I can tell by the way you phrase things. You have something special

My ex didn't think so

On the rare occasions Scott did read parts of *The Doors*, he made me feel as though my attempts weren't worth the laptop they were written on. 'Short stories are more your thing, babe,' he'd say. It was hard to shake the feeling that it was because I was no good.

My phone pings again.

That skato! Fork him

Rage flames through me. *Yeah, fork him.*

Anyway, I say. Thanks for listening. And for doing this cooking thing with me. It helps

No problem. I like making you feel better

You're good at it

Thanks. And btw, it's helping me too

What does he mean by that? Surely it has to be about more than just 'liking the chat', but I don't want to risk scaring him off by asking him outright. He's only been in my life for just over a week, and I already can't imagine him not being there, always ready with some witty remark to make me laugh.

I guess if there was ever a time to ask why he's doing all of this, it's now. But before I have a chance, my phone pings again.

See you tonight for pie time? I've got a killer name ready. Inspired by this chat, actually

Tell me, tell me!

I'm not completely disappointed that our deep moment has passed. It means I can keep the dream of our fun, no-strings-attached banter alive a little longer. I'm not ready to say goodbye to it just yet.

Don't be greedy, Max. Btw, do you know that French silk pie isn't a French recipe?

No. How do you know that?

I know lots of things. Plus, the Oreo crust kind of gives it away, don't you think?

Ha

See you at 8 pm!

The feeling I have in the pit of my stomach is hard to describe. It's unlike anything I've ever felt before – warm and nourished and fed, like my belly is an oven, and a loaf of bread is quietly and contentedly baking in there.

I put my phone down, pick up my glass and take a sip. The wine has grown warm. As I move over to the sink to pour it out, I pass the window, and a streak of purple catches my eye. I peer out to see the rear end of a woman in purple jeans. She's bending down picking up dog poo, a leash wrapped around her wrist. There's presumably a dog on the other end of the leash, but it's obscured by the large fig tree.

I swear Alice has pants just like that. My eyes travel down the woman's legs and stop at her sock-and-Birkenstock-clad feet. Wait a second . . . it *is* Alice!

A moment later, a familiar bulldog appears around the tree trunk.

For some incredibly mysterious reason, Alice is walking Thor, aka the fur baby of the worst neighbour in the world.

Chapter Eleven

*F*ORK HIM.

I stare at the two words on the computer screen in front of me. They stare right back, as if to say, 'Yes, and . . .? You were saying?' The problem is, I'm not sure what it is I was saying – or what I'll ever have to say again.

I sigh and shut my laptop. With Day 8's quiche Lorraine crisping up in the oven, Johnny challenged me to get some words down until the timer went off. As though it was as simple as doing the washing-up.

It doesn't matter what you write about. Get messy with it! You think your ex-ancestors-in-law came up with these recipes without breaking a few eggs first?

I appreciate his belief in me, but my word count is stuck at two. Four, if you count the full stop and page number. Ha!

I cast my laptop aside and stand up. Too quickly. I'm light-headed and dizzy. I'm sure the avalanche of sugar over the past few days hasn't helped. There's been a spate of desserts, Day 6's Bad Apple Tarte Tatin followed by Day 7's Cuntish Crème Brûlée.

I'd burst out laughing at that one. But it was Day 5 that made my insides melt each time I thought of it. True to Johnny's claim, the name was inspired: the Smart, Sassy, Sexy Silk Pie. Its Oreo cookie crust has a rich, creamy chocolate filling, topped with whipped cream and chocolate shavings. I can only assume – hope – that he was thinking of me when he'd renamed it. After receiving that message, I'd gone straight to bed with my Frisky Flutter 2000 and imagined Johnny dripping melted chocolate all over my body, then smothering me with whipped cream before his tongue slowly and expertly licked me clean. It was a welcome reprieve from the thought of my approaching surgery.

I open the fridge to stacks of containers holding various desserts. A sickly sweet scent has claimed the space, over-powering the usual fridge aromas of fresh fruit and veg. I'd considered taking some of the Bad Apple Tarte Tatin into work. Lucy could never resist an office cake. The moment that email hits our inbox – *Help yourself! It's in the usual spot near the photocopier* – she's up out of her chair and rushing to grab a piece. That's the very reason I refrained from bringing in any leftovers (and with my fluctuating appetite, thanks to my meds, there were plenty). I didn't want the office hyenas picking over the last of the pastry to catch Raffie's attention. What if she recognised the recipe as one of the Laurents'? I don't know how I'd go about explaining that one. Not that I owe her any kind of explanation.

I nudge aside the containers of dessert to hunt around for ingredients for a quick salad. Not a display salad – Johnny and I have long since done away with the pretence of props and filters – but something to nicely complement the very cheesy quiche and impress Alice and her mystery guest.

I'd sent Alice a text message immediately after spotting her outside the Nest's window.

Hey, is that you with Thor?

I watched as she slid the phone from her pocket to reply.

Hey! Yes. Will explain when I'm home 😌

But Alice didn't come home that evening, nor the next. I sent her a text this morning to check in and ask if she wanted to have dinner tonight.

How does a Day 8 quiche Lorraine sound?

She replied right away, **Yummy**

Do you mind if I bring someone?

I welcome it 😉

I can hardly wait to meet this mystery man.

~

I'm peering through the oven window, watching the cheese bubbling away, when I hear the jangle of keys outside the front door. A moment later, the door swings open and Alice walks in, followed closely by Maggie.

'Hey!' Alice greets me brightly, like this is any ordinary Wednesday evening and it's perfectly normal to invite our nightmare of a neighbour around for tea.

'Hello,' I reply carefully, and desperately try to make eye contact with Alice. A heads-up that we were going to be breaking bread with the enemy would have been nice. I'm not sure I can trust myself to be polite. Life is increasingly feeling too short for niceties.

I wait for Maggie to throw out a thinly veiled comment about the Nest's 'interesting décor' in her usual stuffy tone, but she remains quiet. Instead, she shuffles closer to Alice, until they're practically attached, like gum stuck to the bottom of a shoe.

Wait a second . . . What's going on here?

'This is Maggie. From downstairs,' Alice says, introducing us like we haven't bitched about her almost every night since I moved in.

'Yeah, hey Maggie,' I say.

My mind is racing, running through a million different scenarios. The only one that really makes any sense is that Alice has rage-quit her agency job and become a dog walker, and Maggie (and more specifically, Thor) is her client. But before I have a chance to worry that quiche Lorraine is too casual for a business meeting, Alice reaches out and grabs Maggie's hand.

Ohhh. Now I see.

'We're dating,' Alice states, just in case the body language didn't already give it away.

Wow, okay, wow. Out loud I say, 'Well, welcome to the Nest, Maggie.'

I step forward, arms outstretched, and wrap them around her. It's a neat hug, because I'm conscious of not crushing her crisp white shirt. I spot a splodge of egg mixture on one of my fingers and quickly withdraw from the embrace, like I've suddenly realised I'm wielding a loaded weapon.

'Thanks, Max.' Maggie smiles at me – a real, genuine smile. 'First off, I really want to say how sorry I am.'

I turn to look at Alice. Her cheeks are bright pink, and she's studying me closely. I shrug. 'For what?' I ask.

'For being such a dick!' Maggie exclaims, and we all erupt into laughter.

'Yes, about that . . .' I joke. I don't want to misread this situation and mess up whatever Alice has going on here, so I steal another glance at her, and she nods her approval. 'What was that all about?'

Maggie sighs deeply. 'Ah, I think I was jealous.'

We're all still standing near the doorway, so I move to the couch. Alice and Maggie follow my lead and flop down next to me. I'm on one couch cushion, and they're huddled on the other. Alice rests her hand casually on Maggie's thigh and gives it a pat, encouraging her to continue.

'I thought that you might be a couple. It just sounded like you were having so much fun up here,' Maggie says.

Now that explains a lot. The green-eyed monster is a hell of a force to be reckoned with sometimes. And the fun part was true – while our late-night dance parties often started in floods of tears, they always ended in pure joy.

'If you call listening to Tay Tay on repeat fun. Not even any of her new stuff – "We Are Never Ever Getting Back Together". Ha!' I say.

'Yes, Alice filled me in on what you've had going on – what you still have going on. I'm so sorry, Max.'

'I hope that's okay?' Alice asks, eyes wide with worry.

'Of course it is.' I give them a reassuring smile. 'There are no secrets between friends.'

I see the tension leave Maggie's body. 'Thanks, Max.'

'It's all good,' I say as I stand. 'Now, who wants a wine? Dinner is about fifteen minutes away. Then I'd love to hear all about you, Maggie. If you're no longer our cranky, stuck-up neighbour, then who the hell are you? Although please forgive me if I ask you all the same questions again in a few weeks . . .'

'Max.' Alice's tone is warning. She hates it when I joke about losing my memory.

'Just ignore her,' I say to Maggie. 'She's having a hard time accepting that she may end up with a goldfish for a flatmate.'

I turn my back and busy myself pouring out sizeable glasses of French rosé, so that I don't have to deal with Alice's pity face.

～

The quiche Lorraine is delicious. The pie crust is lovely and flaky, the eggs fluffy, and the bacon, cheese and caramelised onion filling is perfectly balanced.

Maggie has relaxed into the evening and unbuttoned the top two studs of her shirt; her fluoro-green bra is visible. An hour ago, that would have taken me by complete surprise. Uptight Maggie looks as though she'd sport a matching beige set, not colourful lingerie. But it's taken no time at all to get acquainted with fun, quirky, accomplished artist-not-banker Maggie, who originally knocked on the Nest's door a month ago with a peace-offering of cupcakes left over from Thor's first birthday.

I wasn't home, but Alice gladly accepted them before Maggie realised she'd accidentally boxed up pup cakes instead of the human variety. Alice thought it was hilarious, and the rest, as they say, is history. I can't wait to get all the details as soon as Maggie leaves. I should probably be upset that Alice didn't say something sooner, but it's hard not to get swept up in her excitement. She's kicked off her Birkenstocks and has been playing footsies with Maggie throughout dinner, our plates bouncing up and down periodically like they've hitched a ride on a bumpy school bus.

'Can I offer anyone dessert?' I ask as I stand to clear the table. Every plate is scraped clean. I remember the quiche being a guaranteed winner in the Laurent household. Sometimes all that was needed to impress was eggs, not escargot. Thank God that for all the Laurents' snobbery, they (or rather, their ancestors) weren't partial to snails.

'We have a crème brûlée, apple tart or French silk pie,' I say, and I can't help but repeat the *Smart, Sassy, Sexy* bit to myself.

'Wow! You must really like dessert.' Maggie sounds impressed.

'The Nest is kind of a test kitchen right now,' I explain.

'Ohhh, yes, that's right. The Fork Him project with that online guy.'

My forehead creases. Alice has really told her everything. I'm not sure how I feel about that . . .

Maggie smiles. 'The pie sounds yum.'

'Ew, no, don't,' Alice cautions.

My face warms. How could Alice have any idea about all

the things I've visualised doing with Johnny and that pie? Is she a mind-reader now?

'Didn't you make that a few days ago?' she continues.

Ah, right. For some reason she's suddenly a food safety inspector.

'Just two,' I huff.

Maggie looks at me and then back at Alice.

'How about I take some dessert to go,' she offers, clearly sensing tension. 'Leave you girls to catch up and talk behind my back.'

Ohhh, I like her. I don't know how I got it so wrong. But that's also me, a proven track record of poor character assessments. At least I know what I'm getting with Johnny. A bad boy who wants to remain permanently unattached. I'm happy he was so upfront about that.

'Yeah, take your salmonella to go,' Alice says.

I ignore her and start cutting into the tart. Why is she being so ungrateful when I've been nothing but lovely to her surprise girlfriend?

Thor's muffled whimpers sound from the apartment beneath us.

Maggie sticks out her bottom lip. 'Poor guy. I haven't been home all day.'

'Maybe you can take some extra for him?' I offer.

Alice jumps in. 'Max, no! Chocolate isn't good for dogs.'

'You only learnt that from the Oreo ad,' Maggie says. Alice pokes her tongue out at her.

Yes, I *really* like Maggie.

I arrange a generous piece of each dessert in a Tupperware container. Maggie hugs me before heading to the front door. 'It was lovely to meet you properly, Max. And if I don't see you before your surgery . . . Well, I hope that it goes well. I know it will.'

'Thanks, Maggie.'

Accepting well wishes from near strangers makes my upcoming surgery feel real.

Alice walks Maggie out onto the landing. They bend their heads close, deep in murmured conversation about how the evening has gone, and it's my turn to feel a little jealous.

When Alice slips back through the front door, I'm at the sink, elbow-deep in suds.

'Are you surprised?' she asks.

'Hmm. Not super.' I pull my hands from the soapy water, wipe them dry on a tea towel and turn to face her. It's the truth: sure, Alice has never explicitly said that she's into women, but she's never said she wasn't either.

'Maggie seems great,' I add. 'Not a monster after all.'

'She is pretty great.' Alice grins.

'I'm just happy that you'll have someone to keep you company once I'm go–'

Alice barrels towards me, grabs me by both arms and starts shaking me violently.

'W-w-what a-are y-you d-d-doing?' I choke out.

'Stop it! You need to stop this right now, Max!' she shouts. Spit flies into my face.

I wince. Alice drops my arms, but she doesn't take a step back. 'I need you to listen, and listen very carefully,' she says. Her breath is warm on my face. 'You are not going to die. You hear me? Not on my watch.'

'I'm shit-scared, Alice,' I say, studying my hands. The egg splodge is gone.

Alice doesn't respond, just puts an arm around my shoulders.

'What if they super mess things up, and I end up a completely different person?'

'That's not going to happen,' Alice replies, so calmly and confidently that I almost believe her.

'How do you know that?'

'Well, if this Alexander guy is as brilliant as you say he is, he's not going to let your tiny brain tumour tarnish his reputation, is he?'

I consider this for a moment. 'Yeah, he did say he's operated on tumours the size of oranges.'

'And yours is a pea, right?'

'Two peas . . .'

I know I've been being silly. Still, it feels good to acknowledge the fear that's been festering for months.

'What if we had a secret code word?' Alice suggests.

I laugh. 'What do you mean? Like a safe word?'

'Exactly. If you remember the word and text it to me after you're out of surgery, then you're good to go.'

I laugh. 'I like it.'

'What about "cunt"?'

I think of Johnny's Cuntish Crème Brûlée and smile.

'Maybe something that won't get me kicked out of the ICU?'

'It's got to be something so ridiculous that you can't have fluked it.'

'How about "negative gearing"?' It's the first thing that pops into my mind. 'I'm sure that's the only time I've ever uttered those words.'

'Home ownership in Sydney? You can't get more ridiculous than that! It's perfect,' Alice exclaims.

Our eyes meet. There's a warmth there that could rival the sun. 'Thanks, Alice.'

'Thank *you*,' she replies. 'For being so patient with me and letting me tell you about Maggie in my own time.'

'Oh please, there's nothing to thank me for.' I wave her absurd gratitude away.

'Well, there's no one else I'd rather pretend negative gear with,' she says.

'Ditto.'

I don't check my phone until I hop into bed later that night. There's a message from Johnny with a photo: **Quiche Lorraine Abomination**

I reply: **Nope, this is the Joyful Quiche Lorraine**

I send along a photo of Alice and Maggie smiling widely at the dinner table.

When I eventually drift off to sleep, I'm happy.

It's the simple things: I'm happy that I've finally made a dish that's edible. I'm happy for Alice and Maggie. I'm even happy about Johnny the Tinder Pen Pal who lives in my phone.

I don't think about Scott. And I certainly don't think about the fact that it's just six short sleeps until my surgery.

Chapter Twelve

It's finally Saturday. I haven't set an alarm, but by the looks of the slice of cool morning light peeking through the curtain, it's still early. And it's sunny. That must be a good omen.

I shut my eyes again. It's the last weekend before my surgery, so I feel like that entitles me to an extra-long sleep-in. Even though I'm sure I'll be spending plenty of time horizontal over the next few weeks.

The light appears to have been turned up a few watts and is now piercing through my eyelids.

Why does this always happen? Up at the crack of dawn when I have nowhere to be, yet I can barely rouse myself for weekday starts. The last couple of days have been particularly painful, dragging my butt to work, then ducking and weaving through corridors to avoid Raffie. Thankfully I haven't been called up by HR. I was praying that Raffie would be too ashamed to report my walkout, and it appears my prayers have been answered.

I've finished up at work – for the next six weeks, at least. I gave Lucy a quick hug and ducked out at 5 pm on Friday without saying goodbye to anyone else. My team seemed satisfied enough with my vague explanation that I was taking leave – they only cared that I'd left them thorough handover notes and my work had been done in advance.

I've spent much of the night clutching my belly in pain. Not tumour related – presumably – more to do with Day 10's Fucker of a French Onion Soup. All this rich French food was catching up with my digestive system. Day 9's A Cock of a Coq au Vin wasn't exactly light fare, either.

I'd also had too much red wine. Alice was out with Maggie, so I'd stayed up polishing off a bottle of shiraz, exchanging flirty texts with Johnny. I was dangerously close to the bottom of the bottle and dangerously close to revealing my French silk pie sex fantasies when I was saved by Alice banging on the front door. She'd forgotten her keys and needed her mouthguard for bed. I love that she's fully herself with Maggie, teeth grinding and all.

I rub my temples, trying to massage away the rumblings of a headache. I don't regret a thing, though. After all, it was my last hurrah. There will be no more drinking now. I have the weekend to zen out before a day of pre-admission appointments on Monday. Blood tests to record my blood type, the cardiologist for an ECG to ensure my heart is in working order (heartbreak excluded) and a chest X-ray as proof of fully functioning lungs.

The only regret I feel this morning is that our flirty drinking session wasn't face to face. I know that Alice is right, that it would only complicate things, but if I'm not honest with myself about my building desire for Johnny now, when will I be? I can feel myself getting bolder with every minute inching me closer to the surgery, knowing that I'll soon be smoke-bombing my way out of this little text-uation.

I was even brave enough to ask why he was at home texting me, instead of out on the town enjoying his Friday night with one of his casual lovers.

Well, ma cherie, these onions will not peel and slice themselves, he'd said. **Are you wiping away tears over there?**

The next moment my screen was obscured by a photo of Johnny wearing a snorkel mask. He was grinning, his perfect piano-key teeth stained red with wine. I zoomed in. The dark patch above his top lip looked scratchy. Suddenly my own lips were burning with an incessant itch.

I'm making that my wallpaper, I replied with shaky, wanting fingers.

We texted until our bowls were scraped clean. I was chuffed that my version of the thirty-two-step soup tasted like I'd nailed at least twenty of the steps. By the time I fell into bed, I was drunk. It was only as I was brushing my teeth that I'd realised Johnny had completely evaded my question about his social life – or lack thereof. If he was such a player, it didn't make sense that he was spending a prime Friday night slaving away in the kitchen.

My feet kick at something hard and cold trapped between the sheets at the bottom of my bed.

What in the –? Ahhh, that's right . . . Johnny had challenged me to write again, so I'd taken to my computer in the middle of the night.

I roll onto my side and pull the laptop up, balance it on top of a pillow and open the lid. I've written another IKEA-inspired short story featuring Dennis, the eager retail assistant, that's not half bad. There's also another open Word document, and I lean in to inspect my tipsy ramblings. Perhaps there is some profound genius here to uncover – I need all the words I can get for *The Doors* right now . . . Or, at the very least, the start of something new.

*Curiouser and curiouser he makes me, but nevertheless
I persist, as the delectable rewards satisfy more than just
my stomach. I am full with something far greater than rich*

soups and sauces. A sense that I'm both nourished and hungry, all at once. Is Johnny the electrifying entrée preparing me for the bountiful main course of my new life?

Wow. My eyes scan the page. It goes on and on in much the same way. An entire page of utter drivel. I suppose that's what one bottle of red gets you: some very bad, wannabe Austenesque writing. *Oh, the audacity of me to compare this rubbish to Jane Austen's work!* I notice that I have used the correct punctuation – but that has more to do with muscle memory than my sanity.

I quickly drag the document to the trash, so I don't have to stare at it a second longer.

Now to scrub away the embarrassment with something half-decent . . . Yes, my head could do with some painkillers washed down with coffee, but since my computer is already open, I might as well get started on some early-morning pages. They say your mind is more in tune with your subconscious when you first wake up – and everyone knows the subconscious is where the creative magic is at. There had been no dreams of Johnny and that sexy French silk pie last night, but thankfully no nightmares either, so I'm taking that as a win.

I stare at the blinking cursor, flashing in time with my heartbeat. I'd better get cracking. There is nothing more pressing than a true deadline. Who knows when – or if – I'll be able to do morning pages again?

Still, I start with my normal routine: procrastinating by formatting a new document. I'm inserting page numbers on the unwritten pages when my side table starts vibrating. My phone, still plugged into the charger, is ringing. I stretch over to answer it. I'm expecting Mum, but instead two words, *Hot Alexander*, are splashed across the screen.

'Hello?'

'Hello, is that Maxine Mayberry?' says a clipped voice.

'Yes, speaking.'

'This is Cheryl from Dr Alexander Jock's office. Sorry to call you so early. I was just hoping to catch you as soon as possible about your transsphenoidal endoscopic surgery scheduled for Wednesday.'

I assume that's the name of my surgery. I've only ever heard it referred to as brain surgery.

'Yes?' I say.

'I'm phoning as Dr Jock would like to move your surgery forward to Tuesday. The hospital has done a bit of a number on him, you see, and double-booked the theatre on Wednesday. It's a twelve-hour open heart, so that gets priority, unfortunately.'

'Ah, sure. Okay.'

My head is spinning. I'm having difficulty comprehending what she's saying.

'I know it's a huge imposition, and I'm not sure how you're placed with work and such, but I can see you're booked in for your pre-op appointments on Monday, so you'll be all ready there, and your anaesthetist and surgical team have been advised of the date change.'

'Uh-huh . . .'

Cheryl sounds so casual, like she's rescheduling my manicure appointment by half an hour and not moving my BRAIN SURGERY forward by an entire day.

'That works for you then?'

Do I even have a choice? It certainly doesn't sound as if I do.

'So you mean this Tuesday? The Tuesday that's three days from now?' I need to confirm I'm not hearing things.

'That's right. Unfortunately, if Dr Jock can't operate on Tuesday, it will be at least another month –'

'Oh, no, no, no,' I say. 'That won't work.'

I've waited this long, and I've done all – well, most – of the mental prep I can. I don't think I'll cope if the surgery is delayed. Plus, my work sick leave is all organised.

'Perfect. I'll let Dr Jock know. If you can arrive at the hospital at 7 am? I can see here that you're second on the list. The hospital will still confirm with you twenty-four hours before.'

'Okay, thank you.' My voice is faint and uncertain, like it's coming from the very bottom of a well.

'Thanks, Maxine. And sorry again for the last-minute change. I hope the procedure goes well.'

'Than–'

Cheryl has already hung up.

Somewhere in the course of the conversation I have cast aside my laptop and pillow desk, thrown back the doona and sheets and sat up straight, cross-legged on the mattress. Now I rest my phone in my lap and tilt my head to gaze at the whirring ceiling fan. I watch the blades spin as I try to process the call.

Okay, so three more sleeps, not four. Surely that's easy done. Oh! But that means no Day 14 dish . . . The duck! Of all things, why is the Fork Him project the first place my mind goes?

I pluck the mobile from my lap and start to type out a message, but then I stop. I've never messaged Johnny this early. He's probably sleeping. I don't know what I would say if he replied anyway – I'm not about to mention my surgery. I wish Alice was home so I could rush into her room, dive under the covers with her and unpack everything. We'd go through the pros and cons of the surgery being bumped up earlier and decide that the pros win out. But I'm not going to bother her when she's with Maggie. Let her enjoy her weekend sex.

I really should call my mum, especially as the news completely changes the logistics of the next week. I'm going to stay with my parents so they can look after me post-op. A nugget of guilt forms in my stomach when I realise I haven't spoken to Mum all week. *There will be plenty of time for talking*, I remind myself. I needed some time out to sort my own emotions without dealing with hers as well.

Right, now I need to go somewhere to gather my thoughts. In the last week and a half, it's been the kitchen, or more specifically cooking in the kitchen, that has been my source of calm, but it's too early to make a start on Day 11's artichokes à la barigoule, and I'm not going to find peace pouring out a bowl of cornflakes.

It's time for the next best thing.

It'll take a sharp knife to cut through those artichokes, and IKEA is just the place to source one.

I hop out of bed, peel off my pyjamas and pluck a top and a pair of jeans from the dirty pile on the floor. The mothership doesn't care about crumpled clothes. It accepts people from all walks of life, however and in whatever emotional state they come. Once I'm dressed, I grab my bag and keys off the dresser, but I leave the tube of Love on Top lipstick where it's resting next to my jewellery dish. There's no risk of running into Johnny this time.

Chapter Thirteen

I sit staring at the croque monsieur on the bench in front of me. Part of me wants to gobble it down before my 9 pm fasting cut-off time; the other part of me wants to savour this moment. It's Day 13, the final dish of the Fork Him project – though only by default. Day 14's duck à l'orange will forever remain between the pages.

I'm glad the challenge ended with a simple dish – a ham and cheese sandwich slathered in béchamel and grilled, and not Day 12's Terrorist's Tarte au Citron Meringuée. That was a complete nightmare. First I heated up the egg-white mixture until it basically scrambled, then I overbeat the meringue. Today there would have been no time to start over, pack my hospital bag and do the thing that I've known needed doing from the very beginning of all of this. Johnny has successfully distracted me to this point – the time's come to rip the bandaid off. There's a high chance I won't remember him, or any of this, when I wake up anyway.

So why have I put it off until the very last minute?

I pick up my phone and look at the photo of Johnny's Cruddy Croque Monsieur again.

His hand has snuck into the shot. Strong-knuckled and large. Firm yet soft. I imagine that firm-yet-soft hand cupping my chin, his warm breath tickling my ear as he tells me not to worry. To stop this nonsense. That he'll be there for me, always, always.

I shake my head free of silly fantasies and start typing.

Hey, Johnny. I think our lil challenge has run out of steam. I feel myself losing interest

My thumb hovers over the 'enter' button. *Enough, Max. It's now or never.*

I tap the screen, and my message is sent.

He replies right away.

Okay. Wow

As soon as his message slides into view, I want to take mine back. But what would that achieve? There was never any future here. He made that clear from the beginning.

You're welcome to call it now? No more Forking Him?

Look, I feel there's little point. Cute in concept but . . .

So, no duck tomorrow? Bit ironic for the Mother Ducker, isn't it?

Yeah ☹ No duck

That's a shame, Max

We're too old to spend our time texting internet strangers

I hold my breath, hoping that he'll put up a fight. Demand an explanation for my sudden ripcord on the Fork Him project – even insist that we meet. It wouldn't take much for me to crumble and tell him everything. For whatever reason, it's been so easy to open up to him.

Well then, I wish you well with your writing and everything that matters

My stomach drops. Of course he's not going to fight for me. He doesn't know me, or what I'm about to come up against.

I should at least thank him for helping me get through the hardest time of my life. But it's much easier to keep things light.

Have fun out there. Don't think I've ever farewelled a Tinder pen pal before, LOL. Remember: there's life after 50

Haha, I don't doubt it

I'm debating whether or not to send a single 'x' when my phone buzzes with a final message.

Good luck, Max xx

I can't stop the tears streaming down my face. They pour onto my croque monsieur until it's just a soggy sandwich, damp as the centuries-old cobblestoned streets of wintry Paris.

PART II

Réchauffer

/ ʀeʃofe /

(verb) To reheat.

Chapter Fourteen

Four months earlier

My shaky hands rip at the oversized envelope. Eventually I find a small tear at the top that I can slice all the way along. I slide out the first film and press it up against the passenger-side window. The bright midday sun lights up the ripples of my membrane and its cavities. *Seems normal enough.*

I'm under no illusion that my dedication to *Grey's Anatomy* is equivalent to a degree in medicine, or more specifically neurology, but it at least offers some point of reference. My appointment with Dr Alexander Jock isn't until Thursday, and I need an answer before then.

Brow furrowed, I study one of the jagged passageways. It meanders along like the rest, then sprouts into tiny trails that merge before ballooning into a larger canal. The canal is represented by a void of white space, tarnished only by a black smudge in one of its corners.

I lean in for a closer look. My right pointer finger wipes at the spot. It doesn't budge. Although no bigger than a sultana, it's relatively sizeable compared to the rest of my brain.

A quick comparison of the other films reveals that the sultana is in fact a permanent mark.

Relief whooshes through me, like the breaking of a dam wall.

It was just as Scott had thought. There is something seriously wrong with me.

Chapter Fifteen

One month later

'Scott! Can you come and help me!' I yell, thumping on our front door with my free hand. My other arm is clutching shopping bags filled with Christmas presents for his family. After much deliberation, I've purchased an espresso machine for his mum so she can make her *café au lait* at home (although I'm sure I've gotten the wrong brand) and a fancy hair dryer for his sister, Eve, the kind with so many attachments it resembles one of those AI robots plotting to take over the world. As the least high-maintenance member of the Laurent family, Gary, Scott's dad, has scored himself some heavily discounted luxury shower gel and cologne. There are at least some perks to my job.

I wait for what feels like an eternity before resuming my thumping. 'SCOTT!'

Silence.

He should be home by now. His flight got in hours ago.

Dammit. My keys are at the very bottom of my handbag. I plonk the shopping bags down just as the door swings open.

Scott's designer-stubbled face peers around the doorframe.

'Hello, stranger.' He beams at me.

His Culture Kings T-shirt is crumpled. Not like Scott at all. Unless it's a new thing from Melbourne, and he's purposely scrunching his shirts now as part of his 'manufactured dishevelled' look.

He kisses me on the cheek, and I go to wrap my arms around his waist and cuddle him to me like a teddy bear. We haven't seen each other for six whole weeks – and they have been far from ordinary weeks. But Scott ducks under my embrace to collect the shopping bags at my feet.

'Whoah. These are heavy!' he exclaims. 'Why didn't you call me from the car, Maxie?'

'I did.'

'Whoops. Did you?' Scott shrugs. I follow him inside. 'I got home from the airport and cracked a beer.'

He drops the bags onto the counter, which is littered with at least half-a-dozen empty beer bottles.

Well, that checks out.

'Had a solo tour-wrap party?' I tease. 'You should have texted me. I could have come home from the shops earlier and celebrated with you. I've missed you!'

I don't mention that I left the shopping centre hours ago and have been pacing the aisles of IKEA.

'Sorry, Maxie. I was just hanging out for it after such a stressy few weeks.'

Stressy. The word tumbles around my mind like loose change in a washing machine. I remind myself that not only are emotions completely relative, but that Scott is still in the dark about my diagnosis. I hadn't wanted to ruin his tour.

'I tried calling you a bunch of times today,' I say quietly.

Scott shrugs again. 'Sorry. I'm not sure where my phone even is.' He drops down onto one of the breakfast stools.

My stomach twinges. Scott is very rarely without his phone.

If he's not memorising a monologue saved in his notes, he's checking his views on TikTok and YouTube.

'No worries!' I exclaim with false brightness. It really doesn't matter, with everything that's going on right now. I'm just happy that he's finally home.

'Can I at least have a hug?' I chirp as I flop onto his lap.

Scott yelps. 'Ouch! Max!'

'Sorry,' I murmur, face already buried in his neck. Then my thigh connects with a hard, iPhone-shaped bulge in his pocket. 'Scott! Your phone is here!'

His hand shoots down to his pocket.

'Ah, yes, so it is,' he says, pulling it out and placing it face-down on the counter.

My brow furrows. 'Are you feeling okay?' I know I'm probably acting strangely, but I hadn't anticipated Scott behaving even more oddly.

He responds by squeezing his eyes shut, his fingers going to his temples.

'I'm just tired. Maybe I'm jet lagged.'

'Jet lagged from Melbourne?' I clench my jaw. 'The day-drinking probably hasn't helped.'

'It was a stressful tour!' Scott whines.

Scott has every right to be exhausted, Max. A brain tumour isn't the only ticket to fatigue-ville.

'I'm sure it was,' I say, rubbing his back in big, soothing circles. 'So, how did it go?'

We've spoken almost every day he's been on tour. Either an early-morning call or a text fired off from the office – or the doctor's waiting room. But it was mostly surface-level stuff. *How did you sleep? What's for dinner? Good show?*

I know that I was trying to conceal what was really going on with my brief texts, so there's no telling where Scott's *IT WAS AMAZING, THE CROWD WAS AWESOME* replies fell on the honesty scale.

He's known for hyperbole, so it can be hard to pinpoint the truth at the best of times. It's generally accepted that stand-up comedians exaggerate, to bring out the humour in their anecdotes and get a laugh, but Scott frequently goes next level – especially lately. Like his TikTok that blew up recently, where he filmed a homeless-looking man in a pink bathrobe chasing him down the street. He told his followers the man had gone 'Usain Bolt on his arse' while he was out pounding the pavement, training for the City2Surf. He ended the video by thanking the man for helping him break his pace plateau. The thing is, Scott doesn't run.

'Yeah, it all went pretty well.' Scott's hands find my waist, and he gently manoeuvres me off his lap. 'I think I need to head to bed soon, Maxie. I want to make sure I'm all recovered for tomorrow's festivities.' He yawns.

I chew my bottom lip. He normally takes any opportunity to lap up attention after his shows. But it's Christmas tomorrow, and our week-long celebrations start with the traditional feast at the Laurents', move on to my parents' place for Boxing Day and continue with a full schedule of boozy beach barbecues and cricket matches with friends.

'Can you just tell me how our joke landed?' I ask.

If I was to believe social media, and all the reposts from Scott's show, it had been a hit.

'*Our* joke?' Scott scratches his stubbly chin.

'The tirami-poo!'

How has he forgotten? We'd workshopped a story about a week we'd spent in Rome with food poisoning. Scott had wanted to detail every graphic moment of our explosive diarrhoea, while I had suggested it would be funnier told with some clever innuendo. The episode had been triggered by a suss tiramisu, so when I'd come up with 'tirami-poo', we'd howled with laughter.

'Ah, yes.' A too-quick smile crosses his face. 'They lapped it up. After I gave it a few tweaks.'

'Tweaks?' I ask warily.

I wish I could rewind the clock to those early days when he'd perform just for me in his parents' garage. Now I'm lucky to even get a preview, and I find myself holding my tongue when I do. While I get the need to appeal to a broad audience, I don't think Scott should have to compromise his craft for the fickle TikTok masses.

'If you'd come to see the show, you would know,' he shoots back.

Ouch.

I place my hands on the benchtop and hang my head. It's started thumping – right on cue.

'Sorry,' I mumble. 'I really wish I could have been there.'

Everything will make sense to him soon. Maybe I should just tell him now?

Come on, Max. You can do this. The tour's over, what are you waiting for?

I look up.

Scott is wriggling his eyebrows at me. He has an overbright expression plastered on his face, but the shine doesn't reach his eyes. 'You can come say sorry to me in bed if you like.'

Well, that's a massive change in tune. Now is clearly not the right time to tell him about my tumour. It's almost as if he's calling my bluff . . .

There is part of me that wants to dive straight under the sheets with him, but there's another that's too aware of all the gifts that need wrapping. Even the simplest tasks are taking me much longer to complete. I'm hoping the meds that I'm finally starting next week, now that all the diagnostic tests are complete, will relieve some of my pain, as well as stabilise the tumour's size ahead of surgery.

I give his arm a weak punch. 'Nice try. How about you help me with the wrapping first?'

'Nah. I'm all good, thanks.' Scott takes a step away from me. 'I did make a lasagne for dinner, though.'

He gestures over his shoulder to where a rectangular dish covered in aluminium foil is resting on the stovetop. 'I figured from the number of takeaway containers in the bin that you haven't been eating properly.'

Scott's tone is stern, but in a way that makes my heart swell. He's back, and now he's going to take care of me.

'Oh, yum. Thanks.' I move towards the lasagne dish like a homing pigeon. I'm surprisingly peckish. 'I really only got slack in the last week,' I lie. If it wasn't pad thai or pizza, it was tuna and crackers. Mum ended up dropping in some home-cooked meals the other day, even though I told her it was completely unnecessary. Scott must not have stumbled on the freezer full of quiches and soups.

He shadows me as I open one of the overhead cupboards.

'Hey, so what was with all the post-its?'

I freeze, my hand on a dinner plate. *Shit.*

I had forgotten about the brightly coloured squares stuck all over the kitchen cupboards and drawers. Of course, Scott would have noticed them right away!

The idea had come after googling methods to train your brain. Not only did I want to test whether the tumour had already compromised my brain function (despite Alexander assuring me it hadn't), I wanted to look into whether there was anything I could do to prime it for surgery, like a weightlifter bulking up before an important competition. I found a few exercises that claimed they'd help me 'think faster, focus better and remember more'. I decided to attempt a mix of memory and vocabulary exercises – writing ridiculously long words and their definitions on post-its to memorise. I've been at it for a fortnight, and I've only managed to master three out of the twenty words:

Pneumonoultramicroscopicsilicovolcanoconiosis: the inhalation of very fine silicate or quartz dust.

Hippopotomonstrosesquippedaliophobia: the fear of long words!

Supercalifragilisticexpialidocious: duh, Mary Poppins!

I hesitate, eyes fixated on the perfectly stacked crockery inside the cupboard. How am I going to explain this one?

I take a deep breath and spin around to face him. 'They're just some ideas for my book.'

It's a gamble. How closely he's studied the post-its will determine whether I get away with this explanation.

'Oh, yeah? How is that going?' Scott's gaze wanders to the oven clock.

The time clicks over to 18:00.

'It's going,' I say, conscious of my voice climbing an octave. He's not the biggest supporter of my writing anyway, so I'm purposely vague.

'Mmm, that's great.' But I can tell from his half-lidded eyes that he's barely heard me.

'So where are they?' I ask, glancing around the kitchen.

'Where are what?' Scott stares blankly.

I cross my arms in front of my chest. 'My post-its!'

'Whoah, chill out, Max,' Scott drawls. 'They weren't doing anything for the aesthetic . . . so they're in a pile on the desk in the study.'

I clench then unclench my teeth as Scott's phone vibrates to life on the counter.

He picks it up instantly. 'Hello?'

A few beats later he mouths, 'It's Mum,' and ducks into the hallway.

I'm happy to have a moment to myself. This is not the homecoming I'd envisaged.

I peel back the foil covering the lasagne. It's already been hacked into, with the equivalent of two sizeable slices missing.

I'm using a piece of freezer bread to mop up the last drops of béchamel from my plate when Scott returns. He's whistling 'Joy to the World'.

'So, Raffie is coming to Christmas,' he announces.

The muscles in my neck stiffen. 'What? Why? I don't have a present for her.'

He shrugs. 'I don't know. Apparently Eve invited her.'

I jiggle my head from side to side, attempting to loosen my stiff neck. 'Okay, well, I guess I'll have to scrounge up a scented candle or something from somewhere. I just hope she doesn't want to talk shop. I really need a break from work.'

I walk over to the sink to deposit my dirty plate and find a béchamel-crusted plate and two forks have been added to my morning cereal bowl.

I frown, turning back to Scott. 'Was someone here?'

He's quick to reply. 'What? No.'

My eyes search his, trying to cut through the beery glaze. 'Are you sure?'

He sighs. 'Are you serious, Max? This is what I've been saying to you. You never used to be this uptight.'

I shake my head, attempting to clear the dense fog that seems to have settled permanently in my brain. Scott's right. I'm struggling to think straight at the moment. My little post-it exercise has obviously been futile.

It's Christmas Eve, Max, and you're on borrowed time. Get it together.

'Want to watch the Christmas episode of *Schitt's Creek* while I wrap?' I ask.

Scott grins. 'Now that's more like the Maxie I know.'

He pulls me onto his lap and squeezes me tight.

Chapter Sixteen

The last of the honey carrots glisten in their bowl under the candlelight. In this low light, I can almost convince myself that it's the wine giving me a pulsing headache and that my blurry vision is a symptom of too much of the Laurents' rich, very alcoholic plum pudding.

My pants zipper made its way down after the main course, and I'm wondering if I should excuse myself to the bathroom and press a cold washer to my head before we settle into the dessert wine and gift-giving. I want to ensure I'm still conscious by the time I fall into bed and finally tell Scott what's going on with me.

'Max, can you pass me the custard?' asks Raffie, Eve's best friend, my sort-of boss and the family's last-minute dinner guest.

'Sure.' I reach for the ceramic custard boat. A droplet of thick, yellow liquid falls onto my menu card as I pass the custard across the table, and I quickly wipe it clean with my index finger. The printed menus, which have been arranged next to the place cards, are marked with the Laurent wax seal.

'Are you looking forward to New York, Raffie?' I ask.

Raffie will soon be off on a two-month secondment to Slice Agency's Brooklyn office.

'For sure. I think it's time to inject some local flavour over there. Show them how us Aussies do things.' She winks.

She has clearly visited the hairdresser for a fresh blonding and sharpening of her signature bob ahead of her trip.

Scott burps next to me, and I elbow him.

'Scooott . . .' Helen, his mother, warns.

Coincidently – or perhaps not – Helen also sports a blonde bob. Her straight 'do is perfectly even. Back in her heyday, I'm sure it would have framed her cheekbones perfectly, but now it looks like an ill-fitting wig, drawing attention to her hollow cheeks.

I first met Helen at Eve's eighteenth birthday party, only a fortnight after Scott and I had officially started dating. Helen had embraced me warmly and immediately offered me a glass of Moët. I found out months later that Scott had told her I had a face tatt. I've grown used to Scott's constant jokes since then, but I've never been quite sure if Helen actually liked me, or if she'd simply been relieved that her son's new girlfriend wasn't a Hell's Angel.

Over the years, I've been to many more Laurent family parties and countless celebrations. I'm not yet at the stage of referring to Helen as my mother-in-law, but I'm close. I'm hoping to receive the ultimate seal of approval tonight – being gifted my copy of the famed *Laurent Family Cookbook*.

'Did you know that in China, burping is a compliment to the chef?' Raffie jumps in to keep the peace.

I remember when I used to try to referee; I've well and truly learnt to stay out of things now. At some point, the Laurents always make up, and then you end up on the outer. Except Raffie never seems to be on the outer.

It's hard not to feel out of place tonight. Scott normally sits at the Laurents' dining table with a hand on my leg, and, if I'm wearing a skirt, his hand often makes its way under the fabric. He hasn't even tried to catch my eye throughout dinner, let alone touch me. Is he still angry at me for not going to his show? We'd spoken about me flying to Melbourne for a weekend, to see him perform and then explore the maze of graffitied alleyways together. But it had been near impossible to get leave from work in the run-up to Christmas, especially as I'd spent the past few weeks ducking out for doctor's appointments. Scott would understand once I explained. I couldn't wait to sink into bed and into his arms and come clean about everything. Last night, he'd ended up having two more beers while watching *Schitt's Creek* and passed out almost as soon as his head hit the pillow.

'See, Helen. It's just Scott's way of thanking you for yet another delicious Christmas meal,' says Gary, who holds down the permanent role of family peacekeeper.

'Yeah, your amazing cooking is to blame, Mum,' Eve adds, pushing her blunt fringe back from her eyes. 'I'm stuffed . . . Although I'm sure I could go round two after presents.'

I squeeze Scott's hand, but he doesn't look at me.

~

Helen switches over the Christmas symphony to 'Petit Papa Noël'. She always insists on listening to French music for the gift-giving portion of the evening. I'm now sitting cross-legged on the hard oak floor. Being down so close to the ground makes me feel less dizzy.

The Laurent residence is like a gallery with no art: sparse in furnishings, with expansive white walls that would make the perfect backdrop for a movie projector, but not a warm, family home. The Christmas tree is the one homely exception.

Wrapped up in the heady after-dinner glow, gazing at the Laurents' perfectly trimmed tree, I almost manage to convince myself that this is just a regular Christmas Day. I'm not sure I'm ready to shatter that illusion. My parents and Alice know, but saying it aloud to Scott will make it all the more real. Even though my news isn't the sort you want to share over FaceTime, it had felt so foreign to keep my diagnosis from him.

Scott chooses the spot on the floor next to me, while Eve lies on the couch moaning and nursing her full belly, calling on Raffie to refill her glass of dessert wine.

Helen glares at Scott's dirty trainers tucked up underneath him.

'Scotty! I told you to take those filthy shoes off in here!'

Scott grins. 'Don't worry, Mum, I've sealed the stains with hairspray.'

I try to conceal my eye roll. The longer Scott's been on the comedy circuit, the grubbier he thinks he needs to be. Apparently not bathing gives you more cred. But the dirt on his shoes is so artfully positioned, it just looks like he's bought white designer sneakers and then found a muddy puddle to scuff them up in. There's nothing authentic about it, but, like a good girlfriend, I keep my mouth shut.

'Ho, ho, ho! What do we have here?' Gary booms as he plucks a rectangular package from the pile of presents next to his perch beside the tree.

One of the Philippe Starck Ghost chairs has been relocated to the living room, and Gary has donned a Santa hat. With his white curly beard and sparkling blue eyes, he certainly looks the part. It's easy to imagine Scott carrying on the tradition with our kids one day. If we're afforded the time, that is.

'This one is for Max. From the Laurents,' Gary says.

'Oh, thanks.' I hop to my feet, and Scott whacks me on the arse. Perhaps everything is okay between us? I wait for the room to stop spinning before picking my way through the strewn wrapping paper to collect my gift.

'I think you'll like this one,' Gary says, giving me a wink as he deposits the firm parcel into my hands. It feels exactly like a book.

My eyes search the dark room for Helen, who has decided the music is too loud and has moved to the speaker to adjust the volume. She catches my eye and simply nods.

Once I'm back next to Scott, I shimmy the package out of its gold organza ribbon and rip at the brown paper. After the first tear, and the first glimpse of the familiar black spine with gold lettering, I know exactly what I'm holding. *The Laurent Family Cookbook.*

I'm finally in.

The book is still partially encased in paper when I turn to Scott, eyes shining.

'Now you can't get rid of me!'

He laughs lightly, eyes glazed from too much wine, and leans forward to drop a kiss on the tip of my nose.

Suddenly remembering my manners, I go to stand to thank his parents, but stop as Helen's words slice through the air. 'No need to get up, Maxine.' Then, more warmly, 'Welcome to the family.'

A thrill runs through me. It feels good to be recognised as someone worthy. As family, though not bound by blood. Yes, it has been a long time coming, but it's arrived at the perfect time – right when I really need their support.

'Thank you,' I say. I remove the last of the paper and hug the cookbook close to my chest. 'I'll treasure it always.'

'All right, you're up next, Raffie,' Gary announces. By the looks of the sizeable pile by the tree, we are still hours away from bed. I hope Scott doesn't drink much more.

Raffie unwraps her gift, pulling out a familiar black-and-gold book.

Wait, what? Why is Raffie receiving the Laurents' prized recipe book? She's been Eve's best friend since primary school, but still . . . I didn't realise the sacred cookbook I've waited a decade for was being handed out tonight like party favours.

'Thanks, Mr and Mrs Laurent,' Raffie gushes. She stands to embrace Helen.

'Please, Raphaela – we've gone over this. Call me Helen,' Helen says as they hug. 'Luckily I'd already printed an extra copy for you, so it was on hand when Eve let me know this morning that you'd be joining us.'

Huh? Helen called to tell Scott last night . . .

'And now onto the truly special part!' Gary booms, whipping out a stack of envelopes from underneath his red shirt. He fans out the envelopes and waves them in front of his face like he's in the bleachers at the Australian Open on a putrid thirty-five-degree day. Scott had certainly gotten his knack for theatrics from his film director father. 'Do you want to do the honours?' he asks Helen.

Helen collects the envelopes and begins handing them out. Eve is first, then Scott and then – lucky last – me. As I take the envelope, Helen's grip seems to tighten for a second, like we're in the playground and she's offered me a chip from her bag of salt 'n' vinnies, only to change her mind and pull back, not wanting to share.

I'm still opening my envelope when Eve's shrieks start up. 'France, Mum? Really!'

'Plane tickets? Are you for real!' Scott chimes in, as I see that I've received a ticket too.

'Yes, my darlings. As you know, I'm turning the big six-oh in May, and I thought it would be wonderful to go on a family trip to Paris – a fortnight exploring our French roots!' says Helen, beaming proudly, before addressing Raffie. 'Sorry, honey – this one is just family.' At least a line has been drawn somewhere.

I turn to Scott excitedly, but he's looking at his mother, a stern look plastered on his face. 'I really wish you'd discussed this with us first, Mum.'

What on earth was there to discuss? It's a free trip overseas. Okay, Helen might not be my favourite human of all time, but still, PARIS! *Oh, gosh . . . wait.* I've let myself get carried away for a moment and forgotten about my surgery. I glance warily at Scott. Is that why he's looking so serious? Does he already know somehow? Could Alice have told him?

'It looks like I might have a new show to tour,' Scott says.

Oh. My stomach plummets violently. This is the first I'm hearing of a new show. It hadn't even occurred to me that he might not be available to care for me. Of course, that will change the instant I tell him I'm sick, but we still can't go on this trip.

'Scott, just be bloody grateful!' Eve calls from the couch. She's sitting up now, the excitement of the tickets having raised her from her zombie state.

'Sorry,' Scott shrugs. 'Let me see what I can do. It's just Max, too.' He turns to look me dead in the eye. 'Her work is so busy at the minute, isn't it, babe? Couldn't even make my show . . .'

Okay, so he is mad.

Chapter Seventeen

The springs of the fold-out couch jut into my side as I wriggle around on the thin foam mattress to get comfortable. Helen converted Scott's childhood bedroom into a study when we moved in together five years ago, and replaced his bed with an upholstered settee.

I reach for Scott, but he stays facing the wall.

'Scott . . .' My arm tightens around his waist, my face pressing into his back. I drink in the familiar mustiness of his T-shirt. He normally sleeps naked.

'Hmmm . . .?' The couch bed dips in the middle as he rolls over to face me.

'Can we talk?' I whisper.

We're the only ones down here – Eve, Raffie, Helen and Gary are all passed out upstairs – so there's really no need to whisper, but I don't have the energy to speak any louder.

'Can it wait until the morning? I'm sleeeeepy.' Scott yawns to illustrate his point.

I first tried talking to him when we were in the bathroom brushing our teeth, and then again in the kitchen pouring large

110

glasses of water for bed, but I'd stopped myself. I wanted the comfort of complete darkness and close proximity, so I could cling to him.

'It really can't,' I say, still whispering.

'I'm not angry at you, if that's what you're thinking. I'm just disappointed you didn't make the effort to come to Melbourne.' His breath smells of alcohol, sickly sweet.

Make the effort.

I hook my legs over his. 'It's just that I've had some other things going on –'

'What "other things", Max?' Scott interrupts. For someone who claims he's not angry, he sounds it. 'I really don't get what's going on with you.'

I pull away, and he reaches over and places a hand on my cheek.

'We've always promised to keep it real with each other. I'm worried about you, Maxie. You're a completely different person to the girl I fell in love with.'

Wow. That stings.

We have always said we prefer the truth. We're both far too pragmatic to waste time on bullshit – if we don't like something, we simply tell each other. Except for Scott's jokes, which are off limits.

'How do you mean?' I ask.

'You used to have a sense of humour.'

'Oh, did I?' There's no disguising the iciness that's crept into my voice.

'I just don't get why you wouldn't want to come see my show. You don't work weekends. And don't say that you had to work on your little manuscript.'

His act was off limits, but everything else was open slather, especially my writing. Lately, I've had to constantly remind myself that Scott only has my best interests at heart. He just doesn't want me wasting time on a hobby that isn't going anywhere, when I could be climbing the ranks at the agency.

'Did you go and speak to someone like we agreed, Maxie?' he probes.

He thinks I'm depressed, and that's why I no longer find his jokes amusing. He'd been too wrapped up in rehearsals to notice me wincing at my bright phone screen, but he'd certainly noticed my lack of laughter. How will he react when I tell him what's really going on with me?

Suddenly, I no longer feel like confiding in him. I don't want to give him the satisfaction – to tell him that there's something wrong with me, that I'm the one at fault in this relationship, exactly as he's been insinuating.

'I'm sure it's not a big deal, Scott. I'll go for a check-up soon.'

I kick off the sheets and dangle my legs off the side of the bed, trying to cool down, and to get as far away from Scott as possible.

'Okay, good,' he says. 'We just want you back to normal, firing on all cylinders, right?'

A breeze from the open window catches the curtains, pulling them back to reveal a glowing moon. The light strobes across Scott's face, illuminating his hopeful expression.

'Sure, right.'

I'll tell him in the morning.

~

The house is quiet as I tiptoe up the stairs. My throbbing headache is back with a vengeance. I just want to go home to our cosy two-bedder, but fleeing in the middle of the night wouldn't be a good look. It's the Laurent family's Christmas tradition to stay overnight.

'Scott,' I hiss as I pad across the living room. 'Are you there?'

His side of the bed was empty when I'd woken in a pool of sweat, throat screaming out for water.

I stop at the bathroom door, half-expecting to find him crouched at the toilet bowl, his head resting against the cool tile wall. He had drunk a lot. That excused some of his insensitivity. Not all.

But the bathroom is empty, the slow drip of a leaking tap punctuating the silence. I move towards the sink, turn the tap, cup my hand under it and scoop the water into my mouth.

I drink until the scratchiness subsides, then open the bathroom cabinet to search for some painkillers. *Found you!*

Two white pills slide down my throat, followed by another handful of water for good measure. I wipe my mouth with the handtowel, then pad back out of the bathroom.

I'm about to head down the stairs again when a muffled laugh echoes up the hallway. It's faint, but it's definitely Scott. I make my way quietly up the hall, towards Eve's room, where the noise is coming from.

When I reach the door, it's ajar, so I push it open without knocking.

Scott and Raffie are propped up in bed, a laptop resting on Scott's thighs.

'What are you doing? Where's Eve? What's going on?'

I can't decipher the expression on Scott's face. Nonchalance?

'I'm just showing Raffie my show on YouTube. And Eve's snuck out to see some dude.'

'It's really good,' Raffie exclaims. Her expression is far easier to read. Smitten kitten. *How on earth have I missed this?*

'It's even better on screen than it was in person,' she says.

My heart rockets into my throat. 'You were in Melbourne?'

'Ah, yeah, you remember that new account we've just signed down there – the artisan skin care brand? I was already there for work, so it wasn't like a special trip or anything.' She's talking way too fast. 'And I only dropped around yesterday to give back the jacket Scott lent me. It was much colder than I'd anticipated. Bloody Melbourne . . .'

Scott's face drains of colour, turning as white as the doona they're cowering under.

'And then you phoned last night because you forgot to take a piece of lasagne to go on your way out?' I spit. Raffie's filled in the blanks for me, inadvertently exposing their sneaky plan to spend Christmas Day together. Right under my nose!

I lurch towards the bed and rip the covers off them. Scott has no pants on.

I give the sheet another yank, so there's absolutely nowhere to hide, and the laptop clatters to the floor. I bring my foot down on it so hard that I'm positive I've shattered some bone, then I limp from the room.

Chapter Eighteen

I get an Uber straight from the Laurents' back to our apartment and call Mum.

'Please. Come,' I sob down the phone.

'You're at your place?'

'Yessss,' I wail.

She doesn't ask any other questions. 'Your father and I are on our way.'

I stumble into the bedroom and retrieve my suitcase from the closet. I fill it with a disproportionate amount of undies and socks. I can't think straight. I throw in my favourite polka-dot bikini.

Toothbrush. I need my toothbrush.

I move down the hallway to the bathroom, trying to minimise my steps. It's impossible to know the exact path Raffie trod. Has she stepped in this specific spot? What about on the chipped tile? Did Scott stand with her in the shower, adjusting the taps until the water beat down on them at his ideal pressure? Most things in my life had been customised to Scott's liking.

Now I'm free.

But my body writhes at the thought of no longer having to consider him, compromise for him.

Now I'm lonely.

I pluck my purple toothbrush from its holder. It looks unkempt with its frayed, worn bristles. Scott's toothbrush stands to attention like an orderly soldier.

Now I'm taking the full tube of toothpaste.

I double-back to the bedroom for my laptop. Were they in our bed too? Probably.

I can't be in here.

I wait for my parents in the kitchen. The lasagne remnants from yesterday are still in the sink – including that extra fork.

I slide onto a breakfast stool and open my laptop. If I'd known Scott's routine was on YouTube, I would have watched it immediately.

Why didn't he tell me? Why didn't he tell me *anything*?

He was done with me, that's why.

My fingers punch the keyboard. 'Scott Laurent. Stand-up. Melbourne.'

The video loads, and I press fast-forward to skip ahead to the part I want to see.

Bingo.

Scott delivers the tirami-poo joke exactly as I wrote it. Not a single change – not even to the dramatic pause at the end.

I launch off my stool, then pull a good Murano glass from the cupboard and a bad wine from the fridge.

~

After my parents' early-morning rescue, Alice was kind enough to take me in. Today is the first morning I've gotten dressed.

It's been ten days. Ten days of pretending to function (and by function, I mean showering, drinking endless amounts of coffee and commencing wine time once the clock ticks over to 12.01 pm). On New Year's Eve the drinking kicked off with breakfast mimosas to toast my 'fresh start'. Bless Alice. But the rest of the day passed in a tipsy funk, and I eventually put myself to bed at 7 pm. There's no point making cheery resolutions about 'eating better' or 'learning a language' when I feel like I've just lost a limb. That's the problem with being with someone for so long – they literally become a part of you. Technically I'd been the one to ditch Scott – but what's it called when your hand is forced? A non-decision decision?

Mum and Dad stopped by to see me yesterday. I was still in bed, more or less just a lump under the doona. I'd attempted to brush my hair, but even before my dad uttered a single word, I could tell from the way his forehead creased that I wasn't fooling anyone. It was the same deep line that appeared whenever he examined his credit card statement and realised he'd accidentally auto-renewed his wine subscription for another month.

'How are you, love?' he asked.

'I'm okay, Dad. Still no drinking straight from the bottle. Alice says I'm classy.'

'I always knew he was an insecure piece of shit!'

'You're not helping, Brian!' My mum had shushed him before embracing me, murmuring into the covers, 'Do you want me to run to the servo and get you a pack of cigarettes?'

I haven't smoked in three years. The last time I lit up, at my cousin Lily's wedding, Mum had been ready to disown me. I wasn't about to start again now and have to answer yes to the question about smoking on the pre-surgery hospital questionnaire – I didn't want to risk that kind of judgement, not to mention an actual blood clot.

At this point, I'm starting to look forward to the surgery, just for the break from my thoughts. Maybe I could lie to the anaesthetist and say I weigh more than I do, to get a double dose?

I don't want to die – even at my lowest of lows, I'm still far too rational for that – I just want to escape for a while, and come to when everything is sorted. When I have a new, loving, loyal boyfriend, and perhaps even a book deal.

That's even if I make it to my surgery – I still have months to survive.

I wish I could fold myself into a box and ship myself to the future, past the countless doctors' visits and scans I have in the lead-up.

Alice and my parents have offered to accompany me to every appointment, but it would only remind me that Scott isn't there to squeeze my hand and tell me everything was going to be okay.

There are really no words for the monumental way in which he's let me down.

PART III

Julienne

/ dʒuː.li.ˈen /

(verb) To slice thinly, into small pieces.

Chapter Nineteen

Now

I open the fridge and begin pulling out plate after plate of left-overs. I balance the assortment of cling-wrapped crockery up my arm and tuck the bowl of French onion soup into the crook of my elbow.

I scrape the food into the bin. It seems wasteful, but it's not going to be eaten now. For the next little while, my life will be all apple juice and chewy hospital jellies.

The fridge is cleared, my bed is made, I'm showered, and my hospital bag is sitting packed at the door. There are no more chores left to distract me from the inevitable.

I take a deep breath and delete my Tinder account. Deleting all traces of Johnny along with it.

Chapter Twenty

The admissions area of St John's Hospital could really be more welcoming. I'm not expecting complimentary hot cocoa and shortbread like the lobby of a five-star ski resort, but surely enough chairs for the patients and their chaperones isn't asking too much. My mum stands next to me, one hand on the back of my chair. She's on her phone texting my dad to let him know we've arrived safely.

Next to us a man in a moon boot tries to offer her his seat.

'Oh, no, thank you, it's my daughter who's sick.'

Sick? I'm not sure I love that label, but I guess I'd prefer that to him thinking I'm like one of those bratty schoolkids who doesn't stand up for their elders on the bus.

I give the man in the moon boot a grateful smile. We are comrades, after all.

I look around the room at the sets of anxious eyes tracking every movement of the humans behind the check-in desks. There are no white-gloved concierges or maîtres d'hôtel with pencil moustaches, just kind-faced staff in all blue, occasionally calling out names – friendly smurfs steering us towards the next step of our medical journey. We've all gotten this far – presented to a doctor, received a diagnosis of some kind or another, scheduled surgery, and now we're stuck here, waiting.

I wonder how much collective sick leave is being used up in this room.

I clutch my hospital bag on my lap, trying to pull it closer to my chest, hugging it rib-crackingly tight. It's the same tan duffel that I've taken on countless weekenders with Scott: antiquing in the Southern Highlands; the Hunter for wine-tasting and weddings; the Blue Mountains for delicious Christmas in July Yuletide feasts.

I bend my head discreetly and whisper, 'I'm sorry this is not a more glamorous outing.' My lips meet the soft, supple leather. 'Next time. I promise.'

I think of all the places I still want to visit.

'Darling? Are you feeling okay?' I look up to see my mum's face is creased with concern. Making out with my bag must be a peculiar sight.

'Ah, yes. Just checking I packed my charger,' I say quickly, busying myself with the zip and peering into the dark depths of my bag.

'Maxine Mayberry?' My name pierces the air.

We stand and make our way over to the desk.

The admissions officer is a jolly lady named Rosie. She has tiny black seeds in her teeth like she's had a berry smoothie of some description for breakfast. My own tummy grumbles at the thought of food.

We run through the pre-admission questions – mainly finances and what outstanding sums are still to be paid and when. The hospital is a business, after all, but it's easy to forget that: when your life needs saving, it's not as though you have much choice.

We sit in silence for a short while as Rosie taps away at her keyboard. Mum clutches my hand.

After about ten minutes of hmming and ahhing, Rosie declares me 'all sorted' and directs us to the lift that will carry us up to the pre-op area.

Next stage unlocked: the surgery.

~

I've changed into a blue gown and cap, so I now resemble one of the downstairs smurfs.

My belongings are tagged to be stowed, hopefully to reappear on the other side of this. I watch as my tan bag is wheeled away. I really hope we meet again.

Mum sits by the bedside, distracting me with commentary about my neighbours. I simultaneously appreciate the senseless chatter and want to tell her to shut up.

'Oh, he looks like he's in real pain, doesn't he?' The man in the moon boot has followed us. There's a grimace plastered on his face that I hadn't noticed in admissions.

'Bless her cotton socks, that poor dear. Where is her husband?' Mum has now moved on to the elderly lady on my left. She looks much too fragile to be here alone. My heart breaks for her.

Nurses hum around me taking last-minute obs, confirming my name and birthdate and securing my hospital bracelet. I have to repeat multiple times what procedure I'm here for. *Transsphenoidal endoscopic surgery* is still a mouthful, so I simply say 'the brain'.

I appreciate the thoroughness. I've heard horror stories of surgeries where the wrong leg has been amputated. I hope Alexander remembers that I'm the double pea-sized tumour and not the orange. I'll take one frontal lobe intact, thanks. I'd considered wearing my Love on Top pink lipstick for him, just to lift the mood, but I even had to remove my nail polish, so as not to interfere with the probe that will be monitoring my oxygen levels. I'd much prefer them know I'm turning blue than look cute.

I'm allowed to clutch my phone until the final moments. My finger goes to find the bright red Tinder flame. *He's not there anymore*, I remind myself.

Instead, I send one last message to Alice before I pass Mum my phone for safekeeping.

Okay, I'm going in. Get ready to be negatively geared

'I love you,' Mum mouths as I'm wheeled away.

～

There's more waiting on the other side of the rubber double doors. I'd always envisaged those intimidating doors to be a portal to the medical version of a Formula One pit stop. A streamlined, choreographed dance of passing scalpels, surgical blades and suction. But instead of being whisked straight into the operating theatre, I'm held in a small waiting area. It feels like purgatory. Like the in-between space I've been trapped in for the past few months.

Let's get this show on the road! my head screams, but my heart refuses to keep pace.

I suspect they've given me something calming in my drip. How dare they medicate me without my knowledge! I try to get my body to rage-pump blood through my thirsty veins, but instead I feel as though I'm floating, bouncing around on a fluffy cloud.

I'm tired of waiting. But I'm also tied down to the bed with so many tubes and cords that I don't have a choice in the matter.

A nurse appears at my bedside.

'Sorry to keep you waiting, Maxine. Dr Jock is running slightly behind.'

First he was running a day early, and now he's late . . .

'Your anaesthetist is coming out to see you now, then we'll get you sorted. How are you feeling?'

'I'm okay, thank you,' I croak.

Suddenly, I'm no longer angry, just scared.

'You're going to do great. Let me get you a heated blanket to make sure you're nice and comfy.'

Okay, fine. All of the waiting is forgiven.

I've almost been lulled to sleep by the warmth and weight of the waffle throw when my anaesthetist emerges.

She instructs me to count backwards from a hundred as she administers a syringe of drugs into my IV. My skin feels tight and stretched as a distinct coolness floods the veins down my arm. I begin to count down.

One hundred, ninety-nine, ninety-eight – how fast am I supposed to be going? What if this doesn't put me to sleep, or I wake up mid-surgery?

Ninety-seven, ninety-si –

Chapter Twenty-one

I'm alive! At least, I appear to be. I can feel my throat. It's burning. My mouth is dry. My lips are cracked and stinging. I try sitting up to find some water, then realise I have an oxygen mask over my mouth and nose.

'Aww, Maxine. You're awake. Just stay put for a moment. No rush. Do you know where you are?' I hear a kind voice say. I can feel the warmth of the nurse's body next to my bed, but her voice sounds like it's being transmitted from a submarine at the bottom of the ocean.

'Yes, St John's Hospital,' I'm relieved to hear myself reply.

'That's right. I'm Eliana. You're in ICU, recovering from your surgery.'

'Mmmm.' The initial burst of adrenaline is fading, replaced by a deep aching all over my body. 'Am I okay?'

I've started shivering, and there's a sudden sharp pain digging into my temple, like someone has taken a drill to the bone.

'It says here that everything went really well, but the doctor should be around later. You may feel some discomfort with the anaesthesia wearing off, so I'll give you something for the pain now.'

A few beats later the room goes dark.

When I next open my eyes, my mum is pressing a wet flannel to my forehead.

'Hey, honey.'

'Hi, Mum.' Her touch overwhelms me, sending a flood of emotions coursing through my body. Relief, gratitude, joy. *I did it. I'm still here.* Tears stream down my face.

'Oh, honey, are you in pain?'

I shake my head, realising the oxygen mask has been removed. I still have a dull ache in my head, but it's much more tolerable.

'No. I'm all right.'

With my next breath I ask, 'Do you have my phone?'

Mum chuckles. 'You must be feeling okay.'

'I just promised Alice I'd message,' I explain.

'I already let her know that you're safely out of surgery.'

'Thanks, but I'd really like to message her myself, too.'

'I don't want you overdoing it,' she cautions, but she puts my mobile on the tray alongside my bed, next to a cup of ice chips.

With shaky fingers, I pick it up and type out my message to Alice.

NEGATIVE GEARING

I can't help but smile, despite the pain. If I can remember our safe word, surely that means I'll also remember how to write.

~

Mum stays until visiting hours end and promises to return tomorrow, when – if all goes well during the night – I'll be transferred onto the ward.

There's still no word on the specifics of the surgery's success. The official line is that it went well, but I still don't know if

Alexander was able to remove all of the tumour, and we'll need a few days to get the results of the cell testing.

I wriggle around in my bed, trying to get comfortable. I'm careful not to pull on any of my tubes or knock my nose, which is throbbing and packed with gauze. I wonder if there's bruising under my eyes. It certainly feels that way. I'm glad I don't have a mirror.

Eliana has explained why they can't offer me a stronger dose of morphine. They're monitoring my brain function, on high alert for a post-surgery brain fluid leak. I certainly don't want one of those, but I'm also desperately in need of something to knock me the hell out.

It's like a living graveyard in here. From what I can gather from snatches of the nurses' conversation, the lady in the bay next to me is not doing well. She has been given ketamine after a massive surgery to repair a perforated bowel and is agitated and confused. She keeps hallucinating that she's falling from a building, her piercing screams echoing throughout the unit. The delirium only pauses long enough for her to be sick.

Poor old duck.

I close my eyes and try pretending that I'm midway through a hideous long-haul flight, and that the commotion is standard cabin noise. I've dealt with screaming babies for twenty-one hours at a time before, so this should be a piece of cake. But my imagination is no match for the constant beeping of machines and alarms going off, and the bloodcurdling screams next to me.

I crane my neck, looking for Eliana. I spot her right away, seated at the station just a metre or so from the end of my bed. She's sipping from a mug and nibbling on a pastry. It's bizarre to think of even having an appetite, let alone indulging in a midnight snack. The scene looks so normal, when my life feels the opposite of normal right now.

I almost feel guilty pressing my buzzer and interrupting Eliana's well-deserved moment of peace.

She looks up immediately. 'I'll be right there.' She abandons her mug and hurries over to my bedside.

It's sort of like being on a plane – but with much better service – although I'm not up for a mini bottle of chardonnay or a pack of peanuts just yet.

'Are you feeling okay, Maxine *mou*?'

'Yes, I think so. My last name is Mayberry though?'

'Ah, *mou*,' Eliana says. 'The Greek word for "my". It's a bit like calling someone dear, or love. It slips out sometimes. I can't help myself. I hope you don't mind?'

'Not at all.' I smile weakly. 'I was wondering if I could listen to my audiobook? I just need my headphones from my bag.'

I assume my tan duffel has made it down here somewhere.

Eliana's eyebrows furrow. 'Are you sure you're feeling up to it? You must be the first person in ICU who's ever asked to listen to an audiobook.'

Should I reveal that this is the only way I can prove to myself right now that my brain is still sound? I've pre-downloaded a book by Sally Smyth, one of my favourite authors, and I figure that if I marvel at her usual witticisms, then my brain must be intact.

'I need it to help me sleep,' I say instead. It's a far simpler explanation.

Eliana considers me. I'm finally alert enough to take in her appearance. She looks around the same age as my mum. But unlike my mum, who takes pride in her long locks, her hair is cut short. Not in the curly style popular among many older women, but stacked in ashy layers. She's fastened the wispy hairs at the front with a single pearl clip that gives her a youthful look.

'How about this,' she says. 'You show me that you can keep down a few sips of water first, and I'll fetch your headphones for you.'

Her crinkly eyes are deep pools of compassion.

'Thank you.'

Eliana lifts a cup of water to my mouth, and I suck cautiously on the straw. The cool water trickles down my parched throat.

'I'm sorry I interrupted your break,' I say once I've swallowed.

Eliana waves my words away. 'Not at all, Maxine *mou*, You saved me from that baklava. One of the orderlies has been baking up a storm recently and bringing in lots of cheeky treats.'

Baklava.

How is this the second time I've heard of it in as many weeks, when it's spent close to thirty years not on my radar? Coincidence, or something more? Johnny has lurked at the edges of my consciousness since waking.

'Now why don't we give you a nice, warm sponge bath?'

I nod, suddenly unable to speak.

Eliana fills a shallow bowl with soapy water and brings it over to the bed. She lifts my gown and begins dabbing gently with a washer. She takes extra care sponging my inner thigh, around my catheter.

'We'll leave your face for the moment,' she says, inspecting my bandaged nose. 'It's all looking good.'

'So no leaking brain fluid?'

'No brain fluid.' She doesn't make me feel silly, just reassures me.

'It might feel nice if I do your back, too. Do you mind if I call the orderly to help me get you upright?'

'Okay.' It's strange how much I trust this woman already.

'I'll be back in just a moment.' Eliana returns to her workstation and makes a call.

'Oh, I wasn't expecting you still to be here,' I hear her say to the person on the other end. 'I thought you weren't doing nights at the moment.'

There's a pause. 'Ah, that's a shame,' she responds, then says, 'I was hoping to get some help with a sponge bath?'

Another pause. 'Lovely. Thank you.'

She puts the phone down.

'He'll be right here,' Eliana tells me as she moves to the basin to refill the bowl.

I'm sure it's all the drugs, but I'm suddenly overcome by the feeling that the baklava-baking orderly might be Johnny.

An alarm goes off as my heart picks up pace. It feels like a betrayal. Eliana rushes over to inspect my monitor before clearly deciding it's a false alert and pressing some buttons to silence it.

Good heart, slow down.

I see a tall, shadowy figure making its way across the dark unit towards us, and I avert my gaze, looking at the ceiling.

'Heya, Eliana, how can I be of service?'

The voice is deep, low and melodious; the sound of it stirs something in me.

'We're going to pop the lovely Maxine onto her side,' Eliana says. 'Is that okay?' she asks me.

'Sure,' I squeak.

I don't want to look at him. I can't.

'Okay,' he says, 'I'll just slide a hand underneath you and another on your back. Is that all right?'

'Yes,' I manage again, my eyes not shifting from the ceiling.

He towers over me as his hands slide into position. Firm yet soft.

'There. Easy does it.' He manoeuvres me slowly.

I'm glad it's dark, because I'm sure I'm completely red.

'Anything else you need?'

'I think that's it,' Eliana replies. 'We can manage it from here.'

Suddenly I'm panicked that he's going to leave. I steal a

quick glance his way, breath bated, and see a clean-shaven face that is most certainly not Johnny's.

I focus on keeping a tight lid on my emotions.

Don't cry, Max.

I manage to compose myself, and the orderly continues on his merry way, none the wiser.

Eliana finishes wiping away the stickiness on my back.

'Thank you,' I tell her. 'I almost feel human again.'

'Aww, Maxine *mou*, it's my job to make sure you're comfortable. Would you like to brush your teeth too?'

I nod enthusiastically. I feel like a minty mouth could cure just about anything right now.

I'm spitting into the bowl, the watery toothpaste meandering like a river down my chin, when Eliana says, 'Now, I should be the one thanking you for bringing that Dr Jock into our lives. We don't get enough of the likes of him in here.'

I swallow a strangled laugh. 'Alex– Dr Jock was here?'

'Yes, he came to check on you earlier, while you were asleep.'

'Oh. Did he say anything?'

'Just that he'd be back to see you in the morning.'

That could sound ominous, but the way she says it puts me at ease.

'Shame that I'll be off shift by then.' She winks and flashes me a mischievous smile. 'Now, Maxine *mou*, let me go get you those headphones.'

Chapter Twenty-two

Alexander appears the next morning, like a mirage at the end of my bed. A mirage in a full suit.

'Morning, Max. You're looking well.' He beams. It can't be much later than 7 am.

I'm sure that I look the opposite of well right now. Sally Smyth's dulcet tones had eventually lulled me into a couple of hours of broken sleep; I had giggled in the right places and even picked up on some plot clues before I decided my brain was in working order and allowed myself to drift off. But now I've been awake, counting the beeps, for what feels like the equivalent of another long-haul flight to Dubai.

My neighbour's hysterics quietened around the same time as I heard Eliana gently draw the curtain around my bed. She had spent much of the night crouched by my bedside tallying up the output from my catheter.

I'm sad I didn't get a chance to say goodbye and thank her for taking such good care of me. I now understand why nurses get fan mail. She's the only reason I survived last night.

I wipe the dry spit from the corners of my mouth.

'Thanks, Dr Jock. Although I'm not sure that's true,' I say, thinking of my bruised eyes and bloodied nose, which is still throbbing uncontrollably. Then – realising that's sort of like insulting Alexander's handiwork – I add, 'I'm sure you did a great job.'

Did he do a good job? That's the million-dollar, maybe-my-life-can-resume-as-normal question, isn't it?

'Everything went really well,' Dr Jock says before I ask. 'The tumour was smaller than expected – more corn kernels than peas.' He's moving his hands like a greengrocer describing the latest in-season specials.

I wish my mum was here, as I'm not sure how much information I'm capable of retaining right now, but visiting hours aren't for a while yet. I'm so used to receiving bad news that good news is difficult to process.

Dr Jock unhooks my chart from the end of my bed.

'Bridget says you've had an orange juice this morning.'

Ah, yes, Bridget the sweet Irish nurse who replaced Eliana before I woke up. Perfectly lovely, just not Eliana.

I nod. I'm starting to feel peckish.

'Good, good. We'll send you off for an MRI shortly to make sure we got everything and then get you up onto the ward.'

Okay, so this is where things go south – straight back into my comfort zone of shit going wrong. The MRI will surely reveal that Alexander has missed a bit, and I'll be wheeled back into the operating theatre. Best prepare myself for that now.

'Sure,' I say.

The thought of the MRI scares me as much – perhaps even more – as the idea of further surgery. My claustrophobia has only intensified since the whole Laurent necklace debacle, when I was almost burnt alive.

'You know the great thing about being in hospital, Max?' Alexander asks.

Oh, pray thee, Alexander, do tell. Is it my hourly bladder spasms as I'm milked like a cow for my urine, my house of horrors neighbour or the unrelenting beeping that is quite frankly worse than water torture?

'We can give you a nice dose of Valium to knock you out for the scan.'

Well, now, that is a great thing.

'Thank you.'

I knew I loved Alexander for more than his movie star looks.

'Perfect. I'll let Bridget know to get your drugs arranged, and an orderly will be down shortly to transfer you to your scan.'

~

Fortunately, I'm not allergic to flowers, because right now my hospital room rivals Floriade. Despite the drab walls and overall beige aesthetic of my new room on the ward, it's colourful, fresh and fragrant, which I'm sure I'll appreciate just as soon as I feel a bit better.

Alice and Maggie have sent a bunch of daffodils, Mum and Dad brought in an orchid accompanied by one of those gaudy 'Get Well Soon' balloons and work has sent a giant bouquet of Australian natives. Bloody Lucy and her loose lips – there goes my undercover surgery plan. I'm already nauseous, but I feel even queasier when I see Raffie's name on the card with the others.

Yesterday's scan went well. It felt as though I was in and out in a flash. I was out for the count when they wheeled me down there, but I was alert enough afterwards to notice it was last night's clean-shaven, definitely-not-Johnny orderly who brought me back up to the ward. Then I dozed the rest of the day away, so had another patchy night's sleep and now that it's morning, I'm tired again.

Mum arrives and greets me with a soft kiss on my forehead.

'How was your night, sweetie?'

Her arms coil around my weak frame and my lower lip quivers. I don't want her to leave my side. I rest my cheek on her shoulder.

'Rough.'

'Why don't you try to get some more sleep. Let yourself rest and recover. I'll be right here.'

It's like being back in my mum's presence has given my body permission to sleep properly. I'm vaguely aware of her fussing around my bed as I drift in and out of consciousness.

'Who sends flowers to a hospital with no box,' I hear her mutter to herself. 'Vases don't grow on trees.'

Sleep again.

When I next stir, it's a delicious aroma that coaxes me awake. It smells like my mum's scrumptious pot roast chicken from the Sunday evenings of my childhood. I turn my head carefully to look for her, but the room is empty. My eyes settle on the food tray next to my bed.

I find the remote at the side of my mattress and press tentatively. It tilts my upper body forward slowly, until I'm almost sitting up. I take my finger off the button. There's no searing pain, and everything still seems to be in place – at least my brain isn't slipping out of my nose. I press again, until I'm upright enough to reach for the table and manoeuvre it over my bed. Then I lift the cover off the dinner plate.

A succulent chicken leg stares back at me. It's covered in a glossy sauce and smells absolutely delicious.

What an extravagant hospital meal – and here I was thinking the best I could hope for was powdery potato mash!

I glance at the time on my phone in the bed next to me. My iPhone cuddle buddy. It's 11 am. Too early for roast chicken. But I haven't eaten properly for going on forty-eight hours, and I'm suddenly ravenous! Perhaps a sign that I'm on the mend.

Chicken for breakfast? Why the hell not. I suppose it's like the law of air and sea – a separate set of rules apply in hospital.

The papery skin cracks and crackles as I cut through it with the knife, exposing the velvety flesh beneath. My tastebuds explode as I push the meat onto my fork, then pop it into my mouth. Should I have checked that I'm allowed to eat this? They wouldn't have served it to me if I couldn't, right?

Yummm. The meat is silky and rich, with the perfect hint of citrus. It tastes like sunshine. I'm onto my third forkful when I notice the glistening orange segments and twirly rind. And then it clicks. This isn't chicken. It's duck. More specifically, it's Day 14 duck à l'orange.

I stop chewing and look around the room frantically, my already throbbing head spinning.

How? Where? This is impossible! My heart is racing a million miles per minute. Surely this can't be a coincidence? But how could Johnny know I was here? And, most importantly, is he still somewhere near?

'You're awake.'

I almost choke on my duck.

Scott is standing in the doorway, his hoodie pulled up over his head.

I swallow. The duck skin scratches my throat on its way down.

'I was here earlier, but you were sleeping,' Scott says. Like that explains everything. Like this isn't the first time we've laid eyes on each other in three months.

'What are you doing here?' I finally manage. I should be angry, but I'm too weak. Instead, I have an overwhelming urge to throw my arms around him, to sink my face into my favourite navy hoodie and drink in the familiar scent of the human who still knows me better than anyone.

Luckily, I'm bed-bound, so I can't do anything I'll regret. I've thought about this moment so many times – coming face to face with Scott, and what I'd say, how I'd feel. I expected we'd cross paths at some point – getting petrol or buying toilet paper. I never thought it was going to happen this way. In my hospital room.

He answers my question with a question. 'Why didn't you tell me?'

Is this really happening right now?

'I–I–I was waiting for your tour to finish up, and then . . .'

There's no point me finishing my sentence. We're both well aware what took place after the 'and then'.

'You haven't replied to any of my emails. I could have been here to support you, Maxie.'

I didn't want you here. You broke my heart.

He takes a tentative step towards the bed.

Don't come any closer, I will him silently. I feel like a sitting duck; I can't just kick off the sheets and run away.

'I got you something.' He gestures to the side of the bed, where I've pushed away the tray table with the duck.

My heart sinks. Of course. The duck à l'orange is his family's recipe. Given the circumstances, though, it seems like some cruel joke that he's chosen to cook the duck and not his usual lasagne. His eyes bypass my dinner tray and travel to the shelf on the wall where my temporary Floriade display has been set up.

'I know you love roses.'

Sure enough, a new bunch of red roses has been added to the line-up. Mum has obviously returned at some stage while I was sleeping to sort the vases. I wish she'd hurry back from wherever she is now.

As I go to thank Scott (as clichéd as they are, roses really are my favourite), a woman wheeling a trolley of meal trays comes to a halt outside my door.

'I've got your lunch here, love,' she calls out, stepping into the room and waving her gloved hand at Scott to shoo him out of the way. She stops when she sees the plate of duck on the table.

Her forehead crinkles. 'Oh, there must have been some kind of mix-up. I've got you down as a red tray. Mashed and puréed foods only. Let me just check on that.' She pulls a piece of paper out from underneath a pot of vanilla custard. 'Yes, yes, that's right. Luckily it looks like you've only had a few bites. I'll get that sorted for you.'

As she whisks the duck away, I want to reach out and snatch it right back. I feel strangely possessive as I picture it being scraped into a bin, just as I'd done with the Fork Him leftovers. It's hard to believe that was only two days ago. It feels like it's been a year.

The lunch lady leaves, and the room is silent. It's so different from the chaos of the ICU. The only sounds are the inflation and deflation of my leg compressors, helping to circulate blood, and the beeping of my heart monitor, probably working over-time now that I've eaten unauthorised solid food.

'So you brought the duck?' I ask Scott.

He smiles proudly. 'I wanted you to know just how much I care.'

I'm not sure how I feel. It's a sweet gesture. The type of gesture that I had longed for. Words were easy for Scott. At last, some action. But I'm disappointed, almost ashamed, at the part of me that's still hoping Johnny has somehow found me.

Scott comes a little closer, his concerned eyes searching mine for permission, then takes a seat on the edge of my bed.

'How are you feeling?'

He reaches out to touch my leg, but I flinch, and he quickly retracts his hand.

'They were able to remove the tumour, and it's not cancerous, right?'

'Right. Well, I'm not a hundred per cent sure. But so far, so good. I think?'

It's starting to feel natural to share with him again, just as I used to when our relationship was at its best.

'Well, you're looking well.'

I reach up and gently touch my tender, padded nose. The bandage feels crunchy, like it's covered in dried blood. This is not how you want to see your ex for the first time.

'How did you find out?' I ask.

'That work friend of yours. Lucy? She mentioned something to Raffie.'

Loose lips Lucy strikes again.

'Eve told me, not Raffie,' Scott clarifies hurriedly. Then he hesitates. 'It really was just that one slip-up, Maxie. You have to believe me.'

'Scott . . .' I warn.

'Please, just hear me out. I can't be this close to you and not at least try.'

I consider his words for a moment, then eventually nod. I suppose things can't get much worse.

He pulls his phone from the pocket of his hoodie, clears his throat and starts reading.

'Max, you are way too good for me. You always have been. You're a smart, funny, beautiful dream girl, and I'm still a work in progress. But I'm trying, and I want to keep trying, for us both.'

He pauses for a moment and inhales deeply, as if mustering the courage to continue. His eyes remain glued to the screen.

'I hate myself that things have turned out this way. I've ruined my chance to give you a purely happy existence. That's gone, because I can never say that I've always done the right thing by you. I wish I could, but I'll never be able to. As I've said in my emails, all I want is your happiness. I don't feel any less connected to you now after all these months apart than I did when we were together, and in a heartbeat I would sacrifice everything –'

Crassssssssssssssssshhhhhhhhhh!

The sound of shattering glass cuts Scott's speech short.

Mum is standing at the foot of my bed, her mouth agape, one hand clutching a square vase. A second vase is in pieces at her feet.

'Scott!' she exclaims. 'What are you doing here?' Her face is a mixture of confusion and shock.

'Err, hi, Mrs Mayberry. I just wanted to check on Max,' Scott stammers.

She looks to me.

'I'm okay,' I say, trying to reassure her.

'I'm gone for all of ten minutes, and this is what happens! Honestly, Scott, you're lucky that Max's dad is at work and not here – he'd be escorting you right back out to the hospital car park via the laundry chute.'

'I know, I know, and I deserve it.' Scott hangs his head. 'I owe apologies to you all for what I've put Max through.'

'It's fine, Mum,' I say again.

Luckily, she's a soft touch. She could never quite understand the break-up, or Scott's cheating. She could only see who he used to be – the boy who had made her daughter deliriously happy, who eagerly assisted her with basic IT requests – not who he'd become.

'Well, okay, then,' she says, still sounding uncertain. 'I'll give you five more minutes. I'll be in the bathroom filling this up.' She lifts the remaining vase to show us. 'I finally found something large enough for that ridiculous bouquet from your work. Watch the glass, please, Scott.' Her maternal instincts can't help but kick in. 'I'll buzz someone to come and sort it out.'

Scott waits until the bathroom door is firmly closed before he shuffles further up the bed towards me, then he reaches out and gently cups my chin.

'Look at your little nose, all beaten up.'

For many months before our break-up, I couldn't understand where the person I'd loved had gone. Now, at last, here he is again.

'We're not just going to get back together,' I blurt, because I can't trust my foggy head.

'I know that – I wouldn't ever assume that. I'm just asking for the tiniest sliver of a chance . . . Do you think you can give me that?'

I hear the whoosh of water from the bathroom. Taps being turned on and off, then back on again. The toilet flushing. Bless my mother – after all the pain she's seen me through, she's still giving us our privacy.

'I'll think about it,' I whisper.

My bed bounces violently as Scott fist-pumps the air.

'I'm going to work so hard to prove to you that I'm worth it. That we're worth it. We'll get you all healed and us back on track in no time at all,' he declares. 'Soon this is all going to seem like the tiniest blip on the radar of our relationship.'

He pulls his feet up to sit cross-legged on the bed. I stare at his dirt-stained sneakers resting on the freshly starched white hospital sheets.

Scott sees me looking. 'Don't worry, Maxie – that dirt's not budging. Remember, I sealed the stains with hairspray.'

How could I forget? Three months apart and I seem to have forgotten a lot.

Chapter Twenty-three

Revertigo: defined by the Urban Dictionary as 'a dizzyingly inexplicable reversion to past behaviour in the presence of a lost acquaintance once associated with the behaviour'. I am suffering from a rampant case of it right now.

I've been at my parents' house for just over two weeks, and even my hair has decided to tangle in the same way it did when I was eight. Mum and I also had the same fight as she lovingly brushed my hair – or as I interpreted it, attempted to scalp me.

'Ouch, you're hurting!'

'Honey, I'm being as gentle as I can. It's just so knotty – there may even be few birds in here!'

Despite our squabbling, which was becoming more frequent as I grew stronger, my recovery was going smoothly.

Dr Jock had been happy with my MRI, and the collected cells were thankfully all clear of cancer, so he had sent me home after a week in hospital.

My days consisted of pain meds, sinus flushes and Sally

Smyth audiobooks. I listened to them at double speed to give my brain a proper workout.

At night, Mum and I would snuggle on the couch with a bowl of popcorn in front of a movie – Dad too, as long as we weren't watching a chick flick. I got the coveted three-seater all to myself, my head propped up on a stack of pillows, while Mum and Dad squeezed onto the tiny two-seater.

Each evening I pushed my bedtime slightly later, from 7 pm to 7.30 pm, then from 8 pm to 8.30 pm.

Last night at 9 pm, I snapped. We were all watching *Pretty Woman* (the chickiest of all chick flicks, but also a classic, so Dad had made an exception). Mum had been commenting through-out the entire film about all of the many well-documented continuity issues. The one she was especially fixated on was Julia Roberts' croissant suddenly transforming into a pancake as she ate a room service breakfast. If that wasn't bad enough, the pancake then goes from half-eaten to whole again.

When I was in a good mood, I found Mum's constant film commentary endearing. But last night she was getting on my last nerve.

'It's so distracting for the viewer. I don't understand how mistakes like that get through all the checks,' she commented for what felt like the umpteenth time.

'*Your* commentary is distracting,' I piped up from my three-seater throne.

'Oh, Max, do you think you should head up to bed? You sound tired.'

'I'm not tired,' I'd growled through gritted teeth – even though I knew the disappearing croissant, or more accurately, Mum's opinions about the disappearing croissant, shouldn't be bothering me that much.

'Did you hear from Scott today?' she asked.

I didn't like the insinuation that my mood had something to do with Scott. My dad had sworn under his breath. He'd been less than impressed to hear about Scott's surprise visit to the hospital.

Scott hadn't dared to make an appearance at my parents' house, but he'd been sending almost daily care packages made up of yummy snacks, comfy pyjamas and bunny slippers. He was texting regularly, too, and mostly respecting the boundaries I'd set about not hounding me to get back together with him. But his last message had broken every rule.

Max, would you consider coming with me to Paris to recover? I'll take care of you xx

I hadn't replied. Yet.

'Yeah, I heard from him,' I eventually responded – purposely vague. 'I think I will go up to bed.'

When I'd eventually fallen asleep, I'd dreamt of croissants. No doubt influenced by thoughts of *Pretty Woman* and Paris.

This morning Mum had quietly set out my medications with my breakfast, then disappeared for a shower. I'm still internally seething – and for no good reason. If recovery cycles through stages like grief, then I must be smack bang in the anger part of this journey. I know I should be happy that the surgery went well – and I am – but I'm angry that I'm here. That I have no other option but to crawl back to my childhood home, where I automatically revert to behaving like an eight-year-old.

Housed within these familiar walls, and held in these familiar arms, I feel pressure to feel better for my mum's sake. Yes, physically, I'm doing okay. With the help of constant pain-killers, the pain has been reduced to a dull throb. Whenever Mum asks how I'm feeling (every hour) I respond with 'okay'. Technically, that's accurate, but emotionally I'm not really sure how I'm feeling. I need to be where I have the freedom to make my emotions big.

It's time to stop treating my parents like dirt and send an SOS text to Alice to break me out of here. She'd initially offered to take time off work to care for me, but that was 'BM' – 'Before Maggie' – when she'd had more time on her hands. She came to see me once in hospital, but I'm disappointed she hasn't bothered visiting me here.

My spoon is scraping the bottom of my cereal bowl when Mum reappears, her body wrapped in a towel like a burrito.

'How are you feeling this morning, Max?'

'Okay.' My usual response. I should apologise for last night's temper tantrum.

'You're looking well.' She collects my empty bowl. 'You don't even have your bandage on this morning.'

I reach up to touch my nose. It hadn't been oozing when I woke up, so I must have forgotten to replace it.

I wait for Mum to ask me whether I've taken all my morning meds, but instead she 'tsks' loudly, sets my bowl back down on the table and starts scooping up invisible crumbs.

'I didn't eat toast,' I protest.

She doesn't say anything.

'Maybe it's time I headed home . . .'

'Sure. If that's what you'd like?'

Wow. Not the response I was expecting. I'm used to far more babying.

'Yes. I think that might be best,' I test again.

'Perfect. Well, your father is just getting changed, and then he can drive you home.'

Now it feels as though I'm being kicked out.

'Unless Alice is going to come fetch you?' she asks.

Alice still hasn't responded to the text I sent her yesterday morning.

'A lift would be amazing, thank you.'

'I'll start packing your things. I've also frozen some meals for you to take home, so you don't have to worry about cooking,' she says.

'Thanks, Mum. I really do appreciate everything you've done for your fully grown daughter,' I say.

She pauses briefly. 'I know, darling. It's not easy on any of us. We love you so much – we just want what's best for you. If it's your own space you need, then that's completely understandable.'

I'm not sure *what* I need, but it can't hurt to make a change. I hug her tightly.

An hour or so later I'm dressed, and Dad is escorting me to the car, his arm looped in mine as we slowly ascend the driveway.

'Is Alice going to be home much?' he asks. I can tell he wants me to stay longer.

'I'm sure she will be,' I reassure him, even though I'm not certain of that myself. 'I can't be your full-time couch sloth. It's time for me to start re-entering the society of the standing,' I add with a smile.

'Promise me you'll take things easy, Max. We can't have any more calls in the middle of the night,' he says sternly.

His dig doesn't go unnoticed. Mum must have had a word with him, as this is the first time he's said anything to me – even indirectly – about Scott's reappearance. I'm glad he hasn't asked me outright where things stand with Scott, as I'm not sure how I'd respond. That we're texting again, but that's it? That I might be considering getting back together with him? After everything my parents have witnessed and supported me through over the past few months, I feel embarrassed – almost ashamed – admitting that I'm beginning to wonder if there *is* a world that exists in which I can forgive Scott and give us another go. Thankfully, Dad doesn't persist with his uncomfortable line of questioning.

'Well, I'm glad to have the couch back,' he says gruffly. 'We're playing a test match with Pakistan tonight, and I wouldn't mind putting my legs up.' His contribution consists strictly of swilling beer.

Mum follows behind us with my luggage. My bags have multiplied. In addition to my tan weekender, there's now a collection of reusable green shopping bags, bursting with gifts, food and medical supplies.

'All of your meals are in this one.' She gestures to the bag in her left hand. 'And I've packed your presents in this one.' She raises the bag in her right hand. 'Most of the flowers were on their way out, so I tossed them, but I've kept the natives so you can dry them out.' I can see a spiky yellow banksia peeking out from the bag's opening.

'Thanks, Mum.'

'And I've wrapped up the duck to keep it in one piece.'

What? Don't tell me Mum has been cooking duck à l'orange now, too? What happened to her chicken pot roast?

'Duck?'

'Yes, that little glass duck you have. I found it tucked in the bunch of roses Scott gave you.'

Ohhh. I hadn't realised that had been part of his gift.

'I'll come and collect you for your check-up at the end of the week,' Mum says, 'but please call if you need us before then, okay?'

'Max?' Mum and Dad are staring at me expectantly.

'Oh, yup, sure,' I say.

'Remember, in the face of pain there are no heroes.'

I can't help but laugh at her stern face. 'Yes, Mum.'

~

My lilac eggwhisk is missing.

When I'd arrived home earlier in the day, Alice greeted me like the prodigal daughter and made sure I was comfortable with my couch set-up of a cosy throw and pillows upon pillows. She'd even lit one of our good Amalfi scented candles. But as the room filled with the scent of lemon groves, fresh sea air and the vanilla aroma of an Italian pasticceria, she'd retreated to her bedroom to 'finish up work'.

'Hey, Alice! Did you guys move some stuff in the kitchen?' I call, already knowing the answer but attempting to sound like I'm not out for blood. More specifically, out for either Alice or Maggie's blood – whoever had thought it was a good idea to remove the whisk from its home in the top right-hand drawer with my other prized utensils. I never thought I'd have prized utensils, but here we are.

'Why are you in the kitchen?' she bellows back.

That wasn't an answer.

'Just getting myself a drink.'

That wasn't entirely true. I had tired of re-runs of *Schitt's Creek* and scrolling social media. My Instagram and TikTok were full of healthy people doing fun, healthy things, like going to the gym and eating brunch. I thought maybe a jaunt to the kitchen might make me feel better – to be embraced by familiar surroundings. As I'd rested a hand on the timber bench, I was transported back to one of the many evenings standing in this exact position, either patiently waiting for the oven timer to ding, or for a message from Johnny. At the thought of Johnny, I'd felt strangely content – that things had worked out as they should. It was only ever meant to be a good time, not a long time.

It wasn't until I'd opened the drawer and seen that the whisk was missing that my calm evaporated.

It's not a big deal, Max, I think, trying to reason with myself.

Maybe I'll have that drink after all. I push the drawer closed and open the overhead cupboard. In the spot where my favourite 'M' mug sits are two new mugs, both emblazoned with *World's Best Girlfriend.*

I fix myself a tea and decide it will pair well with a chocolate chip cookie. I pull open the pantry to find that all my food has been shoved onto one shelf to make room for two jumbo-sized bags of dog food.

'I'm going for a walk!' I yell, slamming the cupboard door. I have unlocked a new, fever-pitched anger stage of my recovery.

'Really? Will you be okay on your own?' Alice sounds like she's in the bathroom now. 'If you can wait half an hour, I'll grab Maggie and Thor, and we can go for a family stroll.'

I stand outside the bathroom door. There's no sense in shouting – even though we'll no longer be receiving noise complaints from our downstairs neighbour, as she appears to live here now.

'I think I need some time on my own.'

'Are you sure?' I can hear her tearing off sheets of toilet paper.

'Yes. I went out by myself all the time at my parents' place.'

Lie, lie, lie. I just want to get out of here.

'Okay, well, take your phone and call if you need anything.'

I go to my bedroom to fetch my sneakers. I already have leggings on; I'm permanently in leggings these days. Blood rushes to my nose as I carefully bend down to pull on my socks, then shoes.

I hurry out the door before I hear the toilet flush.

Once I'm downstairs, I move like a baby deer in the snow. I can't risk tripping and falling on the pavement. I shudder as I imagine my nose split open and my brain fluid gushing into the gutter, like stormwater from a broken pipe.

I stop at the local cafe and buy an apple juice. It feels weird to pull out my bank card. I wonder how the bank thinks I've been paying for things over the past three weeks? I know there are alerts for suspicious transactions, but how about *no* transactions?

I sip on my drink and head towards the park, trailing behind a group of twenty-something men carrying six-packs of cold beer. It's almost 5 pm – knock-off time. The tallest of them is regaling the group with tales of his unreasonable boss, who is failing to see 'the big picture' and micromanaging his every task. I don't miss work at all. In fact, I'm relieved I still have three more weeks before I have to return to Slice.

I can feel my vitamin D levels being replenished as the late-afternoon sun warms my back. I pop in my earphones, switch on Sally Smyth and breathe in the glorious fresh air.

I'm back, baby, I think. *Next stop, words on the page!* In a few more days, I'll be well enough to spend the rest of my time off working on my novel.

As I fiddle with my phone to adjust the volume, Scott's name appears on the screen.

'Hello,' I answer.

With each day that passes, it feels more and more normal to hear from him. It's like riding a bike . . .

'Hey, Max.' He pants, like he's been running.

'Are you okay?'

'Hey! That's my line.'

I smile into the phone. 'You just sound like you've been rushing.'

'Well, I have been.' He pauses, like he has something big to reveal.

'Okay . . .?' I take a seat on a park bench.

'First off, though. How are you feeling? Is it nice being home?'

'Yes. Well, yes and no.'

Why is it so easy to be this candid with my ex-boyfriend?

'What do you mean?' His voice is full of concern.

'It's just taking some adjustment.'

I don't mention Alice and Maggie's apparent new living situation, even though I have already updated him on the latest about Alice's dating life. It doesn't feel right to bitch to him about Alice.

'Come on, Max. I know you better than this. What's up? You sound sad,' he probes.

The funny thing is, I do suddenly feel sad, when just moments ago I was enjoying basking in the sun and feeling more like myself than I had in quite some time.

'I guess I am a bit. Not like toaster-bath-bomb sad, more animal-died-in-a-movie sad.'

Specifically Disney-cartoon-animal-Bambi sad, I think to myself. I was toaster-bath-bomb sad the night I found him with Raffie.

There's silence on the other end.

'Scott, are you still there?'

'Sorry, I just had to quickly write something down before I forgot. Now, I have some amazing news to cheer you up. I was so excited that I had to ring you right away!'

'What is it?'

'I've literally just left Mum's place. She's upgraded us all to business class so you can have a comfortable flight over!'

'Scott . . .'

I hadn't responded to his text message, and there'd been no further discussion about me going to Paris.

'Come on, Max. It's the perfect place to recover. All expenses paid. You can just focus on recuperating.'

'But I don't think I'm allowed to fly –'

'Technically you can,' Scott interrupts. 'I've googled, and it says the risk decreases after two weeks. I would have called your doctor to confirm, but I didn't want to overstep.'

'Hmmm.'

'Come on, Max! When is the last time you went on a holiday, or even treated yourself?'

When *was* the last time? I'm sure that flipping my pillow over to the cold side doesn't count as a treat.

'You already have the time off,' Scott continues.

'Let me think about it,' I say, mostly to wind up the conversation, as I can feel someone standing uncomfortably close behind me, like they're waiting for their turn to sit.

'Please do, Max.'

I hang up and swivel on the bench to make fierce eye contact with whoever is standing there. I know it's not obvious that I'm recovering from major surgery, but I still have every right to hesitate for longer than a few minutes on a public park bench.

I am suddenly face to face with Alice. Maggie is at her side, and Thor is at their feet. I can feel the judgement emanating from her pores before she even opens her mouth to speak.

'No, Max. Absolutely not. I forbid you.'

'How long have you been eavesdropping for?'

'Long enough.'

'Can we not do this here?' *In front of Maggie*, I want to add, but I am restrained enough not to.

'You're smarter than this, Max.' Alice scoots around to the front of the bench and slides in next to me. 'You know what a good show he can put on.'

Oh, I'm smarter than this, am I?

'Am I smart enough to ask that your girlfriend start paying her share of the rent? It's clear you've been having a great old time playing happy families while I've been on my deathbed. You couldn't even be bothered checking in on me.'

Alice looks like she's been slapped. 'Excuse me?'

'You heard me. You only visited me once, and you barely replied to my messages.'

'That's not fair, Max. You were with your parents, and you know that I would have been there in a heartbeat if you'd asked me to.'

'I shouldn't have to ask. I didn't need my parents – I needed you!' I'm yelling now.

'Other people's lives don't stop for yours!' She yells back. 'What more do you want from me? You don't even know all the things I've been handling so that you haven't had to worry!'

'Huh? What things?' Sounds like absolute BS to me. Like she's trying to make excuses for being such a shit friend.

'It doesn't matter now, Max. How many late nights have we had; how many bottles of wine have been consumed over *your* problems. I let you move in with me for God's sake!'

'I didn't realise I was such an inconvenience,' I spit. 'Plus, we both know that my mess-of-a-life made you feel better about yours. Your shit was all over the place before you met *her*!' I look pointedly at Maggie. 'I almost prefer loose cannon Alice over this new boring Alice. At least she was a decent friend.'

I immediately regret my words.

Alice clears her throat and stands. 'Right, well I think you've made your point, Max. I'll leave you to enjoy your holiday with your loser boyfriend. You clearly deserve each other.'

'Alice, please. I'm sorry. I'm being an arsehole.' I stand and try to grab her arm, but she shrugs me off and reaches for Maggie's hand instead.

'No need to apologise. You feel the way you feel. Just don't expect me home tonight – you can have your deathbed all to yourself.'

Wow. Now it's my turn to be slapped.

'She's really rubbed off on you, hasn't she?' I try to catch Maggie's eye, to hold her accountable for the wedge she's driven between me and my best friend. But like the coward she is, she averts her gaze. My initial character assessment was evidently accurate.

'Let's go,' Alice says to Maggie.

Tears stream down my face as I watch Alice and her new family disappear around a curve in the path.

PART IV

Mise en place

/ mi zã ˈplas /

(noun) Putting in place.

Chapter Twenty-four

'Great weather for ducks, isn't it, *mesdames et messieurs?*' Our cycle tour leader turns to look back at our party of five and beams.

The rain pours down on us as we pedal. I'm having a difficult time breathing, with my poncho stuck to my face like plastic film clinging to leftover deli meat. It is simultaneously wet and humid, and I am in hell.

If I had thought Paris in spring was all wisteria blooms, leisurely visits to Gothic basilicas to ogle stained-glass windows and cultured evenings at the Nuit des Musées, I'd been horribly mistaken. Oh, there would be markets, that much I'd been promised. I just hadn't realised I'd have to cycle sixteen kilometres to reach them. Had I been properly briefed, I would have skipped the excursion and stayed in bed.

Scott had sold it as a casual bike ride; it was also, in his words, 'the most important day of the entire trip', a sentiment that had been echoed by Helen at dinner the previous night, after complaining about the saltiness of her steamed mussels.

She went on to declare that the Laurents were much more skilled in the culinary arts – and that she 'absolutely could not wait' to prove it to everyone tomorrow in what would be the *pièce de résistance* of the trip. So, yes, in no uncertain terms – and in a very bad French accent – she had made it clear that today's activity was unmissable.

Our cycling journey had begun in the bumpy backstreets of Paris, my bum bouncing up and down on the hard leather seat. Thankfully, it has now been weeks since my surgery – weeks of double-checking that my brain was definitely firmly in place and not about to slip out of my nose like a toddler barrelling full speed down a slide.

Despite the rain, we successfully navigated pothole after pothole until we arrived at the station and boarded a train to Versailles.

Scott helped me lift my bike into the carriage. I was surprised at the lack of whingeing from Helen and Eve as they awkwardly manoeuvred their bikes into the vestibule. Gary was having a fine time wrestling his own wheels. The train lacked any prominent signage denoting the bike section, so we followed Rex, our *charismatique* guide, and propped them up near the luggage section before taking a seat on the adjacent bench. The thin cushion felt like plump buttermilk pancakes on my bruised derrière.

We were immediately greeted with fierce irritation. 'Have you bought extra tickets for those contraptions?' a nondescript man spat. 'If not, stand the fuck up.' Understandably, he assumed we spoke English. The scum on the soles of his leather loafers was very clearly *English* scum.

Rex was quick to respond. He must have gone into bat for many groups before us. '*Monsieur, s'il vous plaît.* Our bikes have every right to be here.'

This was very clearly Rex's homeland too, and he was all set to defend it. With his monocle eyepiece dangling from his shirt pocket, Rex certainly looked the part – in that he was a walking – sorry, cycling – French cliché. I kept thinking his monocle string was going to get caught in his bike chain.

'Yeaaah, shut the fuck up, mate,' Scott chimed in. His broad Australian accent sounded so crass in contrast. 'We have every right to be here.'

I wanted to die inside.

'"We have every right to be here,"' the man mocked under his breath. But he'd put his earphones back in, presumably bored with the conversation.

He'd continued to glare at us as Rex launched into the day's itinerary.

'Our first stop in Versailles will be the famous open-air market so we can buy our lunch. There is so much beautiful produce to choose from, fit for Marie Antoinette herself!' He paused and tipped an imaginary hat to Helen, Eve and myself. 'Once you've made your selection we'll cycle through the château's sprawling park along *le magnifique* tree-lined paths to the Grand Canal and dig into our feast while I give you a history lesson on the French monarchy.'

It wasn't long before the smoking brick chimneys gave way to countryside. The trees looked like illustrations from a storybook; mostly trunk, with leaves sprouting from the top like fluffy bristles on a make-up brush. The rain had made everything an iridescent, shiny green, but I caught myself watching for flashes of blue. A habit, really. IKEAs typically lurk on the fringes of cities. While others seek out the Golden Arches, I look for the blue mothership.

Rex handed out ponchos as we stepped off the train. Again, Scott kindly lifted my bike for me. Stopping to consider whether cycling sixteen kilometres was too much for someone who was still recovering from brain surgery would have been far kinder.

'Are you okay, Max?' Scott calls to me now. He's a few bike lengths ahead and has been checking on me periodically.

'Fine,' I yell through clenched teeth, as the plastic poncho slaps across my face like a wet fish. 'Do you know how much further it is?' But my words are lifted by the spitting wind and sail away.

Rex pulls up next to me. 'We're almost there. You've got this, Maxine.'

A few minutes later we round the corner, and I see market stalls in the distance. I am brimming with a mix of relief and pride that I've made it in one piece and a flood of endorphins from the exercise. It has been months since I've even broken into a light sweat, and I'm sure my face is positively glistening.

We follow Rex's lead and dismount, pushing our bikes towards the bustling market square. It's like a scene out of *Beauty and the Beast*. This is much closer to the France I'd dreamt of.

Scott takes my hand, our plastic ponchos rustling in the wet as we walk towards the decorated square. He's been proceeding with caution – an embrace here and there, a quick peck on the lips, but no other physical advances. I can feel myself slowly warming up. I'd fallen asleep on him on the flight over. Dribbling on his broad shoulder felt familiar and foreign all at once.

'Welcome to *Les Halles de Versailles*,' Rex announces. 'Here you will find the freshest fruit and vegetables you could imagine. The produce is so good that chefs from nearby restaurants pay a visit each morning to collect boxes of ripe tomatoes, earthy mushrooms and perhaps a rabbit or two.'

We trail behind him as he weaves his way through the stalls. Scott clings on to my hand tightly, like I'm going to be sucked into the crowd, never to be seen or heard from again.

Rex stops in front of one of the vendors. 'Can I direct your attention to these amazing artichokes, *s'il vous plaît*. They're the size of a small soccer ball! Or look at these green almonds – they will split and sauté them whole for you, or these olives! Marinated, herbed or oil-cured – you decide! There are also pastries *et du pain*.'

Rex's enthusiasm is contagious.

'You can't get this at the DJ's food hall!' Helen exclaims as her greedy eyes take in the trestle tables laden with produce.

'You most certainly cannot!' Rex booms. I wonder how he even knows what David Jones is, or if he's just familiar with Helen's type – all brand names and labels.

'I will let you browse and make your selections for our picnic, while I pick up a few things for our surprise later.' He winks at Helen. Maybe he's warmed to her more than I'd initially thought.

'Now, some quick *faux pas* to be aware of. Definitely no touching; point to what you'd like to purchase and the very experienced stallholder will select the best produce for you.'

I don't think it's any coincidence that we're in earshot of said stallholder.

'Use French if you can,' Rex continues. 'It's always better to try and fail, than not to try at all. We don't like the arrogance of that. Now, let's meet back in this spot in thirty minutes. Oh, and be careful of pickpockets!'

With the sights, sounds and smells of the bustling markets overtaking my senses, it's easy to ignore the uncomfortable feeling niggling at the base of my belly. The feeling that I've left things on such bad terms with Alice that I shouldn't be enjoying myself here. I squash the thought down as Scott and I splinter off from Helen, Gary and Eve and wander down a crowded aisle.

Traversing the vibrant passageways of the busy market with Scott makes me nostalgic for our past holidays; the shared, unbridled thrill of the unexpected, offset by the safety of each other. There was a time when, together, anything felt possible. It makes me hopeful we can find our way back there.

We find a stall selling macarons and Scott buys half a dozen. He covers my eyes and feeds me bites while I guess the flavours. If I get it right, I'm rewarded with a kiss. Pistachio, white chocolate, lemon meringue, rose, and lavender . . . I struggle with the final flavour. Red velvet! Scott agrees that it tastes like strawberry and gives me full marks anyway. I appreciate how hard he's trying to make me happy.

We return to the designated spot half an hour later, with a backpack bulging with cheeses whose names I can't pronounce. We've managed more snack stops along the way, too. Seafood paella so colourful it bubbled in the pan like a rainbow potion, and paper-thin crepes filled with banana and oozy Nutella.

Rex returns five minutes after us – and five minutes behind his own schedule – with an armload of brown waxed packages in various shapes and sizes. We wait patiently as he pushes his shopping down into his leather satchel. He frowns, securing his monocle in place to shuffle the packages around like an elaborate game of Tetris before fastening the flap and announcing, 'All right, to *pique-nique* we go!'

Scott slings our bodyweight-of-cheese-backpack over his broad shoulders, and I can't stop myself from imagining the muscles rippling under his poncho and shirt. He's wearing one of his stupid vintage hip-hop T-shirts that's not vintage at all, but despite this, my attraction is undeniable. It's been so long since we had sex, but I think I still want to.

Luckily the rain has eased for our ride to the canal. Rex selects a neat patch of grass under some of the storybook make-up-brush trees a few metres from the water. A couple of picnic blankets appear, and we pull packages from our own bags and begin tearing them open.

Helen and Gary have brought some glossy cherries and melon – who knew fruit actually sparkled! Meanwhile, Eve has purchased charcuterie meats and more fromage. (You can never have too much fromage.)

Laid out on the red-and-white check rug, our improvised picnic looks like it belongs in the pages of *Gourmet Traveller*. I can't help but wonder what artful modifications creative director Raffie would make to the shot. I quickly shake my head. So far, I have done a pretty good job of ignoring any intrusive Raffie thoughts, and I'd like to keep it that way.

I reach for a marinated olive, but Helen's arm shoots out to block mine. 'Just a moment, Max. The girls at home need to see this. They'll be green with envy.'

She pulls out her phone and starts snapping. For a boomer, Helen certainly knows her way around an Instagram filter.

Rex is clearly hoping we'll ignore the light sprinkle, so we cast aside our ponchos and dig in. You can tell what hemisphere someone is from by the way they respond to the weather. Alice and I regularly make fun of the very obviously northern hemisphere transplants sunbaking in the park on their lunchbreaks in the middle of winter, while we wear scarves and gloves inside and microwave our pumpkin soup. This year I can level up my soup game and cook us French onion soup! That's if Alice ever wants to speak to me again. She's not responded to any of my texts.

The rain is coming down harder now, and I notice a baguette peeking out from the top of Helen's bag. 'Helen, your baguette is getting wet!' I say, pointing.

'Oh dear!' Gary jumps up to rescue the sodden bread stick, pulling it from the bag and stowing it his jacket.

'Protect that baguette at all costs!' Rex exclaims. 'It's hard to find good-quality ones these days.'

'Isn't all bread the same? It's just a vehicle for cheese,' Scott remarks. I can tell from his smug expression he's proud of his one-liner.

'Absolutely not!' Rex is horrified. 'With market bread, you get a lovely snappy, yeasty baguette, none of this flaccid grocery store business.'

Scott sniggers at Rex's use of *flaccid*, and I elbow him.

'It's not uncommon to see young men having sword fights in the supermarket over the worthiest baguette,' Rex continues.

'Duel in aisle two,' I quip.

Rex laughs. *'Exactement!'*

It's Scott's turn to elbow me. I don't know why – it doesn't seem as though I've offended Rex.

'Why don't you eat the baguette now?' Rex suggests. 'I'm not sure it's going to make it through the rest of day.'

Gary pulls the bread out of the long paper bag and examines the dark end. 'It's burnt!'

'I don't mind having that bit,' I say quickly.

Gary takes a knife and carves off the burnt end. 'I like my bread cremated,' I add.

Rex laughs again, and this time Gary and Eve join in. Scott scowls. Perhaps because he's reminded of the countless times I've burnt his toast. I could never decipher the settings on that Kmart toaster. Oh, how times have changed. I now cook soufflé. Rather, I have attempted to cook soufflé. Flashes of evenings spent cooking in the Nest's kitchen have darted in and out of my mind all day. It's difficult to be in France, surrounded by the delicious food that featured in the Fork Him project, and not think about it. And Johnny.

'What cheese goes best with a French baguette?' I ask Rex as I survey our healthy (or not-so-healthy) selection of hard and soft cheeses. I'm sure there's an art to pairing cheese with different types of bread. But before Rex has a chance to respond, I'm struck with another suddenly very important thought.

'Sorry, Rex, probably a silly question, but if we're in France, is it still called a French baguette, or just a baguette? And French onion soup – is that just onion soup here?'

'*C'est ça.* It's a baguette and just plain onion soup here in France. *Soupe à l'oignon*, to be precise.'

'Has Helen told you that the Laurents have a family cookbook?' I ask Rex. 'It has a recipe for French onion soup. It's delicious.'

'Such good questions, Max,' Helen chimes in. 'Your brain certainly seems to be in tiptop shape after the surgery . . . In fact, you're looking so well. How are you feeling?'

I could be mistaken, but it seems like she's intentionally trying to change the subject. Especially as this is the first time anyone besides Scott has enquired about my health since meeting at the airport in Sydney a few days ago. Maybe we have an unspoken pact to pause time on any discussions about the painful past, pretending that no life-altering events have transpired since we were all together last. At least, for long enough to eat our brie.

'Yes, fine. Thank you. Dr Jock is happy with my progress. I just have to have a scan once I'm back to make sure everything still looks clear.'

I glance at Rex, conscious that a stranger is now privy to my intimate health details, information that some of my closest friends still don't know. But he's busied himself collecting the empty plates and packages and tossing them into a garbage bag. I'm sure he's heard all sorts on group tours before.

'That's great news, Max,' Eve says.

I just smile and take a bite of burnt baguette topped with a camembert-like cheese. We continue munching in silence until Rex, satisfied with his clean-up efforts, gestures to the château that looms beyond the canal and launches into a fresh monologue.

'You are looking right at the ultimate symbol of power and wealth. Built in the 1600s as a palace for the French monarchy, for King Louis XIV, the Château of Versailles is now a national landmark – in fact it's a UNESCO World Heritage site. Once we finish up here, we'll be touring The Hall of Mirrors and the King's Grand Apartments. And Max, you'll be happy to hear, we will *not* be cycling back to the station – a van will be collecting us to take you back to your hotel. After Helen's surprise, that is!'

The relief I feel upon hearing I won't have to muster the energy for the bike ride home disappears at the mention of Helen's *pièce de résistance*. I can hardly wait.

Chapter Twenty-five

It's a cooking class. Because of course it is. My childhood and teenage years were spent watching (and listening to Mum critiquing) rom-coms featuring domestically challenged women ordering in takeout, then pretending they hadn't. They'd transfer the food from aluminium foil packages into ceramic bowls, then carefully dispose of the wrappings. I now have to do the opposite: act as though I rarely step foot in the kitchen and use the oven to store my sweaters, Carrie Bradshaw style – because that's the Max who Scott knows.

After our picnic lunch, we'd toured the château and continued onto Marie Antoinette's hamlet. It was like something out of a fairytale, with adorable thatched-roof cottages spread around a big lake. The balconies and staircases were decorated with flowers, and climbing vines covered the walls and arbours, arching over the quaint entryways. Alice would have loved it. I took a bunch of photos to send to her when we're back on speaking terms.

Once we were done admiring the village, we'd followed Rex down a street off the main road to an eighteenth-century apartment building. We climbed the staircase up three floors to a sprawling apartment and stepped into a gorgeous kitchen boasting beautiful restored herringbone floors, red geraniums in flowerboxes and cabinets filled with pastry tools and antique cake stands. In the middle of the room was an oversized antique French farm table.

'We are lucky to have this kitchen on loan for the afternoon,' Rex announces as he unwraps one of his waxed-paper parcels. 'This,' he gestures to the burgundy-coloured meat on the kitchen table in front of us, 'is duck liver. We will be cooking the Laurent family's famous terrine of foie gras, under my guidance.'

It turns out Rex is not only a tour leader, but an accomplished chef. Not Michelin-starred or anything, or so he tells us, but he knows 'enough to get by'.

I look at Helen, expecting her to be beaming, but she appears unimpressed. 'You'll be taking the class?' she asks Rex, voice thin.

Ah, right. As a Laurent, she would have been expecting Julia Child herself to appear from beyond the grave, or at the very least, a graduate from Le Cordon Bleu.

'*Oui*, Helen!' comes Rex's enthusiastic reply. He's oblivious to the disappointment his apron-clad presence provokes. 'I promise you that you're in good hands,' he says.

As we swap our plastic ponchos for heavy cotton drill aprons, I notice that Rex still looks impeccable in his pressed white shirt and khaki slacks. The only change is his monocle, which has been discarded for a pair of regular round-framed reading glasses, denoting serious cooking business.

I'm now in the awkward situation of having to massively downplay the cooking skills I've picked up over the last couple of months. My first thought is to message Johnny and tell him where I am. Then I remember: not only is that not a possibility, as I no longer have a way to contact him, but I'd have to tell him who I'm with. How would I explain that the Fork Him project has been inverted, and I'm now cooking my way back into the Laurent family?

Thank goodness terrine of foie gras is not a recipe I'm familiar with. When I'd chosen the recipes for the Fork Him project, I'd deliberately skipped right over it. Mostly because I was aware of the questionable ethics of foie gras, but also because it looked like vomit. I don't even eat oysters. I suppose I should be grateful it's not snails. Thanks to my *tres* weak stomach, it will be easy to hide how comfortable I now feel in the kitchen.

We're stationed in pairs at different sections of the farm table. Scott and I are at one end, Helen and Gary are at the other, and Eve is in the middle with Rex. I'm sure she's delighted about that. She'll barely have to lift a finger.

'My favourite technique in French cooking is *mise en place*, which translates directly to "putting things in their place",' Rex begins. 'You must prepare your ingredients, chopping them and measuring them out before you start cooking, so that you are not trying to find the duck fat or the thyme while the potatoes are burn–'

'We're cooking potatoes?' Helen interrupts. 'Rex, must I remind you, this is my sixtieth birthday surprise? I think I deserve something more gourmet. I thought you said we were doing the terrine?'

My hand goes to my mouth to stifle a giggle. *Surprise?* For who? Herself? Plus, I'm instantly suspicious of anyone who isn't excited by potato anything. My dad calls that culinary sacrilege.

'That was just *un exemple*, dear Helen.' Rex grips the table, visibly agitated. One day spent with Helen is clearly one day too many.

Rex portions out the ingredients, along with copies of the Laurents' duck terrine recipe. Unlike the hastily photocopied pages I left in the Billy bookcase at IKEA, the pages have been copied on a colour printer. And laminated.

'Let's get cooking!' Rex announces, his voice like the crack of the starting gun before an Olympic race.

And we're off! Well, at least Scott is. 'You handle the liver,' he says. 'I'll take the apple chutney.'

His competitive streak works in my favour. Scott is so concerned with being top of the class that he's completely focused on peeling, coring and quartering his apples, so he's not watching as I start pulling out the veins from the slimy liver. I follow the instructions, heating the knife on the open flame of the cooktop burner before tearing apart the dense meat into small and large lobes, then cutting into the small lobe. For once I'm not feeling very competitive. Instead, I'm careful not to work too fast, but I'm aware I don't look as clueless as I usually do – like I'm about to amputate a finger. Referring to the page while my hands simultaneously work the ingredients has become second nature to me. I run though the steps methodically until, two hours later, I have a very presentable (although still vomity) dish in front of me. As I peer down at my perfect terrine, goosebumps bite the back of my neck. I feel like I'm standing in the Nest's kitchen, with Johnny right there on my phone. I snap a pic of the finished dish out of habit before realising I have nowhere to send it . . .

We sit down at a dining table laid with candelabras and linen napkins. It hasn't been too long since we inhaled an entire fromagerie, so we attack the terrine with restrained enthusiasm. Our terrines need to firm up in the fridge for the next six days, so we're eating pre-made and probably far superior substitutes. After half an hour of exaggerated moaning and groaning about how positively delicious it is, but how full we are, we admit defeat. Even Helen is nursing her belly as we push back our chairs, leaving the dirty dishes for someone else to deal with, and roll ourselves out the door.

~

Hôtel d'Argenson occupies an elegant eighteenth-century town-house in the 8th arrondissement. It's bigger than our Versailles cooking school, but not by much.

The footprints of these old buildings were not designed to accommodate grand hotels, so the rooms are modest. As is the lift we're waiting for. In fact, teeny tiny would be a more fitting description.

Working out the order in which to send each of us up to our respective floors is like solving one of those silly river-crossing riddles. *Two lions, two wildebeest and a farmer need to cross a river using a raft. Only one animal can go with the farmer at once. The problem is, if the lions ever outnumber the wilde-beest, they'll eat them. How can they all cross the river?*

In this case, it was decided that one lion (Helen) and Gary (most akin to the farmer) would take the lift first, as Helen had a terrible stomach-ache from the gelato we somehow managed to fit in at a touristy ice-cream parlour on the Champs-Élysées, on the way back to the hotel. Truthfully, I think Helen was still miffed that Rex-the-lowly-tour-guide had dared lead us in making her family's beloved recipe instead of some descendent of Marie Antoinette. I can only imagine how she'd react if she ever found out about the Fork Him project making a mockery of the family's sacred text.

Eve is next to go up. She waves to us through the wrought-iron grate as she slowly ascends.

By the time we step into the lift, I've had plenty of time to ponder what's going to happen once we get upstairs, but the jury is still out. *Will Scott make a move?* I wonder.

We start travelling at a glacial pace. The lift is so tiny, my face is pressed against Scott's chest. His arms hug my waist. With its famous monogrammed canvas made from genuine vintage Louis Vuitton steamer trunks and time-worn timber, the lift should be romantic. A thrum of something begins to vibrate through me and I briefly entertain the idea of sharing Scott's bed tonight. But that excitement is quickly eclipsed by terror as I suddenly feel as though I'm back inside the MRI machine, gasping for air. I grip Scott tighter, trying to calm myself.

'Nice coffin, hey?' Scott's bad joke snatches some of the precious oxygen, and even though there's no room to tilt my neck to see his face, I can imagine its self-congratulatory grin.

'Why would you say that?' I mumble.

I thought this trip was supposed to be about winning me back. There have been moments today where he's put in some effort, but I'm not sure how much he's *genuinely* trying.

At last we arrive at the very top floor, where a single attic room occupies the space. It may be extra pokey, but I'm relieved we're not sharing a floor with the rest of his family. I was happy about the twin bed situation at first too, but now I'm wondering why Scott hasn't tried to initiate anything more than a kiss.

'Do you mind if I have the first shower?' Scott asks as soon as we unlock the door. He's already shrugging off his jacket and unbuttoning his shirt. 'You kinda dribbled on me.' He gestures to the wet patches on his shirt.

'I didn't think corpses dribbled,' I say, completely deadpan.

Scott looks at me like horns have suddenly sprouted from my head. 'Are you feeling okay, Max? It's been a big day. Maybe you should lie down?'

'Should I push the beds together?' I test.

Scott hesitates, swallowing visibly.

'Is that what you want?' he asks eventually.

'Do you?' I bite back.

'Of course I do, Maxie!' He drops onto his bed. 'I've been waiting for signs from you.'

Really?

I peer down at the carpet. Yes, there have been glimpses of the fun-loving and highly compatible holidaymakers Scott and Max. But that's all they've been. Glimpses.

When I look up again, Scott is studying me. Our eyes meet, and he cocks his head to the side. 'Get over here,' he growls.

I cross the room in two steps and sink down next to him. His hands are in my hair first. I don't even care that he's messing up my braid. My body does more than remember Scott's; it craves it. It's like our kiss rewinds the last few months – the last few years, even – and we're right back in our uni love-bubble days. We're kissing our way down onto the bed when his phone pings.

'Sorry, sorry,' he breathes, sitting upright. He fumbles in his pocket and pulls out his mobile. 'I need to check this.'

I'm still lying on his single bed, confused about what could be so important, when Scott cheers, 'Yes, yes, yes!' and rushes over to my suitcase.

He pulls my laptop from the zip pocket.

'Do you mind if I borrow this?' he exclaims, already opening the lid of my computer. The bright screen lights up his flushed face as he types in my password. 'I just got a message telling me to check my email and –' He drags his fingers along the trackpad, then gives it a click. 'Yes! Here it is!'

I climb off the bed and hurry over to where he's crouched by the suitcase.

'Max, are you ready to get a load of this?' He's bent over the computer, gaze fixated, like he's in a trance.

'Yes?' I coil the end of my braid around my fingers.

'I've been waiting on some news, but I didn't want to say anything and risk jinxing it.'

I flinch. The last time I was kept in the dark like this, it did not end well.

'Yes?' I say again, with more urgency this time.

Scott finally tears his eyes from the screen and looks up. My stomach drops as I see his eyes are watery.

I fold onto my knees.

'Scott! What is it? Tell me what's going on!'

He grins and jumps to his feet.

'Guess who just signed with the country's biggest talent agency?' He barely takes a breath. 'Me!'

My heart starts beating at a steady pace again.

'Wow. That's massive. Congratulations.' I'm so relieved that it's good news. I stand and hug him. 'So what does that mean exactly?'

'It means Montreal, Edinburgh Fringe – Hollywood! The works!' He's talking a mile a minute.

'Aaaaand . . .' He pauses, like he's waiting for an imaginary drumroll to end. 'They also represent authors!'

'Ah, cool.' I try to sound nonchalant. I don't want to assume he's thinking of me. It's not like Scott has ever actively supported my writing before.

'Max! Do you understand what this means? I can help you get published.' He's still grinning.

'Really?' I think this is the first time he's even properly acknowledged that as my dream.

'Hell, yes, babe. After I get my career sorted, we're going to make you a famous author! Now, if you don't mind, I'm going to grab that shower, to bring me back down to earth.'

I give him another congratulatory squeeze before he disappears into the cupboard-sized bathroom.

Almost immediately, the room begins to fill with steam, seeping from the wide crack underneath the bathroom door. I move to open the small window above the writing desk in the corner. I'm feeling extra inspired to write now. I wonder if I have time to get a few paragraphs down?

The window frames the perfect Paris postcard. Domes, shuttered windows and slanted grey roofs of neo-Gothic buildings punctuate the dusty twilight. The cityscape is interrupted by elm trees with light foliage and branches twisting like the thoughts in my muddled mind.

I'm reminded that I haven't yet had a chance to enjoy the Nest's view of the gorgeous jacarandas. When I'd moved in with Alice, it was already the height of a sticky summer. I'd spent my adult life admiring those magnificent painterly canopies, often looking for excuses to pull my car over and watch as the light changed the blossoms from a soft purple haze to a blue as deep as the harbour. No other blossoming had such a transformative effect on the city. Regardless of what happened with Scott, that was something to look forward to. But before spring came, there was the dropping of leaves . . . I shake my head to propel myself out of my downward thought spiral. Right now, I'm in Paris. And Scott and I *are* making progress. And my career in publishing might be too. And it's spring here. All budding and beautiful and on the brink of becoming thick with flowers. I didn't fight with my best friend and come all this way to not seize this once-in-a-lifetime experience.

I shift back towards the bed and bend down to collect the pile of Scott's discarded clothes, so that there's space to walk around our tiny room. I've spent years picking up after Scott, quickly scooping up then squashing his dirty clothes down deep into the laundry basket and closing the lid. We were always so conscious of each other's privacy. No phone passwords exchanged, minimal questions asked about withdrawals from our joint bank account.

So how does he know my computer login?

Instead of tossing Scott's clothes into his open suitcase, I find myself bringing his jeans to my nose and inhaling deeply. Odours of fatty oils, eau de kitchen, cling to the denim, but there's no lingering scent of perfume. We've been together all today, so I'm not sure what I'm expecting.

My fingers trail down past the waistband to the pocket. There's a solid lump. My heart leaps into my throat. Surely he couldn't be thinking of proposing. That would be . . . insanity.

'Fuck!' Scott's voice is so loud, I almost leap out of the window.

'Are you okay?' I shout once my heart has stopped pounding.

'This is a shower for midgets!' he booms.

He must have banged some body part on the low-slung showerhead.

'Be careful in there,' I call back.

My eyes settle on the bathroom door, but it remains closed.

I hesitate for a few more moments before pushing my hand into the pocket of his jeans and pulling out a wallet.

It's bulky with the wad of cash we needed for the markets. But instead of returning it to the pocket, I'm hit with a sudden urge to take each euro note in my hands and examine every crinkle, tear and mark – and memorise every serial number. I can still hear the water whooshing as I flip open the wallet and a piece of paper flutters to the ground. My breath catches in my throat. It's an age-old story – never go snooping among your significant other's things unless you're prepared for your life to be turned upside down. But things can't get much worse for us, right?

Maybe it's a note from Raffie, professing her undying love, I think as I reach down and pluck the slip of paper off the carpet. At least that would make things easier. A tangible, cut-and-dried reason to hightail it back home to the Nest.

I'm shaking as I glance at the paper in my hands. A page torn from a lined notebook with a few words written in pen. Definitely Scott's scrawl.

A grocery list maybe?

Toaster-bath-bomb
Duel in aisle 2
Cremated bread

~

I'm perched on the edge of my bed when Scott emerges from the bathroom in a billow of steam. He's used both towels. One is twisted on top of his head; the other is wrapped around his waist. I was already worked up, but the sight of *my* fluffy bath towel sitting snugly on *his* head makes my blood boil.

'What's this?' I thrust the piece of paper in his face.

He snatches it from me. 'Where did you get that? Did you go into my wallet?' He's straight into defence mode.

I ignore his questions and repeat mine. 'What is this, Scott?'

'I don't know.' He drops the paper on my side table, next to his wallet, which I've carefully placed there, parallel to the alarm clock, like admissible evidence. 'Maybe there was some mix up at the markets?' he offers.

'So, like a reverse pickpocketing?' I ask. 'Duel in aisle two? Cremated bread? I made those jokes at the picnic today. And toaster-bath-bomb – isn't that something I've said before, too?'

'Okay, okay, you got me.' Scott throws his arms up in mock surrender. I'm afraid the towel is going to slip from his waist.

'I thought I'd help you out, Max.'

'What?' I'm genuinely confused.

He comes over to the bed and sinks down next to me.

'I know you've been having a tough time writing your book,' he says, putting a hand on my shoulder, 'so I thought I'd

179

jot down a couple of funny tidbits for you, in case they could help you on your way. I can be your scribe while your brain recovers. I don't want you to miss out on any opportunities because your book isn't ready.'

I examine his face. I recognise alarm in his eyes – it's the same look he had the night I found him with Raffie. Something is majorly off.

'There's nothing wrong with my brain, Scott,' I say, acidly. 'Tell me the real reason. Now. Or I leave.'

Scott sighs.

'All right, then,' he says, his voice low. 'I've had a bit of writer's block myself recently. I'm struggling to write jokes for this new show, and with the prospect of this new agent –'

'You thought you'd steal mine?'

'No, Max!' He stands up with so much force the towel topples from his head. 'It was just some notes for inspiration!'

'Do you have a dictaphone hiding somewhere, too? Maybe tucked up behind your ballsack!'

'Of course not!' He looks down at me, eyes pleading.

'I watched the YouTube clip from your show, and I saw that you didn't change our tirami-poo joke either. Why did you say that you did?'

Scott's mouth opens, then closes.

I shake my head in disbelief. 'I don't know, Scott. I really just don't know.'

'What don't you know?' His tone is desperate.

'So much,' I say, pausing briefly. 'Like, do you actually even like me? Not even love me, but *like* me? Or have I just been blinded by our history?' My words tumble out in jumbled sentences. 'Did I really think that a handful of dry market macarons would make up for your two-timing arse? How desperately sad of me . . .' I'm muttering to myself now.

'Max . . .'

'No, Scott! Why do you even want me back? Why am I here?'

'Max . . .' Scott repeats, but he doesn't attempt to answer my question. He just stands there, looking helpless in his towel. I turn away, towards the picture-perfect Paris outside our window.

'Yeah, that's exactly what I thought.'

Chapter Twenty-six

Before I leave in the morning, I write a note. Scott is still a ball of tangled bedsheets.

> *Taking the day to myself.*
> *I don't care what you tell your mum.*
> *M.*

The solo trip down in the lift is peaceful – not like the calm before a storm, more like the magical stillness that settles after it, as a rainbow stripes the sky.

In the foyer, I smile at the concierge behind the front desk. I'm about to continue on my way out the door when she addresses me.

'Do you need a recommendation for breakfast, madame?'

I hesitate. Do I? So far, my only plan for the day is to wander until I'm completely lost in the city, absorbed by it.

'Your travel group – the older couple and their daughter – they came down earlier, and I suggested they try the fabulous boulangerie down the street on the right,' she says.

'Okay, thank you,' I say, grateful. She's not to know that my mission is to get as far away from my 'travel group' as humanly possible.

'So perhaps you'd like to turn left, and try out my favourite pastisserie, Pain de Marletti,' she continues. 'The croissants are to die for.' There's a sparkle in her eyes.

My face splits into a wide grin. 'Thank you.'

I suppose you don't spend your days liaising with guests from all corners of the globe and not develop keen observation skills. *She'd make an amazing character in a book*, I think. *The concierge who knows all.*

I exit the hotel and turn left – I don't risk even glancing right and being spotted by the Laurents – and then follow a woman and her tiny dog down the footpath. A chihuahua. It's strutting down the pavement, head held high, butt wiggling like it's on a catwalk. (*Dogwalk?* Ha!) It's taking a dozen steps to its owner's one, but making it appear effortless. If only I could approach life with such unbridled confidence. I sling my bag, weighted down with the day's supplies, my laptop and a giant water bottle, onto my shoulder and pick up my pace. I think of Alice and her new furry charge, Thor, as I watch the dog stop, sniff a tree, then cock its leg and pee. I wonder if she'll ever reply to me?

I keep walking, eyes trained on the ground for any unsightly dog poo to catapult me out of my 'main character takes Paris for the first time' fantasy, but thankfully, the streets are pristine.

A few minutes later, I arrive in front of a building painted blue, a few shades brighter than the sky. I double-check the bronzed sign hanging from the awning – *Pain de Marletti* – before pushing open the door and stepping inside.

I'm immediately greeted by a brusque man behind the counter. '*Que voulez-vous?*'

'Oh, ah, I–I–I . . .'

I was expecting a queue. Some time to get my bearings and figure out what I want to order.

'What would you like?' the man says in English, disdain dripping from every word.

Not even one minute in, and I've been outed as a foreigner.

'I'll have an oat latte and a croissant, please,' I say, thinking fast and making an exaggerated motion to one of the golden croissants sitting on a tray on the counter, like it's the barista and not me who is incapable of communicating properly.

'We only do full-fat,' he says, as he clips a croissant with his tongs and stuffs it into a paper bag. It's like customer service is a crime here.

'Right, right.' I feel my cheeks flush. 'One full-fat latte, then. And it's to have here, *s'il vous plaît*.'

He looks exasperated and shouts something in French to a colleague in the back. The people at the nearby table turn to look at me. Why do I suddenly feel like I'm at the chemist and the pharmacist is confirming the prescription for my herpes cream at the top of their lungs?

'So, to have here?' he confirms in English.

'*Oui, s'il vous plaît,*' I say nervously.

I thought this looked like the type of place you could linger. Isn't that what French people did all day? They lingered. I was hoping to sit in the window and write. *Attempt* to write.

A number is thrust at me, so I collect my croissant and back away from the counter. I scan the room, which is sprinkled with a mix of professionals in suits, presumably grabbing a quick coffee and bite to eat on their way to work, and a few more relaxed types reading quietly or tapping away at laptops. My people.

Okay, you've got this, Max. Don't let this mean man derail your day. After the last forty-eight hours, I need a small pep talk.

There's a free stool at the window bench, so I make my way over and settle in.

Not only is my window seat perfect for people-watching, I love that I'm now part of the scenery to be observed.

When my coffee arrives, delivered by a young woman with glowing alabaster skin and one of those perfect pixie haircuts Alice hates, it's black.

This feels like a punishment, or a cruel Parisian initiation – one of the two. I look over my shoulder back at the counter to check if a jug of milk is coming. Nope, of course not. The mean man has conveniently disappeared.

I take a tentative sip of the coffee. It's scalding hot. I almost spit it back into the cup, but then I manage to swallow. I'm sure I'll regret that later, when I can't taste the day's delicacies. I plan on eating my way through this city.

Thoughts of the deliciousness on offer have me reaching for the croissant. My fingers tear through the crisp pastry. Rex would be impressed.

I pull a soft doughy piece from the middle, lather on a thick spread of creamy butter, then dunk it into my coffee and pop it into my mouth. *Mmm. Delicious.*

I'll get caffeine into my system one way or another! I slept better than I expected, but now that I'm sitting, a fatigue fuzz has settled over me – likely a combination of jet lag and emotional exhaustion.

I'm bathing another croissant chunk in my coffee when I feel eyes on me. Looking around, I see a woman gaping at me. A few minutes ago, she was absorbed in a copy of *Dangerous Liaisons*, but now she's staring like I've just dug into a filet mignon sans knife and fork. I drop my sloppy croissant chunk onto the counter like I've been slapped. I must have committed a huge *faux pas*.

She bows her head over her book again, and I take out my phone.

Calm down, Max. You don't even know her. I'm back on the positive self-talk train.

My phone automatically connects to the cafe's wi-fi, and my fingers head straight for Google, typing in 'IKEA near me' before the blood has even stopped thumping in my ears.

Oh! There's one nearby. A small store in La Madeleine. I go to click for directions before stopping myself. *Don't be a baby, Max. You don't need IKEA here.*

It's so tempting to seek out the comfort of the orderly kitchen and living room displays to sort through my feelings about Scott and the predicament I've landed myself in. But the streets of Paris are waiting to be explored. Streets that invite visitors to slip on new identities. I brush the wayward crumbs to the ground and leap off my stool.

It's time to live *la vie parisienne.*

∾

By late afternoon, I'm a pro at navigating the Metro system. I swipe my all-day pass and walk through the barriers like a local. I've only travelled in the wrong direction once, and hopped off like I hadn't a care in the world, calmly sauntering back through the streets to my starting point. I stop by the Louvre and crane my neck to see over the throngs of tourists for a glimpse of *that* smile, then leisurely browse the gift shop to purchase a postcard of the world's most famous painting for an unobstructed view. I gorge on all variety of delectable pastries – including more croissants – and have invented a sophisticated rating system, assessing the taste, price, appearance, colour and shape. I've noted the final scores in my phone, alongside some random commentary about interesting characters I've encountered.

A man with a handlebar moustache carrying a stubborn mastiff under his muscly arm like it's a chihuahua.

A woman in a headscarf sitting on a bedsheet and surrounded by Eiffel Tower keychains and other trinkets animatedly telling two policemen to mind their own business.

An old man in a straw hat playing an accordion in the outdoor flower market. His instrument is the colour of the fresh-cut red roses.

As much as I want to explore the charming cobblestoned streets of the famed Montmartre, I've given them a wide berth. At the top of the Laurents' itinerary today was a tour of the Sacré-Cœur, the basilica perched on the hill right in the middle of Montmartre. Helen was insisting everyone attend mass there, saying how important it was to her, even though I don't recall her ever going to church in the time I've known her. Even at Christmas.

I've tried to stay in the Parisian moment, only occasionally allowing my mind to wander to Scott and the Laurents. I'm still deliberating over my next move. Do I stick it out and see how the rest of the trip unfolds, or should I change my ticket and fly home?

The sun is starting to set as I head for the Eiffel Tower, the occasional glimpse of the 'iron lady' telling me I'm headed in the right direction. I love how the tower pops up when I least expect it: around a corner, between residential buildings, at the bottom of a staircase. It becomes a sort of *Where's Wally* game in my head. I spot a few real Wallies, too – stripes and round spectacles appear to be the uniform of the French.

With each sighting of the tower, the sun bobs lower, until the final fiery remnants of colour fold into darkness. By the time I reach it, the Eiffel Tower is glittering with light, illuminated in all its glory against the deep blue of the night sky. I've always been a sucker for fairy lights; a cheap string of lights from Bunnings and I melt into a puddle. But this is next-level magical. I alternate between watching the mesmerising light show and the awe-filled faces around me. It's like we're witnessing our wives or hubbies-to-be walk down the aisle. I could stand there all night, but I'm becoming increasingly distracted by the gnawing pain in my belly. Somehow, I'm hungry!

And I know exactly where I'm headed.

A few Metro strops and around twenty minutes of brisk walking later, I stop in front of Bistro Rouge – the restaurant featured in the movie version of Sally Smyth's first book, *Croissants & Other Vices*. Yes, I'm a cliché, but I don't care.

I take the lift to the top floor, step out into the restaurant's foyer and can barely contain my gasp. It's like I'm back at the Château of Versailles. Occupying the entire floor, the bistro is enclosed by a magnificent Art Nouveau glass dome with views over the zinc roofs of the city all the way to the sparkling tower across the Seine.

As I take in the grand, gilded chandeliers and medallion chairs upholstered in leather, I'm suddenly conscious of my scuffed sandals and denim jacket.

I tentatively approach the manicured woman at the counter. Her blood-red lips purse into a tight smile.

'Sorry, I don't have a reservation. Do you have a table for one?'

I'm surprised as her face breaks into a sincere smile. '*Oui, madame*. May I take your jacket?'

She doesn't scrunch up her nose in disgust as I hand it over. She simply slides it onto an ornate coathanger that is definitely worth more than the jacket and then hangs it on the rack behind her.

'Right this way,' she says.

I trail behind her into the dining room, feeling exposed in my lightweight cotton dress.

'How about here?' she asks, gesturing to a table in the back corner. 'This is the table they filmed at.'

I didn't realise how much I've been craving such kindness.

'It's *magnifique*.'

'I'll give you a moment to look at the menu, then I'll be back with some complimentary bread and butter.'

'Thank you.'

As she heads off towards the kitchen, I reach for the leather-bound menu.

My stomach growls as I peruse it. I'm surprised to see many of the same dishes that feature in *The Laurent Family Cookbook*. When my hostess returns to take my order, I request the duck à l'orange. It feels too poetic not to.

I relax back into my chair to enjoy the ambience. At least it's not strange to be dining alone in Paris, the way it would be in Sydney. Instead of taking the easy option and burying my nose in my phone, I leave it on the table next to my water glass and look out over the rooftop of next door's grand Louis Vuitton building. There are some brightly lit windows a few floors down, and I can see people standing at workbenches poring over something of interest – perhaps the designs for next season's runway looks. I'm not close enough to see their expressions, but I imagine them to be alive with that creative inspiration I desire for myself, the kind that is rarely satisfied by my work at Slice. I'm squinting to make out the details when my buzzing phone catches my eye. I lean forward and peer at the screen to see a new WhatsApp message from Scott.

I hope you've enjoyed your day. I'll give you some more space and stay in Mum & Dad's room tonight x

Humph. At this point I don't know how to feel. Do I want him to fight a bit harder? Or am I relieved he's not bothering? I've just finished typing out a hasty 'okay' when my duck à l'orange is placed in front of me.

I focus on one delicious bite after the next and put Scott out of my mind as I wash the duck down with a glass of fine pinot noir – recommended by the sommelier. It's only when I've scraped the plate clean that it occurs to me how similar this five-star duck tastes to Scott's hospital duck. I'm no connoisseur, but there's something very distinctive about the sunshiny citrus flavour.

I finish the last of the bread and moreish truffle butter and pay my bill.

My jacket is no longer on the rack at the entrance. As I wait for a sour-faced woman, who I suspect will be less approving of my denim, to fetch it from the cloakroom, I pick up the restaurant's cookbook, *Rouge Bistronomy: French Fare*, from a stack on the counter and begin thumbing through its pages.

There's a croque monsieur, French onion soup, artichokes à la barigoule, and a terrine of foie gras in the entrée section; a quiche Lorraine, beef bourguignon, bouillabaisse, coq au vin and duck à l'orange in the mains section. I'm flicking through the desserts when it suddenly dawns on me.

I hold my breath as I check the final recipes. There's a chocolate soufflé, crème brûlée, apple tarte tatin and tarte au citron meringuée. All that's missing is the very memorable, very sexy French silk pie.

Holy shit. This is a basically a replica of *The Laurent Family Cookbook*.

Chapter Twenty-seven

A crowing rooster greets me as I step off the train. Literally seconds in and Rouen is upholding its 'magical and medieval' end of the bargain.

A smoky-haired woman dressed in a silky floral housecoat breaks away from the crowd on the platform to greet me. 'Maxine?' she asks. Her accent isn't what I was expecting. Not French. American, maybe?

'Yes.' I let out a sigh of relief. I thought it would be much harder to locate my Airbnb host.

'Suzette. So nice to meet you.'

The rooster crows again.

'That's Maurice,' she says. 'The station's rooster.'

'Do you know all the roosters by name?'

'Only the illegal ones.' She winks. Her eyebrows are arched and darker than her long wave of grey hair, like they've been tattooed on. They suit her. In her housecoat, she looks like she's walked straight off a daytime television set – like she's Rouen's answer to Blanche from *The Golden Girls*.

I can already tell that I'm going to enjoy this woman.

'Thanks for meeting me,' I say.

'You're welcome,' she says, brightly. 'You're my guest. I wouldn't have it any other way. Now, follow me.'

We walk over to a red Mini Cooper, and Suzette takes my suitcase from me. She probably thinks it's excessive for a short holiday – surely I shouldn't need more than a couple of sundresses, a hat and a pair of sandals? Little does Suzette know I have packed up an entire Paris hotel room – including all of the mini toiletries. I suppose I could have left those, but where's the drama in that?

'Let me help,' I say, feeling uncomfortable as I watch the older woman battle my bursting suitcase.

'I have it handled,' she says briskly. 'Your only job here is to relax.'

I've just met Suzette, but I already understand that this is an order, not to be challenged.

Suzette accelerates out of the car park like the siren has sounded in *Mario Kart*. It's been raining. A puddle of water sprays up on the windscreen as we skid around a corner. Suzette jerks the steering wheel sideways to clear the gutter, then stamps forcefully on the accelerator. As we jolt forward, I grip the sides of my seat.

'So, what made you want to visit Rouen? You're from Australia, aren't you?' Suzette asks.

Her voice is smooth and calm – it doesn't sound at all like we're mid-joyride. I hope she hasn't noticed how hard I'm clutching my seat. I didn't survive brain surgery to perish in a car wreck. Although dying in a cute Mini in France would at least make for a better story than dying on the operating table.

'It just looked like the perfect place to escape,' I offer.

Truth be told, when I'd returned to the hotel last night and found both bath towels damp, I'd known instantly I couldn't stay in Paris – but I wasn't ready to return to Sydney either. I'd opened a map of France on my phone, squeezed my eyes shut and launched my index finger at the screen. It had landed on a place called Rouen; upon googling, I discovered that it was the capital of Normandy, a port city on the Seine River, and a comfortable one-and-a-half-hour train ride from Paris. As the tourist website informed me, with its rich medieval history, this vibrant city has plenty to offer: a famous cathedral, Joan of Arc's execution site and, hopefully, a quiet place to write.

'I'm sure there's more to the story than that,' Suzette says. 'Come on, what kind of fool do you take me for? Out with it, my girl!'

I'm a little taken aback by her demanding tone.

'You're right . . .' I pause, debating whether to give her the saccharine version, but Suzette has made no secret of the fact she's interested in the truth.

'I was in Paris with my boyfriend's family for his mother's sixtieth birthday. Well, my ex-boyfriend's family now, I guess, because we broke up. He cheated on me a few months back, but then I had some medical stuff come up, and he showed up for me . . . Well, kind of . . . Like dropping by the hospital with a home-cooked meal, that sort of thing. I thought that maybe visiting the City of Love together would help us to heal. But, honestly, it was a huge mistake. His mother is a nightmare, and he is, well, he's an arsehole. I'm not sure if he's always been that way and I couldn't see it, or if he's changed . . . Or maybe I have. Either way, I can see clearly now that he's a massive dick. So I left. But we're not due to fly home for another week and a half . . .' I trail off, embarrassed.

I knew that I had to get out of Paris – I couldn't risk running into Helen at some outdoor market squeezing all the lovely fresh fruit and veggies, then declaring them 'too bruised' to buy. But as soon as I stumbled across Suzette's listing it became about more than just 'fleeing the scene'. I wasn't running away anymore. I was being pulled away, as if by some powerful magnetic force.

As I browsed accommodation options, it was an image of a cherry-red, floor-to-ceiling bookshelf, the same shade as Suzette's Mini, that first captured my attention. Then I was drawn in by the magical description that danced across my screen:

Enjoy a peaceful rest in this B&B full of charm and natural light. Located just outside Rouen city centre, my home is surrounded by beautiful gardens and nature trails but is still within easy walking distance to shops and cafes. The best of both worlds! The bedroom is small, safe, cosy and comfortable for one travelling on her own. There is a covered porch and a fully stocked library, too. I'm a cookbook author, so book in for breakfast, lunch, dinner or a private cooking lesson with me!

My house is the perfect place to relax or to focus on that book you're reading or writing! It's quiet, unless the crows are crowing or the chickens are squawking about the crows! The garden and house are both big enough to get lost in or find your own private spot for peaceful contemplation, work or naps.

The promise of 'peaceful contemplation' had me booking ten cosy and comfortable nights in a flash.

Suzette is slow to respond to my outburst, her eyes trained on the road. I worry that I've misjudged the situation and offended her with my colourful language. Honestly, I was holding back.

But as we come to a stop at an intersection, she turns to me, face stony. 'What a bastard. More fool him, and lucky me.'

I give her a small smile. I'm glad I've told her, but I'm also relieved she hasn't probed any further. My stay here is about me, and I don't want it tarnished by ugly thoughts of Scott and the Laurents.

'Now, how about we get you sorted with some groceries?' Suzette says.

'Sure. Thank you.'

We continue driving in comfortable silence as I take in the charming buildings of Rouen – a mix of Gothic cathedrals and half-timbered houses with cute flowerboxes on their window-sills. I wonder where Joan of Arc was burnt. Did she have a view of a nice window box?

'Okay, here we are,' Suzette says eventually, flicking on the blinker and pulling into a space in front of a row of shops. 'Would you look at that? Rockstar parking! The Rouen gods are clearly smiling down on us!'

We hop out of the car, and I follow Suzette through the entrance of a tiny supermarket. She nods hello to the cashier, collects a trolley and pushes it through the turnstiles. She's already halfway down the first aisle by the time I catch up with her. For a short woman, she certainly keeps a pace! I feel like I'm a teenager again, trailing behind my mum as she does the weekly Woolies shop.

'Biscuits, should we get some biscuits?' Suzette asks, tossing an armful of unfamiliar blue packages into the trolley before I can respond. 'These ones are delicious with a cup of pepper-mint tea and a good book on the porch. I assume you read?'

I wonder what made her assume that? I suppose her listing would attract mostly bookish types.

'Sounds perfect. And yes, I love to read. Actually, I'm writing a book, too.'

For whatever reason, it's easy to make that declaration – perhaps the anonymity of this foreign supermarket makes me feel safe.

'Excellent. Well, then, you'll need a good cheese for those chapter breaks,' she says.

'Beep, beep, beep,' she calls out as she backs up the trolley and pivots towards a hanging sign that says *L'Atelier du Fromage*.

'There is a small refrigerator in your room,' she says, pulling up in front of a wall of wheels, wedges and blocks in varying shades of yellow and creamy white. The selection is almost as impressive as the market offering in Versailles. 'Feel free to keep a personal stash in your room – I can't say I can always be trusted when it comes to *le fromage*.' Suzette winks. 'I also meant to say that I can cook your meals, if you like, for a small added fee. I can tell you what I'm cooking each day, and you can let me know if it interests you – how does that sound?'

It sounds wonderful, so I tell her as much.

'Excellent!' She beams.

By the time we've looped through the supermarket, I've well and truly gotten the hang of things, grabbing any delicacy that takes my fancy and tossing it into the cart, to Suzette's approving nod. I choose pickled vegetables and gourmet crackers, quince and fig pastes. I think little of the cost, telling myself instead that all this good food is going to – as Suzette puts it – 'nourish my soul'.

She is pushing our full trolley to the register when I hesitate in front of the egg display, feeling a sudden hankering for quiche Lorraine. I grab a dozen eggs and balance them carefully on top of our grocery mound.

'What are you doing!' Suzette screeches, startling me so badly that I only narrowly avoid knocking the eggs from their perch and smashing them on the floor.

'They're free-range?' I offer.

'Did you even open the carton to check if any were cracked?'

I shrug.

'What kind of psychopath doesn't check that?' Suzette mutters. 'We don't need these anyway. My ladies' eggs are the very best in Rouen!'

I stifle a laugh as she plucks the carton from the trolley with an air of disgust and thrusts it into my arms. It's then that it dawns on me. No wonder I feel right at home with Suzette. She's Alice in a different body.

~

As we pull up to the house, it's hard not to feel like the lead in a Hallmark movie. With its white picket fence, gabled roof and wraparound porch, Suzette's home is even more charming than it appeared online.

We bypass the 'ladies' pecking around in the garden, and with arms laden with grocery bags, start down a mossy stone path. Suzette has insisted on taking my luggage and drags my suitcase over the rocks to the front door. She then retrieves a key from her handbag and unlocks the door. 'This is your copy,' she tells me, handing me the key. It's on a chain decorated with a tiny yellow pompom chicken. 'The door is usually unlocked – it's safe as houses around here – but keep the key on you just in case.'

'Thank you,' I say, slipping it into my pocket and following Suzette inside. I suddenly feel like a legit resident of Rouen, as though I've just signed a lease to my new cottage here.

'Leave the shopping bags,' Suzette instructs, setting down the one she's carrying next to an umbrella stand fashioned from a hollowed-out tree stump. 'We'll divvy up the cheese once we've got you all settled.' She flashes me a mischievous smile before swiftly switching back into woman-on-a-mission mode. 'Come along now.'

Suzette starts up the steep, narrow staircase, yanking my suitcase behind her. I already know better than to offer to help.

'Here we are,' she announces as we enter a room at the end of a long hall.

The room is compact, with just enough space for a wooden dresser with an attached oval mirror, a bar fridge and a single bed.

The paisley bedspread matches Suzette's housecoat and is topped with a couple of colourful embroidered cushions. On the dresser are a vase filled with fresh wildflowers, a stack of books and a ceramic dish holding a bar of pale purple soap. I can't help myself and take a step closer, lean down and breathe in. *Mmm, lavender.* Much better than my stolen mini body wash.

'This is perfect,' I turn towards the tiny triangular window over the bed. It looks out to a green garden; the window is open a crack, and a light breeze brushes the wind chimes hung above it. *Tinkle, tinkle, tinkle.* Back in Sydney, the sound would irritate me, but it hits differently here. I'm a regular French zen hen!

'You might like a rest before dinner. Is 7 pm good? The first dinner is always on the house. How does quiche and fresh salad from my garden sound?'

It's like Suzette can read my mind.

'Lovely. Thank you so much.'

At 7 pm, once I've put my clothes in the dresser, tested the bed – the mattress is soft, like fluffy crepes – and had a quick flick through one of the books, *The Most Beautiful Villages of Normandy*, I head down the stairs.

The hallway is bathed in warm lamplight, from proper lamps with linen shades. I follow my nose to the kitchen.

'Perfect timing, Max,' Suzette says as I step into the room. She must have sensed my presence – her back is turned to me as she pulls a bubbling dish from a large, double-door oven.

'Now, would you like me to join you for dinner?' Suzette asks, setting the quiche dish down on the benchtop and turning to face me. She motions to the kitchen table, currently set for one. 'I always give my guests the option. I'm sure they don't come away on holidays to have me yap on at them.'

I'm actually craving company. Maybe not just any company, but I'd bottle and bathe in the warmth this woman emits.

'I'd love you to,' I say, taking a seat at the table.

'Right you are.' Another crocheted placemat appears, along with a set of copper cutlery and a white dinner plate.

Suzette places the quiche in the centre of the table, next to a salad that's practically spilling from the bowl. She cuts me a very healthy slice of cheesy quiche, gesturing that I should pass her my plate, then leaves me to scoop my own salad.

We dig in.

'Ohh, yummmm,' Suzette coos.

Yum is right. This quiche is roughly one thousand times better than my version of the Laurents' quiche Lorraine. Or perhaps more accurately, Bistro Rouge's quiche Lorraine . . .

'Yum, yum, yum, yum!' Suzette smacks her lips together in appreciation.

I stare at her, unable to disguise my amusement. It's not often you see a cook marvelling so audibly over their own creations.

She looks up from her plate at me. 'I only cook this well for people I like.' Her eyes twinkle.

I laugh. 'Well, you must love me! This is delicious!'

'Do you enjoy cooking?' she asks.

I pause. A few months ago that would have been an easy question to answer, but now I'm not so sure. I enjoyed the Fork Him project, or I suppose, more accurately, I enjoyed doing it with Johnny.

'A little,' I reply.

'Really?' Suzette hoots. 'I would *not* have picked that from the way you were stumbling around that supermarket.'

I laugh again. And here I was thinking I'd blended in! 'I was doing a bit of cooking with – um, ah, well . . . a friend – recently. French cooking, actually.'

'Ooohh, would you listen to that stammer. This sounds juicy. Out with it, girl!'

I already feel so at home with Suzette, like I've known her for much longer than one afternoon, so I decide to fill her in.

I start with my break-up with Scott, since I've already mentioned that, then tell her about the prized *Laurent Family Cookbook*, and my tumour, and about Johnny, my Tinder pen pal, who not only cooked his way through the Laurents' recipes with me, but who – completely unbeknownst to him – was really the one who helped get me through my surgery. Then I tell her how Scott lied about changing the tirami-poo joke, the note in his pocket, and my suspicions that he has been using my words as his own material all along. I finish with my recent discovery that *The Laurent Family Cookbook* might be just as phoney as Scott, with its recipes stolen from a famous Parisian bistro.

Her eyes are wide when I'm done. There's not a bite left on either of our plates.

'Gosh, what a hard time you've been having, Max,' Suzette says. 'But that is one hell of a story, if I've ever heard one!'

'I know.' I laugh nervously. Because it does all sound pretty far-fetched.

'So, tell me . . . Have you written any of this down?'

'Hmm, not really. Bits. I'm still trying to find my voice.'

'What do you mean "trying"? I thought you were a writer?'

'An *aspiring* writer,' I correct her. 'All of this brain stuff has set me back a bit.'

'BOOORIIIING!' Suzette exclaims.

I wince. I was expecting compassion, not an outburst like this.

'We don't allow that sort of self-doubt in this house,' Suzette tells me. 'I used to be a pretty young thing like you – I know you can't imagine it, looking at me now, but it's the truth. And I had my own dreams, of running a restaurant where I lived in Montreal.'

Oh, so she's Canadian – that makes a lot of sense, I think.

'There were plenty of naysayers, including my own massive

dick of a boyfriend – yes, unfortunately I had one of those, too. But I went for it, and guess who ended up owning a Michelin-starred restaurant for the better part of two decades? This old girl,' she crows, pointing to herself. 'Then, when I decided it was time for a quieter life, I sold the restaurant for a tidy sum and moved here to rural France with not a regret in the world.'

'Wow,' I gush. Suzette is full of surprises. 'That's so cool.'

'You haven't even heard the half of it! Life is going to throw you some curveballs, but don't you dare let anyone dull that sparkle. You owe it to the world to share your gifts, but more than that – you owe it to yourself.'

I'm quiet for a moment, letting her words seep in. I'm like Alice's thirsty succulent, drinking up rain after months of neglect.

'Thanks, Suzette – for the pep talk and for dinner. That was hands-down the best quiche I've ever eaten.'

'The secret is the butter. Always butter,' she says. She stands to clear our plates. 'You'd have a conniption if you saw how much I put in. And the eggs are from my pretty ladies, of course. I'll take you on a tour of the coop tomorrow.'

'I can hardly wait.' I grin.

Chapter Twenty-eight

I'm in my comfy crepe bed for almost fourteen hours. It's not a restful night, but one of those fevered slumbers from which you wake intermittently, unclear where the imaginary world ends and reality begins.

Time passes slowly, and I check my watch constantly, only vaguely registering the numbers.

My body is aching all over. There's no ensuite in my room, so I stumble out of bed and down the hallway to the bathroom next to Suzette's room. I find a face washer and hold it for a few seconds under the cold-water tap, then wring it out before returning to my room. I fold it in half and press it against my forehead, lying down again, this time on top of the bedspread. Minutes later I'm shivering cold, so I shimmy back under the covers. I wake properly around 2 am, when the wind chimes are whipped into a frenzy by fierce winds outside – and not a moment too soon. In my dream, Alexander was raising his scalpel, about to plunge it into me.

Without the reprieve of sleep, the rest of the night is long. I stay buried under the covers until late morning, when the smell of sizzling bacon beckons me out. I kneel on the bed and peek through my little triangle window to find that it's completely still outside. There are a few leafy branches strewn across the yard, but no rustling trees.

'Well, hello there, sleepyhead!' Suzette chirps as I step into the kitchen. Sunlight stripes across her face, and she squints at me. 'How did you sleep?'

'Like a baby,' I lie. I wonder how I look. I didn't check my face in the mirror.

'It's this fresh country air, I tell you!'

I must look less racoon-like than I thought.

Suzette ushers me to the island bench, where my breakfast is waiting. There's pots and pans hanging low overhead, so I bow my head as I slip onto the stool.

In the light of day, I can better appreciate the country charm of Suzette's lovingly curated kitchen. I note that there's no microwave in sight. An intricately carved cabinet with brass handles flanks the oven, and the cupboard doors are painted a soft duck-egg blue.

'I've cooked your eggs three ways – scrambled, poached and soft-boiled – with some buttered strips of toast, streaky bacon and micro herbs from the garden,' Suzette informs me.

As I glance at the full plate, I feel a sudden pang of home-sickness for my dad's big breakfasts. They're not even tasty. He fries the eggs on the barbecue, so they're always overdone, smothers them in tomato sauce in hopes we won't notice the charred edges, then proudly presents it, like it's the ultimate big breakfast and not a mess of a concoction. He calls it the 'Big Brian'.

Dad was there in the background when I called Mum from the train to fill her in on what had happened with Scott. She thought an escape to the French countryside sounded like a great idea, but cautioned me not to overdo things. I know she'll have a conniption when she finds out that I basically cycled the

Tour de France. Dad was no doubt concerned that this was not the last of Scott, but he let Mum take the floor and didn't say anything besides 'We love you, Max.'

I lift the cute knitted cosy off the boiled egg before deciding to try the scrambled eggs first. They're soft, fluffy and utterly delicious.

Suzette watches me, smiling. 'The secret is more butter and double cream – with a hint of truffle.'

'How do I take you home with me?' I ask, using the linen napkin to wipe my mouth.

'You just say the word, and for a few extra euros I can teach you how to make them – and any other dishes you fancy.'

I return her smile. 'I might just take you up on that.' I thought I was done with the kitchen, but perhaps not.

Ten minutes later, I'm so full that my tummy feels like it's bursting.

'You've been defeated?' Suzette asks. That satisfied smile is back.

'Yes, thank you again. That was delicious!'

'Good,' she says, clearing away my near-empty plate. 'Now, that's enough dilly-dallying. Come with me – I've set you up in the library.'

Set me up?

My first thought is that a dark and brooding Gaston type is waiting for me in the library, ready to show me around town – a meet-cute straight out of the pages of a romance novel.

My stomach lurches as I hurry after her into the front room. A small table has been pulled up to the settee, facing the beautiful bay window. On the table is a single coaster beneath a glass of water, and a fresh notepad and pen.

Oh duh! Set me up a writing station.

'You can plug in your computer over here,' Suzette says, pointing to a power socket. 'And I'll give you this.' She reaches into the pocket of her apron and pulls out a dainty bronze bell. 'Feel free to use it as liberally as you'd like, and I'll fetch whatever you need.'

I look for a mischievous glint in her eye, but her expression gives nothing away.

'Can I get my laptop?' I ask cautiously, unsure if she intends to imprison me immediately.

'Sure. I'll wait here.' Suzette crosses her arms like a strict headmistress while I sprint up the stairs to retrieve my computer from my suitcase.

Once I return, breathless, laptop snug under my arm, Suzette leaves the room, pulling the door closed behind her.

'Happy writing,' she sings, her words striking a slightly ominous note.

I wait a few beats, listening to her footsteps in the hall growing fainter, before I'm drawn to the glorious cherry-red bookcase covering the entire length of the back wall, like a bee to honey. I almost feel like I should bow down to it in bibliolatrous prayer.

Up close, I can see the bookcase isn't handcrafted out of solid wood, as I'd first assumed. It's four IKEA Billy bookcases, joined together! It somehow feels like serendipity, as if I've encountered old friends in the last place I'd ever expect to see them – on the other side of the world.

I can't believe I didn't spot it straightaway. I thought I'd recognise those bookcases anywhere, and I am well-versed in IKEA hacks. I've been wanting to try the genius bookcase hack for myself, but the old-world library look I love so much wouldn't have fit Scott's modern aesthetic.

Suzette has done a fabulous job. The cheap plywood bookcases are elevated on a timber platform, making them a touch taller, and finished with a smart trim. Luxe sconce lights hang above, adding the perfect dash of extravagance. And the colour! It's exquisite. Instead of the duck-egg blue that features throughout the rest of the house, the bookshelves are a show-stopping red. I can almost picture Suzette selecting that specific shade to match the fleshy, jagged comb of her 'ladies', then spending days sanding back the stained oak veneer and applying coat after coat of paint until she was satisfied with the glossy finish.

The sheer number of books also has me mesmerised – there must be more than a thousand volumes on the shelves. I'm practically salivating as I run a hand over their spines. I wonder if Suzette has a copy of Sally Smyth's latest? That would be double the serendipity. I know it was translated into French . . . I lean in to inspect the shelf in front of me, searching for Sally's name, and realise the books are alphabetised by their author's surnames – because of course they are. I'm at 'F.' All the usual suspects are here: Fielding, Fitzgerald . . . I tilt my head back, on the hunt for the 'S' section. On the very top shelf, close to the ceiling, looks to be a collection of rare first editions, identified by their mottled brown and beige dust jackets. There's a library ladder attached to an iron rod that runs the length of the shelves, and I consider climbing it, to get a closer look, but I can't be sure it's not ornamental.

I'm about to take a seat at the small table, where my laptop has sat patiently waiting for me, when I notice a label crafted out of Scrabble pieces stuck on the very bottom shelf: *WRITTEN HERE.*

There are around a dozen books, followed by a gaping length of unoccupied shelf. The vacant space sticks out like a tourist (me!) ordering coffee in a Parisian cafe. It's almost as though Suzette has purposely bunched up the other books to make the empty section more pronounced. It might as well have a label too, or even a blinking neon sign: *MAXINE MAYBERRY'S BOOK GOES HERE.*

~

'I'm going to pop into town for a bit, take in some of the sights,' I say to Suzette when she appears with a fresh pot of coffee. I wasn't expecting to be waited on hand and foot, but she keeps insisting that she was 'making a pot for herself anyway' and that it would 'only go to waste'.

It's early afternoon and I've only left the library twice. To pee. Each time I've felt eyes trained on me from the top floor, despite Suzette saying she'd be tucked away in her study all day writing freelance articles for a magazine, *Taste of France*.

It's like I'm in book-writing prison, but at least it's a highly charming and productive prison. I'd eventually settled down on the sofa, opened the lid of my laptop and started typing . . . and found that I couldn't stop. At last count I've written 5000 words. Even a night of next to no sleep doesn't appear to have affected my writing – if anything, it's helped. Or perhaps the countless cups of coffee have played a part. But now I'm starting to get all bleary-eyed and desperately in need of a break.

'Lovely idea. Why don't you head into the city centre and visit the Old Market Square? Replenish those creative juices. It's so beautiful out,' she says.

I'm surprised by Suzette's enthusiasm. I wasn't expecting her to approve my day release so readily.

'Is it far?' I ask. I was in such a daze yesterday, I hadn't paid close attention to our *Mario Kart* route.

'Not too far, turn left out of the gate and it's a five-minute walk to the bus stop. Any of the buses will take you into the city. It's a half an hour ride. Just tell the driver where you're headed and they'll let you know your stop. Most locals are more than happy to assist pretty tourists.'

I reach up to touch my hair, suddenly conscious of my bird's nest. At some point during my writing session, I've absent-mindedly twisted it on top of my head and fastened it with a pen. Coupled with my bare face (I haven't even managed moisturiser), I'm sure I'm not looking my best. While I'm not really in the headspace to pick up hot French locals, I want to look somewhat presentable – just in case. Who knows what the universe has in store for me. If falling in love with a Frenchman is the universe's plan, who am I to argue with that?

I return to my bedroom for a quick tidy-up, then head out the front door before Suzette changes her mind.

I'm barely out the front gate when her voice booms from above.

'Maxine!'

I turn to see her hanging out of her study window, her breasts squished against the windowsill.

'It's *that* left,' she says, pointing in the opposite direction to the one I've taken.

I grin up at her. 'Whoops! My bad!'

Suzette shakes her head, the light breeze whipping her long, grey hair so that it swirls around her head like a silk scarf.

'I should have written my address on your wrist, child. Do you have your phone?'

'Yes,' I sing-song back.

'Good, good. Well, do your best to find your way back here. I'm already quite fond of you.'

With that, she pulls herself back inside and closes the window.

As I slowly walk the *right* way to the bus stop, I decide that I'm a big fan of Suzette's tough love. As an only child, my parents have only ever mollycoddled me. They'd tried for years to conceive before finally falling pregnant with me. Their helicopter parenting makes sense – and for the most part, I love knowing how much I'm loved – but equally, it's nice to be away from it for a bit. To have room just to be me. Or, as is the case at Suzette's house, to be locked in a room just to be me.

My thoughts morph into daydreams about what it would be like to live here. The homes are so different from the tightly packed terraces of Paris; here they range from sprawling Gothic mansions to cute farmhouses. Every few steps, I'm startled by the crowing of a rogue rooster. It appears there are more poultry than people in this part of town.

The bus comes and once I'm seated I check my phone to confirm that we're headed the right way. I blocked Scott's number the moment I boarded the train to Rouen, but I have a message from Helen letting me know that she'd 'thought more of me than leaving her "all-expenses paid" birthday trip' and that sometimes I needed to 'swallow my pride and turn a blind eye'. I block her number too.

Eventually we reach the Old Market Square and I hop off the bus and follow the signposts to the Place du Vieux-Marché.

I mutter apologies as I elbow through the crowds, trying to get my bearings. *Excusez-moi! Pardon!* So, this is where all the people are! It's quite a shock after my quiet morning in Suzette's library. The charming half-timbered houses are corbelled over the street like they're bent in prayer. In the distance, above the pointed roofs, a pair of Gothic spires stretch up into the clouds – one of the many famous cathedrals, no doubt.

The smiling tourists who spill from the cafes and restaurants fringing the square are being entertained by buskers – a mime artist, a clown twisting balloon animals and a man playing a fiddle.

This is the sort of setting Scott and I revelled in, enjoying the unabashed frivolity that came with being somewhere foreign. I attempt to conjure up a little nostalgic melancholy, but I'm numb. It's like I'm done mourning our relationship. I have no feelings left for him.

The crowd cheers as the balloon animal artist presents his creation to a tiny boy dressed in overalls. It's bright yellow with an orange beak. A rubber ducky.

The carnival atmosphere does seem at odds with the atrocity that took place here. I look around for the towering cross that marks the spot where Joan of Arc was burnt at the stake, and spy it right away just outside a church. I cross the square towards it, moving away from the crowd. A sombre mood descends on me.

Gosh, I wish I knew more about her. I know she was a saint . . . but for what, I couldn't say. I really should have paid more attention in high school history class. Google would be handy right now. I look around for an information centre, somewhere that I can connect to free wi-fi, but instead I see a shopfront with a door the colour of Suzette's bookshelves, with the words *Gryphon Books* spelled out on the awning.

Ah ha! The history section of a bookshop will do nicely.

I float across the square, the bookshop this book-lover's beacon.

When I push open the door, I'm greeted with a scene from a Nora Ephron film. The shop has an authentic, age-old charm, and the higgledy-piggledy stacks of books piled on every surface make me think of my bedroom at home.

'Bonjour.'

I'm immediately put at ease by the warm voice of a young woman crouched down arranging books in the window.

'Bonjour,' I reply.

'Can I help you find something?' she asks in English.

My terrible French accent must have given me away again.

'Do you have anything on Joan of Arc?'

If she had a euro for every time she was asked about Joan of Arc, I'm sure she wouldn't be working in this delightful – but extremely pokey – bookshop. But she just smiles, seemingly unbothered, and points. 'Up there on the left.'

'Thank you.'

'Just watch out for Gryphon,' she says, as I turn to see where she's pointing.

'Gryphon?'

'Our Angora rabbit. The bookshop's namesake. He's hopping around here somewhere.'

I love it. The bookshop has its own bunny.

I find the section I'm looking for and select a book: *Joan: A Novel of Joan of Arc*, by Katherine J. Chen. I open it to a random page and begin to read, and I'm soon swept up. *Gosh . . . what a story.*

I imagine a nineteen-year-old Joan gasping for air, flames licking at her feet. I suddenly feel like I'm back in the MRI machine, and my entire body is on fire.

Maybe I'm not up for a history lesson after all. I shut the book and slide it back into its place on the shelf.

I continue weaving through the aisles, waiting for a shiny pearl of a book to capture my attention among the myriad spines. But I'm so enjoying being immersed in this sea of beautiful books that I make it all the way to the children's section at the back before I stop.

I instantly notice an entire wall dedicated to duck-themed books. How strange. I may be miles away, but it seems impossible to escape Johnny.

I move to the small area dedicated to books in English. There's a copy of Dr Seuss's *I Wish That I Had Duck Feet*, *The Ugly Duckling* by Hans Christian Andersen, the nursery rhyme *Five Little Ducks*, *The Tale of Jemima Puddle-Duck* by Beatrix Potter and Charles Perrault's *The Tales of Mother Goose*.

I reach for the copy of *Mother Goose* and open it. The pages are thick and glossy, the illustrations brightly coloured, and there's a 'Gryphon Books, Rouen' stamp in the inside cover. It's such a gorgeous edition. Maybe I could buy it for Lucy's kid? But I'm still angry at Lucy for telling Raffie about my surgery.

I would never have considered getting back with Scott if he hadn't shown up at the hospital when he did. But then I'd never have come here to Rouen. And I quite like who I am here.

I'm still deep in thought when I feel something brush over my sandals.

'What the hell?' I yelp, jumping back.

I look down to see a mass of white fluff, like a jumbo cotton-wool ball, and my face breaks into a grin.

Gryphon.

'Wrong section, mate,' I say to him. 'I think *Peter Rabbit* is a few aisles over.'

I'm still laughing at how ridiculous I am as I head to the register. And praying that the security camera hasn't captured embarrassing footage for a viral TikTok.

Chapter Twenty-nine

'M ax!'

As I round the corner onto what I've guessed is Suzette's street, her distressed cry rings through the air.

Shit!

I break into a run, clutching the straps of my book-laden pack as it bobs up and down on my back. My first thought is that Suzette has fallen headfirst out of that top-floor window, but when I reach the front fence I see her upright in the yard. She's clutching a chicken under each arm, and her face is bright red.

'What's wrong?' I puff as I scoot through the gate.

'Sorry. I didn't mean to scare you. Not while you're still recovering.'

'It's okay. I'm fine.'

At least I'm fine until my follow-up scan proves otherwise, I think.

'I heard you coming down the road,' Suzette says, 'and I could do with some help. Rumour has it that some nitwit from the council is on their way here this afternoon. Camille from next door has already moved her ladies.'

'Sorry?'

Suzette is speaking so quickly her words run together.

'Here,' she says, transferring one of the chickens from under her armpit into my outstretched arms. I think this is the first time I've held a chicken that's not a raw breast or thigh ready to be seasoned and stir-fried. It's heavier than it looks. *She's* heavier than *she* looks, I suppose I should say. And her feathers are scratchy – or is that her pointy claws? Not at all like Gryphon's soft, downy fur. Apparently I'm now a regular farmyard animal whisperer.

'Tuck her between your arm and your ribs. That will stop her being so skittish,' Suzette instructs.

I put the bird under my arm and hold her tight until she stops wriggling.

'So, where am I going?' I ask tentatively, because I get the feeling I'm supposed to know.

'To the coop out the back. Hurry, now!' Suzette pushes past me, somehow loaded up with three chickens. 'I don't know what time the fool is coming.'

I follow her as she waddles down the path.

'It's illegal to have the ladies free-range in the yard. Isn't that the most absurd thing you've ever heard?' she calls over her shoulder. 'I'm fighting about it with the council, which makes me a prime target!'

We continue scooping up chickens and racing them up the side of the house, then doubling back. I count fourteen ladies in total. No wonder Suzette's speciality dish is eggs every which way. We collect eggs from the nesting boxes, too. With our egg-and-chicken race done, we stack the nesting boxes back in the garden coop and return to the front garden.

Suzette doesn't look great. Small beads of sweat have collected on her forehead, and her hair is a matted mess. I'm about to offer to fetch us a cold drink when she drops down on all fours.

'Suzette! What's the matter?' I sink down next to her. Is it a heart attack? I see my life flash forward to navigating the French hospital system, and then to gaining sudden custody of fourteen chickens.

But instead of clutching the left side of her chest, Suzette has sunk her fingernails deep into the soil and appears to be sifting through the dirt.

'Ah-ha!' she calls triumphantly, extending her arm to show me a few pieces of eggshell resting on her palm. 'Those bastards will look for any excuse to give you a fine. Not on my watch, they won't!'

I must look as dumbfounded as I feel. Suzette explains while returning to her digging.

'Yes, my ladies eat their own eggs. Somehow, they seem to know the difference between a treat I give them, and those precious things burrowed in the straw for me. Mostly, I just scatter leftover shells from the kitchen, but every now and then they get a whole egg, smashed on a rock, and they go nuts!'

I nod enthusiastically while joining in on the digging.

'I tried to tell them last time that I just used the eggshells for my veggie patch, which isn't entirely untrue. If you sprinkle crushed eggshells around – especially near those tender lettuces that you ate for dinner last night – it keeps the slugs away!'

I've collected almost a fistful of shell, so I follow Suzette's suit and dump it in the thick shrub running along the picket fence.

'I'm teaching you a thing or two here, aren't I, Max?' She winks. 'Just some fodder for your book. Plenty more to come, too, I suspect.' She stands to survey the area, then wipes her soiled hands on her apron, clearly satisfied with our clean-up efforts.

'Now, a cold drink? A lavender and lemon spritz?' she asks. 'I hope you drink gin?'

'Love it,' I say, already tasting the aromatic botanicals.

'If I'm going to be fined, we might as well do it in a jolly old fashion.'

As I stand to follow Suzette to the front door, I almost trip over another chicken.

'Wait, how about this one?' I call, glancing down at the feathered friend at my feet.

It's only then that I realise it's not a chicken, but a duck. A very good-looking duck. She's speckled cream and brown, with a dark mark across her eyes and a purple-blue slash on her wings.

Suzette turns and waves her hand. 'Oh, that's a Rouen,' she says. 'She's not mine – just a wild one. She's a funny girl – they're normally so stand-offish, but not this lass. She visits the ladies regularly, like an honorary member of the flock.'

'A Rouen?' I want to double-check I've heard her correctly.

'Yes, this town's namesake. They're layers, too. Occasionally I'll get a pretty blue egg amongst my lot's stash . . .'

But I've tuned out of Suzette's TED Talk.

Of course I've landed myself in a town named after a duck.

≈

Suzette heads straight to the kitchen to pour our gins and get dinner started. We haven't discussed if she's cooking for me again, but given my audible appreciation of every meal she's produced so far, I suppose it's been assumed.

My head is still spinning as I lock myself in the library. Suzette doesn't question it. From the outside it appears all is well, and that I'm knuckling back down to work at my writing desk, but that's far from the case.

That last nugget of information – that I'm literally staying in a place named 'duck' – was one sign too many. The section in the bookshop was one thing (and now it makes a lot more sense!) but this is some next-level woo-woo shit. There is no denying that, for whatever reason, all signs are pointing me towards Johnny the Mother Ducker.

Just a series of coincidences? Maybe. But if I'm honest with myself, I think I've been looking for an excuse to get back in touch with Johnny since I woke up from my surgery. First, there was the ICU orderly, then there was the mystery duck à l'orange breakfast delivery; there have been countless occasions in Paris – and now, Rouen.

There's just one problem. I've deleted my Tinder account, so I have no way of getting in contact with him. After all our messaging, it's crazy to think that we never exchanged numbers, but that was also part of the appeal. We both wanted to protect our anonymity.

That's what you have to remember, Max, I tell myself. *It wasn't just you. We were both hiding parts of ourselves.*

While it all but consumed me at that time, my surgery now feels like a distant memory, but who knows what Johnny had going on. What he *still* has going on. Because who talks to – and cooks with – an internet stranger for that long, and that candidly, with no intention of ever meeting them?

My theories have ranged everywhere from Johnny being a standard commitment-phobe to him not being a him, to him being married, to him having something semi-serious going on himself . . . He'd certainly hinted at that.

It's also very possible that he hasn't given me a second thought since we parted ways on Tinder . . . but there was only one way to find out. I'd resisted until now, but it's time.

I settle on the couch and open my laptop. I bypass my open Word document and type 'Mother Ducker' into the Google search bar.

As the site loads, I feel a disappointing thud in my stomach. I was hoping to be surprised by some avant-garde blog, but it's exactly as I'd envisioned. The site is loud and bright with a chequerboard of viral videos, loud memes and silly photos interspersed with ads for video games and gumboots.

Along the top is a banner, with the text *Vote for the world's hottest duck*. It's all so predictable. Something Scott would be into, actually. I clearly have a type.

Still, I click on the 'Contact Us' link and find myself looking at a form labelled *What the duck are you looking for?* I stare at the blank fields for a moment and begin to type.

Long time, no chats. Just checking in on the life status of my Tinder pen pal. I'm in France. So that's something. I'm staying in a town named after a duck, so it made me think of you. If you feel like messaging me back, it would be great to hear from you. No pressure, though.
    Max

I quickly type my email address and click submit before I change my mind.

As I close my laptop, a deep voice rumbles through the open window.

'Madame, we have gone through this. No chickens out here!'

It's followed by Suzette's cajoling reply: 'Why don't you come in for a nice, cooling spritz, monsieur?'

I grin to myself. *Boy, is she laying it on thick*. I should probably go and assist her with her alibi. I collect my backpack from where I've dumped it by the door.

As I swing the bag up onto my shoulder, one of the sharp corners of my new copy of *The Tales of Mother Goose* digs into my back.

Chapter Thirty

Egg yolk wonton soup, French toast, salade niçoise, vanilla bean pudding, pasta carbonara, toad-in-the-hole – whichever way you can think of having eggs, I've had it. All paired with rich, fatty ingredients. Forget my brain tumour, I'm sure it's now my cholesterol that's the biggest worry. I swear the French must have butter for blood.

All the recipes have come straight from Suzette's cookbook, *Lovely Ladies & Eggsellent Eggs*, which features a particularly haughty-looking hen on the cover. She's a woman of many talents – and a truly wicked sense of humour.

I can hardly believe it's my final day here. The last ten days have passed in a blur of writerly and culinary bliss. Each morning, I retrieve eggs from the ladies for breakfast, then head into the library to write. In the early afternoon, I take a break and either explore the local area or catch the bus into the city. I've walked the trail to Côte Sainte-Catherine for panoramic views of the city and spent more afternoons at the Old Market Square bookshop, thumbing through books with Gryphon at my feet.

It's hard to know if it's the fresh country air, my permanent comatose state from all of Suzette's rich food, or the peaceful home I've found nestled in my words, but as much as I don't want to leave, I'm not fearing it. My check-up MRI is looming when I return to Sydney, and before that I need to face Scott and his family on the plane home. But I now know that it's *because* of these experiences that I have something to write about. I no longer feel like escaping into fantasy worlds; my real life is inspiration enough. The picturesque setting has helped me uncover the beauty in the here and now.

A few evenings ago, I got so carried away with my wandering that I stayed in the city for dinner. Suzette had scoffed when I told her I'd eaten at the pub on the river.

'Ugh. Absolutely terrible food.'

She made her disapproval so clear that I didn't dare try that again. That incident had been the catalyst for the cooking classes. It had been three consecutive days of cooking, and today is my final lesson.

I've requested duck à l'orange.

'Yes, excellent.' Suzette is watching me like a hawk as I slice through the duck. After hours of dicing, lifting, flipping and pounding, I've graduated to her good set of knives. I feel like I'm back at school and have just earned my pen licence. My hands are shaking with intense concentration.

Somehow I make it through all the steps with barely even a spill. Everything seems more manageable here, even complex French recipes, but that could be down to the impressive array of high-tech kitchenware at my disposal and Suzette's patient mentoring. Every time I question a step, she tells me to trust my instincts. Apparently, that's the true mark of an excellent cook. It has been so long since I felt I could trust myself.

'Good grasshopper,' Suzette praises me as we sit down to plates of glistening duck. I'm feeling quite chuffed with myself.

I hold my breath as she takes a bite, chewing slowly and purposefully. She swallows just as slowly and purposefully.

'It's almost as good as Bistro Rouge's!' she announces with a smack of her lips.

I laugh. 'You've been there?'

'*Oui, oui!* And I happen to have their cookbook, too – sorry, I mean "*The Laurent Family Cookbook*",' she says, raising her hands and making air quotes with her fingers.

I roll my eyes. In less than twenty-four hours, I'll see the Laurents, and I could try to get to the bottom of that story – but I'm not sure I can be bothered. I haven't decided yet if the reward of a good story is worth opening that can of worms.

I want to tell Johnny all about the stolen family cookbook. I know he'd lap it right up, but he hasn't responded to my message. I glance wistfully out the window; the Rouen duck is back again, standing loud and proud in the middle of the ladies, like she's addressing an audience. I sigh, and Suzette places a hand on my arm.

'You should try messaging him again,' she says, reading my mind.

I'd ended up filling her in on Johnny and our unique relationship. We've spent so much time together that it was impossible not to.

'Mmm, maybe,' I say.

I've already put myself out there once. It was clearly just a moment in time for Johnny, and that moment has now passed.

Once dinner is done, and Suzette has trumped my duck with a bowl of her spectacular vanilla bean pudding, I return to the library.

I take a seat on the familiar settee, close my eyes and inhale deeply. The room smells sweet and woody. The scent of books new and old. I'm really going to miss it here.

A few minutes of silence pass before I eventually open my eyes. I reach for my computer and refresh my inbox. My heart jumps into my throat when I see a reply from the Mother Ducker. With jittery hands and a churning stomach, I open his email.

Bonjour Max,
I love a sporadic check-in. To be honest, I missed our chats. I was hoping I'd hear from you again.
How goes France?
Johnny

My eyes zero in on a single sentence: *I was hoping I'd hear from you again.*

My fingers find the keyboard and begin to type. I no longer care how desperate an instant reply makes me seem. After being faced with the prospect of never hearing from him again, I'm just so relieved that I have an open line of communication.

Hey Johnny,
I'm happy to hear from you. I do like to check in with my matches every sixty days or so. France has been quite colourful. If you'd like to resume our little pen pal arrangement, I can tell you all about it.
Max

I hesitate for a moment before adding my mobile number, then click 'send'. All I can do now is hope that the intended recipient feels the same way I do.

∾

Ugh. Take that back right now, Max!
Alice's WhatsApp message lights up my screen, and relief floods my body.

I'd snapped a photo of a girl with an immaculate pixie cut sitting in the boarding lounge at Charles de Gaulle Airport and sent it to her on a whim.

She follows up straightaway with another message.

Do you happen to be flying back to the Nest any time soon?

I smile as I type. **I'll be back in exactly 22 hours and 5 minutes**

Really?! Yay. I can't wait to see you. I've missed you

Same, I reply.

I want to make it doubly clear to her that I'm raising the white flag. I don't want to fight with my best friend.

I type again: **NEGATIVE GEARING**

NEGATIVE GEARING, comes her instant reply.

A warm, fuzzy feeling settles in the centre of my chest. All is right again.

As I slip my phone back into my pocket, I vow to make an extra effort with Maggie when I get back. Perhaps I can host dinner again and cook a little doggy meal for Thor, too. Maybe even something out of Suzette's cookbook. She'd handed me a copy at the train station after I'd unfurled myself from her Mini. As I'd waited on the platform, listening to Maurice's crowing, I'd hugged it almost as tightly as I'd hugged her. *Lovely Ladies & Eggsellent Eggs* would be taking pride of place on the shelf by the oven, next to the dead succulents, as soon as I got home.

I glance around the seating area again. There's still no sign of the Laurents. I've been on tenterhooks since arriving at the airport. The first hurdle was check-in. I'd been terrified that my ticket had been cancelled as punishment for going AWOL, but it hadn't, much to my relief. The very pleasant airline lady was super apologetic but couldn't move my seats due to a packed plane. I consoled myself with the fact that the Laurents had probably upgraded to business class anyway.

The flight attendants have begun milling around the gate, dragging the barrier ropes out of the way. We're literally minutes from boarding.

I pull my phone out again and unblock Scott's number, in case there's some need-to-know information I've missed, so that I'm not boarding the flight feeling completely blind. There's a message from an unknown number. My heart picks up pace. In the emotional whirlwind that was saying goodbye to Suzette and my Rouen home, I'd managed to put thoughts of Johnny out of my mind for a while.

I swipe to read.

I'd be delighted to approve this new arrangement

He hasn't signed off with his name, but I know exactly who it is. My cheeks are ablaze, but I don't hesitate. Johnny is living and breathing at the end of my phone right now – I don't want to miss my opportunity.

Any signatures required? JP witnesses? I type.

Blood is pumping so loudly in my ears that it's drowning out the chatter of the packed waiting area. It's like no time has passed – like I never had brain surgery, like I never considered getting back with Scott, like I never came to France. I not only remember how to do this, I remember how good it feels.

My phone lights up again.

Do you have a particular witness in mind? Johnny asks.

That's an in-person situation . . . Which is against the terms of our arrangement

Of course. Are there any other terms I should know about?

We should collaborate on terms. It's a new agreement, after all

Agreed. What do you have in mind?

You first. I initiated

Okay, then . . . Content needs to be of a high level at all times

It wasn't previously?

Just confirming we'll be conversing at the same gold standard

Agreed. Memes?

Of course. They're my livelihood. And now you know where to source the good ones

That I do. Cool site ☺ I lie.

Thanks. Except you did break our anonymity clause

I completely forgot that by visiting the Mother Ducker I was violating our arrangement.

Whoops, sorry!

But I'm glad you did

There's a chill down my spine that's headed dangerously close to my underwear.

As my penance, please ask something of your choosing, I type. Then I look around and realise there is no longer anyone sitting next to me. In fact, the entire area has almost completely emptied out. I stand and rush forward to the gate.

Okay. How about you start by sharing with me why you are in France?

Just tying up some loose ends. Sorry, got to go. Boarding flight home now. Will message again soon x

I type the message quickly as I tack onto the queue of the last few stragglers. *Shit, that was a close call.* Hopefully Johnny won't read into my abrupt exit.

I file onto the plane and find my seat: 42B. Scott should be in 42A, but the seat is empty.

Once I'm settled with my seatbelt secured, I pull out my laptop. I know the flight attendants will shortly be demanding we stow our devices for take-off, but for now all I want is a legitimate distraction in case Scott does turn up. I want to present the perfect picture of a girl with her shit together who has *thrived* post break-up. I check the word count of my document. Fifty thousand words. Heck, yes. *I can get out another quick paragraph now*, I think, my fingers poised on the keyboard.

'Hey, Max.'

His voice startles me, and I fumble on the keys: *asjjksuhd*.

'Hey,' I say without making eye contact.

I automatically stand and move into the aisle to let him into the window seat. We normally swap seats, but I don't want to owe him anything.

'You don't want to sit here?' he asks on cue.

'No, thanks.'

'Does Slice have you back working already?' he asks, eyeing my laptop.

'No. I'm working on my novel. Why? Did Raffie say something?'

'No, Max. Like I've said so many times, I haven't been in touch with Raffie.' There's some sass in his voice, like he's done with defending himself.

Oh, I am so done with it too, buddy. Let's get this flight done and dusted, then go our separate ways.

'That's fantastic you're making progress on *The Doors*,' he adds brightly, seemingly pleased with himself that he's remembered the title.

'Not *The Doors*. Something new,' I say.

'Really? Still fantasy?'

'No.'

'What's it about?'

'I'd rather not say.'

I'd rather not speak to you about anything. Who knows which of my ideas you'll steal.

'So you don't want to chat about things at all?'

'I don't see the point,' I reply, fastening my headphones over my ears and turning to face the aisle.

'Okay.'

We take off in silence. I give Scott full custody of the middle armrest (not that it seems to be up for debate), so there's no risk of any physical contact.

When dinner service starts, I remove my headphones long enough to request the chicken stir-fry. Scott jumps at the chance to speak to me.

'You really don't want to talk, Max?' he asks, as I bite into the dry chicken. The plane food tastes extra bland, thanks to ten days of Suzette's home-cooked meals and my ever-improving palate.

'I don't have anything to say,' I mutter.

I do have one thing to ask, but I'm sure the answer lies with his mum, who I bet is lolling around in business class somewhere, demanding refills of champagne.

'Okay, fine.' Scott turns and digs into his gluggy beef casserole.

I wait for him to swallow before I ask, 'Where's your family?' Curiosity has gotten the best of me.

Scott's fork clatters onto his tray, and he turns back to me with a disproportionate amount of interest.

'They got an upgrade. But I wanted to sit with you.' He's looking at me with puppy dog eyes, like he's expecting a treat for doing a trick.

'Right. Well, I just wondered if you knew that your family cookbook is a rip-off of a recipe book sold by a famous bistro in Paris?'

'Huh?' His forehead crinkles in confusion.

Huh, indeed. I knew he'd be clueless. I turn back towards the aisle and replace my earphones.

Scott peppers me with questions at each meal service, to which I give one-word answers.

'Did you leave Paris?'

'Yes.'

'Where did you go?'

'Rouen.'

'Did you enjoy yourself?'

'Yes.'

Heck, yes.

'How are you feeling?'

'Well.'

We have a quick layover in Singapore, and I make myself scarce, purchasing expensive perfumes for Mum and Alice and a cologne for Dad; ironic, considering France is known for its *parfums*, but I'd completely forgotten to buy gifts, and I don't want to arrive home empty-handed. I decide not to message Johnny again until I get back. It's 3 am Australian time anyway. I'll make contact when I'm feeling ready – when I've kicked the jet lag and worked out something clever to say. Johnny expects clever.

The second leg of the flight passes quickly as I drift in and out of sleep. Every time my head starts slumping in Scott's direction, I manage to startle myself awake just in time.

I'm starting to breathe easier, knowing that I've almost made it home, when Scott reaches over and places something on my tray table.

I look down to see Duck, our Venetian glass memento.

'Max, can I please say something?'

At least that's what it looks like Scott says. I still have my audiobook blaring. It's been a twenty-hour flight. Isn't he too exhausted for this? But I pause Sally Smyth and remove my headphones.

'I got the duck from your apartment before we left. I hope you don't mind?'

'What? How?'

'Alice.'

Oh, great . . . I bet that's what Alice meant when she said she was 'handling' something for me while I was recovering at my parents. So that was true after all.

'Let me get this straight, Scott . . . you went to the Nest and Alice handed the duck over to you?'

'Yes. Well, no. It wasn't as entirely straightforward as I would have liked. Initially, I told her I was going to propose to you, and she slammed the door in my face. But the next time I stopped by I –'

'Wait,' I interrupt. 'You were going to *propose*? Why?'

I seem to have lost control of the muscles in my face but I'm not sure whether I'm about to laugh or cry.

'What do you mean, *why*? Because I love you, Max!'

'You don't love me, Scott.'

'I do! That's why, despite what a pain Alice was being, I didn't give up. When I went back again, I pretended I was busting for a pee, and she finally let me inside. I snuck into your bedroom and found Duck. The plan was to slip the ring over his bill and ask you at the top of the Eiffel Tower, but since that didn't go to plan . . .'

'So, where's this ring now?' I ask, looking at Duck's bare beak.

'Well, I decided to hold off actually buying the ring – insuring that thing for travel would have been a total nightmare. But I have something even better for you,' he says, sliding a piece of paper under Duck's butt. 'You're going to lose your mind.'

My heart races as I tug at the piece of paper. I turn it over and begin to read.

Netflix Comedian Service Contract Agreement
    This is a contract between **Scott Laurent**, *referred to here as* '**PERFORMER**', *and his show* **The Trials and Tribulations of IKEA**, *referred to here as* '**PERFORMANCE**'.

I stop reading and pause for a moment while my brain plays catch-up.

The emails. Scott asking me to come to Paris. The duck à l'orange at the hospital. Poor abducted Duck on my tray table. *Could it be . . .?*

I turn to Scott. 'So *this* is what it's all been about.'

'Yes, baby! It's a contract for my new show. *Our* new show,' he clarifies. 'My agent is the bomb. This show is why the agency signed me and now they've already locked in the Netflix special they promised – can you believe it? It's inspired by those little IKEA stories you've been writing. We'll need to make them much funnier, but I know you can do it now that you're almost recovered.'

I take a shaky breath. 'Are you serious?'

'Very!' Scott chirps, clearly misunderstanding my tone. 'I believe in you, Max. I know you have what it takes. I thought the show could be a stepping stone to you getting back on track – and getting your own book agent one day.'

'How did you get my stories, Scott?'

He shrugs. 'You read them to me. Remember?'

'And then you helped yourself to them from my computer?'

'Well, they needed some samples . . .'

'That's stealing, Scott.'

His face turns ashen.

'Huh? No, it's not – you'd already shown them to me. Max? Why are you being like this? This is not still about punishing me for Raffie, is it?'

'Not at all. In fact, I should be thanking you for *finally* helping me make sense of things. I couldn't wrap my head around why a man I'd loved for so many years was making zero effort with me – *cheated* on me – but at the same time was continually declaring his love for me.'

'What are you talking about?'

If he really wants me to spell it out for him, I will. I'm done with protecting his feelings and building up his ego at the expense of my own.

'You were hell-bent on keeping me small, trying to convince me that I don't have what it takes to write a book, all the while masquerading as my biggest supporter. In reality, you were so jealous you were stealing my material – you're *still* stealing my material, for fuck's sake – under the guise of "helping" me! When in actual fact you need *my* help!'

'That–that's not what I was doing,' Scott stammers. He looks shocked. The reality of the situation seems to be dawning on him at last.

'Would there be a Netflix special without me?'

He hangs his head. 'Well, no, but –'

'Then you were using me, Scott,' I spit.

'Can I just say –'

'No, Scott. I'm done with your meaningless words.'

Suddenly, I'm struck by a new theory.

'Actually, there is just one final thing. And I'll need the truth, please. Do you think you can handle that?'

'Sure,' he says, despondent.

'Was it you who delivered that duck à l'orange to me in hospital?'

Scott's puzzled expression is the only answer I need.

Twenty minutes before landing, I'm suddenly desperate for a wee – and so is Helen Laurent, apparently. She gives a curt nod as I approach the toilet – like we are strangers. I consider returning to my seat, but the mood in row 42 is just as hostile. Scott has spent the last hour alternating between huffing and puffing and urgent whispers, *still* attempting to defend his indefensible actions.

I tuck into the space near the emergency exit and pray that Helen will leave me be. I never responded to the text she sent while I was in Rouen.

'Oh, it's you Maxine.'

Shit.

'It's so dark, I didn't recognise you. I don't know why they insist on dimming the cabin lighting when it's almost lunchtime in Sydney.'

'Hi, Helen.'

I'll keep things nice and civil.

'How's your flight been back there? Everything all worked out between you and Scott, then? Here, let me give you a baby wipe for these disgusting lavatories. Can you believe the business-class toilets are out of order?' She peels back the sticker on the plastic packet in her hand, pulls out a wipe and passes it to me. 'Rose blossom scent.'

'Thanks.'

Will she want it back when she finds out I'm definitely never getting back together with her son? Or will I get another fugly necklace?

'So, Scott told you about the amazing deal he got you both? I'm very proud of him.'

'He did, yes,' I say through gritted teeth, and stare at the *Occupied* sign on the toilet door.

Will whoever is in there hurry the hell up?

'Unfortunately, I can't allow it to go ahead,' I say.

'What!' Helen's mouth forms an O. 'Why?'

I fold my arms across my chest.

'Because your son took my work without my permission.'

Helen wrinkles her nose, like there's suddenly a smell worse than the pungent odour of BO, bad plane food and dirty socks that settled in the cabin shortly after take-off.

'Don't be daft, Maxine! Sometimes to get what you want in life you need to get a little creative . . . Do you think I'd be sitting in business class right now if it weren't for a few calculated moves of my own?' She smooths down her bob, which is still looking immaculate even after hours in the air.

'Like stealing Bistro Rouge's cookbook and pretending it was yours?'

Helen takes a sharp breath in. 'Oh Maxine, you really shouldn't speak of things you know nothing about. I simply *adapted* it; I even added some recipes of my own. I couldn't exactly turn up to the Laurent mansion to meet Gary's parents empty-handed now, could I?'

Wow. Just wow.

'A nice box of chocolates wouldn't have done the trick?'

Helen smirks. 'That's how I got the idea. I went to DJ's food hall to pick up some chocolate truffles, but then I came across the most delightful French cookbook and thought that it would help me craft the perfect backstory. I knew Gary's parents were keen on his partner having French heritage, too.'

'So you're not French?' I ask incredulously. 'And you didn't even buy the cookbook from Bistro Rouge?'

'*Non* and *non.*'

Unbelievable! Why am I hit with a sudden urge to burst out laughing?

'You're not to mention a word of this, Maxine. I'm only telling you to help you see sense.' Helen eyes me sternly. 'My gift left quite the impression, and when Gary and I married, the Laurents couldn't have been more delighted that I renamed the cookbook after their family and got new luxe printed editions for everyone – even for Grand-mère and Grand-père. It's a shame they are no longer with us . . .'

The door to the toilet slides open and a sheepish man in socks scurries back up the aisle. Helen doesn't make any move to go in.

'And how is this helping me exactly?' I ask.

'Take Raphaela, for example. She wasn't just offered a secondment to New York. She sought it out. It's the French blood in her, I'm sure.'

A light bulb goes off in my head. *Ahh . . . no wonder 'Raphaela' can do no wrong in Helen's eyes. She's part French.*

The plane suddenly lurches and the 'fasten seatbelt' sign switches on.

'Am I making any sense to you, Maxine?' Helen asks, reaching for the wall to steady herself.

'Perfect sense. A fish rots from its head.'

Helen's eyes widen. 'Whatever do you mean?'

'Scott never really stood a chance, did he? I'm not excusing it. He's a grown man who's had plenty of time to course-correct, but he comes from a family of liars.'

'I never lied. I just went after what I –'

'Enough, Helen,' I interrupt. 'I've heard enough. Now can you kindly get the fuck out of my way, I'm about to wet my pants.'

Helen remains rooted on the spot, presumably in shock, as I push past her.

Maybe she would have preferred it if I was a Hell's Angel after all.

PART V

Faire fondre

/ fɛʁ fõdʁ /

(verb) To melt.

Chapter Thirty-one

Dad has layered the expensive airport cologne on top of his pre-existing golf stink, like the chemically sweet pine scent of an artificial freshener working overtime in a strange-smelling Uber. I'm just grateful that he's come to collect me, and I don't have to battle public transport with luggage.

I sneeze into my elbow.

'Are you okay, sweetie?' Dad glances in the rear-view mirror at me.

I'm sitting in the back seat like a paying passenger after he insisted there was more room to stretch out my economy-class legs.

'Yes, all good,' I reassure him, as I put the window down. 'It was just a bit nippy on the plane.'

I don't have the heart to tell him that I'm sneezing because he's doused himself in cologne. One stroke of a match is all it would take for him to go up in flames.

Dad had been so excited about his gift that he'd ripped open the packaging and poured half the bottle on his wrists before we'd even exited the terminal.

I'm sure Antaeus would approve of such liberal use if it meant more sales. I'm due to start work on another campaign for them in a few days. I suppose I need to start getting my head back into work-mode. I'm looking forward to resuming some sort of routine – just not seeing Raffie. I wonder if Scott has already been in touch with her? Helen will be much happier with the choice of daughter-in-law. Raffie could have her fake family with their fake cookbook.

'Max . . . Maxie, are you okay back there?'

I've completely zoned out. 'Oh, yup. Sorry, Dad. I'm just a bit tired from the flight.'

I sprinted off the plane and somehow managed to breeze through customs and collect my bag without seeing Scott or any of the Laurents. At least there's no Tupperware to be returned this time. I even left the poor glass duck in the plane seat pocket.

'I was just saying that if you're feeling cold, shouldn't you put the window up?'

He has a point. I press the button to close the window, sealing us in our cologne chamber. Good thing I'm not asthmatic.

'Am I taking you straight home? Or do you want to say hello to your mum first?' Dad asks. 'She'll be home from work by the time we get there. We can even stop for a cheeky thirty cent cone first?'

I snort. 'Daaad . . . Maccas put their prices up, like, a decade ago. They're a dollar now.'

'What? Really?' We lock eyes in the mirror, and he grins. 'Well, offer withdrawn. I'm not made of money.'

It's like we're delivering lines from a rehearsed skit.

'The ice-cream machine is probably broken anyway, like it bloody always is,' he mutters. 'Plus, I'm sure you're now accustomed to outrageously expensive French delicacies.'

'The food was spectacular,' I volunteer. 'In Rouen, I stayed with this woman who cooked the most amazing things. We had fresh eggs from her hens for breakfast every morning.'

'Not better than the "Big Brian"?' he asks in mock horror.

'Definitely not.'

He glances into the rear-view mirror. 'So, how was your trip? Terrible company aside. Not that lady of yours – she sounds lovely.'

I register the hesitation in his voice. 'Dad, it's done. You don't have to worry. I'm not going back there,' I say, responding directly to his subtext.

I love that he's trying to show some restraint and not peppering me with a bunch of questions about what exactly went down. I gave Mum and Dad the headlines when I was over there, but I know they'll want the details eventually. Dad can barely follow the plot of *Pretty Woman*, so he's going to struggle with this one.

'Okay, darling. So, home . . . or?' he asks.

'Actually . . .' I pause. 'Do you mind taking me to drop something off to, um, ah, a friend, first?' I say, surprising even myself.

'Sure,' he says without hesitation. Dad's taxi service has been going strong since the nineties. 'Where to, then?'

Whoops, minor detail. We'll be needing a destination.

'Um, just a sec. Let me check.'

I'm glad I'm hidden in the back as I open the browser on my phone and type 'Mother Ducker' into the search bar. I scroll to the bottom of the contact page and find the details I need:

Name: Johnny Kalos
Entity Name: Anatidaephobia Pty Ltd.
Address: 72 Johnson Street, Marrickville

Anatidaephobia? A quick google and the Urban Dictionary informs me that it's 'the fear that somewhere, somehow, a duck is watching you'. I snort with laughter. That name has Johnny's fingerprints all over it. Johnny *Kalos's* fingerprints all over it. Learning his surname makes him seem so much more real.

'Do you have the address?' Dad asks, an eager finger hovering over the dashboard's GPS.

'Johnson Street, Marrickville, thanks,' I say. 'But let's swing by Maccas first. This fancy French palate could do with some nuggets.'

~

The nugs may not have been the best idea. As we pull up to the Marrickville address, one shoots back up out of my stomach like a pinball and lodges in my throat.

'Do you want me to wait here, or?' Dad is looking at me expectantly. Innocently. He's completely unaware that we're at the home – well, assumed home – of my internet stranger crush, and not an actual friend.

'Sure, thanks. I shouldn't be long.' I'd like a getaway car just in case. I'm not sure what to expect.

I hop out of the car and try to swallow the nugget back down. Success. My legs are shaking as I walk towards the house. It's a beautiful, three-storey historic home – not at all the type of place I pictured Johnny texting me from, or as the Mother Ducker's HQ.

The grand old-world charm of the home envelopes me as I travel up the stone path to the front door. The nerves hit me with full force as I reach the entry and I nearly run back to the safety of the car. It also suddenly occurs to me how awful I probably look. I reach up to try and at least smooth down my hair. I typically go straight home after a long-haul flight and pray no one sees or smells me. I didn't even think to spritz myself with Dad's new cologne. I suppose love makes you do crazy things. Except it isn't love. Yet.

The front door is wide open. An overpowering scent of sweet honey, like there's bees nesting in the walls, beckons me inside. I look down the stretch of hallway, but I don't see anyone.

I search for a doorbell. There isn't one. Just a plaque screwed into the brickwork next to the door: *Daphne's Cooking School*.

I'm relieved to see Johnny's story checks out so far. That also explains the delicious scent. Baklava.

'Hello?' I call softly. I wait with bated breath for a reply. Nothing.

I'm too scared to call any louder. I want to meet Johnny as much as I don't want to meet him. At least now I can say that I tried and it just wasn't meant to be.

I grasp the strap of my bag and turn back down the path. But instead of following it back to the kerb, I turn left and walk along the side of the house. I stop in front of a bay window and peer in.

The room is large and decked out with a run of stainless-steel benches. It's abuzz with people, presumably students, marked by their matching blue-and-white striped aprons.

In front of the room, at a separate bench, is an older woman with grey hair. Maybe fifty or so. The sleeves of her linen top are scrunched up to her elbows and her hair is scraped back with a stylish tortoiseshell clip.

'Today we are going to learn how to make a meze spread, moussaka, bougatsa and – to end – baklava, before we sit down to enjoy the food together, Greek-style,' she announces, her voice curling out through the open window. I edge closer to the side of the building, flattening myself against the wall next to the window. She isn't facing this way, but I don't want to risk being seen. How would I explain my creeping? I can only imagine how it looks. Why pay for a cooking class when you can take one for free?

'First off, hygiene housekeeping. Please wash your hands in the basins at the back. I want you to get nice and intimate with your dough. You will need to really move your hands through it to understand how dramatically the weather can alter its texture. How even the little bit of air here and there can change everything.' She has a direct approach to her teaching. Suzette and this woman would get on well.

The students disperse in the room, some moving at an eager trot. I take the opportunity to lean closer to see if I can spot any signs that Johnny has ever occupied this space. If I'm to believe his messages – and he's never given me reason not to – this is the very space where he cooked the Fork Him dishes.

I'm not sure what I'm looking for, but as I survey the room, I accidentally make eye contact with one of the students returning from the basin, their hands still dripping.

Okay, you are in creep territory now, Max.

I lurch away from the window and scurry back around the house to the entrance.

I've just reached the entry when someone comes hurtling out the front door, almost taking me out. They manage to step off the path milliseconds before we collide. My first thought is that it's the cooking class teacher coming after me to demand I either join the other fee-paying students, or scram.

But when they swing around to face me, I see a woman wearing scrubs. Her short grey hair is fastened with a pearl clip and the skin around her eyes is crinkled with concern.

'Maxine!'

Eliana!

'Are you okay?' she asks.

'I'm fine,' I croak.

I'm a little lost for words. Considering the long list of patients she's cared for I'm taken aback that she remembers me at all. But even more than that, I'm confused. What is she doing at Johnny's house?

'Oh, Maxine *mou*! It's so good to see you. Have you recovered well?' Her voice is warm with concern.

It's like we're back in the ICU and she's doing her hourly checks.

'Yes, I think so. I have scan next week to check on everything,' I answer in a daze.

She leans in and squeezes my arms.

'Fingers crossed then. That Dr Jock is a miracle worker. I heard that you've been in France? How exciting for you!'

My brow furrows. *How does Eliana know I was in France?*

'Giannis is my nephew,' she explains.

Who is Giannis?

'Johnny. Sorry, Giannis is his Greek name.'

Oh.

Wow.

Right.

Okay.

But wait. How does Eliana know that I know Johnny?

'He lives with us – my sister and I – here.' She gestures to the beautiful home behind us.

I'm quiet as I digest what she's saying. I'm so confused.

'Did you tell Johnny I was in hospital?' I ask.

I hope my question doesn't sound like an accusation; I owe so much to this woman – I'm just trying to make sense of everything. My long-haul-flight brain fuzz is not helping.

'Oh no, Maxine, I'd never do that!' Eliana exclaims. 'He works part-time at the hospital as an orderly and took you for your post-op MRI. He told me right away that he thought he recognised you even though you were asleep. Asked me if you'd said anything about being a writer, and I mentioned your audiobook . . .'

I stare at her vacantly, unblinking.

He took me for my scan!?

She eyes me carefully. I must not look as haunted as I feel because she continues, 'I discouraged him from saying anything to you while you were in such a vulnerable state. Told him it was highly unprofessional. But he managed to find his own way of sending you a message.' She pauses again. 'I wasn't happy at all when I found out about the duck. I'm sorry, Maxine *mou*. I've said too much. I'm sure you're in shock what with all of this new information. Can I assume that you came here looking for him?'

'I did.' The two words are all I can manage.

'He's not home right now. I'm not sure where he is. But I know he'll be happy to hear that you stopped by. Do you want me to give him a message?'

She's right – I am in shock. I came here on a whim, carried by a swirl of emotions, but now I'm ready to get to the bottom of who Johnny is – and what his intentions were with me. Was I just a fun distraction, or was I something more? *Am* I something more? I mean, how does Eliana know that I was in France? Johnny must have spoken about me. I have so many questions that I'm sure Eliana could answer, but I know that I need to ask Johnny himself.

'Oh, dear!' Eliana says as she glances at her watch. 'I'm sorry to do this to you, Maxine *mou*, but I've got to run. Shift starts in . . . gosh, would you look at that, fifteen minutes!'

She leans in to embrace me. 'I'm sure we'll be seeing each other again soon enough.' Eliana gives my arms a final squeeze before turning and power walking down the path. She breaks into a jog as she reaches the letterbox.

Dad is probably watching from the car and wondering why on earth a middle-aged woman dressed head-to-toe in scrubs is sprinting up the front lawn, like a light-blue gazelle.

As I turn to head back to the car, I stop and pull the copy of *The Tales of Mother Goose* from my bag. I've been carrying the book around in my backpack since leaving Rouen. I couldn't even say why.

I take a pen from my bag's front pouch and open the front cover.

I scrawl a quick message on the first page, underneath Charles Perrault's name and the original French title: *Les Contes de ma mère l'Oye*, or 'The Tales of My Mother Goose'.

I close the book before I can second-guess myself and slide it under the doormat.

There's no two ways about it, Johnny and I need to talk. IRL this time.

Chapter Thirty-two

I'm checking my phone for a message from Johnny for the seventeenth time this morning when the lift opens into the Slice office. Head down, I step straight into the path of a scooter whizzing down the tiled hallway.

'Fuck!' I gasp, as I leap back into the lift to narrowly avoid a collision.

I vaguely recall seeing an email while I was off about scooters being introduced to navigate the office's long hallways. I've been back at work for a few days and this is my first time seeing one in action. I'd assumed they were a gimmick for when important prospective clients came to visit and were not intended as substitutes for legs. *Hell, when did Slice turn into Google?* I shudder involuntarily.

Perhaps the cool factor is wasted on me. I remember when I used to lose my mind over the foosball tables and the secret meeting room hidden behind a bookcase (okay, that is still pretty cool) so maybe I'm the one who's changed. Give me a simple desk, a laptop and a dash of creative freedom and I'm good to go. I've been adding to my novel's word count since arriving home. The jet lag has meant some extra early-morning writing time so I've just cracked 60,000 words – I can hardly believe it.

I take a tentative step back into the hallway, my sandals making a delicate tap-tap on the tiled floor. I'm still wearing my French uniform of a wrap dress. It's nice to have a bit of the French countryside with me here in Sydney. Especially today, when I want to be feeling my best. HR hasn't said anything to me yet about my casual attire, and I plan on donning my usual pair of heels for any client-facing stuff.

Squeeeaaakkk! The painful sound of rubber grinding on tiles warns me that another scooter is approaching. A spray of WD-40 wouldn't go wanting.

Tiny butterflies spring to life in my stomach at the sight of Raffie's blonde bob swinging back and forth with the momentum of the scooter. The person I've managed to avoid for days, but had hoped to avoid forever.

The scooter has almost reached me when I notice Raffie has a passenger clinging to her back. It's Zac. He mustn't be as tall as the six-foot measurement given on his comp card, as his head has been obscured by Raffie's.

Shit, shit, shit. My first thought is that Friday's Antaeus shoot has been moved to today, and I am woefully unprepared. I may no longer find this job inspiring, but I still need it to pay my rent. And who knows what other new medical expenses I'll have after my follow-up scan.

The scooter stops in front of me.

'Hey, Max!' Zac greets me over Raffie's shoulder.

'Hey, guys.'

Raffie's grinning like a Cheshire cat. My eyes trail down her sleek dusty pink pantsuit to find Zac's arms are still wrapped low around her waist. Completely unnecessary now that they are no longer moving.

Well, well, well. How the plot thickens. I clear my throat to disguise a giggle.

'The shoot isn't today, is it?' I ask.

'Oh, no,' Raffie says. 'I invited Zac in to take these new babies for a spin. They're great, hey babe?' She twists her head to look at Zac.

Babe . . .

I'm careful not to smile.

Just because she's found a new boyfriend doesn't mean we can be besties now. It was Scott's responsibility to keep his dick in his pants – but that doesn't mean all is forgiven and forgotten with Raffie. I wonder how Scott feels about her new situationship? I'm sure the news has made its way to him via Eve by now.

'I can't believe I finally convinced them to get a fleet. The New York office has had them since 2012. We're living in the Sydney Stone Age.' She rolls her eyes.

A *fleet?* I pinch my wrist to stop myself from smirking.

'Anyway, how *are* you? Were we expecting you back so soon?'

I hate her use of the royal we.

'I'm fine.' There is no way I'm going to let on a thing about this afternoon's scan. 'Thank you for the flowers,' I add, remembering the giant bunch of Australian natives that arrived after my surgery. 'And yes, I was always due back to work this week.'

If she knows about my swift Paris exit she doesn't let on. The starry look in her eyes tells me that her mind has been elsewhere.

'That's great to hear, Max,' she says.

'Thanks.'

I appreciate her attempt to be a nice and normal human being, but if she hesitates any longer it's going to get super awkward.

On cue she says, 'I might keep showing Zac around the place. Can you believe he's never been up here? You know what they say, all work and no play . . .'

They push off and Zac waves goodbye. As they glide down the corridor, I note how natural Zac looks. His broad back is ironing-board straight and his muscled arms are casually looped around Raffie's waist like he'd shot out of his mother's birth canal on a scooter. But the only back I'm interested in clinging to is Johnny's.

'Don't you go getting yourself killed,' a voice to my left sings out. I turn to see Lucy walking towards me. *Will I ever make it to my desk this morning?* Her throwaway comment sounds particularly ominous given my lunchtime scan. 'I saw your close call just before. Don't worry, you'll get used to it. It took me a hot minute, but they've been darting around here for weeks now. I can give you a quick lesson.'

'Thanks. I'll need one.'

'Will have to wait until I'm more awake, though. I've been up all night with Master Four and I feel like a walking potato.'

I laugh. 'You could be a scootering potato!'

Lucy and I were back on good terms. The second I stepped into the office on Monday morning she'd apologised for blabbing about my surgery. It was impossible not to forgive her. I'd deduced that she was a gossip, but not an ill-intentioned one. I almost regret impulsively leaving *Mother Goose* under a doormat in Marrickville and not giving it to her for her son's bookshelf. *Almost.*

Lucy flashes me a look that clearly says, *over your dead body*. Why does my brain seem so intent on thinking about dead bodies today?

'Your scan's this afternoon, right?' Lucy asks, as if reading my mind. 'How are you feeling?'

'I'm doing okay, but I'm sure I'll feel even better after a coffee . . .'

'I thought you'd never ask!' Lucy says. 'I could murder a latte. By the way, I swear I have not told a soul about your appointment. Pinky promise.'

'I know. Thank you,' I say.

We link arms and turn back to the lifts.

~

'Le sigh.'

'*Le sigh?*' Alice asks. 'So, two weeks in France and you now sigh in French?'

'I was trying not to be dramatic,' I say.

'Well, you failed miserably at that. More drama than the *Titanic*, I'd say. Five-star drama.' Alice chuckles as she grabs my hand and gives it a squeeze. 'It's going to be fine, Max.'

'If it's going to be fine then why did you just compare my life to a sinking ship?'

'Ah, but you see there was nothing wrong with the ship – it was that stupid captain who sealed those passengers' tragic fate. Need I remind you that you have the finest captain of them all, *Al-ecks-an-duh*!'

'Alexander,' I say, correcting her ridiculous pronunciation.

'Yes, I was trying out the French thing.'

'Well, don't. Also, are you basing your knowledge on the movie? Or is that fact?'

I realise my line of questioning is rich, coming from someone who a couple of weeks ago didn't know why Joan of Arc is a patron saint of France.

'Do the history books show the captain was a weakling who couldn't stand up to pressure from his boss when they hit that iceberg, who knows? What I do know is that Kate and Leo were busy having steamy car sex.'

'Le laugh,' I say.

'That's the spirit. Am I doing a good job of distracting you?'

'The best.'

I'm so grateful Alice insisted on meeting me at the hospital for my scan. Mum had offered, but I'd told her that it wasn't a big deal. I'd be in and out and wouldn't get the results on the spot anyway. But as much as I was trying to downplay it to myself and everyone around me, I was scared. So I didn't resist when Alice told me she would be there. She had her unique 'A-way' of keeping things light.

She was running late and missed me going in for my actual scan, but that ended up being for the best. I was desperate for the loo so I couldn't concentrate on much else – which is the entire point of the Full Bladder Method™. It never fails me. This MRI was slightly different from past scans, though. As I clenched my pelvic floor trying not to wet myself, I still had the tightness in my chest, but my mind looped with images from France. The entire trip was spooling out before me, a replay of all the most significant moments, starting with the claustrophobic Paris lift, moving to Bistro Rouge and the copycat cookbook, and ending in my little library room in Rouen, messaging Johnny. It is a well-known trope in books and movies: a protagonist's life flashing before their eyes just before a near-death experience.

When I'd walked back into the waiting room after the scan and spied Alice's familiar pixie crop, I'd burst into tears.

'Come on, my outfit is not *that* bad,' she'd murmured into my shoulder as she'd hugged me tight.

Choking back my sobs, I'd stepped back to judge the day's fashion choice. No Birkenstocks with socks, but a T-shirt featuring an otter in glasses and a striped scarf with the words 'Hairy Otter' printed underneath.

'It's truly hideous,' I said.

'Why, thank you.' She'd curtsied. 'I was wearing this tee the day Scott came to ask for your hand in marriage – the first time.'

'Gosh, I'm surprised he didn't run the other way.'

Alice had poked out her tongue. 'Apparently even Hairy Otter couldn't stop him. What a dick!'

At that, we'd burst into a fit of manic laughter, doubled over, knees weak. No one in the waiting room – not the reception staff nor the anxious patients – batted an eyelid at us. I suppose hospitals are the one place you have permission to come as you are. For me, it was an unexpected release of the waterfall of emotions that had cumulated over the last few months: fear, excitement, terror, relief, disappointment and hope. I've felt it all.

We're now sitting quietly in our seats waiting for my films to be developed.

'The radiographer was making grunting noises and stroking her chin a lot,' I whisper. I can't help analysing every moment of the scan. 'That's what the television doctors do when they can see the tumour's returned but they're not allowed to tell the patient.'

'I stroke my chin a lot to check for rogue hairs,' Alice replies matter-of-factly. 'If I don't stay on top of the plucking Maggie says it's like kissing her aunt.'

'Well, she must *really* like her aunt,' I shoot back, once again grateful for Alice's swift subject change.

PDA may as well be Alice and Maggie's middle names at this point, but I've not only come to accept my new mushy Alice, I love her.

'You better be using Maggie's tweezers, not mine,' I add.

'Sure.' She winks at me.

Maggie and Thor are moving in with us next month and my only request is that I get a dedicated drawer for my cooking utensils. Theirs is that I cook for them on Sundays. Alice has added an extra caveat that I deliver her meal with a chapter of my book. She did one of her silly elfin jigs when I told her I'd found my novel-writing groove in Rouen.

'Maxine Mayberry?'

My stomach does a somersault as the medical receptionist calls my name.

I stand and go to collect the oversized envelope.

'Remember, this is to be opened by your referring doctor only,' the receptionist instructs. 'The report will be sent to them in the next few hours. Do you already have an appointment to see them?'

'Yes, next week,' I say diligently, knowing full well I'll be opening it as soon as I'm alone.

In the hospital car park, Alice gives me another squeeze.

'You did it, Max! I'm so proud of you.'

'Let's not count our chickens just yet,' I say nervously. 'We still need to wait for the results.'

'Sure, sure.' She waves a hand in the air, swatting my concerns away. 'But you should still celebrate that you've reached another milestone. And you've been feeling fine, haven't you?'

'Well, yes . . .' Once the last of the jet lag subsides I'm sure the fatigue will disappear with it.

'Then we'll be thinking positively, thank you.' She links her arm in my mine. 'Now, what time are you meeting Johnny?'

'We don't know if he's even going to show up.'

'Again! *Positif*, Max!'

I cast my mind back to the message I'd scrawled inside *Mother Goose*:

IKEA
Wednesday, 7 pm
Max
x

'Seven, I think.'

I really wish I'd thought to take a photo so I could be sure of what I wrote.

Alice drops my arm and swipes her hand across her brow in a dramatic fashion.

'Le swoon. It's just all so romantic!'

Alice's one-eighty on Duck Boy has been nothing short of outstanding.

Once I'd told her about my visit to Marrickville and the conversation with Eliana (Johnny's aunt! What in the actual heck) confirming he'd sent me the duck à l'orange, I'd handed over my phone and let her read our string of recent messages.

Her verdict: *Oh, shit. The man likes you! Like, proper likes you.*

'I'd love to go and hide out behind a Kallax shelf and watch this all go down,' she says, gleefully.

'Please don't,' I plead.

'Don't worry, I have to go straight home after work. Maggie is working back late tonight and a huge storm is on its way – Thor is petrified of thunder. Speaking of work, I should probably get back. Can I give you a lift back to your office?'

'I've actually taken the rest of the afternoon off.'

Alice lets out a low, appreciative whistle. 'I am loving this new relaxed, French-whimsy Maxie.' She flicks the bottom of my dress playfully. 'So, what's the plan, Stan?'

I'm not sure how she can call me relaxed after the emotional rollercoaster she's just accompanied me on – but I'm not going to argue.

'I was thinking I'd head to the shops to find something new to wear tonight.'

'Oh, yes, yes, yes! Approved.'

'That's if he even shows up.'

'He will. I have every faith in good ol' Duck Boy.'

As I walk Alice to her car, she gives me her hot take on what I should buy: 'Something revealing that still leaves a little to the imagination – like the fact you actually have boobs.' Apparently, I 'can't go wrong with a classic LBD', especially when teamed with my Love on Top pink lipstick.

For someone who wears socks with their sandals, she suddenly has a lot to say about fashion. She's also forgetting that the so-called date is taking place under the bright fluorescent lights at IKEA.

'I cannot wait to hear how this goes,' Alice exclaims as she hops into her car. I'm standing at her open driver's-side door while she fastens her seatbelt. 'But remember that Thor and I can be there in an instant if you need us. You just have to send our two magic words.'

I laugh, but I know that the fact Alice is just a message away will help settle my nerves.

'Oh, and Max?' Alice says as she pushes her keys in the ignition and reaches to pull the door closed.

'Yes?'

'No peeking at that scan, okay?'

'Okay,' I promise.

Chapter Thirty-three

In my defence, I last three whole hours before I rip open the envelope.

I first try to examine the scan in a change room while trying on a floaty blue dress with spaghetti straps, practically identical to the one I'm already wearing. But for all its unflattering lighting, the change room is not the best place to determine which dark grey and white blobs belong in my brain, and which do not.

I purchase the doppelgänger dress, so I at least have something fresh to wear, and relocate to the storefront window, which is backlit by spotlights trained on the scantily clad mannequins. Crouched in a quiet corner furthest from the entry, I hold the scan up to the light. Again, I search for something recognisable before giving up and sliding the thumb-smudged scan back into its envelope. Making anxious humans wait for medical test results should be a punishable offence.

So, I do what I always do when I'm on the cusp of a crisis: I catch the train straight to the mothership. I had planned on going home before meeting Johnny, but the comforting distraction offered by IKEA is too tempting.

Time passes quickly as I bounce around different departments, eavesdropping on the conversations of strangers. Everywhere I turn, someone is experiencing some sort of relationship milestone. Trying out a mattress together. Deciding who has better taste in rugs. Debating who cooks more to determine who gets the final say on the rangehood.

I watch a couple browsing light fixtures. The guy points out a bamboo pendant lamp that he 'really likes'. He goes on to say that 'he wouldn't mind having it in our home one day' as he grabs the hand of the man he's with, and they exchange a knowing smile.

I oscillate between feeling hopeful that Johnny will turn up and being certain that he won't.

At 6.40 pm, I change in a toilet stall, then make my way to the Billy bookcase – the one near the entrance where I did the cookbook drop. Rather than standing there waiting and feeling incredibly exposed, I turn my attention to the shelf. I pluck a golf pencil from my bag and start doodling on an order form. My penmanship is nonsensical, but it calms my nerves while the ticking hands of the alarm clock on the shelf in front of me creep closer to the hour.

I wonder if our landlords would consider letting us build bookshelves at the Nest? We could always ask. Hmm, if Billy is 80 × 28 × 202 cm, I wonder if two bookcases would fit along our living room wall? We'd need to move the couch.

I start sketching a terribly scaled floor plan of how it might fit. It helps to pretend that I'm doing something productive with my tiny golf pencil.

Once the alarm clock's hands are positioned on the 7 and 12, I ditch the keen renovator cosplay and pocket my paper and pencil. I reach up to my hair to check for flyaways and feel something sticking out of my bun. Another golf pencil. I must have stuck it there absentmindedly while deep in diagramming. I pluck it from my hair and add it to my denim jacket pocket stash.

I must look like quite a sight: bird's nest hair with writing utensils hitching a ride, a dress that's way too thin for IKEA's industrial air conditioning (my hero of a denim jacket only just sparing the other shoppers from a mosquito-bite high beam), and a backpack that won't zip up due to the oversized envelope poking out the top – because everyone brings their medical information along with them when meeting their crush for the first time, right? At least it isn't a urine sample. Still, I wouldn't blame Johnny for assessing my chaotic vibe from afar and deciding that I'm not for him.

My eyes dart to the clock: 7.05 pm. He's late. He's probably not coming. Maybe he never found the book wedged under the doormat? But surely Eliana would have seen him by now and mentioned our run-in – so he should have at least messaged. Unless he's decided against meeting me?

Don't go too deep into storytelling mode, Max, I caution myself.

I resolve to give him five more minutes before calling it. A ten-minute window is reasonable.

I count down the seconds playing a version of 'he loves me, he loves me not', but instead of plucking petals from daisies, I'm silently chanting to the beat of the ticking clock. *Will he, won't he?*

When the clock hits 7.10, I have my answer.

If he was going to stand me up, he could at least message, I think, looking down at my phone, anger bubbling to the surface.

I suppose to stand someone up you need to know you had a plan in the first place. What if he really didn't find the book? My anger dissipates as quickly as it arrived.

I'm about to pocket my phone when an image of a duck appears on the screen.

The Mother Ducker would like to share a photo, reads the notification.

I grin and press accept. Splashed across the image is the text:

Why don't ducks make plans?
They like to wing it

'It's funny, right?'

I slowly peel my eyes away from the screen to see Johnny standing in front of me.

My first thought is that he looks exactly like his photos. My second, updated, thought is that he looks *better* than his photos. It's like photoshopping in real time: the background of IKEA is blurring out as Johnny's tall, manly figure sharpens. Every part of me is focused on every aspect of him: his olive skin, his salt-and-pepper beard, his dark curling hair, the naughty twinkle in his eye, his easy smile. That smile is pretty much all about his cheeks. He has lovely white teeth, a great chin and eyes that seem to lighten the longer I look. He's sprouting a wide grin now, his cheeks becoming round, flushed and absolutely adorable.

Wow. Pull yourself together, Max.

I don't want his first impression of me to be of a gaping idiot. But, despite my best efforts to say something – anything at all – I find that I'm suddenly mute.

He's in a wrinkled denim shirt and ripped jeans, like a Canadian tuxedo that's been mauled by a bear. There's something inexplicably sexy about a guy who can pull off 'hot' even when they're totally scruffy.

Max! Focus!

'Ah, it's not your best,' I finally manage.

He looks down at the ground and shuffles unevenly on his feet. I'm surprised. I was expecting easy charm mixed with bad boy confidence. But the moment is fleeting; his head snaps up, eyes extra twinkly.

'You know a goose isn't a duck, right?'

And there he is.

'I'm glad you liked my gift,' I reply.

'My airdrop was an apology of sorts. For being late. I'm normally a wing-it kind of dude, I'm not accustomed to making plans via seventeenth-century French fairytales. Or receiving recipes that way either.'

So he recognises the book and it's significance . . . I'm thrumming with energy but instead yawn performatively, covering my mouth with what I hope is a dainty-looking hand in my best efforts to channel Marie Antoinette. 'Texting is just so pedestrian. We did enough of that, don't you think?' I say.

'Agreed,' he replies.

He agrees.

We stare at each other, drinking in the newness. I've spent so much time zooming in on his photos – memorising every expression, imagining how his voice sounded, how those strong hands looked as he stirred and chopped his way through all the recipes – that it's surreal for him to be here in the flesh. No amount of analysing his photos could have prepared me for the way I feel now.

He's first to break eye contact and I feel his hot gaze run the length of my body.

I want to track where his eyes are going (Right down to my sandals? Shit! When was the last time I got a pedicure?) but I can't seem to tear my eyes from his face.

'So, you're not fifty,' I say, eyes still locked on him.

'I'm not. And you're very pretty. For a stalker with green eyes.'

He thinks I'm pretty.

I can feel his compliments weakening my knee joints like a bout of scurvy. Love scurvy, if you will.

'Thank you.' Now I'm the one suddenly very interested in the lino floor.

'I could still live in a basement,' he says.

'You don't. I saw where you live,' I shoot back.

'So I heard . . .' His eyebrows arch.

Does he want to get into it right away? I'm sure he has as many questions for me as I have for him.

'Should we head to the cafe so we can talk properly?' I ask.

'You lead the way,' he says. His voice is taking some time to adjust to – it's more butter than gravel.

'Now, everything the fluorescent light touches is our kingdom,' I joke as we follow the arrows out of the kitchen section.

Johnny snorts, and gestures to a crate filled with pillows. 'What about these polyester inserts, Mufasa?'

'Everything,' I say solemnly.

'Well, you'll need to show me these lands,' Johnny says. 'I've only ever been here once to collect a cookbook.'

'What!' I gasp, breaking character and coming to an abrupt stop in the middle of the pathway – much to the displeasure of the customers trailing behind us. They grunt in disapproval, quickly sidestepping our conversation.

'How are you only now telling me that you're an IKEA virgin? How has this happened?' I demand. 'What's wrong with you?'

Johnny shrugs and his face pulls into an adorable half-smile. 'I guess I've just never found the right person to come here with,' he says in his thick butter voice.

Ahhh. The love scurvy is back in my knees.

'And, I've also never moved out of home.'

I come crashing back to earth. *That is slightly troubling.*

I hate that this comment reminds me so much of Scott. If

it wasn't for me forcing him to move in with me, I think Scott would have freeloaded off his parents forever.

'Why do you like it here so much?' Johnny asks, interrupting my thoughts.

I shrug. 'What's not to like?' I answer. I don't want to scare him off by revealing how I really feel about my little safe haven.

'What, crowds and shoddy craftsmanship do it for you?'

'Nooo!'

'So, sell it to me then.'

Fine. If he insists on trolling me like this, then I will.

'Firstly, it is amazing for people-watching. Take these guys, for example,' I say, pointing to a young couple to our left. 'You have to wonder why they're looking at nursery furniture. Do they have a baby on the way? Or just a future 2030 dream of a baby? IKEA is the best way to play house without having to clean your room. And it's romantic! There is nothing better than sharing a paper tape measure – *Lady and the Tramp*-style – to find out if a piece of furniture is going to fit into your home. It's also a great way to vet future partners. If you can't handle this place with patience and grace, you will not be able to handle *me* with patience and grace!'

I can't read the expression that's settled on his face. Bewilderment? Awe, even?

'Have you brought me here to vet me, Max?'

My stomach flip-flops.

'That depends. Do you want to be vetted, Johnny?'

'Maybe.'

It's like fire between us.

'Well, okay then. Let's try *us* out.' I can't believe how bold I'm being, but I decide to just go with it.

Johnny nods and obediently follows me to the bathroom section where we sketch out a morning at home. I poke my head out from behind a shower curtain while Johnny sits on the toilet (sealed and labelled DISPLAY ONLY) and calls out to me to bring him breakfast 'on the throne'.

I storm out of the shower and tell him that's disgusting, and I'm not his house slave! I then announce that perhaps it's better if he sleeps on the Ektorp sofa tonight. A fierce thrill rushes through me as we role-play an unravelling couple.

Next, we head to the living room section and see if we can fit inside a Pax wardrobe. First, one at a time and then together. We're so close I can feel Johnny's warm breath on my face. He puts a hand on my back to steady me as we step out of the wardrobe. His touch is electrifying.

We head straight to the bedroom. Section. The bedroom *section*. To test mattresses. We lie side-by-side on the Valevåg pocket sprung mattress, and I remark on how comfortable it is for sleeping. Johnny disagrees.

'I'm looking for a multipurpose mattress,' he says. 'It really needs to be conducive to activities *other* than just sleeping.'

I have to bite the sides of my mouth to stop myself from yelping.

I'm on a high. I feel like I'm Zooey Deschanel in *500 Days of Summer*. All that's left to do is make out with Johnny in one of the many hidden corners.

I lead him through a secret shortcut back to the kitchen area and we recommence our role-playing. There's something about the familiar setting that makes it feel like real life.

'Can I smell something burning in there again, honey?' Johnny asks.

'Again?' I bite. *Damn he's good at baiting me.* 'I don't think so . . .'

'Oh, apologies. I'd just heard that your cooking is fire.'

I try not to give him the satisfaction of laughing as Johnny wriggles his eyebrows and pulls open one of the kitchen drawers.

He plucks a fork from the cutlery tray and holds it aloft like a trident. 'Nothing like saying "fork him" with a slight char.'

Fork him.

Shit, I'm going to have to fill Johnny in on that whole thing. How I stopped wanting to fork Scott for a while there, but how I'm back with a vengeance.

'I think you'll find most people like their dinner a tad crispy,' I say. 'It adds a whole new sensory experience.'

Johnny smirks. 'If you say so.'

We make our way to the cafeteria and grab one tray to share between us. I'm not sure whose idea that is. Maybe his? But I don't argue with the opportunity to be closer to him. He looks scruffy but smells a million bucks. Sweet. Like baklava.

Our elbows bump as we choose our food from the sad selection baking underneath heat lamps. I let him lead: Chicken tenders (great for sharing!), meatballs (I convince him!) and some token greens. None of it looks particularly appetising, but I'm too nervous to eat much anyway.

There are plenty of seats in the dining room. Apparently, IKEA's cafeteria on a Wednesday evening is not the hot place to be. As soon as we sit down, the adjacent party of five finishes up their slices of chocolate cake and departs.

'Lovely ambience,' Johnny says, glancing around. 'Would you say it's a cross between a P&O cruise and a Las Vegas buffet?'

I laugh. 'A little too generous, I think.'

I can't get over how our banter flows even better in person than it did in our messages.

'At least we've selected the Chef's Tasting Menu tonight,' Johnny continues, surveying the plate of the randomly selected food on the plate between us. He dollops some sweet lingonberry sauce over the meatballs. 'I assume you take sauce on your horse?'

'It just so happens that I do.' I grin at him. Because it's impossible not to smile. I've never been one for fancy dinner dates, so this is utterly perfect. Low-key and perfect. There's no laughing quietly so as not to disturb the other diners battling their way through six courses; we can ditch the airs and graces and start peeling back those layers.

'Mmm, ugly but delicious,' I say, chewing a meatball.

'Come on, now. That's a bit rude. Ugly? Really?' He adjusts the collar of his denim shirt and sits up straighter in his chair.

I receive his subtext loud and clear. 'I also said delicious,' I reply, staring him down.

Again, he's the first to break eye contact. Like he can't finish what he's started.

'The chicken tenders are nice and plastic-y,' he says, looking back down at the plate.

'Yes, you went a bit rogue there. I never co-signed chicken tenders as part of the official IKEA tour. They're no Macca's nuggets.'

'Ah, I love a good nug.'

'They were my meal of choice while I was recovering from my surgery,' I say.

Okay, Max. So you've decided just to come right out with it.

'Not the duck?' Johnny doesn't skip a beat.

'That duck was a true highlight,' I say. 'After I worked out where it came from, that is . . .'

Johnny shrugs, a sheepish smile on his face. 'It wasn't obvious?'

'I mean, of course it was. Day 14 was duck à l'orange . . .' I don't say anything about also suspecting Scott. 'I was just struggling to work out *how*.'

'That was a wild coincidence, wasn't it? *My* aunt being *your* nurse. I wondered why you cut me off so suddenly like that . . .' He trails off. 'You're recovered okay now, yeah?' His voice has a faint wobble.

He cares. You can't fake this.

I hesitate before answering, my mind going straight to the scan that's stashed in my bag. 'I think so,' I say. 'Seriously though . . . the duck . . . thank you. That was so thoughtful.'

'You're welcome. Do you know how hard it was not to rush to your bedside when Theia Eli confirmed that it was you?'

Gah. I can't handle this sweetness.

'You have to admit to being slightly stalkery yourself . . .' I tease.

'Just a tad,' he admits, eyes shining. Before I can probe any further about the duck and the intentions behind it, he pushes the plate towards to me. 'Here. This one has your name on it.'

I grin and take the last meatball. 'Thanks.'

Johnny's bouncing knee shakes the table as I chew.

'Are you okay over there?' I ask once I've swallowed.

He responds by unfastening another button below his shirt collar. 'Is it super hot in here?'

One more button and we're headed into pervy territory. Not the least bit unwelcome, but also not very IKEA cafeteria-friendly. I shift my gaze to his face. He is looking dewy.

'Hmm, not really.' I pull my jacket tight across my chest. 'They could probably turn the AC off.'

'Oh, yes, right, right.' Johnny swivels in his chair, presumably on the lookout for a yellow-shirt employee to adjust the air conditioner. He snaps back to face me and blurts, 'Will you let me take you out for dinner tomorrow?'

My breath catches in my throat. So this is why he's acting so jittery.

'Like, on a date?'

'Yes, on a date.' His voice gains a more confident tone. 'I want you to try some proper meatballs. *Keftedes.*'

'*Keftedes?*'

'Greek meatballs. Made with pork, beef or lamb. Seasoned with Greek herbs and spices like oregano, commonly, and served with tzatziki sauce and pita bread.'

'Sounds delicious.' Almost as delicious as the evident passion in his eyes.

Once we've handed our tray back to a hair-netted employee we walk down the stairs to the marketplace hall and through the checkout.

'Do we need to add a $1 hot dog to our IKEA tasting menu?' Johnny asks as we come to a stop outside a strategically placed hot dog stand.

I groan and rub my belly. 'I don't think I can.'

Johnny laughs. 'Neither can I. Plus, I need you to keep some room in there for tomorrow night.'

I raise my right hand. 'I solemnly swear to fast all day.'

Johnny leans in and slaps my hand. 'See you then, then.'

'Wait! I get a high-five as a goodbye, not even a kiss on the cheek?'

'Good things come to those who wait, Max,' Johnny says gruffly and my stomach flip-flops.

'I'll text you the details,' he calls to me as he strides towards the exit. 'Or maybe I'll slip a book under your doormat . . .'

'You don't know where I live!' I exclaim.

'Let's rectify that soon,' Johnny calls over his shoulder.

I'm still floating as I reach into my bag for my phone. I find it hiding at the bottom. As I pull it out my hand grazes against my scan. I have a new message:

Please call Dr Jock's rooms ASAP

Blood rushes to my head as the ominous words sink in. Of course, I can't just enjoy this glorious moment.

With shaky hands I punch out a message to Alice. It's back to le *Titanic* we go, and there's another iceberg up ahead.

Chapter Thirty-four

'Where are the plates?' I ask, my eyes darting around the dining room. We're at a taverna a few suburbs over from Johnny's house. The restaurant is beautiful and bright, with blue and green furnishings reminiscent of Greece's sparkling oceans and sunny hills.

Johnny's gaze shifts to the impressive spread covering our tiny table. There are so many plates of food that I've taken to nursing my wine glass to make room.

'What do you mean?' he asks, smoothing down the linen napkin that's tucked into the collar of a fresh denim shirt.

'I thought you were going to throw plates at me?' I tease.

Johnny scrunches up his nose. 'Oh, that.' Disgust plumps his cheeks in the same adorable way delight does. 'That's only for the tourists.'

'Excuse-moi!' I exclaim.

'*Signomi*,' he corrects, eyes sparkling. 'You're in Greece for the night.'

Our in-person banter is still top-notch, I think. I'd almost convinced myself that our IKEA date involved too much make-believe to be real, but if this is what a future of dinner dates with Johnny looks like, I'm all in. There is just the small matter of the other women he's seeing . . .

How many are there? Has he seen any of them since our IKEA date? Surely they can't have the same level of connection he has with me! I don't want to risk ruining the perfect night so I force the thoughts aside.

'*Signomi,*' I repeat, completely butchering the pronunciation. Johnny chuckles. 'We'll make a Greek out of you yet.'

'So, the plate-smashing thing isn't really a thing?' I ask. 'I googled it and it said that it symbolises new beginnings. I quite like that.'

Johnny quirks one of his thick eyebrows. 'You think we're in need of a new beginning, Max?'

I take a sip of my wine, mouth suddenly dry. 'I think we've sort of had one already?'

I phrase my sentence as a question. Johnny's harem of women aside, I need him to at least confirm he feels the same way I do.

We lock eyes and a silly grin creeps across his face.

'Agreed. The whole seeing-you-in-3D thing really upped the ante.'

There's a delightful fizzing in my chest. 'So, would you say that the movie is better than the book?'

I can't help myself. Johnny responds by reaching under the table and placing a hand on my knee. My whole body tingles as my legs slowly part. *Wider, wider.* My knee edges closer to his. I'm suddenly grateful that the table is so small, and for the surplus fabric of my red A-line dress. But just as the sides of our legs touch, Johnny retracts his hand. My legs snap back together, and I sag in my chair and try to stop my chin quivering. I've obviously misread his signals.

'Sorry, but they've used way too much olive oil on that

haloumi. I don't want to stain your dress.' Johnny swipes a hand across his napkin bib. His hand is back on my leg so quickly it surprises me. I can't help but jump.

'Is this okay?' he asks.

I manage a nod, mute in my relief.

'I just want to make sure that you're here in the flesh and you're not going to disappear on me again.'

'Like Cinderella?' I'm somehow able to locate my voice.

'If you're Cinderella, does that make me your dashing prince?' he says, voice low and buttery.

'How many princes do you know who wear bibs?' I tease.

Johnny doesn't skip a beat. 'It's not a bib. It's a medieval tunic.'

I love that he doesn't immediately rip the napkin from his collar, instead leaving it unashamedly and firmly in place.

'Well, shouldn't you at least fit me with a sparkly glass slipper?'

Johnny ducks his head under the table. 'Isn't a pedicure a princess prerequisite?'

'Hey!' A flush creeps across my cheeks, but luckily Johnny is too busy examining my chipped toenail polish to bear witness. I should have slipped my tired travel feet into boots, not open-toe mules.

I quickly recover my composure. 'Unless you are planning on sucking my toes, my polish is not your concern.'

'Ooh. Are you into that sort of thing?' Johnny's voice is muffled, but I can still feel the tension building.

My tongue darts out of my mouth and I lick my lips. There's something about the fact that Johnny is basically addressing my crotch that floods me with liquid warmth.

'Wouldn't you like to know,' I say, voice trembling.

'I would, actually.' His grinning face emerges from under the table. He's red, too, but I can't tell whether the colour is from excitement, or the blood that's been rushing to his head.

He scoots his chair closer to me, then reaches out to tuck a blonde curl behind my ear.

My hands clench at my side. I want to abandon the rest of our meal and get an Uber back to the Nest.

'Seriously though, Max. That was very naughty of you' – *Is my mind that translucent?* – 'just disappearing from Tinder like that,' he says.

Oh.

'I did let you know,' I say weakly.

'Yes, you did.' He rubs a warm palm over my knee. 'Although, it was right at the eleventh hour, wasn't it? And in the most dramatic fashion. It's almost like you did it for the sake of a good story . . .'

I love the way he seems to know me better than I know myself. I didn't plan it this way, but my surgery and Johnny's part in it has made its way into my work-in-progress novel.

I shuffle in my chair, unintentionally bucking his hand off my knee. 'Sorry.'

Johnny rakes his fingers through his beard. 'What am I going to do with you, Max?'

'Take me for dessert?' I suggest, trying to keep things light.

'Not so fast, sunshine.' He waggles a finger at me. 'How can we make sure you're not going to run off on me again?'

Before I can answer, his grin shrinks and he presses his lips together.

'I just can't stop thinking how you must have felt – breaking up with your ex and having to deal with surgery on your own.'

I open my mouth to answer, then pause, considering exactly what it is I want to say.

'Not that you're not completely capable,' he adds hurriedly.

'I didn't feel alone,' I say eventually. Carefully.

'And why is that, Max?'

He knows. I can see it all over his face.

'Because I had you,' I whisper.

A pair of matching, knowing smiles spread slowly across both of our faces. For a while we sit in silence, sipping our wines. After all the words that have been exchanged, it's nice just to *be*. The restaurant's soulful music provides the perfect soundtrack to our disgusting eye gazing until we're interrupted by a rowdy hen's group next to us attempting to divvy up their bill.

'But I didn't have any ouzo slushies, Tracey,' comes one high-pitched voice.

'I knew we should have gone to the Turkish place instead,' sings another.

'You're right. We would have at least got belly dancers. I can't believe they don't do plate throwing here. I'm sorry, guys, I should have done more research.' The last girl is sporting a bright pink 'Maid of Honour' sash. She must be the group's chief organiser, Tracey.

I shoot Johnny my best 'told you so' look.

He rolls his eyes. 'If it's really that important to you, we can go to IKEA and get some Gladelig plates to smash on the road outside.'

'Ohh, someone has been studying the catalogue. I'm impressed!'

'Not bad for an ex-virgin, right? Someone I know has a highly alarming attachment to IKEA. Luckily, I'm quite fond of her, so I'm willing to overlook it.'

I poke out my tongue.

Johnny clears his throat and takes a sudden interest in the Greek salad dregs. He spears a chunk of feta and pops it into his mouth.

'This is why I like this place,' he says, stabbing another piece. 'This feta has been made the traditional way – sheep's milk, not cow's milk. Unlike so many other spots in Sydney. Here, have a taste.'

He waves the fork in my face, and I obediently open my mouth.

I squeeze my eyes shut as I chew. 'Yummm.' I'm conscious of speaking with a mouth full of cheese.

'Can you taste that perfect balance of saltiness and tanginess?'

I feel his eyes on me and I nod, savouring the morsel.

'It's the brine that gives it that pungent, full flavour.'

'Have you picked up some tips from living above a cooking school?' I ask.

'Mmm . . .' He's already taken another bite.

I watch his mesmerised face as he chews. It's like he's under some kind of spell.

I can't tell if he's having an extended moment with the feta or if he's not interested in elaborating.

I take another sip of wine and for the first time since sitting down, my mind wanders to tomorrow's appointment with Alexander.

I sigh involuntarily and Johnny's eyes pop open.

'Sorry, I know I can get carried away with food,' he says, rewarding me with an adorable half-smile. 'Especially Greek food. It takes me straight back to being a kid in the kitchen with Mum.'

'That's lovely.' Warmth enters my voice before it cracks. 'I'm a bit distracted myself.' Out of nowhere I'm blinking furiously to keep myself from crying.

Oh, no, no, no, Max . . . The evening was going so perfectly.

Johnny's eyebrows draw together. 'Why? What's going on?' He pushes the bowl of salad away and reaches for my hand.

'I–I–I . . .'

A tear slips down my cheek. *Dammit.*

'It's all right. I'm not going anywhere. Take your time.' He squeezes my hand as his concerned eyes search the table. 'Do you want a dolma?' he asks, plucking one of the leftover vine-wrapped rolls from the centre plate. It's been sitting in its own juices for an hour and now it's heavy and limp. I can't help but laugh. It comes out like a strangled sniff-snort.

'Are you trying to pacify me with food?'

'It's worked before, hasn't it?' Johnny winks and I can feel my body relax.

'As appealing as that looks . . . I think I'm full. But thank you.'

'So, what's going on, Max? You can talk to me.' Johnny gently places the droopy dolma down on its plate.

'I had a follow-up scan, and I don't think it went very well,' I blurt before I can second-guess myself.

A palm goes to his chest. He's silent for a beat.

'Okay. And what makes you think that?' he asks eventually, voice measured.

'I've been asked to go into the surgery early to talk about my results.'

'When are you going?'

'Tomorrow.'

'And how are you feeling?'

I'm grateful that he's asked, and not just delivered the stock-standard 'Let's think about tomorrow, tomorrow' line.

I pause for a moment. My heart is hammering hard in my chest, but I think that's more to do with Johnny's steadfast gaze than fear.

'I am scared. I think that's obvious,' I laugh as I wipe away the last tear. 'But I've done it before and been okay. So there's that . . .'

Johnny breathes out. 'That's true.'

'So I know I can face it again.'

'Hell yeah, we can!'

We.

'You know, the funny thing is,' I say while fidgeting with my napkin, 'I was petrified the first time around that they were going to mess with my brain so much that I'd become a new person. It helped me realise how much I like who I am. My ex almost had me convinced that I needed a personality change.'

'That *skato*!' Johnny's hand balls into a fist.

I laugh, reaching for him. 'It's okay.'

My fingers caress his fist until it relaxes into an open palm. I trace a finger down to his wrist, drawing slow circular movements at the base of his hand. 'It's worked out fairly well, wouldn't you say?'

Johnny's eyes widen.

'Shall we get out of here?' he asks.

'Let's,' I say.

'Nightcap back at mine?'

'Dessert?' I ask.

'Why not both?'

'Bourbon and baklava!'

'And breakfast,' he adds with a smirk.

'Presumptuous, much?' I'm loving every minute of our flirty exchange.

'I have your volumising shampoo.'

My heart feels like it's ground to a halt for a few beats.

Johnny pays for dinner and we walk a few hundred metres down the street to where he's parked outside a second-hand bookstore.

It's a classic green Vespa, not the motorbike I pictured when we first matched on Tinder. Now that I know Johnny, this makes much more sense.

'Are you okay on the back of this?' he asks.

'We'll find out.' I smile. 'These were everywhere in Paris. Road rules also appeared to be optional there.'

Johnny opens the compartment on the back of the scooter and hands me a pink helmet. 'Gotta protect my precious cargo.' He winks.

I try to ignore the niggling feeling that this helmet has graced the heads of countless women before me.

'So, what took you to France? A holiday or . . .?'

I fasten the strap under my chin and swallow hard. It's time to tell him. 'I was with Scott. The ex.'

'Oh.'

His body stiffens.

'I almost gave him another chance, but I decided not to,' I say quickly.

The last thing I want to do right now is give Johnny the impression that I'm not interested in exploring this thing between us.

'And that involved following him to France?'

'Sort of, yes.'

Gah. It's more complicated than it seems. How can I possibly explain to him that I thought there might still be a chance for me and Scott when he showed up after the surgery and I was convinced he had made the duck à l'orange? Especially when Johnny was the one helping me cook my way through my heartache? I wish I'd never mentioned Paris.

'I wonder if they have a copy of *The Tales of Mother Goose* in there?' I say, turning my attention to the shopfront behind us and attempting to get our conversation back on track. Back to baklava, breakfast and volumising shampoo.

Johnny gives a half-hearted shrug in response.

'Actually, you'll be happy to hear that I made great progress on my book while I was away,' I continue, my voice bright.

I'm not sure what I'm trying to prove to him. That his words of support weren't wasted, I guess. That they meant something to me. That I did something productive with them.

'Great.'

I can tell from his flat tone that he's checked out of the conversation. He probably thinks I'm one of those girls who will forever be hung up on their ex and has decided that I'm no longer worth his time.

'Are you okay?' I ask.

'Not really.'

The entire mood has shifted. I can feel that he wants to tear the helmet off my head. I save him the trouble, unbuckle the strap and hand it back to him.

'I promise you that Paris was not what it sounds like.'

'It's okay. I'm the one who's obviously misconstrued what this is.'

'You haven't!'

Weeks of messaging, months of all this build-up . . . It had been going so perfectly, until it wasn't. Why do I want to cry? I fixate on Johnny's feet, blinking back hot tears. My eyes settle on his socks. They have a quirky duck print.

I'm not ready to give up yet.

'I like your socks,' I say eagerly.

'Thanks,' Johnny mumbles.

'So, what *is* your duck obsession all about?' My intention is to reignite our fun, flirty banter, but desperation combined with breathlessness makes it sound judgy.

Johnny stares at me. 'That's not something I want to talk about right now, Max.'

His matter-of-fact statement pierces my heart like the sharpest chef's knife.

'I think I'm going to go now,' he says.

'Okay.'

The hot tears I've been holding back spill down my cheeks as Johnny swings a leg over his scooter and swivels towards the road. His jeans inch up above his ankles, the tiny ducks on his socks taunting me as he rides away.

Chapter Thirty-five

It feels like Groundhog Day. If Groundhog Day involves being diagnosed with a brain tumour over and over again. To be fair, it's the same tumour. Some wayward cells apparently found a place to hide in my nasal tract and decided to make a sudden reappearance, six weeks after the surgery. 'Getting the band back together', so to speak.

'I'm so sorry, Max, but I'm going to have to go back in,' Alexander says.

'Into my brain?' I say.

Where else, Max, into your pants? I swallow down my snort. My Alexander wet dreams are a distant memory. I think Johnny has ruined me for all current and future crushes, at least for the foreseeable future.

Mum confuses the strangled sound as a sob and offers me a crumpled tissue.

I wave it away. I'm actually fine. Maybe because I was half-expecting it. I'm very clearly at the dramatic turning point of my story, when things go really bad. But my overwhelming angst over Johnny has numbed my feelings to this disaster. It's like he's the full bladder and I can't focus on anything else but my heartbreak.

Heartbreak. Do you have to have loved someone to suffer heartbreak? And how could I have possibly fallen for someone I've only just met in the flesh?

I need to appreciate these new cards I've been dealt for what they are. Another chapter. Writing material. If it wasn't for Suzette, I don't think I could have looked at my life this way. 'Write what you know,' she'd said. 'You've been gifted a storied life for a reason.' But it's Johnny who made me feel like my brain was beautiful.

'Yes, into your brain,' Alexander replies. 'Unfortunately, this happens sometimes. I'm happy to do the surgery free of charge.'

'Okay.' I think I nod too. I have no energy left to worry about the cost.

'Your dad and I will help you out anyway,' Mum whispers to me.

'So, you're sure you can get it all this time?' I ask.

Albert Einstein said it best: the definition of insanity is doing the same thing over and over and expecting a different result.

'We can never make any promises, but I'll do my very best. We want to avoid radiation if we can.'

Radiation? No, thank you.

'Why don't you head out to reception to see Cheryl. She'll book you in for a surgery redo date. In the next few weeks if we can.'

Redo.

Once Cheryl has re-booked me for some futile date in the future (I write it in my phone, but it still doesn't feel real), Mum informs me that she's going to get the car from where she's parked it a few blocks away and will meet me at the entrance.

'I'm not an invalid,' I protest. 'I honestly don't feel any different. I can walk to the car!'

'I know, honey, but I'm your mother. Why don't you go to the cafe while you're waiting and grab us a coffee each?'

'Okay.' It's easier to do as she says. I wonder if she's already thinking what it's going to be like having me back at the house as a patient for round two. At least there will be no Scott hanging around this time. And I can busy myself with writing – that's if my brain bounces back for a second time.

But who will send me duck for breakfast? A tear threatens to roll down my face, but I manage to hold it back.

I have barely stepped foot inside the hospital cafe when a voice calls out to me.

'Maxine *mou*!'

I turn to see Eliana sitting at one of the tables.

Gah. It hasn't crossed my mind that I might run into her here.

I give her a small wave and walk towards her.

'What are you doing –' she cuts herself off. 'Oh nooo, don't tell me!'

'Yup,' I say. 'It's back.'

'Oh, Maxie *mou*. Are you okay?' Her eyes widen like saucers.

I nod.

'Why don't you sit down?' She motions to the bench across from her.

I'm not sure I have the strength to hear about Johnny right now, but I also can't help myself. I glance at the counter. It's empty. I should be able to grab coffee quickly before I go.

'Okay, just for a moment.'

I slide into the seat opposite Eliana, my eyes settling on the crumbly pastry on the table. Baklava.

'Would you like some?' she asks, pushing the plate towards me. 'Johnny baked it.'

I shake my head. 'Johnny did?' I'm conscious of how high-pitched my voice sounds.

'Yes. It's the way I could tell how much he liked you. He started cooking again.'

My stomach somersaults.

'Again?'

I'm aware that I'm parroting back her words as questions.

'Yes, again.' She has a puzzled look on her face. 'He has mentioned to you that he's a chef, hasn't he?'

'No.'

That definitely has not been mentioned, just a career in duck memes.

'Oh, that strange boy. Anyway, not to worry. Enough about him – tell me, what's happened? And how are you feeling? Just know that you're in the very best hospital in the country, I can promise you that,' she says.

I hesitate. It's not that I don't feel comfortable revealing personal medical information to Eliana – she's milked my catheter, for goodness sake – it's just that there's something else I'd prefer to talk about. Something that I'm desperate to know.

'If you don't mind, I was hoping I could ask you a question?'

'Sure. Go ahead.'

'Has he said anything about me? It's just that we met up for dinner last night, and it was going so well until it wasn't . . . And now I haven't heard anything . . .' I trail off.

'Oh, Maxine *mou*. I warned him against hurting you.'

'I think I may have hurt him,' I tell Eliana. 'I told him I was in Paris with my ex, then he couldn't get away fast enough.'

Eliana's eyes dart around the room and her voice drops to a whisper.

'He wasn't always so closed-off,' she says. 'Well, he never seemed interested in much outside of cooking, but it was when my sister – his mother – passed away last year that he really lost his way. He took it hard – as he should – but it's more than that. It's like he lost faith in the world. They were so close, running the cooking school together. He had grand plans of eventually taking it over from her, but all of that came to a halt when she left us. My other sister, Tina, has stepped in temporarily but we're hoping that he finds his way back soon. I got him the orderly job here just to keep him busy, but I've so loved seeing him cook again.'

I must look as stunned as I feel, as Eliana stops speaking and clamps a hand over her mouth.

'*Panagia mou*, I've said too much! He's at home now. Please go to him, Maxine *mou*. But if he asks, I didn't tell you.'

~

Mum is taking me back to work. I spend the car ride processing everything Eliana's just told me, but it's impossible to recalibrate my thoughts about who Johnny is, and what we could possibly be, in a twenty-minute journey. Mum doesn't ask me where our coffees are, and after a few grunts in response to her questions about how I'm feeling she leaves me to sit in the passenger seat in silence. When we pull up outside my office, I get out of the car, barely mumbling goodbye. I'm sure she assumes that it's the news of another brain surgery that's thrown me, and not a mysterious duck-loving, six-foot chef.

A chef! This entire time.

When the office elevator doors open, I bypass the row of scooters and make my way down the long hall to my desk.

I sit and check my email, clicking and typing with a vigour more suited to 10 am, right after my morning latte. It's like the louder I drum, the more I'll be able to block out the swirling thoughts in my mind.

That's so awful about his mum.

Should I go over there, like Eliana said?

Would he even want to see me?

I glance at the clock. It's 3 pm. I have no idea how I'm going to get through the rest of the afternoon with my mind in such a mess. ASOS shopping might have to take it from here. But before I open a new tab to browse the latest sundresses, my eyes focus on the screen in front of me. I've been copied in to a new email:

Hi all,

> *Excitingly, we've just signed a new client: D'Artagnan Ducks – an online service focused on delivering the finest natural and organic poultry to five-star chefs and gourmet homes.*

I skim the rest of the email – *team coming in for a kick-off meeting, blah blah blah, need all hands on deck, blah blah, please everyone leave the scooters free for the client on the day, blah.*

I've read enough. This is the sign I needed.

I spring up out of my chair and scurry across the room to Lucy's desk.

'Can you cover for me?' I hiss at her. 'Say that I've gone home sick or something.'

I barely wait for her confused 'sure' before I'm off again. I've spotted a lone scooter in the corner of the office.

'Wait, where are you going?' Lucy's question almost jars me back to reality as I hurry towards the scooter, but the thought of Johnny sends an unstoppable wave of adrenaline pulsing through me.

Let's do this!

'I'm off to see a man about a duck,' I call without turning back.

I feel Lucy's amused eyes on me as I push off towards the elevators.

Chapter Thirty-six

When my Uber pulls up to the house in Marrickville, I feel sick. I almost tell the driver to turn around and take me straight back to the office.

A cooking class must have just finished as there are people milling around outside, holding plastic takeaway containers.

I wait on the street a few doors down while the crowd disperses into their cars, strapping their culinary creations into passenger seats.

When the coast is clear, I creep on my tiptoes up the driveway, as though demi pointe will somehow help settle my nerves.

Johnny's Vespa is parked at the end of the driveway – a stark reminder of the previous night. I approach the door, still on my tiptoes, and press the doorbell. My neck and shoulders are tense.

After only a few minutes, the door pulls open. I hold my breath, expecting to see the woman from the class, presumably Johnny's other aunty, Tina, standing there. But it's Johnny. His hair is ruffled like he's just woken up from a nap.

There's an unfurling warmth in my stomach. He looks so sweet.

'Max,' he breathes.

His voice vaults through me.

'What are you doing here?'

The question is direct, but his eyes stay soft.

'I–I–I . . .'

Where are all your words, Max? You've had so many of them recently.

'How did your appointment go?' He asks, soft eyes desperately searching mine.

Water pools in my own eyes.

'You remembered . . .'

'Of course. I've been thinking about it non-stop. Thinking about you.'

My insides twist.

'So how did it go?' he persists.

I blow out a shaky breath trying to compose myself. I'll fall to pieces if I tell him about the second surgery now.

'I think there are a few things we need to discuss,' I manage eventually, like I'm here for a business meeting.

'Okay.' He nods, understanding that now is not the time. 'Are we even on speaking terms?'

Oh.

But his mouth curves into a slight smile and I feel instant relief. *Hello there, cheeks.* He's teasing.

'Do you want to come in?' he asks.

'Yes, please.' I don't care if I'm too eager. For once, I'm putting my self-doubt and thinking on pause and following what feels right. It's Johnny who feels right.

I step inside, wiping my sweaty palms down my sides. Johnny watches me, his gaze unnerving.

'Mind your step,' he says as I almost trip over the hallway rug. His arm shoots out to steady me.

I flush, laughing to cover up my embarrassment. 'Thanks.' My pulse races erratically at his touch.

He removes his hand from my shoulder and gestures in the direction of the cooking school wing. The skin where his hand rested tingles. 'I need to finish cleaning up,' he says, seemingly unaware of the affect he's having on me. My entire body is zinging and zapping. 'Tina has had back-to-back classes so she's having a siesta. Tina's my aunt.'

'Oh yes, I know.' *Shit*. 'I mean, Eliana said . . .' I've definitely outed her.

I'm surprised by Johnny's tinkly laugh. 'Relax, Max. She's not in trouble.' His expression turns serious. 'I think I wanted her to tell you.'

'Well, she didn't say much at all,' I say carefully.

'Honestly, it's okay, Max. I've been struggling to find the words – that's what I need you for.' He steps in close and takes my hand. 'Come on, we can chat while we scrub.'

I stare down at our fingers entwined in each other's. My hands feel all jelly and boneless.

He leads me into the stainless-steel kitchen and over to a pair of deep double sinks filled with a jumble of pots and pans. He looks down as he turns on the hot water. 'You know, I tried to quit you.'

My heart is thudding so loudly that I'm sure he can hear it.

'You tried to quit me?'

Johnny lifts his gaze to meet mine, eyes grim. 'I did.'

'First off, why are you quoting *Brokeback Mountain*?' I ask, trying to lighten the mood. 'And secondly, why?'

The crease running along his forehead deepens. 'I liked you too much,' he says.

Goosebumps creep up my neck.

'If you hadn't done it first,' Johnny continues, 'I was going to cut you off after Day 14 anyway. It's why I took so long to write back to your website message, and it's why I left you standing on the side of the road last night . . . I'm so sorry about that by the way. I overreacted. You're obviously free to do as you please. I was going to text you tonight after your appointment – I didn't want to add any extra stress to your day.'

My mouth opens but no sound comes out. I'm the one who should be sorry.

Johnny inhales, shifting on his feet.

'I knew that it wasn't going to work out,' he continues. 'It couldn't . . . I–I–I –' he returns his hands to the dirty water like he's searching for the right words among the food muck and bubbles. 'I wasn't in the right place,' he finishes eventually.

'Because of your mum?' I ask carefully.

He looks at me. No traces of anger, just sadness. After a beat, he murmurs, 'Yeah. She was the one who made me sign up to Tinder.'

'Oh?'

'She was always nagging me about settling down. I've never really dated seriously – you could say that I'm married to the job. It's difficult when you're working all hours of the night. But she stepped up her nagging when we got her prognosis. She was so worried I'd be left with no one to take care of me. For the record, I never needed her to wash my undies.' He laughs, but his face is grief-stricken.

'Sure, sure,' my voice is light, but my heart squeezes.

'A few weeks before she passed away, she demanded I download an app one of her cooking students had told her about: "Tindle".' He laughs again. 'She had me sign up then and there and made me promise I'd use it to meet someone. It was her dying wish.'

'Gosh. That's intense.' I'm not sure what else to say.

'Yeah, anyway,' he says, clearly wanting to change the subject. 'Did Theia Eli tell you that I used to run this place with Mum?'

'She mentioned it.' I try my best to sound casual.

'So, I'm not sure how Mum thought I'd have time to date *and* take over the cooking school on my own. As it turns out,

I couldn't even manage one of those things. I'm not sure what I would have done without my aunts.'

He looks so haunted I can barely take it. I need to do something.

'So, you basically cheated your way through the Fork Him project?' I tease. 'You never once let on that you were a professional chef.'

When he finally cracks a smile it's like the clouds have parted after days of rain. A physical weight leaves my body.

'What if I told you I cooked everything with only one hand?' He smirks.

'You did not!'

'Okay, you got me. I didn't.'

'I'm writing about it by the way,' I say. 'The Fork Him project.'

'Oh, *really*,' Johnny says, drawing out the word like he's turning the idea over in his mind. 'I don't doubt that it's going to be every bit as brilliant as you, Maxine Mayberry.'

My hands slip into the water, sending a tidal wave over the lip of the sink and onto the floor.

Johnny clears his throat. 'And – ah – I wanted to thank you for helping me find the joy in cooking again. Before we started chatting, I hadn't even turned on a cooktop since she passed away.'

'It showed,' I say playfully. I hate that I'm much better at banter than the heavy stuff. That doesn't stop me from desperately wanting to know more – more about his mum, more about his feelings towards dating now. More specifically, his feelings towards me.

'I'm actually running a cooking class next week. The first one in a year. The theias – that's what I call my aunts – went a bit crazy when I told them. I don't want to get ahead of myself – I have to see how I go – but I may trade in my "memologist" title for chef again soon.'

'That's great, Johnny,' I say. Then, keeping my voice cool, I ask, 'Are you planning on updating your occupation on your Tindle account?'

He arches an eyebrow. 'I don't have a Tindle account, Max.'

'Tinder then.'

'No Tinder anymore either.' His eyes zigzag around the room. I can tell there's something else he wants to say, so I wait. Johnny runs a sponge along the rim of the pot he's scrubbing, then continues speaking.

'I deleted the thing after you dumped me. I tried for Mum, I really did. But it was a bit like driving a taxi with its light on, but no intention of ever picking up any passengers. Sorry, that's a shit analogy.'

I snort, and a shadow of a smile crosses his face. I'm glad he's a bit more at ease.

'It was easy enough to swipe. It just felt like a game, and I could tell myself I was keeping my promise. But I never felt like messaging anyone.'

His eyes flick over me. 'Until you.'

The air suddenly feels heavier, making it hard to breathe.

'So there weren't any other girls?' I ask shakily, my emotions threatening to spill over.

'No. I said that so I wouldn't get too close to you. I didn't think I was ready to date and I didn't want to mess you around.' He swallows hard. 'I'm ready now, Max. But the question is: *are you?*'

His steady gaze doesn't leave my face.

There's no reason to pause. 'I am,' I whisper hurriedly.

Johnny throws his tea towel down on the bench and moves behind me, setting his hands on my shoulders. Every nerve in my body is on high alert.

'How about some of that baklava I promised last night?' His warm breath brushes my neck, all light and feathery. 'This mess can wait.'

~

We step into Johnny's apartment – the entire top floor of the house – and are instantly enveloped by soothing tones, soft earthy shades and rich wood accents. There's also the familiar dusty warmth of books. They're not in my line of sight, but I can *feel* them. *Smell* them.

'Why don't you take a seat here,' he says, gesturing to a leather settee.

Now that we're upstairs, the flirty mood shifts back to serious. I sink into my assigned seating and a cloud of dust puffs into the air. Maybe it's mothballs I can smell, not books.

Johnny looks down at me and scratches the back of his head. 'Can I fix you a coffee with your baklava?'

I study him, conscious that I'm barely blinking. I explore all the details of his face – eager eyes, flexed and bearded jaw.

I shift my gaze to my lap and fold my hands. 'That would be lovely. Black, thank you.' I hear myself request. *Black!* I really have come back from France a changed woman.

'I won't be long. Just make yourself at home.'

As Johnny busies himself in the kitchen, I take in the artwork that decorates the walls. Among what appears to be a collection of happy family photos are a handful of framed duck prints.

When Johnny returns with two steaming mugs and a plate of baklava balanced in the crook of his arm, I stand to help him.

He brushes up against me as we sit. My heart races as I feel what's coming. I'm trying to think my way through it, but I also know that my brain has no power in this moment.

He takes a sip of coffee. His throat bobs as he swallows.

'Your place is lovely,' I say eventually.

'Thanks. It's Mum's stuff, mostly. And Yiayia's before that.' His eyes shine with pride. 'She left her husband in Greece, came here from Lesbos in the fifties with practically nothing. She managed to scrape together enough money from her factory job to buy this house. It was falling down, but she spent a few years fixing it up, then opened the cooking school. Unheard of, really. Taught herself English, too. All three of her daughters are – or in my mother's case, were – just like her: strong, independent women.'

'Wow. That's amazing.'

'There's a reason why I'm attracted to fierce, intelligent women, Max.' His glistening eyes darken as he looks at me.

My cheeks burn and I lower my head briefly. I can't believe he's putting me in the same category as these incredible women he loves.

'Mum took the greatest interest in the cooking school – which is why it was eventually passed on to her. The theias supported the decision. Said she'd earnt it. She used to help out Yiayia every day before school, washing plates and bowls from the classes and helping prep ingredients like chopping the walnuts and almonds. I started even younger – imagine, a three-year-old wielding a knife!'

I love the image of small Johnny in a tiny apron. Johnny's tongue flicks over his lips, swiping the flaky pastry crumbs away. I haven't touched mine yet.

He doesn't mention anything about his father, so I don't ask. I'm hoping there will be plenty of time to share every detail of our lives and how we've arrived here. I want to know every part of him.

'And the ducks?' I point to the colourful pictures.

He leans back into the couch, like he's stretching away from painful emotions. 'Also hers,' he says.

'Oh? Really?' I try not to sound too surprised.

'Yes. Her name was Daphne – Daffy. So, everyone called her Duck. She didn't like it at first, especially when her sisters insisted, but it grew on her – she ended up collecting all sorts of duck paraphernalia. Most of it is packed away now with her other stuff. I found it too hard to look at every day. I've only recently unpacked her cookbooks.' He picks up his coffee again and swirls it around in the mug. 'A Tinder wife wasn't Mum's only request. She also wanted me to rename the school once she was gone – but I could never erase her memory. I think it's the only fight my mother ever lost, aside from the one for her life.'

Sympathy blasts through me. Daphne's Cooking School. With no Daffy.

I fight to keep my voice even. 'She sounds wonderful.'

'She really was. The sicker she got, the more her sense of humour grew.' A sad smile plays on his lips and it's all I can do to stop myself from reaching out to him.

'That's where your funny comes from, then?' I ask.

His eyes flare. I enjoy seeing the brief return of joy to his face. 'So, you'll admit that I'm funny?'

'Just a little.' I think back to those fear-filled days at the Nest when it was only his daily quips about the latest Fork Him dish that kept me afloat. He's not just funny, he's strong and stead-fast, and compassionate too.

'Can I ask how she passed?' I ask.

He looks away. 'Cancer.' His voice trembles and his raw emotion skates down my spine.

I blink back tears. 'I'm sorry.'

His eyes are still dark, but there's a new sheen to them. 'She left this world laughing, though. I started the Mother Ducker for her – she reckoned she'd seen every duck meme in existence, so I tasked myself with creating more.'

My breath catches in my throat. *It was all for her.*

'And you've kept the site going in her honour?' I ask, shame burning fiercely. I can't believe I'd judged it so harshly.

'Partially. But mostly because it makes a bit of money now, too. I donate it all back to the hospital's cancer research centre.'

'That's lovely of you, Johnny.'

There's a thrumming rising in my body. I'm not sure how to make it stop or where to look, so I take a bite of the baklava.

Johnny looks at me expectantly as the sweetness explodes in my mouth, eclipsing my other senses.

'Delicious,' I say.

'Mum's recipe,' he says, pupils flaring. 'Passed down from Yiayia.'

His gaze trails to the crumbs that have fallen into my lap, then continues down my bare legs. I freeze. I don't want to move an inch and ruin this moment.

Johnny thaws first. 'Let me grab you something to clean yourself up,' he murmurs as he stands.

Without thinking, I stand too. The crumbs spill onto the carpet.

'Shit, sorry,' I say. 'Do you have a Dyson or something?'

He nods and I follow him through the living room. He opens a cupboard and pulls out a vacuum, handing it to me. I'm hit with a shot of adrenaline as our hands touch. *So, a vacuum is turning me on now, huh?*

I swallow down a laugh and Johnny lifts an eyebrow at me.

'You okay there?'

'Yup, yup,' I say hurriedly, turning back to face the room. Then I stop. Propped up against the wall next to me is a Billy bookcase.

I feel his eyes on me and glance sideways at him.

'I thought you didn't shop at IKEA?

Johnny runs a hand over his beard. 'Someone sold me the dream.' The corners of his eyes scrunch up handsomely. 'I went back this morning. I needed somewhere special for Mum's cookbooks.'

Sure enough, there's an allen key resting on the shelf at eye-level.

'It wasn't the same without you there vetting me,' Johnny continues, his intense gaze boring into me.

My insides burn. *He's going to lean in and kiss me*, I think. I set the vacuum down.

Instead, the corners of his mouth flinch downwards.

'I am sorry that I left like that. I got scared that you wanted to get back with your ex. I just don't think I can handle another loss right now.' His hoarse voice spears into my knees and they weaken.

My teeth sink into my bottom lip. 'It's okay,' I say. 'It was my fault. I should have been upfront about it as soon as you asked. I only went to Paris because Scott managed to convince me we had unfinished business. As it turns out, I should have trusted myself. It was a huge mistake.' I fix my eyes on his, intensity burning brightly. 'I'm not going anywhere, Johnny. I promise.'

I reach out and put a hand to his cheek. It's damp with tears. He slowly peels my hand away. His touch is warm. 'I've never met anyone like you, Max.'

He cups my chin and tilts my face up to his. I think he's about to press his lips to mine, but instead they brush my temple.

'That beautiful, sexy brain,' he murmurs.

I close my eyes and inhale deeply, drinking in his already familiar scent of honeyed baklava mixed with woody after-shave. His mouth moves down to my neck and he scrapes his teeth lightly against my collarbone.

Mmm. I could pass out from happiness.

My eyes are still firmly shut as he finds my lips. His kisses start slowly but build steadily until I stumble back into the bookcase.

A delicious heat ripples through my body.

Johnny's hands tug at my hair. 'I have been wanting to do this for forever,' he whispers between kisses. His hands slowly inch over my dress to cup my breasts.

My back arches as he pushes me up against the bookshelf. It nudges backwards a fraction, then tips back into place.

'Holy fuck,' he moans and nibbles on my earlobe.

'Wait, wait,' I pant.

He pauses. 'What is it? Is this not okay?' he asks, voice urgent.

'No, no, it is.' I shiver.

'Thank god,' he breathes out. His ear nibbles turn into sucks. His hand slips under my dress and slides up my thigh.

I gasp. He jerks closer, and my hands tighten around his firm torso. His body melts deeper into mine, sliding up and down, and the shelf rocks back and forth to the rhythm of his motions.

'Johnny,' I huff between thigh strokes. 'I know this is very unsexy . . .' I'm caressing his chest. It's as deliciously chiselled as I'd imagined.

'Nothing about you is unsexy, Max,' Johnny growls.

'. . . but is this thing anchored to the wall yet?'

His hands lift from my thighs to my shoulders to tug at the straps of my dress. He swaps his hands out for his mouth.

'Ah, no, I'm a bad boy,' he mumbles, spaghetti strap between his teeth. 'What are you going to do? Call the IKEA police on me?'

I want to laugh but his words only make me more restless. My hands fumble down to his crotch. It's hot and hard.

'As much I enjoy having danger sex, it is an OH&S issue,' I breathe.

'What did you say?' Johnny asks. The straps finally come off, and my dress pools at my feet. He looks at me for a moment with dark eyes then runs his hands down my body before getting down on his knees.

'Huh?' I can't think straight. His mouth is tugging at my underwear. I don't even care what knickers I'm wearing. 'Sex,' I say. Every muscle is tense. My fingers sink into his shoulders. I need something firm to hold onto.

'No, the other word.' He pulls back to look up at me. Everything throbs and aches.

'OH&S?' I gasp as he buries his face in my body.

'God, I love your mind,' he groans.

The world narrows as I sink back into the shelf, until it lurches behind me.

'Johnny, the bookcase!' I manage.

'Right. Let's take this to the kitchen.' He stands and scoops me up, easily carrying me into the next room.

My legs are still wrapped around him as he sets me on the counter, the cold granite a delicious shock against my bare skin.

'It's better in here. We have toys,' Johnny says, gleefully opening a drawer.

As he starts tracing my nipple with a whisk, I finally succumb fully to the love scurvy and slink off the counter, onto the floor.

~

'Did you know that one Billy bookcase is made every three seconds?' I say as we lie on the floor at the base of the bookcase, basking in our afterglow, limbs still in a tangle. Somehow, we found our way back into the living room and, thankfully, avoided being crushed.

'Why did three seconds have to come to mind in this exact moment?' Johnny's indignant voice tickles my ear.

'Sorry, just a random fun fact.' I giggle, wriggling out from the crook of his arm and flopping onto his solid chest, my fingers winding into his beard. 'And it wasn't just you. I was a tad overexcited, too.'

'Good thing we'll get to do it again then, hey?' Johnny's chest rumbles with his low voice, sending shockwaves down to my toes. 'Although, I might need a few more minutes' recovery,' he says, pulling my face up to his and kissing my temple. I love the way he kisses me there. 'Now, are you going to tell me how your appointment went?'

I prop myself up on my elbows so that I'm looking down at him. 'I thought you'd forgotten about that. I can see your nose hairs, by the way.'

He tugs me back down. 'Oh no, don't even think about trying to distract me, Max. I know all your tricks.'

It was worth a shot.

I sigh into his chest; a sweaty saltiness has eclipsed the scent of honey and wood. 'Well, the tumour is back. But I really am feeling okay about it.'

Johnny's body stiffens beneath me. 'You should have told me before!'

'Before?' I wriggle up his body so our faces line up.

'Before I did *that* to you,' he exclaims, sounding half-panicked, half-amused.

'Do we need to have a little anatomy lesson, Johnny? So, the brain is up here.' I touch my head. 'And the clit is *all* the way down here.' My hand trails slowly down my body.

'Where is it, exactly?' Johnny asks gruffly.

I move my hand back to rest on my stomach.

'Tease!' he rasps.

'We need to think about poor Mother Goose,' I say with a saintly smirk, spotting the book at my eyeline. 'Who knows what she just witnessed.'

'*Lucky* Mother Goose,' Johnny corrects. He dots another firm kiss on my forehead. 'In all seriousness, though, Max, you do know that I'm going to be here for you every step of the way, right?'

The heat that's been loitering below my hips rushes to my chest. 'I do. Thank you.'

I tilt my head with the intention of kissing the tip of his nose, but I end up kissing his nostrils.

'Eww, gross,' he says.

'Gross yourself,' I say, collapsing back onto his chest.

His arms go around me, and I nuzzle into his downy, duck beard. He feels safe and warm; he feels like home.

Epilogue

'So, how is this going to work? I get half of the royalties, right? Considering you've taken my Tinder messages and basically printed them verbatim . . .' Johnny teases me as he plucks one of the copies of *Duck à l'Orange for Breakfast* from the Billy bookcase.

'I wish they were verbatim! That would have saved me a whole lot of much-needed brain power!' I reply.

Johnny gives me a stern look. My second surgery had come and gone. Both Alexander and the multiple MRIs I've had since deemed it a success, and I'd promised Johnny I'd stop making jokes about my bung brain.

'If I'd known how everything was going to pan out, I would have definitely taken screenshots.' I wink.

'Come off it!' He rolls his eyes. 'You're telling me that you never took screenshots of my *many* witty messages to send to Alice?'

'There was no need. She was usually sitting right next to me.'

'Was that before or after she hated my duck guts?'

I poke my tongue out at him. 'Why don't you ask her yourself?' I say, pointing to where Alice and Maggie are setting up the snack station on the island bench opposite us. 'Plus, you got a dedication! What more do you want?'

His eyebrow ticks upward. 'A kiss wouldn't hurt.'

I laugh, stand on my tiptoes and plant a quick kiss on his lips.

It's not our first IKEA kiss. I've been dragging him here every month since we made things official on the pretence of needing things for the Nest, when my real goal is just to plant one on him in every single one of the store's perfectly styled nooks. I'm sure it won't be long until we get a place of our own, and all our role-playing will pay dividends when we know the exact shower curtain we want.

Evidently not satisfied with his peck, Johnny closes the space between us, face warm and hungry. I take a step back and my hip collides with an Ekedalen table.

It's still surreal that I'm having my book launch here – all credit to Johnny's fierce negotiation skills. I've enjoyed seeing this side to him; in addition to agreeing to a regular weekend kitchen-showcase chef gig, he'd requested we have exclusive access for tonight's event. Everyone was happy to come at 10 pm, after the store had closed. There is already a distinct *Night at the Museum* vibe in the air.

Johnny tries again, this time sweeping his arm around my back to dip me. His touch is as electrifying as ever.

I laugh as sweeps me off my feet. 'Watch the duck!' I exclaim as my head is launched at the papier-mâché duck.

In lieu of flying in duck à l'orange from Bistro Rouge or Suzette's kitchen, I asked Maggie to fashion a replica duck from newspaper and glue as my book launch centrepiece. Johnny and I had agreed to keep the hospital duck sacred – only to be cooked on our anniversary. If the last ten months are anything to go by, I'm confident that we have decades upon decades of ducks à l'orange in our future. Baklava had arrived after my second surgery, but that had been hand-delivered.

'Behave,' I caution Johnny playfully once I'm upright again. 'I want to look professional in front of Sally.' I smooth down the lapel of the bubblegum-pink suit I've donned to match my book's cover. 'She should be here any minute now.'

It was a major coup getting Sally Smyth to host my book launch – mostly thanks to Lucy. In her new role as Head of Marketing at Arc Publishing, she'd not only helped me secure my dream deal by sneakily manoeuvring my manuscript to the top of the slush pile, she'd also ensured I had five-star pro-motional support. Not bad for two ex-Slice employees!

I move over to the Gladom tray table to arrange the flowers Suzette's sent. Sunflowers, in exchange for one copy of *Duck à l'Orange for Breakfast* for her cherry-red bookshelves. Her name is on the cover too, for the recipes she's generously provided for *The Laurent Family Cookbook*, retitled as *The Blanchet Recipe Book* – the only real tweak I've made to the story. I can't risk legal trouble with Bistro Rouge, or the Laurents.

Johnny and I had attended Scott's comedy show a couple of nights earlier. Curiosity had gotten the best of me when I'd spied a poster for his latest tour taped on a telegraph pole outside the Nest.

We had sat at one of the bar tables at the back in the shadows, and when Scott sidled up to the microphone in his hairspray sneakers, my skin crawled. Johnny kept a steady hand on my knee to stop me from launching up onto the stage in rage and taking control of the mic.

'I was recently in Paris,' was Scott's opening line, and I was immediately on high alert.

'The Eiffel Tower, more like the awful tower! Who built that thing anyway? What a bloody eyesore, am I right? It's basically a scar on the face of Paris. Like, get rid of the tower and maybe I'd want to fuck it. The Hunchback of Notre Dame would stand a better chance, and there's no way I'm letting *his* baguette anywhere near me. Even if he has a fancy, crunchy market baguette and not a flaccid grocery store baguette. You're with me, aren't you? *Baguette!*'

He was no longer using my jokes, but he'd apparently taken a shining to tour guide Rex's.

'Before you moan, I'm French, so I'm allowed to make fun of my own people. The name is Scott Laurent. Or, as my people say, Scott Lau-*ren*,' he said, using an exaggerated French accent.

'You see, we swallow our consonants like we're in a constant state of hunger. Which is ironic, really, because it makes us sound constipated. Must be all that cheese.' Scott paused for applause, but the room was quiet.

The show was a complete train wreck, but I at least left with the confirmation that I never want to see Scott Laurent ever again – that includes his Netflix special, if that ever even happens.

'I hope Scott reads this,' I say to Johnny as I straighten the towering pile of books, pink spines facing out.

I'm not above Scott knowing that he is the unfunny arsehole ex. I've also included my brain surgery, the ill-fated Paris trip, the delightful Rouen surprise, and of course, my Tinder pen pal.

'And I hope that he knows I'm the hot Mother Ducker,' Johnny replies. 'You *have* made it clear that I'm really hot, right?'

I grab one of the hardbacks and whack him in the shoulder. He yelps in mock pain.

'Of course I have,' I say.

'And a baklava extraordinaire?'

'*Oui, oui.*'

Johnny, Eliana and Tina had collaborated on a version of Daffy's baklava recipe for my book.

'And your creative muse?'

'Now you're pushing it.'

~

The evening is a success. Many books are signed, all the food is eaten.

As the crowd starts to thin out, I spot Johnny and Mum huddled together on a Slatorp three-seater sofa, giggling like naughty schoolkids. Meanwhile, Dad has corned Sally Smyth near the bathrooms and is speaking animatedly about something or another. Probably pitching 'cricket fiction' as the next big thing. I'm on too much of a high to feel mortified.

The afterparty is still going at 1 am when I get word that there's been an attempted break-in at the cafeteria. Apparently, my highly tipsy nearest and dearest have a hankering for Swedish meatballs.

I text Alice. **NEGATIVE GEARING**

I watch her across the room as she pulls her phone from her pocket.

You sounded the alarm?

Yes, it's an emergency, I snort-type. **Are you by any chance wearing Hairy Otter under that surprisingly tasteful blazer?**

Alice looks up and locks eyes with me before opening her jacket and flashing me her T-shirt, and a wide grin.

Perfect. I'll need you to use that ugly spectacled otter to shut down this party. It's late, and Johnny and I still have some celebrating of our own to do . . .

Ooh la la! Consider it done!

Thanks A ♡

I look around the room and smile. These are the people I trust most in this world, the ones who helped me trust in myself. Everything I need is right here.

Acknowledgements

A h, Oscar speech time. There's no 'getting it right' so I'm going to launch right in.

To Geordie Williamson for the dream publishing experience that I thought only existed in the movies or on *Younger*. I really can't thank you enough for believing in me and my writing. Dreams can come true y'all!

To the entire team at Pan Macmillan, especially my editor Belinda Huang. I loved every moment of working with you; you made this book so much better. Thank you also goes to Elizabeth Cowell and Lucy Heaver for your meticulous copy-editing, Christa Moffitt and Lucinda Thompson for my gorgeous cover, and to Candice Wyman, Adrik Kemp, the distribution and sales teams and all the amazing booksellers for getting the word out there about *Duck*. Working with 'the experts' has been an absolute privilege.

Thank you, as always, to the amazingly talented Penny Carroll, who not only sharpened my words but helped me elevate this story. If you hadn't pointed out that French Silk Pie was not in fact French, I would never have come up with the cookbook twist!

JoJo Swords, I could write pages and pages about how much I adore you as a human and a writer. Thank you for being my forever cheerleader. Bring on the Cotswolds! And to January Gilchrist, you are a trusted advisor and an absolute crack-up. I'm so grateful to 'sprint' and 'retreat' with you. Danielle Townsend, thank you for lending me your eagle-proofreading-eyes – a truckload of warm yoghurts for you!

To my chef, Christopher Alagna (and to my wonderful friend Pip Lynch for facilitating our 'working' relationship), thank you for cooking your heart out and bringing the 'Fork Him' recipes to life. Your passion for French cooking helped this non-cook inject much needed culinary colour into the story: *artichokes the size of soccer balls!*

I also want to thank my brother-in-law, Jim Kormas, for being at the end of WhatsApp/the bat phone to help me with all things Greek. A huge thank you also goes to Stavroula Kormas for sharing her family's special baklava recipe, and to Lemonia Kormas for translating said recipe and auditing Johnny's 'Greekness'. I'm also grateful to Chlöe Brault for checking my French. Any butchering of languages, food or places is most certainly my own doing! *Pardon!*

To the 'flattie' and the 'squatter'; Natasha and Marissa Saroca. Where do I even begin? You're like sisters to me. The idea for the Fork Him project would never have existed without a chain of events that I'm not going to reveal here, LOL. Mush mush to you. Thank you also to Natasha Grainge for always believing in me, and for inspiring 'the devil's' chocolate soufflé.

It really takes a village to pursue a creative life and I'm so honoured to have the very best villagers. Donna Armstrong, not only do you have amazing hair, but you know the song in my heart and sing it back to me when I forget the words. Our craft angel,

Sylvia, knew what she was doing when she hired you. Danica May, you are a sister and a best friend. Thanks for listening to my early 'Duck' ramblings while plant shopping and dodging water dragons/dinosaurs. Your enthusiasm over the years has motivated me to keep writing. To my lifelong bestie, Lauren Cheney, you never waver in your loyalty and love for me, and to Kylie Hunter, the most reliable beta reader and dear, dear friend. Thank you to all my tent poles/inner circle – you know who you are.

My deepest gratitude goes to Clare Fletcher, Rachael Johns, Jessica Dettmann and Ali Berg & Michelle Kalus for the 'pinch-me' early endorsements (I cried happy tears!). I also want to thank the incredibly supportive Australian writing community, especially Kimberley Allsopp, Victoria Brookman, Vanessa McCausland, Penelope Janu, Pamela Freeman, Clare Griffin, Natalie Murray, Chrissie Bellbrae, Sandie Docker and (my almost name twin) Kaneana May, as well as all the members of the 'Not So Solitary Scribes' writing group and 'Beaches' book club.

I have been blessed with the most loving family. Life would be nothing without my favourite *skatoulakis,* Lexie and Nora, and delicious eggs, Arlen, Finn and Donovan. Thank you, Cassie & Jim and Jeremy & Laura, for always letting me crash family dinners and activities. I hope you know how much you all mean to me. And Dom, don't worry, I haven't forgotten you. Thank you for five-starring books you've never read. Danica, I've already thanked you (and look, it's in print!).

My parents are endlessly proud and supportive, and without their guidance I would never have believed I could actually do this – and I would never have done it. Thank you, Mum and Dad. I love you.

Lastly, this story draws on a tiny slice of my own personal life, including brain surgeries I underwent in 2019 and 2020. Just like Max, this experience set me on a path of self-discovery and acceptance. I stopped choosing what wasn't choosing me and started embracing what was meant for me (still a work in progress, but we're getting there!) Thank you all – including you, dear reader – for embracing me right back.

P.S. If you're reading this in a bookshop, copies to the front of shelves – please and thank you!

P.P.S To all the girls and guys who need to hear it: YOU'RE FUNNIER THAN HIM.

This book was written on Guringai and Gadigal Country. I acknowledge the Traditional Custodians of these lands and pay respect to Elders past and present.

RECIPES

The Fork Him Project

Johnny and Max's updated and improved recipes from *that* cookbook.

Cheaper than therapy, and more delicious than any relationship . . . except theirs ♡

Day One: The Devil's Chocolate Soufflé

Where it all began!
This chocolatey goodness shits all over sex with that unfunny ex.

Serves 6

Prep time: 20 mins
Cook time: 25 mins
Special utensils: 6 ramekins, stand mixer

75 g high-quality dark chocolate*   ***The fancier the**
   (85% cocoa solids)   **packaging, the better.**
115 g (½ cup) caster sugar
250 ml (1 cup) milk
6 eggs, separated into 6 egg whites and
   4 yolks (discard two yolks)
2 tbs plain flour
20 g unsalted butter
icing sugar, for dusting
granulated sugar, for sprinkling

Preheat the oven to 220°C.

Melt the chocolate with 75 g of the sugar and 1 tablespoon of the milk in a small saucepan over low heat. Add the remaining milk and gently bring to the boil. Remove from the heat.

In a separate bowl, whisk together two of the egg yolks. While whisking, slowly add 2 tablespoons of the remaining sugar, followed by the flour, until you have a paste.

Add the hot chocolate milk to the paste and stir until well combined, then pour the mixture into the pan and return to low heat. As soon as the mixture starts to boil, remove the pan from the heat and pour the mixture into a large mixing bowl.

Place the egg whites and a pinch of sugar in the bowl of a stand mixer with the whisk attached and beat until stiff peaks form. Slowly add the remaining sugar and beat until combined.

Add the two remaining egg yolks to the chocolate mixture, then gradually fold the meringue into the chocolate mixture until you have a combined light and fluffy soufflé batter.

Grease six ramekins with butter and lightly dust with icing sugar.

Divide the batter evenly among the ramekins and sprinkle the tops with granulated sugar (this helps the soufflés puff up). Transfer to the oven, immediately reduce the temperature to 190°C and cook for exactly 12 minutes. Do not open the oven door during cooking – the hot air is important for the rise of the batter.

Open the oven door, turn the oven off and leave the soufflés for 5 minutes. Serve immediately out of the oven to enjoy the gooey centres.

Dust the tops of the soufflés with icing sugar before serving. Remember, the more sugar the better the sex!
Remove oven mitts to resume marathon texting sesh . . . just joking, those days are long over.
Give Max a big fat kiss, then fetch us big, fat bowls of vanilla bean ice cream!

Recipe credit: Christopher Alagna

Day Two: The Dishonourable Beef Bourguignon

One glass of wine for the beef . . . and one for Max.
No 'two buck chucks' – pls get the good stuff, babe!

Serves 8

Prep time: 20 mins
Cook time: 2½ hours
Special utensils: large flameproof casserole dish with a lid

olive oil, for cooking
150 g bacon, diced
1 kg rump or chuck steak, cut into cubes
1 onion, diced
2 carrots, diced
3 garlic cloves
2 tbs plain flour
100 ml Cognac
500 ml (2 cups) red wine (something you would drink)
250 ml good-quality beef stock
1 tbs tomato paste
1 bouquet garni of thyme, parsley, bay leaves and 5 cloves,
    tied in a muslin bag
sea salt and black pepper
2 tbs unsalted butter
4 eschalots, quartered
250 g mushrooms, left whole if small, otherwise quartered
chopped parsley, to serve
roast potatoes, to serve

*

Preheat the oven to 200°C.

Heat 2 tablespoons of olive oil in a large flameproof casserole dish over medium heat. Add the bacon and cook, stirring, until browned. Remove the bacon to a plate and set aside. Working in batches, add the beef to the dish and sear until browned on all sides, adding more oil if necessary. Transfer to the plate with the bacon.

Reduce the heat to medium–low, add the diced onion and carrot to the dish and sauté for about 7 minutes, until soft. Add the garlic and cook for 2 minutes.

Return the beef and bacon to the dish, then stir through the flour for 2 minutes. Pour in the Cognac and stir to deglaze the dish, ensuring nothing is sticking to the pot's bottom. Add the red wine, beef stock, tomato paste, bouquet garni and salt and pepper to taste, and bring to the boil – the liquid should just cover the meat and vegetables. If more liquid is needed, add additional beef stock. Cover with a lid, transfer to the oven and braise for 1½ hours.

With 15 minutes to go, melt the butter in a saucepan over medium heat, add the eschalots and brown for 10 minutes. Add the mushrooms and sauté for a further 5 minutes.

Remove the dish from the oven, add the eschalot and mushroom mixture and stir through the beef bourguignon, then return the dish to the oven and cook for another 30 minutes.

Once cooking is complete, sprinkle some chopped parsley over the beef bourguignon, and serve with roast potatoes.

Recipe credit: Christopher Alagna

Day Three: The Vile Bouillabaisse

It's pronounced 'Boo-yuh-bes', babe.
Sure, whatever. DO NUT under any circumstances cook this if
Alice and Maggie are coming over. Maggie is deathly allergic to
crustaceans.
Ooooooh donuts!
Argh, Johnny. You know that was a typo. DO NOT!

Serves 8

Prep time: 50 mins
Cook time: 1 hour 10 mins

1 French baguette, cut into thin slices
1 kg mixed whole fish, such as scorpion
  fish, flathead and sand whiting, gutted
  and cleaned, cut into large chunks
1 kg raw king prawns
500 g mussels or clams, cleaned
aioli, to serve

In lieu of flaccid baguettes, try Bakers Delight's end-of-day specials.

Bouillabaisse soup
125 ml (½ cup) olive oil
1 onion, diced
1 leek, cleaned and diced
1 fennel bulb, diced
1 carrot, diced
2 garlic cloves, finely chopped
500 g tomatoes, diced
3 kg large fish heads, gills removed, cleaned and cut into large
  pieces
1 bouquet garni of thyme, parsley and bay leaves, wrapped in
  a leek leaf

2 tbs tomato paste
pinch of saffron
sea salt

To make the soup, heat the olive oil in a large stockpot over medium heat. Add the onion and sauté for about 7 minutes, until golden. Add the leek, carrot, fennel, garlic and tomato and sauté, stirring frequently, for 5 minutes.

Add the fish heads and bones and bouquet garni to the pot and stir to combine. Pour in enough water to just cover the fish (about 2 litres), then cover with a lid and cook for 40 minutes. Remove the pan from the heat and leave the soup to cool for 2–4 hours.

Preheat the oven to 160°C.

Place the baguette slices on a baking tray and dry out in the oven for 15 minutes.

Meanwhile, strain the soup back into the pot and discard the solids. Bring to the boil over medium heat and stir through the tomato paste and saffron. Season to taste with salt.

Add the scorpion fish and flathead to the pot and cook for 2–3 minutes, then add the sand whiting and cook for 5 minutes. Add the prawns, followed by the mussels or clams, and continue to cook for about 7 minutes, until all the seafood is cooked through.

Using a slotted spoon, remove the fish from the soup and divide among shallow bowls. Ladle the soup over the top and serve with the toasted bread and aioli on the side.

Recipe credit: Christopher Alagna

Day Four: Crap Comedian's Cassoulet*

*Amended name: Crap Comedian Official Headliner of Netflix's Worst Ever Stand-Up Special Cassoulet.

Serves 8–10

Prep time: 30 mins
Cook time: 4 hours (it's nice to prepare everything the day before, then just add the confit duck legs the next day and reheat)
Special utensils: cassoulet dish, made of clay (if you don't have a special cassoulet dish, you can use the same casserole dish as for the beef bourguignon)

500 g dried white beans, such as cannellini or Tarbais, soaked in plenty of cold water for 24 hours

Max, honey, giving them a quick boil for 5 minutes is not the same as soaking them for a day. You're fooling no one.

1 garlic bulb, cut in half horizontally, plus 5 garlic cloves, unpeeled
250 g tomatoes, quartered
1 tbs tomato paste
1 onion, quartered
2 carrots, roughly chopped
1 tbs red wine vinegar
150 g pancetta or smoked ham
1 litre chicken stock
1 bouquet garni of thyme, parsley, bay leaves, 5 cloves and 10 peppercorns, tied in a muslin bag
sea salt
2 tbs duck fat
a total of 1 kg pork including pork sausages, pork belly, ears, trotters or anything you find at the butcher

Please, no trotter, Johnny – vom!

small handful of thyme sprigs
4 confit duck legs

Drain the beans and place in a large saucepan with the garlic bulb, tomatoes, tomato paste, onion, carrot, red wine vinegar, ham, chicken stock, bouquet garni and a pinch of sea salt.

Add enough water to fully cover the beans, then cover with a lid and bring to the boil over medium–low heat. Reduce the heat to a simmer and cook for 1 hour 20 minutes until the beans are just cooked.

Meanwhile, preheat the oven to 220°C.

Place the whole pork pieces in a large roasting tin and smear the duck fat over the meat. Scatter with the garlic cloves and thyme sprigs, then transfer to the oven and roast for 20 minutes. Remove from the oven and reduce the temperature to 200°C.

Using a slotted spoon, remove the cooked beans from the stock and transfer to a bowl. Strain the stock into another bowl and discard the solids.

Cut the pork into bite-sized pieces and place in the bottom of a cassoulet dish or large casserole dish. Add the beans, then add enough stock to cover the beans. Cover with the lid, then transfer to the oven and cook for 1½ hours.

Remove the lid and add the remaining stock if the cassoulet is starting to look dry. Return to the oven for 30 minutes, then set aside to rest, covered, until ready to serve.

Twenty minutes before serving, place the confit duck legs on top of the cassoulet and return to the oven for a final 20 minutes until the duck legs are heated through.

Now it is ready to serve!

Recipe credit: Christopher Alagna

Day Five: The Smart, Sassy, Sexy Silk Pie

Best consumed in the bedroom 😉
Voulez-vous coucher avec moi, ce soir?
Oui, oui.
Whoever said this dessert wasn't French?! Pop on a negligee and meet you in there.
Don't forget the whisk!

Serves 12

Prep time: 20 mins
Chill time: 2 hours
Special utensils: Large pie dish, electric beaters

125 g dark chocolate chips
250 g unsalted butter, at room temperature, chopped
220 g (1 cup) granulated sugar
30 g (¼ cup) cocoa powder
¼ tsp vanilla extract
4 eggs
250 ml (1 cup) pouring cream
1 tbs icing sugar (optional)
1 Cadbury Flake

Oreo crust
2 packets of Oreos
125 g unsalted butter
pinch of sea salt

To make the Oreo crust, use the end of a rolling pin to crush the Oreos under a clean tea towel. Transfer to a bowl.

Melt the butter in a small saucepan over medium heat, then slowly pour the butter over the crushed Oreos, stirring to combine. Season with the salt.

Grease a large pie dish with butter, then press the Oreo mixture into the base and side of the dish, using the back of a wooden spoon or spatula to flatten and tightly pack the mixture. Set aside in the fridge for 20 minutes.

Meanwhile, melt the chocolate chips in the microwave on High in 15 second bursts, stirring between each burst. Set aside to cool slightly.

Using electric beaters, beat together the butter and sugar until soft, then add the cooled melted chocolate, cocoa powder and vanilla extract and continue to beat until combined.

Beat in the eggs, one at a time, making sure each egg is fully incorporated before adding the next.

Spoon the mixture on top of the pie crust, then refrigerate for 2 hours.

Clean the electric beaters, then whip the cream to stiff peaks, adding a little icing sugar if you'd like it sweeter.

Dollop the cream on top of the chilled pie, then crumble the Flake over the top.

Recipe credit: Danica May

Day Six: Bad Apple* Tarte Tatin

*Did you know this saying originated from Chaucer's *The Canterbury Tales*?
I've said it before, and I'll say it one million times over, Max. I love your brain.

Serves 8

Prep time: 20 mins + 2 hours minimum if you are making your own pastry
Cook time: 30 mins
Special utensils: cast-iron ovenproof frying pan, pastry rulers (to get the thickness just right)

8 large pink lady apples, peeled, cored and quartered
100 g brown sugar
100 g unsalted butter
splash of freshly squeezed lemon juice

Pâte sablée (sweet pastry)
250 g (1²/₃ cups) plain flour, plus extra for dusting
120 g cold unsalted butter, chopped
120 g caster sugar
1 vanilla bean, split and seeds scraped
½ tsp baking powder
1 egg

To make the pâte sablée, combine the flour, sugar, vanilla seeds and baking powder in a large bowl. Add the butter and use your fingertips to rub the butter into the flour until the mixture resembles breadcrumbs.

Make a well in the centre of the mixture and add the egg. Gradually incorporate the egg into the flour mixture until a rough dough forms. Turn out onto a clean work surface and bring the dough together into a smooth ball.

Lightly dust your work surface with flour. Using pastry rulers to assist you, roll the dough out to a circle of 5 mm thickness. Set aside in the fridge for at least 1 hour before using.

Preheat the oven to 180°C.

Ensure that you can fill a cast-iron ovenproof frying pan with the apple quarters resting on their side, fitting together snugly.

Melt the sugar and butter in the cast-iron pan over medium heat for 2 minutes, until butter is melted and sugar dissolved. Carefully add the apple quarters, along with the lemon juice, and cook for 7 minutes.

Remove the pastry from the fridge and cut out a circle about 2 cm larger than the diameter of the cast-iron pan. Cover the apples with the pastry and very carefully tuck the edge of the pastry between the apple and the edge of the pan. Transfer to the oven and bake for 20 minutes or until the pastry is golden brown.

Allow the tarte tatin to cool in the pan for 5 minutes, then place a large upside-down plate over the top of the pastry and invert and serve.

Apples up!
Steve Jobs up!?
No, Johnny. Just no.

Recipe credit: Christopher Alagna

Day Seven: Cuntish Crème Brûlée

This deliciously delicate brûlée is certainly not deserving of its vulgar name . . .

I love how you blush every time you say it, Johnny. It's too adorable to rename (sorry, babe!)

Serves 6

Prep time: 10 mins
Cook time: 35 mins
Chill time: 2 hours
Special utensils: 6 small ramekins, small blowtorch

3 egg yolks
300 ml pouring cream (for whipping)
50 g white sugar
1 vanilla bean, split and seeds scraped
boiling water
100 g brown or raw sugar

Preheat the oven to 110°C.

In a large bowl, whisk the egg yolks, cream, sugar and vanilla bean seeds until well combined.

Divide the mixture among six small ramekins. Place the ramekins in a large baking dish and pour enough boiling water into the dish to come halfway up the sides of the ramekins – this is known as a bain-marie. Carefully transfer to the oven and bake for 30 minutes.

Place the crème brûlées in the fridge and chill for at least 2 hours (you can also make them the day before).

Allow the crème brûlées to come to room temperature for 30 minutes. Sprinkle the brown or raw sugar over the top of each ramekin and use a small blowtorch to burn the sugar, leaving a solid caramel top.

Return to the fridge until cold, then serve.

Recipe credit: Christopher Alagna

Day Eight: The Joyful Quiche Lorraine

To cook when Alice and Maggie come around.
So every Sunday?
Yes! Sunday = Alice and Maggie quiche fun day!

Serves 6

Prep time: 20 mins
Cook time: 1 hour
Special utensils: 1 × 23 cm tart tin, ceramic baking beads or dried chickpeas, 5 mm pastry rulers

1 tbs unsalted butter
200 g bacon pieces
4 eggs, beaten
250 ml (1 cup) double cream
50 g sour cream
½ teaspoon grated nutmeg
sea salt and black pepper

Pâte brisée (shortcrust pastry)
250 g (1²/₃ cups) plain flour
½ tsp baking powder
pinch of sea salt
120 g cold unsalted butter, cut
    into cubes
1 egg

You can always use store-bought shortcrust pastry if it's easier, babe. Amazingly, kneading helps my book #2 creativity rut. That's my girl!

To make the pastry, combine the flour, baking powder and salt in a large bowl. Add the butter and use your fingertips to rub it into the flour until the mixture resembles breadcrumbs. Create a well in the centre of the mixture, add the egg and

3 tablespoons of water and mix with your hands to form a shaggy dough.

Transfer the dough to a clean work surface dusted with flour and use the heel of your hand to press firmly on the dough and incorporate any remaining flecks of butter. Bring the dough together into a ball, wrap in plastic wrap and set aside in the fridge for 1 hour.

Allow the dough to come to room temperature, then roll it out between two sheets of plastic wrap using pastry rulers to create a 5 mm thick circle large enough for the tart tin. Return to the fridge for 10 minutes.

Preheat the oven to 200°C.

Grease the base and side of a 23 cm tart tin with butter, then lay the pastry over the top, pressing it into the base and side of the tin. Prick the base of the pastry with a fork. Line the pastry with baking paper and fill with baking beads or dried chickpeas. Transfer to the oven and blind-bake the pastry for 15 minutes. Remove the baking beads and baking paper and set aside to cool.

Melt the butter in a small frying pan over medium heat, add the bacon and cook for 5 minutes, until crisp. Drain the bacon on paper towel.

Combine the eggs, double cream, sour cream and nutmeg in a large bowl and season with salt and pepper.

Scatter the bacon over the base of the pastry shell, then pour over the egg mixture. Transfer to the oven and bake for 30 minutes, or until the filling is golden and set.

Serve the quiche hot with a light salad.

Recipe credit: Christopher Alagna

Day Nine: A Cock of a Coq au Vin

Don't forget to pour some vin in with that coq ;)
Rude! Cooking is stressssssssful, Johnny. Let a girl unwind.

Serves 5–6
Prep time: 20 mins
Cook time: 1½ hours
Special utensils: Large flameproof casserole dish

1 × 2 kg 'poulet fermier' (free-range or organic chicken)
sea salt and black pepper
2 tbs olive oil
150 g bacon, diced
1 onion, diced
2 carrots, diced
3 garlic cloves, finely chopped
250 g button mushrooms (small left whole, bigger ones
    halved)
2 tbs plain flour
50 g unsalted butter
splash of Cognac
500 ml (2 cups) red wine, something you
    would drink
250 ml (1 cup) chicken stock (see page 327)
1 bouquet garni of thyme, parsley, bay leaves
    and 3 cloves, tied in a muslin bag
20 g butter (optional, to thicken)
20 g flour (optional, to thicken)
chopped parsley, to serve
roast or mashed potatoes or rice, to serve

Again, Max if you're cooking this get two bottles!

Chicken stock (makes 2 litres)
1 chicken carcass
1 onion
1 carrot
1 celery stalk
½ leek
1 bouquet garni of thyme, parsley, bay leaves and 3 cloves,
    tied in a muslin bag

Take the 'poulet fermier' and remove the breast, wings and legs from the carcass, cut the breast pieces in half, and remove the thigh pieces from the legs. Keep the carcass (plus the head, feet and neck if you have them) to make the chicken stock. Pat the meat dry with paper towel and season with salt.

Preheat the oven to 180°C.

Heat the oil in a large flameproof casserole dish over medium–high heat. Add the bacon and cook for 5 minutes or until crisp. Remove from the dish using a slotted spoon and set aside on a plate.

Working in batches if necessary, add the chicken to the dish and brown for 2–3 minutes on each side. Remove from the dish and set aside with the bacon.

Reduce the heat to medium, add the onion and carrot to the dish and sauté for about 7 minutes, until golden. Add the garlic and sauté for 2 minutes, then add the mushrooms and cook for a further 5 minutes.

Return the chicken and bacon to the dish and stir through the flour for 2 minutes. Deglaze the dish with a splash of Cognac, scraping any bits stuck to the bottom, then add the wine, chicken stock and bouquet garni and season with salt and pepper. Bring the boil, cover with a lid and transfer to the oven for 35 minutes or until the chicken is cooked through.

Using a slotted spoon, remove the chicken from the dish and set aside. Place the dish over medium heat and reduce, stirring frequently, to a nice thick sauce. Remove the bouquet garni. Put the saucepan back on the stovetop on medium heat and reduce for up to 10 minutes until you get a nice thick sauce. You can add 20 g of butter and 20 g of flour if it looks thin.

Return the chicken to the reduced sauce and top with some chopped parsley. Serve the coq au vin with roast or mashed potatoes or rice.

Or Johnny's special Patates Riganates (Greek-style lemon potatoes with garlic and oregano – nom, nom, nom!)

Chicken stock

To make the chicken stock, place the chicken carcass in a large saucepan, cover with plenty of cold water and bring to the boil. As soon as the water starts to boil, immediately remove the carcass and rinse in cold water. This removes any impurities from the carcass.

Wipe out the saucepan and return the carcass to the pan. Cover with cold water and bring to the boil again. Add the vegetables and bouquet garni, then reduce the heat to a simmer and cook for 2 hours.

Remove the pan from the heat and allow the stock to cool for 2 hours. Strain the chicken stock into containers and store in the fridge for up to 3 days or in the freezer for up to 3 months.

Recipe credit: Christopher Alagna

Day Ten: Fucker of a French Onion Soup

Babe, I've made this as toddler/Max-friendly as possible.
It doesn't look very friendly . . .
If you want me cook it for you, just say the word.
Word!

Serves 4

Prep time: 10 mins
Cook time: 1 hour

1 tbs unsalted butter
900 g onions, diced
5 tsp plain flour
splash of Cognac
2 litres chicken stock (see page 327 for method)
French baguette, for toasting
sea salt and black pepper
grated Gruyère, to serve

Melt the butter in a large stockpot over low heat. Add the onion and gently sauté, stirring occasionally for 30 minutes or until the onion is dark golden and completely collapsed.

Preheat the oven to 160°C.

Add the flour and cook, stirring, for 2 minutes, then deglaze the pot with the Cognac, stirring to scrape any bits stuck to the bottom. Pour in the chicken stock and simmer for 30 minutes. Season to taste with salt and pepper.

Cut the baguette into thin slices and place on a baking tray. Transfer to the oven and toast for 15 minutes until crisp.

Divide the toasted baguette slices among four deep soup bowls and pour the onion soup over the top. Sprinkle with grated Gruyère and serve.

Recipe credit: Christopher Alagna

Day Eleven: Asshole Artichokes à la Barigoule

What happens when you eat artichokes? It breaks their hearts!
Are you responsible for that bad joke, or am I?
Maybe it was your ex . . .
Nah, way too funny for him.
Well, then it was my genius.

Serves 2

Prep time: 10 mins
Cook time: 45 mins

5 cloves
2 star anise
2 large artichokes
2 lemons, sliced in half
sea salt and black pepper
aioli, to serve

Fill a large stockpot with water, add the cloves and star anise and bring to the boil.

Meanwhile, break the stalks off the artichokes and remove any dry-looking leaves. Slice off the top third of the artichoke flowers. Immediately rub one of the lemon halves over the cut surface of the artichokes.

Add the artichokes and lemon halves to the boiling water, cover and simmer for 45 minutes, until the artichokes are soft.

Once cooked, remove the artichokes from the water, and cut in half. With a teaspoon, remove the hairy choke in the middle of the flower.

Drain the artichokes and divide between two plates. Serve with aioli on the side for dipping the leaves or a light vinaigrette sauce.

Recipe credit: Christopher Alagna

Day Twelve: Terrorist's Tarte au Citron Meringuée*

*Johnny to cook only – unless you fancy your lemon curd and meringue scrambled!

Serves 8

Prep time: 1 hour
Cook time: 50 mins
Special utensils: 20 cm tart ring, silicone ovenproof mat, pastry ruler, ceramic baking beads or dried chickpeas, kitchen thermometer, stand mixer, piping bag, small blowtorch

Pâte sucrée (shortcrust pastry)
210 g plain flour, plus extra for dusting
pinch of sea salt
½ tsp baking powder
30 g almond meal
120 g cold unsalted butter, cut into 1 cm cubes
120 g white sugar
1 large egg
1 vanilla bean, split and seeds scraped

Lemon curd
3 eggs
150 g caster sugar
juice of 3 lemons and the zest of 2
50 g unsalted butter, cut into cubes

Swiss meringue
3 egg whites
200 g caster sugar (1½ times the weight of the egg whites)

To make the pastry, combine the flour, salt, baking powder and almond meal in a large bowl. Add the butter and use your fingertips to rub it into the flour mixture until it resembles large breadcrumbs. Add the sugar and vanilla bean seeds and mix through. Make a well in the centre of the ingredients and add the egg, then use your hands to bring the mixture together to form a shaggy dough.

Transfer the dough to a clean work surface dusted with flour and use the heel of your hand to press firmly on the dough and incorporate any remaining flecks of butter. Bring the dough together into a ball.

Lay out a large sheet of plastic wrap and place the dough on top. Using a pastry ruler to assist you, roll out the dough to a 3 mm thick circle. Transfer to the fridge to rest for 1 hour.

Place a silicone mat on a baking tray and grease a 20 cm tart ring with butter.

Cut out a circle from the chilled pastry about 2 cm larger than the tart ring. Lay the pastry over the tart ring and gently press it into the base and side. Using a sharp knife, remove any excess pastry, and return it to the fridge for 20 minutes.

Preheat the oven to 170°C.

Line the chilled pastry shell with baking paper and fill with ceramic baking beads or dried chickpeas. Transfer to the oven and cook for 22 minutes total, carefully removing the baking beads and baking paper after 15 minutes.

Allow the pastry to cool, then carefully remove the tart ring. Reduce the oven temperature to 150°C.

To make the lemon curd, combine the eggs, sugar, lemon juice and zest in a heatproof bowl. Place the bowl over a small saucepan of simmering water and heat, whisking constantly for 10 minutes, until thickened. Do not to let the eggs cook or the mixture boil.

Pass the mixture through a sieve into a clean bowl, then add the butter and stir until melted and you have a silky curd consistency. Set aside to cool a little, then pour into the cooled tart shell. Transfer to the oven and cook for 10 minutes.

Max!!!! If you are cooking, this is where you *always* go wrong. What can I say? I like lumpy lemon curd.
And I like your lady lumps.

Allow the tart to cool slightly then place in the fridge for at least 10 minutes or, better yet, overnight.

To make the Swiss meringue, combine the egg whites and sugar in a heatproof bowl, then set the mixture over a saucepan of simmering water. Heat to exactly 71°C on a kitchen thermometer, then transfer the mixture to a stand mixer with the whisk attached. Beat on maximum speed for about 10 minutes, until the mixture thickens and cools into a glossy meringue.

Transfer the meringue to a piping bag and attach your favourite nozzle. Pipe the meringue over the lemon tart, then use a small blowtorch to brown the tips of the meringue.

Return the tart to the fridge for 1 hour, then slice and serve.

Recipe credit: Christopher Alagna

Day Thirteen: Cruddy Croque Monsieur

Serves 4*

*Or 2 depending on how hungry Max is.
Wait until I'm eating for two!
!!! Do you have something to tell me?
Haha no. But hopefully one day . . .
Mother Goose is standing by.

Prep time: 30 mins
Cook time: 5 mins

8 slices of your favourite bread
100 g thick-cut ham
200 g grated Gruyère, plus extra for sprinkling

Béchamel
500 ml (2 cups) milk
5 bay leaves
½ onion
pinch of grated nutmeg
50 g unsalted butter, plus extra for spreading
50 g plain flour

Combine the milk, bay leaves, onion and nutmeg in a saucepan and place over medium heat. Gently heat the mixture until bubbles appear around the edge of the milk, then immediately remove the pan from the heat – do not let the mixture boil. Set aside to cool for 30 minutes, then strain into a bowl. Discard the solids.

Melt the butter in a small saucepan over low heat, add the flour and stir until the mixture resembles a paste. Add the cooled milk and whisk constantly for about 3 minutes, until the sauce begins to thicken.

Preheat a grill to high. Line a baking tray with foil.

Now we are ready for the ham sandwich. Toast the bread and remove the crusts. Butter both sides of the toast and divide the ham and grated Gruyère among four slices. Top with the remaining toast and transfer to the prepared tray. Spoon the béchamel over the sandwiches, sprinkle with a little extra Gruyère and pop under the grill for 5 minutes, until golden and bubbling. *Voilà!*

Recipe credit: Christopher Alagna

Day Fourteen: Duck à l'Orange

The most sacred recipe of the 'Fork Him' project – also known as 'hospital duck'.
To be cooked on our anniversary each year – following an entrée of IKEA meatballs.

Serves 5–6

Prep time: 30 mins
Cook time: 1½ hours
Special utensils: large flameproof casserole dish with a lid, meat thermometer

8 oranges: 2 diced; 2 juiced; 4 peeled, deseeded and cut into
     1 cm thick slices
2 celery stalks, diced
2 carrots, diced
1 × 2 kg whole duck
sea salt and black pepper
50 g unsalted butter or duck fat
100 ml Grand Marnier
200 ml duck or chicken stock
2 tbs caster sugar
2 tbs red wine vinegar
sprigs of rosemary or thyme

Preheat the oven to 180°C.

Combine the diced orange, celery and carrot in a bowl.

Remove the wishbone, wings and neck from the duck. Generously season the inside and outside of the duck with salt and pepper, then fill the cavity with the orange and vegetable mixture. Tie the duck legs together with kitchen string to secure the cavity.

Melt the butter or duck fat in a large flameproof casserole dish over high heat. Add the duck and seal for 1 minute on all four sides. Remove the duck from the heat and add the stock. Cover with lid, then transfer to the oven and cook for 40 minutes. Drizzle the Grand Marnier over the duck and continue to cook for a further 5 minutes. Remove the duck from the dish, cover with foil and set aside to rest. Use a thermometer to check the internal temperature of the meat has reached 75°C before straining the juices in the dish into a bowl.

Combine the sugar and vinegar in a small saucepan and stir until mixed. Add the orange juice and strained cooking juices and set over a medium heat. Cook, stirring occasionally, for 5–10 minutes, until reduced. You now have your sauce!

Next, heat the sliced orange in a saucepan with some of the sauce until warmed through, then layer in a large serving dish. Top with the duck and fresh rosemary or thyme.

When carving the duck, start with the breast, followed by the legs. Thinly slice the breast pieces at an angle and serve with the sauce.

Recipe credit: Christopher Alagna

Daffy's Baklava

**An actual family recipe for The Mayberry/Kalos Family Cookbook.
Made with love** ♡

Makes 30

Prep time: 1 hour 15 mins
Cook time: 40 mins
**Special utensils: one baking dish the same size as the filo
pastry sheets; alternatively, trim the pastry to fit your dish**

375 g (3 cups) coarsely chopped walnuts
155 g (1 cup) coarsely chopped almonds
2 tsps ground cinnamon
½ tsp ground cloves
185 g unsalted butter, melted
185 ml olive oil
1 × 375 g packet filo pastry
2 tbs granulated sugar
30 whole cloves, to decorate

Baklava syrup
690 g (3 cups) caster sugar
½ cup glucose or honey
zest of 1 lemon
1 cinnamon stick

Preheat the oven to 200°C.

Combine the walnuts, almonds, ground cinnamon and
cloves in a bowl. Set aside.

In another bowl, combine the melted butter and olive oil.
Generously grease a baking dish with the butter and oil mixture.

Lay five sheets of filo pastry in the base of the dish, brushing with the butter and oil mixture between each sheet. Leave the top layer plain. Sprinkle a thin, even layer of the nut mixture over the top sheet of pastry, then add another two sheets, brushing with the butter and oil mixture in between the layers and then sprinkling the top with more of the nut mixture. Repeat this process until all the nut mixture is used – this is how you achieve the multiple layer effect of traditional baklava.

Finish the layering with another five sheets of pastry, brushing between each layer with the butter and oil mixture. Do not brush the top layer. Using a sharp-pointed knife, score the top layers of filo pastry into small diamond-shaped pieces, then stick a clove in the centre of each piece. Brush the top with the remaining butter and oil mixture and sprinkle with some drops of warm water to prevent the pastry from curling as it bakes.

Bake the baklava for 30–40 minutes, until golden brown.

Make the syrup while the baklava cools. Place the ingredients and 500 ml (2 cups) of water in a saucepan over medium heat and allow the mixture to boil for 5 minutes.

Slowly and evenly, ladle the hot syrup over the cooled baklava until the entire baklava is covered.

Store the baklava in an airtight container at room temperature for 10–14 days, or in the fridge for several weeks.

Recipe credit: Stavroula Kormas